# SEVEN YEARS DEAD

## CHUCK DRISKELL

**Seven Years Dead**

Copyright © 2016 by Chuck Driskell
Published by Autobahn Books
Cover art by Nat Shane

First Edition: February 2016

autobahn
BOOKS

*For Charles Sims,*
*one of the finest men I've ever known.*

# Other Books by Chuck Driskell

Demon's Bluff

Doppelgänger

Lahn's Edge

The Diaries (Gage Hartline #1)

To The Lions (Gage Hartline #2)

Soldier of Misfortune (Gage Hartline #3)

In Her Defense (Gage Hartline #4)

*Revenge proves its own executioner.*
*-John Ford*

# Chapter One

Journal Entry

After so many years of torment, after all the nightmares, after the days upon days spent shaking in my sweat-soaked bed, after the rage-filled nights when I could do nothing to avenge my friends—after all of that, I am finally here.

Dammit, I am back.

I want to scream it to every kraut I see.

I wish I could reach out to my fellow soldiers' families, just so they could know that the possibility of vengeance exists.

Not vengeance against the masses. Vengeance against one. I want the man, the sonofabitch, the murderer who gave the command that killed all my friends.

I want him regardless of the price I have to pay. In my mind, I've already paid it. And this journey is the payoff.

Consider this journal the story of my death. And my life after death. I know that sounds strange, but the reality is that I've been dead for seven years now. Keep reading and you'll understand what I mean. When I'm gone, I want this journal to serve as a record of what I did. And why I did it.

My name is now Marty Elder, but I was born Thomas "Tommy" Whiteside. I was the lone survivor of a massacre during the Second World War. It's recorded in the history books as the Massacre at Kastellaun.

And, according to those history books, there were *no* survivors.

I agree with those history books.

My physical body, in a miracle I'll never fully understand, somehow made it through that massacre. Because I was the only one given the "gift" of life, I feel a special duty to do something to bring justice for my friends.

And no, the gift of life doesn't feel like a gift at all. It's a curse. An albatross. A cross to bear.

I've borne it. I'm still bearing it.

Know this: I'm not crazy. Though the massacre destroyed my soul, it didn't wreck my mind, or my judgment. I know exactly why I'm here in Germany. My mind is clear, as is my mission.

Though history already knows the basics of what happened at Kastellaun, I want to tell the entire story. Not for glory—I'd rather my name not be mentioned. I want justice. I want to tell this story for the children of tomorrow, so it will never happen again.

Probably a ridiculous notion, but even I have to admit the world is a far better place than it was even a hundred years ago. However, the cruelty of man still exists. Flourishes in many instances. It's hard to imagine that, in modern society, incidents such as the Massacre at Kastellaun still occur.

It sickens me.

I'm on a train as I write this and we're passing through a decent-sized German city right now. As I peer out, beyond the rail lines, I can see that most of the buildings have been rebuilt. Despite the piles of rubble in the streets, many of the structures are shiny and new. Even the old buildings seem to have enjoyed a fresh coat of paint. It's as if everything's been wiped clean.

Like the abrupt newness can somehow erase all that happened.

Well...it can't.

Hopefully I'll be able to complete this journal before my mission is over.

And I will complete my mission. It's my destiny.

***

Marty stabbed the journal with his pen and glanced around. The click-clacking of the old train had gone on for hours. Miserable hours. Like rocks in a tumbler. Over and over. Grinding. Sanding away at Marty's nerves like coarse sandpaper. On and on the stuffy train blundered. In through the north of Germany, over the slick wet plains in the early morning and, as the passengers unwillingly soiled themselves with their own sweat and body oil, into the brilliant, rolling green of the eastern German hills.

To the other passengers, Marty might have appeared foreign or, most likely, they didn't even notice him. A man of average height with standard-length sandy blond hair, he went to great lengths not to stand out from the crowd. His traveling clothes were nondescript. His hats were plain with no adorning feathers. Even Marty's shoes were old and lacking polish. He was an "everyman"—which was exactly what he'd intended.

Unable to sit any longer, Marty stood and made his way rearward. Five different flights. A ferry trip. And now, crammed in a worn bench seat next to some blathering Englishman, going on and on about himself and about how treacherous his piss-ant thirty-mile trip across the Channel had been. Marty had tried to give polite signals. Even as Marty was journaling, the man kept on chattering. Now at the rear of the car, Marty watched as the fat old Brit turned, frowning at Marty's hasty exit. The Brit then mumbled unkind words about the "dodgy Yanks."

The sudden lack of one-way dialog was blissful.

Nestled into the rear of the compartment, in the nook beside a bench seat and the door, Marty studied the passengers, heads swaying back and forth in a synchronous union with the movement of the old train. The forward ten or so passengers were together. Businessmen, probably in their late thirties, their rack suits giving them away as middle managers. They'd been passing around a bottle of brown liquor, several of them sporting rubicund faces from all the travel booze. Marty had heard them early on the voyage, speaking in what sounded like Boston accents, telling bullshit war stories and ruminating about how easy getting laid was going to be during their eight-day business trip.

"Those krautahs ain't got no money and their men've all been planted undah the ground," one said.

"Fish in a barrel," another had cackled. "Watch n' see. Jennings from civil said he was shacked up with two skinny frauleins a night."

"Jennings?"

"Yeah."

"Well, if Jennings got a shot of ass, I'll nevah be alone," a fourth one laughed as he flicked his Zippo open, igniting a smelly cigar.

Marty would bet his travel check that they all would head back to Boston with bad hangovers and aching blue balls.

In the next group of passengers, Marty noticed a morose-looking old lady who had quietly cried throughout the journey, sniffling into a tissue. Marty had not heard her speak and there was nothing about her to indicate an origin. In Marty's mind, she was German, traveling to Berlin to claim the body of a loved one. Though he had no quarrel with the woman, he hoped she was going to claim a dead kraut.

*The world, minus any one kraut, is a better place.*

Marty violently shook his head back and forth.

*Just listen to you, you sadistic sonofabitch.*

*Blame that prick, Nadel. It's his fault.*

*Raban Nadel...author of my nightmares.*

Marty tugged downward on his face, ready to be there, ready to clear his mind.

The passengers occasionally stood, making their way rearward to use the small, odorous bathroom with the toilet that didn't flush. Navigating on a train, especially an old, pre-war train running on sketchily repaired tracks, can be tricky. One of the tipsy businessmen negotiated the aisle. As the train lurched, he tried to grab for a seat back but inadvertently knocked a woman's hat off, and nearly took her wig with it.

"In-shool-dig-can!" he yelled, drawing riotous laughter from his pals. Marty despised the krauts, but drunken Americans like these bothered him, too. He did his best to ignore them.

As the outer reaches of Berlin had begun to slide into view, a train attendant had finally made his way to Marty's rearward car. After clicking the front door shut, the attendant announced his presence, kindly asking the passengers to remove their tickets and to have them ready. *"Wir sind fast zu Berlin,"* he said with a smile.

The smile.

*My God, is that him? Is that Nadel?*

Marty had to turn away. His heart thudded in his chest. His mouth was suddenly wet. Very wet. The saliva collected in his mouth, becoming more than he could bear. Then, matching the reaction in his mouth, his stomach began to undulate. It's a feeling that every person—no matter their social position, their wealth, their good health— eventually comes to know in life. Even the president of the United States knows the critical urge of impending puke.

Before lurching from where he stood, Marty took one last look at the man's face. No...no...it wasn't Nadel. But combined with the uniform and that simpering grin—those damned squared-off teeth surrounded by sharp canines—the man could pass for Nadel's brother.

Regardless, the puke was imminent, the spike of fear having already found its mark.

Marty shook the handle on the bathroom—locked. Then he remembered the American businessman had staggered in there minutes before. What the hell was taking so long? Marty realized there wasn't time. Flinging the rear door open, he found solace on the windy platform between his car and the caboose.

Cooler, velvety air assaulted Marty as he flung his upper body over the rusty rail, spewing the remnants of his breakfast onto the blurry railroad ties and rocks below. When he finally stopped, he turned his watery eyes to the sky, wondering how he would ever get through this.

Minutes passed as Marty had another coughing spell but managed to keep the rest of his stomach down. Just as he was beginning to feel normal again, a voice...

"*Kann ich Ihnen helfen?*"

Marty kept his eyes on the horizon, paralyzed, afraid to turn around and join eyes with the man.

"*Mein Herr?* Should I zpeak English, inztead?"

Fingers clawing inside his coat, Marty found the dog-eared ticket, handing it over his shoulder. He could hear the attendant's stamp punch the paper. The bastard lingered like some nosy old woman that had to know the whole story.

"You're just not going to leave, are you?" Marty muttered in German.

"I just want to make sure you're well, sir," the man answered, also in German.

Marty turned, wiping his lips with the back of his sleeve. He joined eyes with the attendant, watching as the man cocked his head.

"What's wrong with you?" the attendant asked, curling his lip and making his German rapid-fire.

Well, at least Marty's language training had paid off—this bastard now thought he was a local. Might as well give it a full go. Marty spit over the rail before turning back. "I drank too much last night, and then the stuffy train and all the movement..."

The attendant frowned as he tucked his stamp back onto the loop of his belt. "I'd watch myself, if I were you. There are two American soldiers in the caboose...rail guards. You know the Amis don't take well to German drunkards. Especially war veterans who can't hold their liquor." The attendant's reference, "Amis," was the common German nickname for Americans.

"How do you know I'm a war veteran?" Marty asked, sticking with his German.

"You're of age and seem to be healthy other than a hangover," the attendant snapped, motioning up and down. "What German fitting that bill isn't a war vet?"

Marty nodded. "I'll be fine."

"Go back inside and sit down," the attendant said sternly. "There's no lingering allowed between the cars."

Marty waited.

"Did you hear me, son?"

Marty switched to American English. "I'll go when I'm damn good and ready, *kraut*." He straightened and put his hands on his hips.

The attendant's mouth parted while his eyes went wide. "I'm sorry, sir. I mistook you for a German. Your accent is...is quite..."

"My *Berlinerisch* accent is damned good because I know my *enemy*. And I'm about as far from being a German as a human can be. Thank—God." Marty put his finger on the man's tie and pushed him away. "Now, piss off."

Then Marty was alone. He stayed on the platform as the piles of rubble, and new construction, of Berlin slid into view.

Though he was arriving with the paperwork and legal identity of Martin Vincent Elder, in actuality, it was Thomas Wayne Whiteside who had returned.

And his mission would soon begin.

\*\*\*

On his third evening in Germany, a Friday night, Marty endured another train ride. This journey was much shorter, from the south suburb of Steglitz, where he'd rented an apartment, straight into the heart of Berlin. Stepping off the S-Bahn at the bustling Friedrichstrasse station, Marty queued with hundreds of others at a checkpoint for passage into the Soviet sector. It was quite warm and many in the crowd smelled of sweat. Since arriving in Berlin, Marty had learned that plumbing and sewage were still deficient in a number of homes damaged by the war. Showers and baths were hard to come by.

While he waited, Marty lit a cigarette, his mind wandering to his "job" here in Berlin. Marty had been a double major at East Central State, in Oklahoma, majoring in German and Sociology. Because of his fluency, and the dire need for degreed Americans in Germany's reconstruction, Marty had been hired by a Dallas construction firm after only sending in a résumé and enduring a ten-minute phone interview.

The salary they'd offered him was more than adequate, especially for a man with no experience. The salary was almost certainly made better because few Americans had any desire to live in Germany. As a single man with no family ties, Marty was the perfect candidate. His new boss, a Texan named Jimmy Gallotte, seemed a nice enough man, although he was visibly put off by Marty's "not having served" during the war.

"You didn't serve in any capacity?" Gallotte, incredulous, had asked Marty on his first day.

"No, sir. I was injured on the farm as a teen and classified 4-F."

Gallotte rubbed his chin, frowning. "Most of our boys here served, and served well. Shootin' you straight, I'm not sure how they'll take to you at first."

"I tried, Mister Gallotte. No matter what I said or did, Uncle Sam wouldn't take me."

Gallotte poked a cigarette between his narrow lips. He was a hulking man with sandy-gray hair and a permanent five o'clock shadow on his lantern chin. He lifted Marty's right arm, viewing the scars on his hand. "Was it just your hand?"

"No, sir. The scars run up my arm and onto my chest and back."

Lacy smoke enveloping his head, Gallotte unbuttoned Marty's cuff and pushed his sleeve upward. His head peered all around Marty's scarred arm, not unlike a rancher inspecting a potential purchase at a livestock auction. Finally, he dropped Marty's arm and let out a low whistle. "Damn boy, you're lucky that thing even works."

"Yes, sir," Marty answered, flexing his fingers and trying not to remember the tracks of the Tiger tank that had ground his arm into the loamy German soil.

Gallotte's mouth ticked up at the corners. "Nice scar like that'll get you off the hook with the boys." He pointed the cigarette at Marty. "But make sure they know you tried like *hell* to serve."

"Will do, sir."

Gallotte already seemed bored with the exchange. He cracked his knuckles. "Anyone give you the lay of the land yet?"

"Not really, sir."

"Pretty easy duty here, son. I nearly died in two wars and spent the rest of my time busting my hump in Fort Worth tryin' to put food on the table for the wife and five boys. Took this job thanks to a friend of a friend and damned if it wasn't the best decision I ever made." He placed a meat hook on Marty's shoulder and turned him to the window. Gallotte swept his hand left and right. "Out there's the American Sector and we're tasked with rebuilding a big ol' slice of it. That's real money for Mister Buddy Day, our owner…*real* money. It's also a secure livin' for a fella like you."

"Does Mister Day live here?"

"Nah. Comes about twice a year. He's got stuff goin' all over Texas. Plus, his son's a hot shot golfer, always playin' in tournaments with the country club set when he's not chasin' skirt." The meat hook squeezed Marty's shoulder. "You need to learn, right quick, that things here in Germany are a little different. We won the damned war and I'll be damned if we ain't gonna have our spoils of victory. Now there's some bleedin' hearts tryin' to take that away, but by my estimation, we gotta 'nuther decade of good livin', and earnin', before this place goes to pot like everything else always does. By that time Day Construction'll be outta here, anyhow." Gallotte turned Marty to face him. "You stick with it here for five years, you'll go home with a pile a'money and a satisfied grin on your face."

"Sounds like a great plan, sir."

He swept his hand to the city again. "Now we got krauts out there bustin' their collective asses for us. Make no mistake, they're some of the hardest workin' bastards on earth. Smart, too. Sumbitches can build anything. Get their panties in a wad over our cavalier ways but that's beside the point. The problem is that most'a their younger men are maggot food or so damned broken down that they can't swing a sledge. That's why we've taken to importin' the Turks for the manual labor. You'll see 'em, darker skin and all. They work hard and usually keep to themselves."

"Yes, sir."

"So, just pay attention, do your nine to five, and you'll pick things up. I ain't too worried about you."

"Thanks, sir."

Gallotte audibly ran his tongue over his teeth as his eyes twinkled. "Now, on to the important things, like your nights and weekends. First off, even if you did get stuck back in Okie shovelin' manure on the farm, we won the war, so don't take shit from anyone who ain't American. You can go any-damn-where you want, no matter what a limey, a Russkie, a frog, or *especially* a kraut tells you. Always remember—we, the Americans, *won* the damned war. It was sorely in doubt till we hit that damned beach. Hell, I bled for that victory and for your right to clip ass anywhere you want in this burg. Got it?"

"Clip ass?" Marty asked.

"Yeah, get your stinger wet. Damn, son, don't tell me you ain't never had some." Gallotte snorted as his eyes flicked to Marty's midsection. "Your syringe still works after that accident, don't it?"

"Er—yes, sir."

"Well, you're really gonna love it here. Look around and you'll notice that most of us left the wives back home. Good reason for that. There's a sausage shortage in Germany, son, and it's your duty to go out there and service those fraus and fräuleines. They're pretty trustworthy and they'll probably want a dinner or two, or somethin' for their young'uns. That's okay, 'cause you'll pay for a wife someday, too. Believe me. So, get out on the economy here, give it a few weeks, and you'll figure out the score." Gallotte raised his index finger. "But be direct with the fraus. Ain't no need to beat around their bush."

It was right then that Marty knew he'd taken the right job and had exactly the right boss to unknowingly cover him while he was here on his true mission. Jimmy Gallotte's career at Day Construction was probably sixth or seventh on his list of life priorities.

He was the perfect supervisor.

His mind coming back to the moment at hand, Marty had finally reached the head of the queue. It was manned by two Russian soldiers who'd turned at least half of the people away, sending them back to the train station. They spoke rough German to Marty, though Marty didn't even try to understand. He simply removed his ID card and shoved it in the face of one of the Russians. "I'm American. I'm here to spend money at the bars on the Spree."

The soldiers, who couldn't have been more than twenty, looked at one another before one hitched his thumb, allowing Marty to pass.

Outside the bustling Friedrichstrasse station, Marty felt the energy from this vibrant quarter resonate in his bones. Revelers were everywhere, many of them soldiers. Within a minute, Marty saw a soldier from each sector. He walked to a street corner and lit a cigarette. From where he stood, Marty counted nine pubs, seven prostitutes, two men passed out cold, and he distinctly heard three different sources of music. While others came here for good cheer, Marty was here for business and he was well aware of his pulse thudding in his neck. The moment was nearly upon him. He dropped his cigarette into a sewage grate and checked his watch.

"I hope he's still there," Marty muttered to himself.

Earlier, using a detailed roster Professor Walden had created, Marty called his target's place of business. Acting as if he were an old friend, Marty asked to speak with the man. The young lady on the phone told Marty that the man had already left for the evening. After some gentle coaxing, she informed Marty of the bar Marty's target would likely visit before heading home.

Marty crossed the Spree River and walked two blocks to the west. The riverside area had clearly been heavily damaged in the war. New construction was everywhere, along with obvious repair work. Down the length of the river, there were a number of festive beer gardens lit by strings of lights and the cherry tips of hundreds of cigarettes. He found the bar the young lady had referenced, viewing it from the street. It had an enclosed bar area with a beer garden out back, by the river. Marty checked the items in his pocket one last time then stepped into the bar. He ordered a beer before taking a small table by the door.

The bar was old, although unstained plywood made up most of the far wall. A screen door on the new wall led outside, to the riverside beer garden. Inside, several of the mirrors behind the bar were cracked, and one was completely gone. The bar had probably once been quite handsome, with arched brick ceilings and deep mahogany wood throughout. The resident smoke was as thick as a San Francisco fog, whirling each time a current of wind came in through the screen door. The bar was mostly populated by soldiers and women who looked like working girls. It was a merry atmosphere and, judging by the activity of the bartenders and the ringing of the cash register, a popular place.

Marty removed the sheet of paper from his pocket and concealed it in his lap. At the top, held by a staple, were two photos of his target. One was a service picture from 1943 and, the other, a more recent photo. Marty studied the photos before surveying the room.

It only took a few seconds.

The target sat three tables away, braying loudly as he laughed at someone's joke. His tablemates were older than he was, but he seemed to be the straw that stirred the drink. Marty dialed in on their conversation, hearing their telltale Berlinerisch accent. He glanced down at the dossier: his target hailed from the Berlin suburb of Pankow and had been a decorated paramilitary soldier during the war.

That was a polite description for what the man really was. He was Schutzstaffel—the notorious Waffen-SS.

Marty's target was a tall man, quite handsome with an aquiline nose and broad shoulders. He was the kind of man a person would expect to find wearing a spanking suit in a New York investment firm; the kind of man who might ascend to the upper ranks of an organization based on his looks alone. Watching him, Marty noticed how he spoke with confidence and his clothes were superior to those of his German brethren.

Most important to Marty, his target had been there, at Kastellaun, on the evening in question, filling the billet of a Scharführer in the Waffen-SS. Marty didn't remember the man, thank God, but he'd definitely been there, doing his part, acquiescing to Nadel's unlawful orders.

Sipping his beer slowly, Marty checked the two items in his side pockets at least three more times, anxious about this first encounter.

"Be brutal," Marty whispered to himself, echoing the words from his training.

"Swift and ruthless and brutal."

***

The former Schutzstaffel drank until well after one in the morning. Finally he staggered from the bar, rubbing his eyes and yelling goodbyes to his drunken friends. He stood in the middle of the street, struggling to light a cigarette, cursing his lighter before pocketing it and asking for a light from a passing couple. The area was still teeming with roisterers, making Marty's job of tailing the target all the easier. Although shadowing him was no problem, approaching would be more difficult. The target began making his way to the north as Marty followed from half a block back. Heavily painted, yet stunningly attractive hookers stood on the street, spaced a hundred feet apart. Not a single one said a word to the target, and every single one spoke English to Marty, cajoling him to come and enjoy a half-hour with them in bed.

They're ignoring him but speaking English to me. How do they know I'm not German?

Marty knew he'd have to devote some thought to this problem later. He couldn't afford to be recognized.

Pushing the distraction from his mind, Marty plowed on ahead. The pace was slow as the target trudged along in a zig-zag trajectory. Though the professor had created a nice dossier on this individual, he wasn't able to ascertain his home address, leaving Marty with no idea of how far the man had to go. For all Marty knew, the target could stagger into his apartment at any moment. And the streets here were still too crowded for Marty to approach him.

Feeling his palms growing wet with sweat, Marty could feel himself panicking. What if his home is nearby? What if tonight's not the night? Then, thankfully, the target had a rendezvous with nature.

Singing "Lili Marleen" to himself, the former SS pivoted into an alleyway. Up ahead, Marty could see the signs for the Nordbahnhof, another train station, probably two hundred yards away. But no one occupied this block other than a hooker standing fifty feet ahead on the street corner. Her eyes were averted, locked onto two uniformed soldiers crossing the street.

Marty's tongue felt like a one-pound steak clogging up his mouth. He turned, walking into the dark alley, seeing his target ten feet in, urinating on the wall as he continued his poor rendition of the famous cabaret love song. With slack eyes, the target twisted his head around and saw Marty approaching. The target then mumbled something about not being a homo.

Be swift. Be ruthless. Be brutal.

Marty reached into his pocket and palmed the leather-wrapped lead sap. He released it, wiping his hand inside his pocket, then gripped it again.

"You didn't hear me?" the target slurred as Marty continued coming. "I'm not a damned queer."

Planting forward on his left foot, Marty swung full-force, catching his target on the back of his head, sending him tumbling to the earth and dousing Marty's trousers and shoes in a spray of smelly urine.

When he regained his senses seconds later, the target screamed.

***

The former SS had fallen forward, striking his head on the ground. As a massive knot on the right center of his forehead visibly grew, Marty mounted the man. He reached into his other pocket and produced an ear dagger—a pointed, compact knife resembling an icepick. With his right forearm on the target's throat, Marty held the dagger in the target's right ear and growled, "Stop screaming."

"What do you want?" the man rasped.

"You're Jan Rheinsdorf, formerly of the 101st SS Heavy Panzer Battalion?"

"Yes," Rheinsdorf answered, his voice gurgling. "And I was thoroughly investigated after the war and was not prosecu—"

"Speak softly," Marty hissed. "Listen to me, Jan. Unless you want to die, you'll quietly cooperate with me."

"I don't want to die," the man sobbed.

"Your last commander, Raban Nadel, the man who killed Sturmbannführer Peter Weber in cold blood..."

Rheinsdorf's eyes opened wider.

"Where is he *now*?"

"Who are you?"

Marty jabbed with the ear dagger, pricking a quarter inch into the soft tissue at the ear opening. The German moaned and tried to squirm away.

"Listen to what I'm saying. If you talk, you walk. You got that?" Marty readjusted his forearm on his throat. "But if you hold out, if you hold *anything* back, you'll die right here and I won't lose any sleep about it, you murdering sonofabitch. So, I ask you again, your final commander, Hauptsturmführer Raban Nadel—where is he now?"

Rheinsdorf's expression couldn't have been more horrified. He tried to shake his head as he muttered, "I don't know," three times in succession.

"You're lying."

"I was never in that inner circle!"

Marty again told him to lower his voice and, in return, he eased the pressure on his target's throat.

Rheinsdorf took several gasping breaths. "I didn't change my name, nor do I commiserate with *Die Bruderschaft*." Rheinsdorf was referencing "The Brotherhood," a small detachment of ODESSA, the criminal legion of former SS. Marty knew *Die Bruderschaft* was exclusively made up of men from the 101st SS Heavy Panzer Battalion.

"Do you ever speak to anyone in *Die Bruderschaft*?"

"No," Rheinsdorf said forcefully. "After the war, I turned myself in as SS and was never tried. I now run our family's business. I interact with the Americans and the British on a daily basis. Please don't kill me." He began to cry in earnest.

Rheinsdorf had ceased all struggling, leading Marty to relieve almost all of the pressure on his throat and ear. He had a distinct feeling this man was telling the truth. But, while he had him here, he might as well glean all he could. He gave him a little shake.

"Who would know where Raban Nadel is?"

"What?"

Marty spoke through clenched teeth. "If you stall one more time, Jan, they're going to find a corpse with scrambled eggs oozing from his ear tomorrow morning."

"The only two men I know are in *Die Bruderschaft* are Roth and Zeckern."

Marty had the 101st unit roster and a number of dossiers back at his flat. He knew who Zeckern was, and he remembered reading something about Roth. Regardless, he asked, "Who are they?"

"Roth...his first name was Felix. I hated him. Everyone did. He was a true *Unmensch*...a butcher who found a way to feed his bloodlust in the SS."

"More."

"He was very close to Nadel. His pet. We called him Nadel's *Schwanzlutscher*."

Marty repeated each fact in order to memorize the information. "And Zeckern?"

"Zeckern was the battalion commander. I don't remember his first name, but he never liked Peter Weber, and Raban Nadel was one of his prized recruits."

"Why?"

"Zeckern and Nadel were criminals, like so many who served with me. They used the war as a smokescreen for looting and other criminal activity."

"Oh, but *you* were a professional," Marty remarked sardonically, unable to help himself.

"I joined the Waffen-SS to be an elite soldier and that's how I fought."

"What about the Massacre at Kastellaun? You took part in that."

Rheinsdorf winced. "The worst day of my life."

Marty closed his eyes for a moment, trying not to respond to what he'd just heard. "Your actions that day..." he growled.

"I was disgusted by it."

"But you didn't dissent. All dissenters were killed on the spot."

"No, I didn't, but I didn't kill or maim, either. I stayed behind the fray."

Marty leaned close, his nose an inch from Rheinsdorf's. "Doing nothing is the same as following orders." Marty must have unconsciously jabbed the ear dagger because Rheinsdorf let out a brief yelp.

"I'll always regret what happened at Kastellaun. It's the lowest point of my life. I drink it away every night."

"You're acting contrite now," Marty growled. "But back at the bar you sure were having fun."

"Because I'm drunk. It's the only time I can numb myself."

Marty moved on. "So, you avoided prosecution. What about Zeckern and Roth?"

"Like Raban Nadel, Zeckern went underground but I've heard he's still in Germany, in *Die Bruderschaft*, living under a different name. I haven't heard anything about Roth but, if he's alive, he'd still be in contact with Nadel even though he would have to have changed his identity. Otherwise, he'd have been prosecuted for numerous crimes. He was the top henchman in the entire unit. He's a very dangerous man and I wouldn't doubt that, by now, he's either in prison or dead."

"Where were they from?"

"Zeckern was from the south...I don't remember where. Roth was from Hessen."

"Who else would know where Nadel is?"

"I don't know of anyone, nor do I talk to anyone about such things. I'm ashamed of my role in the war."

"You said you heard Zeckern and Roth are in *die Bruderschaft*. Who told you that?"

"Years ago, they tried to recruit me into their society."

"But you didn't do it?"

With genuine anger, Rheinsdorf said, "I'd rather die than be associated with them."

Marty took a look back over his shoulder before increasing the pressure on Rheinsdorf's throat. "I know where you live," Marty lied. "I've seen your wife, and I've seen your two little girls. If you breathe a word of this to a single soul, I will come after you and your family."

Rheinsdorf began to sob. "I won't! I won't!"

Marty pulled the dagger from Rheinsdorf's ears and nicked the bridge of his nose, drawing blood. "You remember what I said."

Rheinsdorf cried openly as he nodded.

Slipping his implements into his pockets, Marty exited the alley and walked back the way he'd come, towards Friedrichstrasse. Halfway there, he leaned into another alley and vomited explosively.

Then, on the train ride back to Steglitz, Marty whispered to himself all he'd learned.

Over and over, burning the facts into his mind.

# Chapter Two

My final days of the war, up until the massacre, bring back many positive memories. Of course it's a struggle not to let what happened drag my memories down. But, before the massacre, things were truly looking up. For nearly a year, my unit, the 32nd Field Artillery, had bravely fought, moving eastward from France, through Belgium, and on into Germany. As the brutal winter of '44-'45 finally began to abate, a feeling of optimism eventually descended upon all of the troops of the 32nd Field Artillery's "Proud Americans"—our unit's motto.

German civilians, people who'd lived with war for so long, began to emerge from their homes, bringing with them paltry peace offerings in the form of what little food they had. Some brought trinkets and, in some cases, a few provided bodily favors. Many of them were scared of us—and I don't blame them. I never took anything except chocolate and I'm proud to say few from Able Battery, 32nd Field Artillery did either. Several did and, though I didn't agree with it, I can't bring myself to blame them.

Our battery commander, Captain Scott Rook, constantly reminded us to display appropriate decorum around the Germans. He led by example. In fact, I cannot remember a soul from our unit who didn't respect Captain Rook. Unlike our previous commander, who was killed shortly after the beachhead at Normandy, Rook possessed true empathy and a warrior spirit. Not only did he know my name, but he knew my mother's name. He knew my dad had died when I was young. He knew we were from North Dakota, and he often joked that, if a person faced north from South Dakota, they could watch North Dakota blow by in the form of tumbleweeds. Rook was from Tennessee. He was a good man.

For soldiers of a regular artillery tube unit, the men of Able Battery, 2nd of the 32nd Field Artillery, were rugged from all the close combat we'd endured. I can't count the number of times I found myself in a trench, or behind a tree, or—yes—taking cover behind a dead body, fighting the Germans while my 105 mm Howitzer sat idle in the woods a half a mile back. No, we didn't see as much close-quarters combat as the infantry boys saw, but the war was the damned war. Each and every day was an adventure and a person had no idea what hell that day might bring.

By March of 1945, we knew it was just a matter of time before Hitler's so-called Thousand Year Reich fell. By the time a few bundles of the Stars & Stripes eventually made it out to us, we learned that even some of the most pessimistic generals were beginning to talk like the war was almost over. Hell, I bet I talked to a dozen German soldiers, men who had surrendered, who were completely stunned that their leadership hadn't yet admitted defeat.

You should have seen these German guys, too. Their regular line soldiers, what was left of them, were emaciated and most of them sick, making this barking sound like the seals I'd once seen at the Minneapolis Zoo. Like I mentioned, the previous winter had been hell, worst in fifty years, from all we'd heard. According to those kraut prisoners, if a German unit was deemed disposable, or didn't have an influential commander, they didn't get much food or medicine delivered through the supply lines. And when we heard those things time and time again, we began to realize that our enemy couldn't hold out much longer.

That's what made the massacre so shocking.

***Stop it! It's not time. Don't uncork those horrors yet. Telling it now will make the motivation for justice/revenge seem senseless. Besides, you can't handle opening that Pandora's box this early in your hunt. Go into detail about the massacre when your mission's almost complete. Remember...erase this paragraph!

Proceed...

Like I mentioned before, by the time March of '45 rolled around, the weather was beginning to warm up. I don't want to give you the wrong idea, either. When I say "warm," I mean the snow began to slowly melt. A person could actually wash himself without fear of getting frostbite. I remember, just before our final action, when we were bivouacked just outside of a town somewhere inside the border of Germany, taking off all my clothes and showering under a Lyster bag out in the forest. The bag probably only held a few gallons—and it didn't come close to removing half of the grime that coated my body.

Still, it was blissful.

There were still firefights, but by this time we were marching eastward at such a rapid pace that our role in the war had actually gone back to what we were trained to do—contribute artillery support. We would speed forward to a designated position, set up our guns, and send hot steel over the battle line in support of our forward troops. This was a far cry from the close-quarters combat we'd endured back during the winter in the Ardennes.

So, the weather was warming. The generals seemed optimistic. And the only German soldiers we were encountering were either already dead, or being shuttled backward as POWs. Things were looking up.

I remember the big canard going around in March that the Germans would surrender in April and we'd all get to sail back to the U.S. on a sun-splashed ocean liner.

Boy...how little did we know.

***

Marty's flat was located on the sixth floor of a Steglitz apartment building. Other than the constant grind of the steep flights of stairs, he was satisfied with his new temporary home. It had two bedrooms, a small kitchen, a private bathroom and even a small balcony overlooking the buildings across the way and the German plain off to the south. The S-Bahn was only a few minutes away, the small city center of Steglitz just beyond that. The street, Feuerbachstrasse, was quiet and had been tree-lined before the war. Those trees, like so many others in urban centers, had been cut down for firewood during the war. New, smaller trees had been planted and would someday again provide shade to the street's residents.

Steglitz was a suburb of Berlin. It was situated in the American sector, southwest of the city. Marty had chosen Steglitz because it was slightly out of the way and had good train service. It was low profile and afforded ease of travel—perfect for his needs.

Though he didn't normally sleep late, Marty slept until nearly ten this morning, his first Saturday in Germany. The week had been exhausting and his body clock still hadn't adjusted to the seven-hour time difference. After last night's intense encounter, his body and mind had shut down like an overheated machine. When he awoke, Marty thought about what he had done to that former SS in the alley. Then he saw his journal, pen on top, on his nightstand.

Marty didn't even remember journaling last night. After brewing a small pot of coffee, he sat at the small breakfast table with a cigarette and reviewed his brief entry...

After all the waiting and planning, it's finally begun! I located my first target. I waited. I followed him. I knocked him senseless. And, once he'd been neutralized, he gave me what could turn out to be critical information. And not once did that former SS seem to suspect I was anything other than a German with a Berlin accent. Keeping my American identity secret is the key to pulling this off and finding Nadel.

Marty had no idea how many interrogations his mission would require. At least he was off to a good start: after only one sortie, he'd learned far more than he'd already known. Once he'd read his entry and added a few small notations, he ate an apple and a piece of bread, then showered and walked into Steglitz to purchase food for the week. Marty felt as good as he had in years.

That done, Marty stored his groceries in the flat and carried his journal downstairs to the stoop, where he sat and performed risk assessments about his next move in the back of the notebook. Several residents came and went, including another American businessman who tried to engage Marty in some friendly conversation. Having no desire to make friends, Marty rudely brushed him off. Fifteen minutes after he'd sat down, Frau Schaal, the landlady, appeared on the stoop. She wore an apron and carried two garbage pails.

"Good day, Mister Marty!" she said cheerily, speaking English.

Irritated, Marty closed his eyes for a moment. He looked up and offered a pinched, plastic smile.

"You like to write?" she asked, dumping the contents into the large can by the tree stump.

"When I have *peace* enough to do it."

"Oh," she said. "You want to be alone. Excuse me for interrupting."

Marty didn't respond. She stood there for a moment before quietly making her way back inside.

He'd met her, of course, when he'd finalized his lease on the flat. Day Construction backed his lease, which was six months in length, so Marty's meeting with the landlady had been nothing more than a formality. As long as his flat was secure and close to rail transit, Marty couldn't have cared less about its features.

On that first day, after giving him his keys, Frau Schaal had tried to chat with him, probably trying to glean whether or not he was a German hater. Rather than converse, Marty had remained silent as she told him her sob story of her husband in the Luftwaffe who'd never come home. He couldn't help smirking when she'd told him of her misfortune.

But it appeared she'd not gotten the hint, due to her joyful disposition today.

The last thing Marty needed to do was create a high profile at his residence. He was here in Germany for one thing and one thing only. Drawing attention to himself could only serve to add risk to his mission.

*Forget it…get back to work.*

Marty slid a Camel between his lips, lighting it with his Zippo before making more notes in the back of the journal.

A terrific crash interrupted his train of thought.

Across the street, a boy of perhaps eleven or twelve had wrecked his bicycle. The bicycle lay there straddling the sidewalk. The front tire was partly off the rim and the tube was shredded. Next to the bike, its rider squirmed about, trying not to cry as he surveyed his bodily damage. Marty could see that both of the kid's elbows were torn open and bleeding. The boy looked plaintively at Marty.

"I can't get a damn thing done!" Marty yelled to the sky.

Smacking his journal on the porch in disgust, he crossed the street, speaking sternly to the boy in German. "You tried to jump onto the sharp edge of the sidewalk and popped your tire, didn't you? Well, maybe you'll learn that a bike like this is meant to ride on a flat surface." Marty jerked the old bike up and leaned it against the spindly tree. Then he brusquely helped the boy up. While the boy had been doing a fine job of holding back the tears, Marty's rebuke had put him over the edge. He began to silently cry as his face contorted.

"Ahhhh shit," Marty mumbled, producing a clean handkerchief and handing it to the boy. "Here…for your elbows."

"*Danke,*" the boy said, hissing as he touched the white cloth to the scarlet blood. Marty flicked his Camel to the sidewalk and knelt. He produced his pocketknife, taking the handkerchief back from the kid and splitting it into two pieces. Then he folded the pieces and gently wrapped each elbow, using the ends to make a loose knot.

"Those should help stem the bleeding," Marty said. "Don't do jumps on that bike." He pointed to the front tire. "Tire's flat anyway."

The boy touched the tire and said, "Ahhh shit!" He said it in pitch-perfect English.

Marty cocked his brow at the boy. "*Sprichst Du* English?"

"A little," the boy replied in German, smiling despite the tears on his red cheeks. He repeated the curse again, adding the flourish of a pumped fist.

Marty frowned. "You shouldn't say that."

"You just did."

"Doesn't matter. Anyway, I was busy when you interrupted me," Marty replied, finding his Camel and sticking it back into his mouth. He crossed the street, resuming his spot on the stoop and opening the journal.

He could hear the scrape of the rim matched by the accompanying footsteps. The footsteps stopped in front of Marty. Marty ignored them and started writing.

"You're the new American in Six-A."

"Brilliant deduction," Marty mumbled.

"Do you like it here?"

Marty clenched his eyes shut. "Is it everyone's mission to disturb me today?"

"No, sir," the boy replied, switching to English. "I want speak you at thank you." He grinned once he had it out.

"It's, 'I want to say thank you.'"

"I be Josh," the boy said, proffering his right hand. He pronounced Josh in the German way, making it sound like "Yosh" with a long "O."

"Good to meet you," Marty answered perfunctorily, his eyes going back to his journal.

"What are you doing?" the boy asked, switching back to his native tongue.

"*Trying* to write."

Josh leaned his bike against the stoop and opened the trap-like cellar doors. He was gone for several minutes, making Marty think he'd finally found his peace. Just as Marty lit another cigarette, starting to hit his stride with his next set of plans, the boy reappeared with a grease-stained wooden toolbox, an air pump and a bucket of water.

Marty tried to ignore him. The boy hummed a tune as he removed his front wheel, diligently sliding his tire halfway off the rim and taking the tube completely off. He then set about patching the tube with a small patch kit. Marty lifted his eyes, shaking his head.

"You're doing it wrong, kid."

"I'm patching the holes."

"Some of them."

"All of them," Josh countered.

"You can't know that yet. You need to pump the tube up *first* and then move the tube under the water. You look for air bubbles, you mark the holes, then patch each one. You had a number of holes in that tube and if you try to do it by sight alone you're going to miss one. Trust me."

"Will you help me?"

Marty slapped his journal shut. *Screw it!* After he helped this mini-kraut, he'd go upstairs and write on the patio. In peace.

Once the bucket was filled and the tube was pumped, it only took a few minutes to identify and patch the three large holes. When the tube was holding air nicely, they found two other pinprick holes that would have amounted to a slow leak and patched them as well. Fifteen minutes later, Josh's bike was in fine working order.

Lifting the front of the bike, Marty slowly spun the wheel. "See that?" he asked, referencing a slightly warped rotation. "It's rideable, but your wheel's outta true. I don't have the tools to true it up. You'll need to take it to a bike shop."

"But it's okay to ride?"

"I guess…as long as it's not rubbing. But it won't ride well until the wheel has been trued." He wagged his finger at Josh's arms. "Be careful with those elbows."

Josh mounted the bike awkwardly, nearly falling as the bike lurched forward and struck Marty in his midsection. Grunting, Marty bent forward with his hands on his knees.

"Are you okay?"

"Yeah," Marty mumbled. "Jeez, kid, you drilled me right in the family jewels." Marty spoke this in German.

"*Familien Juwelen?*" Josh asked.

"*Family Jewels* in English. Come on, kid…you're a guy. Think about it. It's another way of saying *balls*. You know…nuts, gonads. In other words, pain."

Laughing, Josh said, "What is your name, sir?"

"I'm busy, okay? Just run along."

"You can't tell me your name?"

"It's Marty," he said.

Josh extended his free hand, balancing himself with his other. Marty reluctantly shook it before grabbing his journal and making the trek up the stairs, lamenting the interaction.

*Stupid little kraut.*

\*\*\*

Three hours later, while Marty planned a reconnaissance run to scout his next target, there was a knock at his door. He eyed the door for a moment before his eyes came back to the map, marked by pushpins at the alleged locales of each of his targets. Just today, he'd added new pushpins in the middle of Bavaria and Hessen, the states Zeckern and Roth hailed from. Due to Rheinsdorf's "advice," Marty was hopeful he might find the two wayward SS near their homes of record.

The knock came again.

Marty walked to the door, asking who it was.

"Frau Schaal."

"And Josh!" a second voice chimed in.

Dipping his head, Marty unchained the lock. When he opened the door, he did nothing to conceal his exasperation.

Frau Schaal's hand was on her son's back and she nudged him slightly forward. "Thank you for helping Josh today. He said you patched up his arms and fixed his tire."

"No big deal," Marty said dismissively.

"Well, it was," she replied. "He cherishes that bicycle more than anything."

"Bicycle is very cost," Josh added in his broken brand of English, smiling up at Marty.

"Well, you're welcome," Marty replied mechanically. "Now, if you'll excuse me." He tried closing the door but Frau Schaal put her hand out.

"Herr Marty, we want to repay you by having you for a meal this evening."

"I can't," Marty said, shaking his head. "I have other plans."

"Dressed like that?" Josh asked, switching back to German. Then he sniffed several times. "And you've certainly not been cooking. It smells like a barn in there."

"Josh," Frau Schaal admonished.

"Thanks for the offer," Marty said, again trying to close the door.

"Herr Marty, this was Josh's idea," Frau Schaal countered, gently holding the door. She tilted her head to her son as if trying to tell Marty more than she was saying. "You can eat quickly and leave if you like." Her eyes pleaded with Marty.

"I can't."

"Please." Josh clasped his hands in a prayerful pose as he again butchered the English language. "Mister Marty, with us you walk the stairs for eat and be happy."

Marty's shoulders sagged and he couldn't believe the words that emerged from his mouth. "What time?"

\*\*\*

Despite being a poor piece of bottom round—beef was not good in postwar Germany—Frau Schaal had slow-cooked the cut in the style of traditional roast beef, making it tender enough to eat with only a fork. She'd added carrots and potatoes and a great deal of black pepper. Something was missing, however, and her efforts had created a meager cousin to the beef stew Marty's mother had once made nearly every Sunday.

They'd begun eating soon after Marty arrived. The conversation was sparse and Marty made his answers succinct. He wasn't going out of his way to be unfriendly, but he didn't want to give anyone the impression he was outgoing, either. It was his intention, as Frau Schaal had suggested, to eat quickly and leave. If he offended them, well, so be it. Perhaps then they'd get the message that he was their tenant and nothing more.

The Schaal flat was larger than Marty's, as were all flats on the opposite side of the building. Most of their furniture was antique, probably handed down from relatives. As he ate, Marty noticed only a single photo of Frau Schaal's husband. In the photo, he was standing on the wing of a large German warplane, probably a bomber of some sort. He didn't appear to be the prototypical dashing pilot. In fact, with his round face, balding pate and portly body, he seemed the type of man a person would find pushing pencils in an office somewhere.

"That's my papa," Josh said, following Marty's gaze. "His name is Hauptmann Ulrich Schaal. He flies transport planes."

*A transport—not a bomber.*

Frau Schaal plated her fork and knife, dabbing her mouth. "Josh has not yet given up on his papa's return." She spoke these words in a practiced manner, without noticeable melancholy.

"A recent story in the *Zeitung* said there are thousands of men still alive in the east," Josh added, his eyes coming to Marty's. "The Russians could release him any day now."

Marty shoveled green beans into his mouth and said nothing.

"So, Herr Marty, where are you from?" Frau Schaal asked, clearly trying to change the subject.

"Oklahoma," Marty said, alarmed that he nearly slipped up and said North Dakota.

"That's near Texas?" she asked.

"Yeah."

"Cowboys and Indians!" Josh shouted, shooting mock pistols at both adults.

"Josh loves cowboys and Indians, and cactuses, and wagon trains, and ghost towns," she said, viewing her boy with a motherly smile. "I don't care for the guns but I guess imagining himself a cowboy or Indian is relatively harmless."

"Do you horse drive?" Josh asked in English.

"No."

"Fire gun?"

"No," Marty lied.

"Josh, please," Frau Schaal said. Her green eyes came back to Marty. "Where in Oklahoma?"

"You wouldn't know it if I told you," he replied flatly.

As her eyes slid back to her food, she asked the next question delicately. "Were you in the war?"

"No. And can we not talk about me?" Marty asked, rushing to finish his food.

"Why weren't you in the war?" Josh asked in German, cocking his head. "Every man was in the war."

"Josh, my goodness. That's personal," his mother said.

Marty shoveled a massive piece of roast beef into his mouth, grinding it with his rear teeth as his German hosts watched him. When he'd finally gotten it down, he sipped his water and said, "The military wouldn't take me because of injuries I'd sustained as a teen, on the farm. Okay?"

"Injuries?" Josh asked, looking Marty up and down. "You look okay to me. Is it because of the scar on your hand?"

"Josh," his mother admonished.

"My hand, and other injuries," Marty answered.

"What kind of injuries? Can you show me?"

"Josh, stop it!" his mother scolded.

Marty pushed his half-eaten plate away and placed his napkin on the table. "I appreciate the meal. I must be going now." He stood and walked to the front door.

Josh and his mother followed him into the sitting room, both seeming somewhat bewildered at his abruptness. "Herr Marty, I have coffee and dessert. Please stay. It will only take fifteen minutes. I'm sorry about all the questions."

Marty opened the door. "Like I said earlier, I have plans and I'm *already* late."

Josh grasped Marty's uninjured hand. "Mister Marty, I've been sweeping the stairs and emptying garbage cans for a month and this week I finally had enough money to buy a model airplane. It's American, but it's similar to the plane papa flies. I was hoping you'd help me put it together after Mutti clears the table." He squeezed Marty's hand. "Please help. It'll be fun!"

The boy's eyes sparkled. Marty looked at Josh's mother, seeing great sadness in her face as she pleaded with her eyes.

"No," Marty said, disentangling his hand. "Too much to do." He stepped out the door and slammed it shut.

After jogging up to his apartment and going inside, Marty leaned against his door from the inside, rubbing his temples. He was angry. As his anger faded, Marty soon felt lousy over his rude departure. He could just see his own mother, her lips knotted up, shaking her head in disappointment—no matter how much he despised the Germans.

Marty didn't perform his reconnaissance that night—he stayed home, drinking himself into a stupor on his small patio. Out there, in the light of a hurricane lamp, Marty journaled about a friend he'd lost.

An hour later, Marty stumbled back inside. Drunk, he tripped over a throw rug and passed out cold on the hardwood floor. When he finally awoke at first light on Sunday morning, with no memory of his last hour of wakefulness, Marty would view himself in the mirror and find salty stains trailing down his cheeks.

# Chapter Three

Before I explain the massacre, or how I came to be here in Germany, I want to tell you about my closest friends. They're my namesakes. These men were my section-mates, my fellow soldiers…but, mainly, they were my brothers. Any soldier who served during war, and probably even peacetime, will speak about his best friends in the same manner as me. Believe me when I tell you, when you're together with other soldiers 24 hours a day, months on end, you get to know one another like family. My brothers and I laughed together and, as I'll soon tell you, we cried together.

And, eventually, we died together.

As I mentioned, the war seemed to be winding down. It was mid-March of 1945. We'd rotated off the front line for a day of maintenance and recovery. That night, although we weren't supposed to build fires, we built one anyway. Boy, were we feeling confident. We also knew that we were ten miles behind the front line and burning a fire wasn't such a big risk.

Me and my best friends—my "brothers"—Staff Sergeant Kenny Martin, Sergeant John Vincent and Sergeant Danny Elder—sat around the fire, desperately needing sleep but enjoying the moment for what it was. Despite our collective exhausted state, it was nice to be able to converse without the constant threat of dying. Once the fire had burned down to a comfortable level, we spread an extra blanket on the wet ground and started in with some gin rummy, enjoying it with a pilfered bottle of vinegary local wine.

Kenny Martin inserted himself at this point. Somewhere along the way he'd found a shot glass and, rather than let us take big slugs of that rot-gut wine, he administered it to us one shot at a time, so we'd each get our fair share.

"Gotta make it last, gentumennnnnns," he'd said, mocking the first sergeant and his syrupy-thick southern accent. Our first sergeant always addressed the men of the unit as "gentlemen," but his accent made it sound exactly the way Kenny repeated: Gentumennnnnns.

By the time we'd each had a few shots of the wine, it was obvious that Danny Elder was once again the class of the field when it came to gin rummy. So we put the cards away and performed our favorite activity: talking about home. We loved to talk about our families, growing up, foods we missed, peculiarities about people from our hometown—and, of course, girls.

Maybe it was the coziness of the fire, or the loosening effects of the wine—I don't know. But what really set that night apart was the story that Danny Elder told. Though we all considered ourselves brothers, he revealed something about himself that he'd never mentioned before. It was a shock to hear it for the first time, especially the way he told it.

We'd all been carrying on, laughing, talking about all manner of things when, all of a sudden, Danny turned serious. His face grew stony, as if he were thumbing through a bunch of happy photos before stumbling across one that brought back bad memories.

"I got a son but I don't know where he is," Danny said flatly.

"What?" I asked.

"I got a son."

"A son, my frost-bitten ass," Kenny laughed. We all laughed, too.

Danny didn't laugh. He didn't seem angry, didn't even react. Just stared into the fire.

"What're you talking about?" John asked.

Danny just kept staring, his chest slowly rising and falling.

"You okay?" Kenny asked, touching Danny's shoulder.

"My last year of high school, I'd been courtin' a girl named Darla. She was a nice one, a real looker, from a pretty well-to-do family." Danny licked his lips. "Yeah, her family was one of the richer ones in Troy. Parents didn't like me much, knew we were poor. Prob'ly figured I was trouble. Her daddy was the town dentist and her mama—man, was she pretty—was in charge of the garden club and junior league and all that kinda stuff. You know...white gloves and tea and flowery dresses." The corner of Danny's mouth turned up in a humorless smile. "Anyway, her parents had forbidden her from seein' me. Darla gave in after a few weeks and told me to quit comin' around."

"Dentist sounds like a dickhead," Kenny said.

"I guess he was just looking out for his girl," Danny said with a shrug, continuing to peer into the fire.

"What happened?" I asked.

"Not too long after she broke it off, in late September of my senior year, they had the homecoming dance at the school. I showed up, alone, miserable as hell, standin' in a stag-line, watchin' Darla take turns dancin' with all the rich boys."

"Trying to make you jealous," Kenny offered.

"She wasn't like that," Danny whispered. "And, boy, I was surprised when Darla waved at me and secretly motioned me out the side door of the gym. I followed her out and she kissed me, standing right there in the shadows, before she'd said nary a word."

"Nice young lady," John said, elbowing me.

"It was the best kiss of my life," Danny said, tilting his head back to the sky. "But that wasn't all of it. She took my hand and we went up to the ball field."

"And?" Kenny asked.

"You know," Danny said, his tone still melancholy.

"What, she had her rich beau waitin' up there to beat you up?" John asked, chuckling.

"Don't joke about it," Danny snapped.

"Whoa, sorry," John said, glancing at us and shrugging.

Danny rubbed his face. "Sorry...I'm not mad. I know this story's kinda out of left field. It just...it just hurts." He paused a moment. "Anyway, that was the only time. We'd never done that before and, afterward, it was kinda awkward. We went back inside the dance and didn't talk no more that night. Days later, when I'd see her in the hallway or around town, she'd smile at me then look away. It wasn't fun not bein' with her, but I understood."

"That sounds like a raw deal," Kenny said.

"It was," Danny replied, swigging water from his canteen. "Then one day, 'bout two months later, her daddy came to see mine. Boy did he give me a death stare when he crossed our yard. I didn't know why he was there…all I knew was Pop made me go out to the barn. After the dentist left, my pop beat the ever-lovin' shit outta me. Told me I done knocked that rich girl up. Said her dad vowed to ruin our lives if we ever told a soul."

"Damn," I muttered.

"What then?" Kenny asked.

"They made a big deal tellin' everybody she was goin' off to Virginia to a girls' school that catered to people all into that equestrian stuff. Darla had a pretty nice jumpin' horse she kept down at the stables." Danny shook his head. "Heck, for all I know she did end up at that school. She wrote me a letter right before she left, telling me she was gonna have that baby and keep it with her aunt, a widow, there in Virginia."

No one said a word.

"Almost a year later her mama got word to mine that Darla had a son. Said she wanted us to know he was healthy but she reiterated that it was to be a big secret and all. At the end of the note her mama got nasty about things, about what I'd done and how it was gonna make Darla's entire life one big lie."

"What a witch," John remarked.

"Did Darla ever come back?" I asked.

"Not before I left. When I was in 'cruit training, I got to thinkin' about my boy a lot. I wrote my mama and asked about Darla and my son and my mama wrote back and let me hold it real good, tellin' me to just forget 'bout her and my kid or the dentist would wreck everything."

None of us knew what to say. It was easy to see in that dim firelight that this was extremely difficult for Danny to put into words. We all just looked around at each other, unsure of how to comfort our friend.

Then Danny put his head between his knees and began to shudder. It was awful to watch him grieve that way, just plain awful. I wanted to help my friend that night, to take away his pain. But it was so real, and so deep, that all I could do was put my hand on him so he'd know I was there.

"I got me a son somewhere and he don't even know who his daddy is," Danny cried, his voice full of anguish. "I just want him to know his daddy loves him. I wanna hold him. Just wanna hold my boy one good time and tell him that I do care about him. Tell him that someday, somehow, I'll make him proud of his worthless, no good daddy."

We listened to Danny go on and on about wanting to throw ball with his boy, wanting to teach him how to fish, how to hammer a nail, and someday how to drive an automobile. Boy, did he really let loose.

Despite all the death we'd experienced, that night was one of the most gut-wrenching of the entire war. What made it more powerful was, in two years of service, no one in our group of friends had ever cried in front of each other. Even when those around us were killed. That night, when I finally crawled in my sack, I shed a tear for Danny Elder, and for his son. Danny's distress was truly visceral, from the depths of his soul. I felt for my friend, I really did. And I felt for his son, a kid who had no idea what a good person his father actually was.

Sadly, now his son will never know.

\*\*\*

*Kriminaldetektiv* Werner Eisch was just returning from his doctor, having visited him on his midday break. While many people, especially those with the relative freedom of a detective, would have visited the doctor during working hours, Werner had scheduled his appointment to coincide with his lunch meal, and had eaten his sandwich and apple on his walk back to the station. This way he wasn't cheating his employer, which happened to be the Berlin Polizei.

After he'd walked under the Brandenburg Gate, eyeing the mottled, war-torn areas where the colossal monument had been hastily patched, three American soldiers, manning a security checkpoint, stopped him.

"Papers," one said, snapping his fingers. "And use your left hand, Fritz, not that lobster cracker you've got on your right." This drew riotous laughter from the group. Werner laughed with them, having long before learned that the Americans were an easy sort to handle as long as he was cooperative.

Werner recognized two of the American guards. He felt almost certain they remembered him, especially due to his steel prosthetic. He also wore an identifying badge on his left pocket, signifying that he was a detective in the Polizei. They were just having a little fun with him to kill time. They won the war—in Werner's mind, they had the right to make things occasionally difficult on the Germans. He didn't allow it to irritate him.

Dutifully, Werner used his left hand and produced his papers. "I hope you men are having a fine day," he said, waving his prosthetic to the crystalline sky. "We don't get many cloudless days here in Berlin."

The senior soldier, a staff sergeant, quickly ducked down and looked up into the sky as his face grew concerned. "Careful movin' that meat hook up into the air, Fritz! The Russkies might pick up all that steel on radar and scramble their Migs." This comment brought on another round of uncontained amusement and back-slapping. Werner laughed with the Americans, acting as if he'd never heard a joke about his prosthetic.

"Good one, Phil," one of the soldiers said. "Radar...I gotta remember that one."

"Alright, Fritzie, get on outta here," the staff sergeant said. "Go play pretend cop with your Crackerjack badge and that empty gun we let y'alls carry around."

Werner nodded politely at the three soldiers, continuing on to the east. A widower from the war, he was perpetually thankful that his wife had been unable to bear children. While their lack of offspring had been a source of pain prior to her passing, Werner didn't know how he would raise children without her, especially in the war-torn remains of Berlin.

A cheery soul, he didn't allow his wife's death to weigh on him. Though she had been a tiny lady, she'd have surely given Werner the business for any extraneous grieving—she'd have wanted him to be happy, even if she'd had to "beat it into him," something she had always joked about. On the one-year anniversary of her death, Werner had viewed his bleary eyes in the mirror and decided to live the way she'd have wanted. Since then, he'd remembered her only with joy. And he'd never remarried, nor given it a fleeting thought. Now Werner lived a prosaic life, marked only by his profession and his desire to reach his professional goal.

After walking around a two-story pile of broken, unusable bricks, Werner made his way up the worn stone steps to the Third Directorate, also known as the Mitte Precinct, of the Berlin Polizei. He removed his hat, nodding at the desk sergeant. Sitting next to the desk sergeant was the American adjutant, a military policeman. He was sound asleep and snoring—typical behavior for him. If Werner were to get close, he'd surely smell the cloying remains of the Ami's alcohol from the night before.

Passing through the door to the detective bureau, Werner wended his way through the serried rows of desks and partitions, unable to ignore the odor of perspiration on this unusually hot summer day. He'd just sat at his neat desk, attacking an orderly pile of cases, when a uniformed officer appeared.

"Detective Eisch?"

"Yes?" Werner said, trying his best to control his annoyance.

"Got a guy downstairs whose story isn't matching up. The duty lieutenant wants him questioned further and you're next on the list."

Werner quickly eyed the three pink note slips on his desk. They could wait. He stood, noticing the street cop gaping at the clamp prosthetic. As was his habit, Werner lifted his arm and snapped the pincher a few times. "Satisfied?"

"Sorry, detective, I've just never seen one like that. War?"

"An eagle-eyed sniper on the eastern front. Took my arm off with the efficiency of a butcher knife. My hand is still out there, somewhere, crawling back to me," Werner said, quite good at poking fun at himself. "Now, tell me about this man."

"Yes, sir. Name's Jan Rheinsdorf, born and raised in the Berlin area. The file on him says he's thirty-two, married with kids. He's—"

"Does he have a record?" Werner interrupted.

"No, sir."

"Then why is there a file on him?"

"Lieutenant mentioned that Rheinsdorf was *Schutzstaffel* during the war: Waffen-SS...Panzers. He was cleared afterward and charged with no crimes. Nothing since. As you know, we've got files on—"

"Anyone who was SS," Werner nodded and twirled his prosthetic. "Go on."

"Yes, sir. Says he works with a cousin and an uncle in the commercial bread business. Biggest customers are the Brits and Amis." The policeman shrugged. "I took his statement and, other than some inconsistencies, he seems like a straight fellow to me."

"Your name?" Werner asked.

"Herzog, sir."

"Herzog...what was this statement about?"

"Oh," the officer said with a chuckle. "He came in with his wife, due to *her* insistence. She's a real looker but seriously uptight. They reported his being mugged a few nights ago. He admitted that he was drunk and said he was only filing the report to give his wife some peace."

Werner frowned. "The lieutenant wants me to work a mugging? What was stolen?"

"That's part of the problem. It was cash and a watch, but he changed his story."

"When?"

"Inside of an hour. I didn't even bring it to his attention. He first told me he was robbed of sixty marks and that the robber had taken a Gibraldi watch."

"And?"

"Later, when I was writing the report, he said he lost seventy marks and, after pausing for a moment, he told me the watch was an American Timex."

"So, he's either confused or he lied."

"He seems real distracted. With his background, sir, since he was SS...I just thought..."

Werner nodded. "You were right to tell the lieutenant."

Five minutes later, Werner entered the plain office where Herr Rheinsdorf sat with his striking wife. "Hello, Mister and Missus Rheinsdorf, I'm Detective Eisch. I have a few more things I'd like to ask you about the—"

"Can't we just go?" Rheinsdorf snapped. "I already gave a statement and a description. What else is there to discuss?"

"Honey, please," his wife murmured. The husband pinched his lips together and stared at the floor.

"This won't take but a moment," Werner said, resting his prosthetic on the battered table to quell any curiosities. He eyed Rheinsdorf. With an angular face and a compact, muscular body, he looked like a man who could handle himself. Werner also noted the scab on the bridge of his nose.

After clearing his throat, Werner said, "Sir, you were mugged late Friday night after having drinks in a bar near the Friedrichstrasse train station?"

"Yes."

"Which bar?"

"I don't know the name. It was once called *Die Zwiebel*. It's changed a few times since."

"I see. And who were you with?"

"I already gave him the names," Rheinsdorf said, pointing to Herzog.

"He did," Herzog confirmed.

"Friends of yours?" Werner asked.

"Old friends."

"War friends?"

"You mean, were they Schutzstaffel?"

Werner arched his eyebrows.

"No," Rheinsdorf said.

"You're certain."

"Yes, dammit. Is this about my mugger, or about me?"

"Honey…"

"This is just routine, Herr Rheinsdorf." Werner took the report from Herzog, patiently reading it in its entirety. He looked up, sliding his reading glasses down his nose. "May I see your ear?"

His frustration evident, Rheinsdorf turned his head. Werner let out a low whistle. There was a rusty scab inside the man's ear, almost as large as the tip of a finger. The area around the scab was bright pink. It looked almost like a bullet entry wound. It was larger than the scab on Rheinsdorf's nose.

"Interesting place for a mugger to hold a knife on you," Werner noted.

"Well, why don't you find him and ask him about it?" Rheinsdorf demanded. His wife whispered encouragement to him.

"We'll certainly try. Did he make the wound on your nose, too?"

"I guess. I don't recall."

Werner glanced at the report again. "What did the mugger take?"

"Already told him, dammit."

"Honey…" his wife said again.

"Just for my edification, please," Werner said soothingly.

A loud breath. "Money and a watch."

"How much money?"

"Uh, sixty marks."

Werner didn't react. He did notice the wife turn her head to her husband. "And the make of the watch?" Werner asked.

"An American Timex."

"Not a Gibraldi?"

Rheinsdorf blinked several times. "Wait...what'd I say before?"

"Gibraldi once, Timex twice."

Rheinsdorf shrugged. "I'd have to go home and look at my watches. I have quite a few. He took a watch from me, let's just say that."

Werner nodded. "And was it sixty or seventy marks?"

Massaging the scab on his nose, the victim said, "I don't know. As I've already said, I had too much to drink. I don't remember how much I had left, okay? I'm embarrassed about it. My wife wanted me to come down here...okay?"

"Okay," Werner said, eyeing both citizens. If he had a wife that looked like Frau Rheinsdorf, he might follow her off a cliff. Werner cleared his throat. "Herr Rheinsdorf, did you know your assailant?"

"Are you kidding me? Hell no."

"You're sure?"

"Yes, I'm sure. I don't remember exactly how much cash, but I would remember that."

"Of course," Werner replied, looking at the report. "So, he was short?"

"And Turkish," Rheinsdorf said. "Those little bastards are quick to pull a blade."

"The Turkish people are certainly in a difficult socio-economic position," Werner remarked. "Brought here to rebuild our country but immediately shuttled to the bottom of the social ladder."

"I'm not a xenophobe, detective," Rheinsdorf remarked. "Just speaking facts as I know them."

"I'm sure you are," Werner said, straightening the papers. He looked up. "Was the man facing you as he robbed you?"

"Yes," Rheinsdorf said, but not without a stutter.

"So he mugged you by holding a knife in your ear?"

Rheinsdorf hesitated briefly. "Yes."

"While you were standing?"

"*Yes.*"

"You're a capable-looking man..."

"I was very drunk," Rheinsdorf said, his voice rising. "That's part of why I'm here. I drink so much because...because of the memories..." He pointed to Werner's prosthetic. "I'm guessing you understand. It's hell on my wife. And, because of that, I don't mind giving in when she demands I do unpleasant things...such as reporting this."

"I see." Werner smiled at the wife. "Madam, what did your husband tell you when he got home that evening?"

"He was shaken but he wouldn't tell me what happened."

"Did you see his injuries?"

"Yes. After I wouldn't allow him to go to sleep, he finally told me he was mugged."

"Anything else?"

"No, he then—"

"That's enough," Rheinsdorf said, raising a hand to silence his wife.

Werner turned to Officer Herzog. "Would you please take Frau Rheinsdorf outside for some coffee or perhaps a cigarette?"

"I want to stay," she protested, gripping her husband's arm.

"Your husband will be free to go in ten minutes, ma'am," Werner said in a reassuring voice. "I just have one more thing to discuss with him that I wouldn't want to sully a lady's ears with. It's nothing bad; just not something for mixed company. You'll pardon me, please."

Nonplussed, Frau Rheinsdorf exited, staring inside the room as the door closed.

When they were alone, Rheinsdorf opened his hands and shrugged. "What?"

Werner leaned back in the chair, crossing his legs and narrowing his eyes at the mugging victim. By habit, Werner flexed his bicep, making his prosthetic click open and shut a few times. "Herr Rheinsdorf, you're not telling us the complete truth."

"Who the hell are you to accuse—"

"You didn't even bother to get your own story straight about the money and watch. Normally, I'd buy that as the excuse of a drunken man. But muggers, my friend, don't hold punch knives in their victims' ears. That's an assassin's tool. Somebody wanted more than a watch and cash."

Rheinsdorf's eyes widened and his chest expanded and contracted with great heaves.

"What did your assailant really want from you, Herr Rheinsdorf? Information? Did they require you to do something sexual?"

"Hell no. You're crazy."

"Possibly. But I'm correct, aren't I?" Werner offered a wan smile. "You look like a man of means. Did this person extort you, somehow? Are you too embarrassed, or too scared, to tell me what he did to you?"

"I said no."

"I cannot help you, Herr Rheinsdorf, unless you tell me the truth."

The former SS stood, knocking the chair backward. "Am I free to go?"

"Yes, sir," Werner said. "And we'll certainly brief our squad of Friedrichstrasse patrol officers about this..." he eyed the report, "...this short Turkish mugger with a crooked nose and a deep scar across his face." Werner eyed Rheinsdorf. "I would imagine this clever Turk uses this ear technique on everyone he mugs. He shouldn't be hard to find."

Rheinsdorf walked around the table to the door.

"Herr Rheinsdorf," Werner said, extending his card between the fingers of his only hand. "I can tell you're haunted by something, sir. If you ever want to cleanse yourself by telling the truth, and you want me to keep it confidential, I'm your man. I won't use the truth to harm your good name."

Rheinsdorf eyed the card for a moment. Then he left.

Werner let the card drop on the table. The only sound was the ticking of the clock.

"What was all that about?" he eventually asked the empty room.

# Chapter Four

Journal Entry
Sergeant John Vincent was from the town of Anderson, located in the upstate of South Carolina. When I first saw John, I remember being struck by his appearance. He had sandy blond hair, hazel eyes and extremely tan skin. It was an odd combination and, as I later learned, that was just the way his skin was pigmented. John was a handsome devil who, as we soon learned, had an easy touch with the women. Before heading overseas, the few times we went out on the town, I stayed right by John's side—he was a true lady magnet. But neither John's skin nor his good looks were his best asset—it was his wit and good humor. The man could charm any soul on earth.

Sometime back in '44—it was in the late fall—we were in Belgium. The war was still well in doubt at that time. Casualties had mounted, soldiers were exhausted and everyone's nerves were frayed. We'd been temporarily pulled off the battle line, tasked with making repairs to our equipment and what not, when we got a visit from a brigadier general named Duke. General Duke, as he quickly made sure we knew, reported directly to General Patton.

We also learned that Brigadier General Duke was a red ass of the first order. He had no intention of winning friends.

Now, keep in mind, we'd just come off two straight weeks on the front line. That's two weeks of nonstop hell with little food and no sleep. Two weeks of constant shelling and being shelled. Two weeks that left four of our men dead and a dozen others critically wounded. Two weeks of wondering when the grim reaper was going to drop down outta the sky, riding an artillery round with one of our names engraved on it. So believe me when I say we were in no mood for what this Napoleonic general waltzed in and did.

The brigadier caught us in the midst of manic preparations to "green-line" all our equipment—get it operational. He made us stop, since it was actually his initial order we were following.

"My damned orders you're following!" he roared at Captain Rook. "If I want to stop you, then I'll damned well stop you." Brigadier Duke spoke with a high-brow southern drawl and carried a swagger stick. When he had his back turned, John asked our crew if we wanted to make guesses about how lacking the brigadier was in the manhood department.

Once Captain Rook summoned all the Able Battery soldiers, the brigadier performed a general inspection on our unit right out in a farmer's field while malnourished cows mooed all around us. Literally, there we were, standing in a formation, nearly 200 exhausted men and eight sickly cows. It was about as out of place a scene as anything you'd find in wartime: an egotistical little brigadier general opening our ranks and inspecting our weapons and personal gear like we were shave-tail recruits back at Fort Sill.

There's a reason militaries don't do that crap in wartime, and I shudder to think of what might have happened had a German artillery round hit amongst us. What a pair that brigadier had to pull such a stunt.

So, when the brigadier was a quarter of the way through the battery, having chewed the ass of every single soldier he'd inspected, he finally came to Sergeant John Vincent. John went through his little spiel: spouting off his name, then inspecting his M-1 and presenting it to the general. While the general looked it over, he began to question John about various crap, the way big-headed generals always do. Before John even answered the general's first question, John cocked his head and said, "Do I hear some Alabama in there, sir? I'm guessing north Alabama, certainly above Birmingham."

The general's head snapped up. "Don't you ever question me, soldier."

John narrowed his eyes and grinned. "Yep. Think I've got it."

"Got what?"

"Decatur? Maybe Huntsville?"

The general's eyes widened. "How th'hell did you know I was from Decatur?"

"I spent a bunch'a summers there, sir."

I remember furtively breaking the position of attention and watching John Vincent shatter regulations as he tapped his lip with his finger, eyes up to the heavens.

"Let's see...I knew at least one Duke," John said, drawing it out. "But it's been a while...was it Frank, or Furman, or maybe it was Henry? Dangit...what was that man's name?"

The general's face was bright red. "Who are you talking about?"

"Older gentleman...maybe it was Thomas...no..."

"Was it Roy?"

"Roy!" John yelled, grinning at General Duke. "Plays checkers down at the mercantile."

"Probably," the general muttered, clearly bewildered. "You actually know him?"

"Know him?" John asked. "We were close friends. Heck, he looked after me like a kind uncle."

"Roy Duke's my father," the general said, his voice rising to a yell.

"Your father?" John yelled back, a wide grin splitting his face.

"Sure is."

"Has false teeth?" John asked.

"Sure does. A load on the top and bottom."

"Well, general, sir, I feel like I already know you!" John blew everyone's mind as he grasped the general's right hand and pumped it heartily. After the handshake, the general removed his helmet, rubbing his head. We were all beginning to shuffle around by this point.

"Sir," John continued, "all Mister Roy could ever do was talk about his son, the Army officer. Every time he did, he was about to burst like a ripe July tomato after too much rain."

"I don't believe this," General Duke murmured. "You really know my old man?"

"Honest injun."

The brigadier still wasn't convinced. He viewed John from the corner of his eyes. "What's he look like?"

"Had graying hair, rawboned man, not too heavy, lotsa sun spots."

Plopping his helmet back on his head, the general said, "That's him, alright."

"Let's see, sir, it's forty-four now. That'd make those summers when he and I played checkers...probably thirty-seven and thirty-eight? I think he said you were a major then."

By this point, the inspection had lost all its steam. Soldiers were turning and gaping at the exchange. Our first sergeant had put his k-pot on the ground and was sitting on it, shaking his head at the peculiar situation. And Captain Rook, our battery commander, stood wide-eyed next to the general, listening to this fantastic coincidence with what appeared to be a mix of relief and trepidation.

"Uh, the inspection, sir?" Rook eventually asked.

"Ah, to hell with the inspection," Duke replied offhandedly. "You got a fine unit here, cap'n. Send 'em back to work," he said, shooing Rook away. The general turned to his adjutant and told him to make sure some hot chow was shuttled out before our battery went back up on the line. The adjutant hustled away as the general turned back to John.

"I'm just glad to finally meet you, sir," John said. "You were all he could talk about."

The general lit a smoke, gave one to John, lit it for him, and the two stood there for fifteen minutes talking about summers in Decatur, Alabama. We heard them discuss the general's old man and people around town. John even relayed sordid tales of a few Decatur girls who were quick to neck down by the creek—he didn't mention any names, of course. At one point, John told the general a story about a married mother of three who'd gotten awful fresh with him during Decatur's annual Independence Day parade.

"I was only fourteen or fifteen then, sir. She took me back behind the fillin' station and said she could teach me 'the works.'"

The general, his neck and cheeks suddenly flushed, spent five minutes just trying to guess who she was.

We all eventually watched the general clap John on the back, telling him to send word if he needed "any damn thing at all," before again telling Captain Rook he had "a helluva fine unit" and that he'd be adding a nice hand-written note to Rook's file.

What had started as a disaster of an inspection, and a serious waste of time, ended up being a boon for our unit. Captain Rook seemed mystified afterward and gently told us all to finish what we were doing so he could report our readiness by sundown.

When John Vincent came sauntering back over to our Howitzer like the cock of the walk, we all circled around him.

"I thought you told me you were always going to that Myrtle Beach place during the summers," I said.

"Yeah," Kenny Martin chimed in. "And you'd already told me that crap about the mother of three—which, by the way, I'm still on record as calling it utter bullshit—but you said that happened in the winter, at the Christmas parade, in Anderson. You never said shit about Decatur."

John, smiling, lit another cigarette and dragged deeply, exhaling twin lines of smoke from his nose. He seemed extremely satisfied with himself.

Danny Elder snatched the Lucky from John's mouth, taking it for his own. "Stop smokin' and start explainin'."

John lit another smoke and continued to illuminate the gray late afternoon with that crooked smile of his. "I was just making a connection with the general, that was all."

"But you never told any of us about Decatur friggin' Alabama," I said.

"That's 'cause I ain't never been to Decatur friggin' Alabama," he laughed. "In fact, I've never been to Alabama in my life."

Those of us who truly knew John Vincent weren't shocked to hear this.

When the rest of the battery heard our roaring laughter, they began to meander over, listening as John told his tale in greater detail. "When he got outta his Jeep," John said, "I heard him bitching at his driver."

"So?" someone asked.

"I thought I recognized that distinct accent from a family, the Kilgos, who moved to Anderson when I was a kid."

"Bullshiiiiiit," someone else said.

"Were they from Decatur?" I asked.

"No clue. I just know they were from north Alabama. If you know southern accents, then you know North Alabama's accent is pretty damn distinct."

"How'd you know to use Decatur?" I asked.

"My mama didn't raise a dummy," John answered archly. "Huntsville, which if you'll remember I also guessed, and Decatur are the two biggest cities in north Alabama. I'd guess better than fifty percent of the population in that part of the state lives in one of those two places."

"Playin' the odds," Danny Elder said admiringly.

"Yup."

"But how'd you know his father's name?" someone asked.

"I didn't. I was guessin' all over the place. Didn't you hear me hemmin' and hawin'? He's the one told me his pop's name." John took a final drag on his Lucky before pressing the nub to his tongue, saving it for later. "I just laid a little groundwork, that's all."

"But what about rawboned and sunspots and false teeth?"

"He was looking at the general and making educated guesses," Danny said, beaming with pride over his friend's ruse.

"But what was the point?" someone else asked. "Get yourself in a heap'a trouble if'n he finds out."

"Well, he didn't find out," John said with a shrug.

"But if he did?"

"It's called self-entertainment," John answered. "Sometimes I like to do things like that for fun."

Just because he could.

Captain Rook was standing behind the mob as the group broke up. Though his hands were on his hips in a defiant pose, he was grinning ear to ear. How could he not find amusement in his unique and gifted soldier? John Vincent, with his charm and world-class ability for schmoozing (a.k.a. bullshitting) had singlehandedly gotten our battery out of a bad situation. His little game kept us laughing for days.

You know, I'd give anything to spend one day with John again. Heck, even just an hour. He was one of the smartest, funniest, most unique people I've ever run across.

But I can't. John is dead.

***

Two weeks after enduring the dinner with his kraut landlord and her kid, Marty rode on another train. This one was much newer and ticked along, moving steadily to the southwest, running with the efficiency of a sewing machine. Marty was in the belly of the train, seated in the center car and facing rearward.

He was excited.

Since his first encounter two weeks before, Marty had interrogated two other former members of the 101st SS Panzer Battalion, using the same method he'd used on Rheinsdorf. Like Rheinsdorf, the two men had not been prosecuted after the war. They were living under their born names and, like Rheinsdorf, both claimed to be walking the straight and narrow in German society.

And just like Rheinsdorf, both men independently told Marty the same key detail: if he wanted to find the murderous commander, Raban Nadel, he should also search for former battalion commander Oskar Zeckern, along with Nadel's protégé and chief henchman, Felix Roth. The two distressed men spoke of *Die Bruderschaft* and one said he'd heard Nadel was in charge of the group, despite being Zeckern's subordinate during the war. They gave up other small nuggets, but Marty felt the Zeckern and Roth intel—especially now having come from three different men—was too coincidental to ignore.

At Marty's most recent offensive, last Sunday night, his third victim had wept openly at the tip of Marty's knife. He confessed to Marty that he regretted much of what he'd done in the war, saying that he now saw the error of his ways. Though Marty never clued any of the former Waffen-SS to the fact that he was American, this one spoke in great detail about the Massacre at Kastellaun, telling Marty it was the low point of his life and had made him consider suicide on a number of occasions.

Thankfully, like he'd done with Rheinsdorf, Marty had accosted the third man in a dark and secluded location. When he'd been confessing his sins about the massacre, had the man seen the expressions on Marty's face, it might have tipped him off.

So, earlier this week, on Monday just before quitting time, Marty lingered on the top floor, waiting for his boss, Jimmy Gallotte, and the other senior managers to depart Day Construction for their three-pilsner "end of day meeting." Minutes after Gallotte departed, his secretary, a shapely young German, exited with a gaggle of other senior secretaries, discussing which bar they should visit to let the Amis buy them drinks. When Gallotte's secretary was gone, Marty had deftly slipped into Gallotte's office, placing a transatlantic phone call.

Marty could have made the call from his own desk, but it would have been routed through the switchboard. He would have to give the company operator the client name and number, so the call could be billed. But Gallotte, along with the rest of the senior managers, didn't have to go through this process. They were allowed to make international calls for business reasons—but they weren't audited. It was more evidence of just how much free cash was flowing through the reconstruction of Germany. Marty doubted Gallotte's calls were ever even scrutinized.

If they were, wouldn't the upper management be curious about why someone called Greece?

Marty checked his watch while the operator patched him through to the long series of numbers. It was early evening at Aristotle University of Thessaloniki and a young lady answered, speaking Greek. The operator spoke to the Greek operator and informed her that she had a call from Berlin for Professor Mocaata. After a moment of listening and relaying what was said, Marty's operator told him it would be a moment.

Marty's palms were sweating.

Several minutes passed before a pleasant-sounding gentleman answered the phone, speaking English.

"Professor, I'm a friend of Dr. Len Walden's," Marty replied. "He told me to call you if I needed assistance."

"I've been expecting a call. I'm pleased to know you're in Germany."

"I've made progress," Marty said, "but I need help in locating several *friends*."

"I'll certainly try to help. Who might these friends of yours be?"

Marty read three sets of three-letter initials. For instance, Felix Roth's full name was Felix Leonhard Roth, making his initials F.L.R. The code for Roth's initials was Z.T.J. Before his passing, Professor Walden gave Marty a coded alphabet and told him Professor Macatta had the only other key. Professor Walden assured Marty there was no pattern and, provided he used this initial method, no one else would have any idea who Marty was seeking—assuming someone was listening in.

Professor Macatta had Marty repeat the three sets of initials. Then he said, "As you're aware, we searched high and low for these two friends of yours." He was referring to Nadel and Zeckern. "They cannot be located."

"What about the third friend? Z.T.J.?" Marty asked, referring to Roth. "Has any effort been spent looking for him?"

"Not that I'm aware of. He wasn't thought to be of great importance."

"Well, according to some of the locals I've spoken with, he could be key to finding the other two."

"I see. Please allow me to make a few calls."

"Should I call back?"

"No need. May I have your home address?"

Marty gave it to him.

When the professor had read it back to him, he said, "You have a pleasant evening, young man. And be careful."

"Thank you, sir."

The line had clicked dead. That had been Monday.

On Thursday evening when Marty had arrived home from work, just after he had gruffly disentangled himself from the landlord's kid, he spotted a small envelope on the floor just inside his apartment. He tore it open to find Felix Roth's coded initials, along with an address in a Hessen settlement called Krofdorf-Gleiberg. Below Felix Roth's coded initials was the name Michael Rüdin—most likely the name Roth had assumed after the war.

Marty had scanned his map for the settlement of Krofdorf-Gleiberg, known to the locals simply as Gleiberg. He found Gleiberg situated in the shadow of the city of Giessen, an American military haven. It had only taken Marty a day to create his plan.

Now on the train, Marty turned his eyes away from the rushing German landscape, viewing the typed ticket affixed to the back of the seat in front of him. It was labeled with his destination of *Gießen hbf*, the Giessen train station. Marty would be there in two more hours, just before nightfall.

It would soon become a night Marty would never forget.

***

Krofdorf-Gleiberg is a settlement on a distinct hill, two miles north of the small city of Giessen. Though Marty brought a map, he soon put it away. The hill was easy to find, especially since it was topped by a medieval castle—easily the highest landmark anywhere near Giessen. The early evening was warm and breezy with a clear sky marked by emerging stars. In the distance, a row of clouds could be seen, the summer pattern pushing them west with the sun that had already set. The slick streets told Marty that rain had recently passed through. Wending his way out of Giessen, with another mile to walk before he reached the settlement, Marty smelled the pleasant tang of freshly-cut grass and the distinct aroma of wet asphalt: the essence of summer.

Two Shetland ponies raced at Marty as he walked beside a small pasture. Like exuberant dogs, they pranced beside him, frolicking, probably hoping for an apple or some generous petting. His mind on the brute that awaited him, Marty continued forward, the stark medieval castle looming closer with each stride. It was now nearly 10 P.M.

Having memorized the route, Marty ticked off the street names as he drew within a few hundred meters. He had no idea if the address the Greek professor had provided was accurate. And even if it was, Felix Roth might not be at home—it was Saturday evening, after all. Or, worst of all, what if this Michael Rüdin fellow wasn't even Felix Roth? Thankfully, the exhaustive dossiers created by Professor Walden before his death contained a single picture of Felix Roth. Marty had studied it for hours, memorizing every feature of the man's face.

The walk to Gleiberg went faster than Marty would have liked. As the last faint brushstrokes of twilight dissipated into the blackness of a moonless evening, Marty ascended the steep main road until he saw the stone marker denoting Felix Roth's—or Michael Rüdin's—street.

Turning left on Unter der Burg, Marty counted the house numbers on the tidy street. It was odd finding an entire settlement that seemed to have been untouched by the war. Berlin, strategic target that it was, had suffered under the world's most powerful weaponry—including many crushing blows from its own military. The results were catastrophic. These homes, however, were old and unscathed, paling only under the might of the ancient castle.

Two boys raced by Marty, startling him, yelling something about a game of nighttime hide and seek. Marty walked on, counting the houses. "10, 12, 14, 16..."

*There.*

Rüdin's home was the second to last one, nestled back against the stone facing beneath the castle's foundation. The home itself had good bones but seemed unkempt. It had twin gaslights on the front porch but only one was lit. Off to the side, a single light bulb burned in a small shed, displaying a plethora of woodworking tools hanging from a pegboard. On the workbench were two wooden toolboxes, both with heavy grease stains from the hands that had carried them.

According to the dossier, Felix Roth, despite being a thug, had been a valued mechanic and woodworker during his time in the SS.

Without giving himself time to reconsider, Marty continued past the house, removing his Sauer 38 pistol and threading the small custom suppressor to the barrel. He'd purchased the handgun in Oklahoma, told by the obsequious dealer that it had once belonged to a German spy named Ritter. Marty didn't care who it had once belonged to; he only cared that the suppressor quieted the gunshot. He tucked the Sauer into his pants at his rear, mildly concerned about the suppressor catching on his waistband in the event of a fast draw.

"Just give it a mighty yank," he said to himself, charging up the stone walk at the Rüdin household. As the lone gaslight flickered beside him, Marty looked down at his clothing. He'd decided to wear an old pair of dungarees from his college days. They were well-worn but comfortable and, combined with his threadbare button-down and old shoes, he looked like most any post-war German, still struggling to make ends meet. He made a fist and rapped three times on the door. Without consciously thinking about it, he stepped slightly to the right, subconsciously cautious of a shotgun blast.

There were several seconds of silence before the thud of a person suddenly standing, followed by the rhythmic thumping of feet heading in Marty's direction.

Marty could barely wet his mouth.

He wiped his hands on his dungarees.

His left eye began to twitch.

The door opened, showing only the hint of reddish light from down the hall. Then, slowly, the space was filled by a person leaning against the door. It was a woman. A blonde woman. She wore a frayed summer nightgown and a short robe.

Marty could only see half of her due to the door. She arched her eyebrow and, quite harshly, asked Marty what he wanted.

"The woodworker, is he in?"

"You mean Michael."

"If he's the woodworker."

"What do you want with him?"

"I want him to give me a price to build cabinets in my house."

"You've come here on a Saturday night to talk to him about cabinets?" the woman asked. Her accent, known as Hessische, was quite pronounced. From all his time studying the German accents, Marty found it comparable to a strong southern American accent.

"My frau has been after me about those cabinets for weeks." Marty removed his hat and shrugged. "She got onto me again tonight and, frankly, I'm sick of hearing about it. So, partly just to get out of the house, I came to see—er—Michael."

The woman eyed him for a moment before opening the door all the way, displaying a heavily bruised and swollen left eye. Her jaw was swollen also, on her left side. It appeared she'd taken several vicious right hands.

Marty stiffened. "Your face."

She lifted a damp rag to her eye, dabbing it several times before flicking her eyes upward. "Michael's up there at the *Schloss*, doing what he does best—getting drunk. You'll find him in the beer garden."

"Are you okay?"

"This is nothing," she replied, using the tone of a person who's quite used to pain. It was a tone Marty understood.

"Up there drinking, you say?" Marty asked, stepping backward and looking up at the ancient castle.

"A word to the wise…I'd be wary about hiring him. If fact, if I were you, I'd go back to Giessen and maybe find some nice old man to build my cabinets."

"Why do you say that?"

"Michael hates people."

"Fair enough." Donning his hat again, Marty backed off the bottom step. "Thank you for the advice."

As he turned on the street and began climbing the hill toward the castle, he heard the woman curse him before slamming the door.

*Did you hear that? He hates people. Get your mind in gear, boy. This one's not going to be like the first three. He's not going to roll over.*

His thoughts now solely on his target, Marty climbed the steep corkscrew turn to the castle's base. There, inside the crumbling walls of the ancient structure, was a small beer garden resting on uneven cobblestones that might have been a thousand years old. The drinking establishment consisted of a half-dozen picnic tables situated between two straggly hedgerows. At the rear of the beer garden, a plywood Licher Pilsner stand was manned by a tired-looking elderly bartender and a middle-aged waitress. The tables were filled with people, but one voice—deep and throaty and confident—rang out above all others.

It belonged to that massive fellow sitting at the middle table. He was big and swarthy and sported a thick forest of stubble over a cruel face scarred by years of brawling. His eyes were those of a savage. The man was wearing workman's overalls and palming a large stein of pilsner with a hand that seemed cartoonish it was so massive.

Marty was in the presence of Felix Roth, formerly of the 101st SS Heavy Panzer Battalion. Marty was in the presence of Felix Roth, murderer.

After sitting at the rearmost table, Marty raised his thumb to the barmaid who nodded and walked back to the beer stand. Next to Marty was an older couple having a quiet conversation. Turning back to Roth, Marty closed his eyes, opening that horrid treasure chest of memories.

Though he hadn't remembered Roth from looking at his photograph, Marty remembered him now. It was the voice. It was his rough manner. It was the unmistakable presence of his person. In those first moments after sitting down, Marty's first memory of Felix Roth was watching Roth kill his own fellow SS, the ones who didn't want to participate in the massacre. Marty's second memory came from the end of the massacre, after the SS had run out of ammunition. Roth had walked from corpse to corpse, casually stabbing each one. Marty recalled hiding between his dead friends, peering, utterly horrified, as the big man roared laughter with each strike of his knife.

After asking the older couple to save his seat, Marty hurried to the bathroom where, like on the train ride to Berlin, he vomited.

\*\*\*

Though he hadn't planned to drink, Marty allowed himself to slowly sip the pilsner beer. The carbonation actually soothed his stomach, settling him somewhat. Eventually, he even made idle chit-chat with the older couple. He had no interest in them but needed to talk to someone in order to blend in. It only took a moment for Marty to glean that the old krauts had grandchildren—lots of grandchildren. While they babbled on about some granddaughter in Mainz, Marty kept one eye on Felix Roth, playing cards with three other older gentlemen at his table. Roth would occasionally yell, usually in frustration, bellowing curses that no one dared complain about. After two long hours had passed, Marty counted eight large pilsners delivered to his target.

"We've stayed too long and must be going," the older man said. He held out his hand, which Marty reluctantly took.

"They'll be closing soon," the man's wife informed Marty.

"Thank you," Marty replied dismissively, turning his eyes to Roth.

"We enjoyed meeting you," the man said. "You're originally from Berlin?"

"Yeah. Moved here after the war."

The man narrowed his eyes at Marty. "Your clothes seem…different."

"Oh, these are just old rags," Marty said with a shrug, smiling politely so they'd leave. When they did, Marty furtively compared his clothes to the few remaining Germans.

*My clothes!* Silently cursing himself, Marty thought back to his final preparations. He'd made sure to bring older, less flashy clothing, assuming they would blend in with the Germans' clothes. But as Marty compared his clothes to the other patrons, he noticed small differences in cut and shape and even color. His clothes were a far different style from German clothes.

*That's how the hookers knew I wasn't German.* Marty made a mental note to visit one of the numerous used clothing stores he'd seen in Steglitz. For now, however, he was here and needed to refocus on the task at hand.

Within the next ten minutes, several other patrons settled their tabs. Soon thereafter, the card game broke up and the trio that had been with Roth departed.

*Now or never*, Marty thought, taking a deep breath. He stood and walked to the table where Roth sat. Other than one couple who were in the process of paying the server, Marty and Roth were the final patrons in the beer garden.

"Buy you a beer?" Marty asked.

Roth glared, his ferocious eyes glowing with a lacework of red. "I don't know you."

"True, but I need another beer, and I hate to drink alone."

The bloodshot eyes narrowed. "You're gonna buy a stranger a drink?"

"Got a little bonus yesterday from my American employer. Nothing like money in the old pocket, even if it does come from an Ami."

The big man sneered but turned to the exhausted barmaid and gestured for two more. Probably ready to close up and go home, she slumped at his signal. A minute later, she hurried the beers over, both with an extra inch of head from the fast pour.

"Closing in five minutes," she said without humor.

Marty dug out a handful of Deutsch Mark coins, simultaneously displaying a wad of bills. "How much?"

"Bring us two more," Roth commanded the barmaid. "This guy'll pay for everything and you two can leave. I'll get the lights."

"Viktor doesn't like us doing that. You know—"

"Then tell Viktor to see me about it!" Roth bellowed, turning back to Marty and signifying to the barmaid and bartender that there would be no argument about it.

"Who's Viktor?" Marty asked.

"Nobody," Roth said. "He's the little shit who owns most of this little shit town and he knows wayyy better than to tell me what to do."

Marty lifted his beer, blowing some of the head from the top before clinking it into Roth's stein. "Here's to two more beers."

Roth didn't appear amused, and drank a third of his beer in several large gulps, belching afterward. "Haven't seen you up here before," he said, wiping foam from his stubble.

"Never been up here before."

"What do you do for the *Americans?*" he asked, saying "Americans" as if it were the dirtiest of words.

"Construction work. We rebuild things that their bombers blew up from a cowardly 24,000 feet." As soon as Marty had said it, he wanted to take it back. He was by no means an actor and the line came out sounding forced.

"Yeah?" Roth asked. "Well, if *they* were so cowardly, where were *you* during the war?"

"Western front."

"Where and which branch?"

"I was Heer, Army Group H, 25th Army," Marty replied without hesitation. This was one of the covers Marty had memorized. He knew the cover down to many intricate details.

Seeming disinterested in Marty's answer, Roth sipped his beer and turned away. The two beer garden employees shuffled through the darkened archway of the castle. One of them murmured a goodbye.

"And you?" Marty asked.

Roth turned back, sneering again. "Oh, don't worry, bub, I was in the war. And for much of the time, I *was* the war."

"Where and which branch?" Marty asked, mimicking Roth and wanting to bash his beer stein into the big man's face.

Roth finished the beer, belched again, and slid the next beer in front of him.

Trying to keep his hatred and anger in check, Marty shrugged. "You wanted to know about me, but now you won't tell me anything."

"Maybe I don't want you to know."

The air had turned cool, matched by the growing frigidity of their exchange. Marty glanced around. "No one else up here?"

"Nope. Just me and you." Roth took a mighty pull on his fresh beer, eyeing Marty the way a hungry man eyes a rare ribeye.

Then, it hit Marty. He'd mentioned a bonus and flashed his wad of cash by buying the beers. Now Roth planned to rob him. Once Roth had the money, he'd probably threaten Marty's life to keep him quiet. This was how a man like Roth lived. In fact, Marty would bet Roth employed the same tactics in his carpentry business. He'd probably quote a low figure, finish the shoddy job, then double the price. With his size and intimidating nature, who would argue?

Following a few steadying breaths, Marty guzzled his beer while glancing at the castle exit. It was nothing more than a massive stone archway that led away from the castle's inner courtyard and back to the corkscrew road Marty had climbed on his way in. Setting his stein down, Marty quickly stood, taking a few steps back.

"Sorry, friend, but I sense you don't want to talk. Guess I'll head home now." He tugged on the brim of his hat. "Thanks for having a drink with me, and feel free to drink that extra beer."

Marty thought Roth might panic at his standing. Instead, he slid the third beer in his own direction and mumbled something.

"Excuse me?" Marty asked.

"I said, I don't believe a thing you've said to me."

"Your opinion doesn't matter to me," Marty said. "I don't know you."

Roth's expression changed to one of curiosity. "25th Army, you say?"

"Yeah."

"Which unit?"

"Second rifle."

"You were a rifleman, huh?" Roth asked, as if he didn't believe Marty possessed what it took to be a rifleman.

"Yeah, just a regular line soldier."

"Who was your commander?"

Marty glanced around. "I need to go."

"Tell me who."

Marty breathed his answer. "Ulrich Kleist, why?"

"Ulrich Kleist? *The* Ulrich Kleist?"

"I don't know if he was '*the*' Ulrich Kleist, whatever that means. Why?"

"Ulrich Kleist, of the 25th, was from Kassel."

"How do you know that?" Marty asked, suddenly concerned. Building this cover, he'd memorized quite a bit about Kleist, the last commander of Second Rifle. Kleist was indeed from Kassel—how the hell did Roth know? Blind coincidence? Of all the damned luck! Marty adjusted his trousers, hoping he could get his hand back behind him, under his shirt, and get the pistol out with ease.

"I served with Kleist's younger brother," Roth said.

*Oh shit. I missed that connection...what a piss poor mistake.*

The big German eyed Marty. "And Ulrich Kleist had another relative...also in *your* unit—a cousin. His brother told me all about it. Ulrich kept him close to keep an eye on him. His brother said the man was a tad slow but, under Ulrich's recommendation, the man achieved the rank of *Feldwebel*, despite his stupidity. You see, I have an excellent memory, even when I'm drunk."

"Oh?" Marty asked, perspiring.

"Yeah. I actually remember the man's name, too...unlucky for you."

Suddenly, Roth lifted his right hand from under the table. In it was a Walther P38, aimed steadily at Marty's chest. It must have been concealed in the hip pocket of the former SS's overalls.

"The question is," Roth said, "do *you* remember his name? Or are you a lying weasel?"

"There were a number of—"

"At best there were only five men of *Feldwebel* rank in Second Rifle. Name them."

"Why are you doing this?" Marty asked.

Roth cocked the hammer. "Because I think your clothes are weird. Because I can feel the lies oozing from your pores. Because I don't like strangers talking to me. And because I'm trying to decide whether or not I should kill you." His grin was malevolent. "Name the five *Feldwebel*."

Marty shook his head. "It's been years."

"Yet you snapped off Kleist's name in half a second."

"He was my commander."

"I remember the name of *every* man in my unit."

"Okay," Marty said through heavy breaths. He tried to recall some of the names he'd memorized. "There was Sielbach. Stern. Bingen." Marty opened his hands. "I can't think of any others at the moment."

"You haven't named *him* yet."

"That's all I remember. We were losing men at a high rate. There were lots of replacements."

"The one I'm referring to didn't die. If you weren't a liar, you'd know him." Roth stared as if he were divining the contents of Marty's soul. "Why did you really come up here tonight?"

As much as Marty hated to admit it, he could see why Roth would have been Nadel's henchman. Despite being a caveman, he was damned good at reading, and handling, a nerve-wracking situation.

A bead of sweat had gathered on the tip of Marty's nose, glinting in the light. He opened his hands plaintively. "I came up here because I had a fight with my frau and I wanted a beer."

"I don't believe you."

"Why?"

Roth moved the pistol to his left hand, wiping his right palm on his overalls. "You're a stranger, and you took interest in me. I don't like that. Besides, people are usually scared to talk to me. But you wanted to. That makes me instantly suspicious."

"Can I just go?"

"No. I have to do something about my anger. I have to work it off."

"With a gun?"

He wagged the pistol between Marty's eyes. "Most people turn and run once they get a load of me, so you're either queer, or you have some sort of agenda."

*He's going to move the pistol back to his right hand—an action that'll waste a fraction of a second. When he does, I have to draw and shoot. Have to! Otherwise, I'm going to die, sure as this castle is a thousand years old. Roth is not a talker. He's not a blusterer. He's a killer. And once he finds out why I'm here, or even if he doesn't, he's going to kill me for that money I flashed.*

Continuing to hold the pistol in his left hand, Roth's voice grew louder and he bared his teeth. "Last time, you sonofabitch: *why* did you come here?"

"I already told you."

"You're about to get shot."

"Please...I had a fight with my frau. I went for a walk. I saw the castle, knew there was a *Biergarten* here, and I came up to have a beer. That's it." Marty continued to eye the pistol, waiting for Roth to move it back to his right hand. With each twitch of Roth's body, Marty fought not to act prematurely.

Roth licked his lips. "How much money do you have on you?"

"Maybe thirty or forty marks," Marty lied.

"Thought you just got a bonus. And I saw a wad in your pocket."

"That was all fives and tens. I don't have the bonus money with me."
*Time! Keep buying time.*

"How much was the bonus?"

"Four hundred."

"Hmm," Roth pondered, running his tongue across his teeth. "I'll take it."

"What do you mean, 'take it'?"

"We're going to walk to your home, and you're going to get it for me." He smiled, displaying dark spots behind his canines where he had no teeth. "And that will buy you more days on this earth. It's a good deal compared to the alternative." The gun was still in his left hand. He raised his right index finger. "And, afterward, if you think about calling the Polizei to report me, think again. I'm in a club...a fraternity...that the cops look after. Some of them are in it, too. I'll *know* if you try to report me. And then I will come for you."

"I don't want any trouble, friend."

"Then let's go get my money."

Purposefully appearing to struggle to come to the decision, Marty eventually nodded. "Promise you won't hurt me?"

"Promise? What are you, eleven years old? No, I won't hurt you, you pussy. Now, let's get moving."

"I live about four kilometers away."

"Then let's get moving." Roth slid the bench backward and, in the same movement, switched the pistol back to his right hand. As he did, Marty reached back and yanked at the Sauer 38 with all his might. As he'd worried earlier, the lip of the suppressor caught at the top of his pants. He jerked it free with a ripping sound as thread and fabric gave way.

Marty had the pistol nearly around his body by the time Roth processed what he was doing. In his own movement, Roth had turned to the right to get out of the space between the bench and the table. His face contorting, he wheeled his own pistol around to Marty.

The two men moved in slow motion, their brains far ahead of their bodies' capabilities. Marty was a study in concentration, his piercing eyes framed by a flushed and sweaty face.

Roth, on the other hand, was the picture of fury with blazing eyes and snarling mouth. Judging by his anger, his inner voice was screaming in rage over the confirmation of his own suspicions. Roth's pistol came up, its line of fire nearly on Marty as the first dart of flame blasted from its barrel.

The bullet whizzed by Marty. It missed.

Marty had already pulled his own trigger. The first bullet, its impact marked by a small burst of pink foam, caught the big German in his left shoulder. Marty fired again. His second bullet hit Roth in his upper chest, near his heart. Though the .32 ACP rounds possessed meager stopping power, they knocked Roth backward, dropping him over the bench seat to the cobblestone floor of Gleiberg Castle.

The subsonic, suppressed shots from Marty's pistol amounted to nothing more than metallic coughs. As Roth fell, he squeezed off three more rounds on his descent. All of the rounds missed Marty, rocketing into the sky and falling harmlessly somewhere outside the walls of the castle. Roth's shots were not suppressed. They weren't subsonic, either. Inside the walls of the castle, and probably anywhere nearby, they might as well have been cannon thunder.

Diving over the table, Marty landed on the squirming German, striking him in the face with hammer blows, using the butt of his pistol as the hammer. He reached to his left, knocking the Walther from Roth's grip.

Then, bringing the pistol back to Roth's face, he asked one simple question: "Where is Raban Nadel?"

A trickle of blood ran from the corner of Roth's mouth. Other than his labored breathing, he didn't budge.

"Where is he?" Marty yelled. "Where is Raban Nadel?"

Despite his condition, Roth smiled. His smirk was a haunting, bloody rictus that somehow suited him.

"I was there, you piece of shit," Marty growled. "I was in the artillery unit you massacred. *Ich bin Amerikaner.*"

Roth's breathing was wet, but he managed to maintain his bravado as he rasped, "Thought we killed all you squealing little pigs. Guess we didn't do our job that day." As soon as he got the words out, he burped out a mouthful of dark blood.

"Where is Raban Nadel? What's his new name?"

When it was obvious Roth wasn't going to answer, Marty dug around on the big German's shoulder until he found the bullet wound. As if he were plugging a hole, he jammed his index finger into the hole and scratched his fingernail in all directions.

Despite all his earlier swagger, Roth screamed, his body contorting wildly.

"Where is he?" Marty asked, removing his finger.

Roth began to cough. When he finished, his breathing sounded somewhat clearer.

"Where is Nadel?" Marty repeated, his finger going back to the bullet hole.

Just as it seemed Roth might answer, a voice reverberated through the castle. *"Hallooo!"*

Marty's head whipped to the right.

*"Hallooo!"*

Someone was yelling from a distance. A man. He'd probably heard the gunshots and the yells.

"*Is everything okay?*" the man yelled again, speaking German. There was an echo inside the stone walls, making it hard to gauge the direction of the inquisitor.

"*Hilfst Du Mir!*" Roth suddenly yelled, his mouth spraying blood as he did.

Marty brought his pistol down on Roth's forehead with terrific force, knocking the big man cold.

The situation had gone from bad to worse. Roth's distress yell had been quite loud. Whoever was outside the castle walls would have heard his plea and would now certainly be coming to investigate. Or, at a minimum, they'd be calling the Polizei.

Either way, Marty was very much in danger of having his cover blown.

And very much in danger of going to prison.

With a frantic glance around the interior of the castle, he crafted a hasty plan.

# Chapter Five

Journal Entry

You've already heard me mention Staff Sergeant Kenny Martin from Texas. I actually met Kenny a few days before I met John and Danny. We'd both been through basic training in different places and arrived there at Fort Sill before our advanced artillery training was to begin. Since we were early arrivals, they put us in a holding platoon. As you might imagine, even though we had nothing to do, the cadre wasn't keen to let us sit around, take afternoon naps or play gin rummy. Over the balance of those waiting days, they worked our fingers to the damned bones.

It's just the Army way. Idle soldiers make incredible handymen, primarily because they have no choice in the matter. We polished floors, toilets, desks, awards, windows...we painted buildings, we raked lawns, we dug holes—you name it. And through it all, me and Kenny got to know one another.

And, boy, did I like that fella. Anyone would have, a true man's man.

Kenny was a few years older than the rest of us, hailing from just outside of Midland, Texas. He'd played a few years of college football at Texas Technical, in Lubbock. While there, Kenny had gone through reserve officer training and, even though he dropped out due to a little trouble he'd gotten into, he was able to fulfill his commitment by entering the Army a few pay-grades higher than the rest of us.

Kenny was built like a brahma bull, especially compared to the rest of us scrawny eighteen-year-olds. He stood better than six feet tall and probably weighed 210 or 220 pounds. So, when he and I arrived at Fort Sill in the hellishly hot June of '43, the cadre put us straight to work. While the rest of our still-arriving platoon was tasked with repairing the sheet metal on a Quonset hut, me and Kenny were charged with whitewashing the outside of what was to be our barracks building. We'd been at it a while when this nasty little sergeant with a thin mouth showed up and gave us hell for removing our tops.

Know this: an hour before, the staff sergeant who'd put us on the job said we could get "damned buck-assed naked" if we wanted to, but by the time we heard "To The Colors" played, meaning the American flag was being lowered, he said we'd better have the outside of that entire building sparkling like Judy Garland's choppers.

We were simply doing as we'd been told.

So, the mean little sergeant walks up and yells at us to "drop." "Drop" is Army lingo, an order to assume the pushup position. Having been through recruit training, neither of us was very surprised to be treated this way. In the Army, especially during training, this type of confusing leadership is pretty typical. One cadre will tell you one thing and another cadre will come along and punish you for doing it. It was usually deliberate and wasn't a big deal. Mind games. With us having come straight from basic, we could easily knock out fifty pushups in a row, and that's what the mean little sergeant told us to do.

It was around 1600 hours and, morons we were, we were painting the west side of the building last. Had we had any sense, we would've started on the western half in the morning, and done the eastern half in the evening. Too bad Danny Elder wasn't there—he'd have thought that out for us. Kenny and I, unfortunately, didn't think that far ahead.

So there, on the western side of the building, the temperature probably a hundred degrees, Kenny did his fifty like it was nothing and just kept right on going. Didn't say anything, didn't call attention to it, just counted in that low voice of his while he banged out those pushups as if his big arms were hydraulic pumps. That little sergeant started tapping his boot and asked Kenny if he was some kind of smartass. Kenny paused and looked up at him and said, "I just passed seventy and I'm gonna keep going if you don't mind, sarge. It's good training."

"I do mind, you fresh piece'a shit."

Kenny stayed right there, rigid as a board while his hands and toes supported his powerful body. He nodded, then said, "Well, sarge, I got a five-spot that says, even though I just did seventy-two pushups, that if you'll drop on down here with me, I can still do more than you can without stopping."

I was still down there next to Kenny, done with my fifty, so I was up on my knees and pretty damned surprised by the brassiness of Kenny's challenge. But this wasn't basic training and that sergeant damn sure wasn't wearing a campaign hat—meaning he wasn't a drill sergeant. I later learned that he was the training battery's supply sergeant.

There wasn't a soul around when Kenny issued the challenge and, as you might imagine, you coulda heard a damned pin drop. Had Danny Elder been there with our platoon, he'd have already handicapped the challenge and been taking side and prop bets from anyone with loose cash.

But it was just us three. Me, stunned and waiting. Kenny, still in push-up position. And that foul-mouthed little supply sergeant, quivering at Kenny's insolence.

I'll tell you this much, that supply sergeant sure as hell didn't take the bait. If he had, I'm certain he'd have lost. But he did step around the building and come back with a rake handle—the thin, grass-rake kind. He walked back over, slapping it in his hand while Kenny was still pushing. Kenny eventually stopped at 125. He stood, recovering his wind as sweat poured from his body.

"You're a real smart guy, aren't you?" the sergeant growled, stepping toe-to-toe with Kenny. The sergeant was a full head shorter.

"Just painting this building, sarge."

"You're 'bout to finish it with some red welts," the sergeant said, twirling the rake handle.

"If you're gonna hit me with that, sarge, then get on with it." Kenny's voice was calm and cool, like a movie actor's.

"You're really asking for it, peckerwood."

"No, I'm not, sarge. But I don't like bullies. And you're a bully."

"What'd you just call me?"

"A bully," Kenny said with a shrug. "We're just two soldiers out here, working like we were told. We took off our tops because Staff Sergeant Whitmire said we could. And, besides, you know it's boiling hot. You're just being an ass because you can, because of that rank on your arms." Kenny had been staring straight ahead, but he breached Army regulations for soldiers at the position of attention when he lowered his eyes. "You're a small man, sarge, and that's fine. If we were in any other environment, on equal footing, I wouldn't bother you. What would be the point? Live and let live. But here, because Uncle Sam gave you a few stripes, you go around picking on people who you would never approach in the real world. And that, sarge, is the epitome of cowardice."

"Cowardice?"

"Yes. It means you're not brave. You, sergeant, are a coward...and it disgusts me."

The little sergeant's thin lips opened as he gritted his khaki teeth in fury. He took a full step backward, pivoting as he planted his left foot forward. Then he took a mighty swat with that rake handle. He was aiming for the side of Kenny's head. The rake handle whistled through the air, slicing a shrill arc through that overheated Oklahoma atmosphere.

It might have killed Kenny.

Had it hit his head.

Kenny's feet never moved. He simply raised his left arm, taking the whack on the back of his muscled forearm, breaking the rake handle, sending it whirling for me and making me drop to the ruddy Fort Sill dust in an effort to avoid any collateral damage.

The sergeant took a few steps backward, seeming stunned at his own actions. Kenny calmly lowered his swelling arm and said the following: "Sergeant, I understand at the end of training, on the evening of getting our assignments, that all soldiers have the opportunity to call any cadre to the sawdust pit." Kenny let it linger for a few seconds. "I'll be calling your name, sarge. There's no rank in that sawdust pit. Anything goes. When you and me get into that pit, we're all going to see what kind of man you really are."

Watching that little bully take gasping breaths while processing the terrifying thought of having to tangle with Kenny made the entire incident worth it. Without a word the sergeant turned and unsteadily walked away, disappearing around the building.

I lifted Kenny's left arm. The blow had left a hot-pink welt at a diagonal on the side of his wrist.

"Is it broken?"

He flexed his hand. "Nah. It's fine." Then Kenny, in that dogged way of his, lifted his brush from the bucket and resumed his painting.

I followed suit and, after a few strokes of painting, I asked him a question. "Kenny, are you really gonna call that little prick out after we finish recruit training?"

Kenny was working his way around a window, pressing the brush into the nook of the sill. "Nah," he said. "Fight like that wouldn't be fair at all."

"But he'll think you're yellow, won't he?"

"Nah."

"Why not?"

"He won't be there."

"He won't?" I asked.

Kenny straightened. "I doubt it. And don't tell a soul that I'm not going to call him out. Let's let that little acid pill burn in his belly till we finish training, got it?"

I chuckled, nodding my head. Kenny, in that gentle giant way of his, was going to teach that sergeant a lesson without ever raising a fist to him. And, just as Kenny had predicted, the little sergeant wasn't there when we finished training. Two weeks after he'd swung that rake handle at Kenny, the sergeant got himself transferred from the unit, clear to the other side of post. He left without fanfare and never showed his face around our unit again.

Word had it that he called in every favor he could to get that transfer.

When we heard about it, Kenny just winked at me.

He'd been blessed with strength, athleticism, and charm—and he used all those gifts in a responsible manner. His actions that day, and at other times, taught me a lesson.

Oh, how I wish I could spend another day in the sun with my old Texan buddy Kenny Martin.

***

As Felix Roth lay unconscious below him, Marty frantically scanned the interior of Gleiberg castle. It covered at least an acre, marked by the ruins of numerous rooms and chambers. Just beyond the beer garden, in the dark shadows of the castle's center, Marty could see the large, round tower—the castle's centerpiece, an icon visible from many miles away. Adjacent to the tower, and half as tall, were the remains of an inner building, perhaps the residences, marked by soaring gabled stone walls. At the base of the front of the remains, disappearing down into blackness, was a curved stairway. Hopefully that led to the old cellar—a place of refuge, then and now.

Grasping the massive man under his arms, Marty drug him across the cobblestones, having to jerk him when his overalls caught on the edges of the broken cobblestones. When Marty reached the steps, he saw the slick trail of blood behind Roth's body.

*If whoever yelled brings a hand torch...*

Time was running out and there was nothing Marty could do about the blood. Pulling the big man at a faster, gravity-aided rate, Marty descended the steps, feeling the earthy cold envelop him as he reached the bowels of the cellar. In complete darkness, except for the lighter gray rectangle from the stairwell, Marty continued to lug the man backward until he reached the far wall. He paused, feeling Roth's chest. Though he was quiet, Roth was still breathing.

Marty raced back to the entrance, falling hard over something, sending him into a painful sprawl. He heard his pistol clatter away in the blackness. Knowing his time was severely limited, he pressed on, rushing up the steps as he felt the burning of his skinned hands.

Back in the courtyard, Marty found Roth's Walther, palming it as he sprinted behind the plywood bar. There, gripping the electrical cord for the strung lights, Marty eyed the blackness of the cellar entrance, making sure he had his bearings. Then he pulled the plug, satisfied with the resulting darkness.

Marty made a beeline for the steps, slowing as he neared in an effort to avoid another tumble. When he reached the drop off, he heard footsteps scratching on the asphalt, just outside the castle entrance. Then the man yelled another hello.

Gripping the Walther, Marty backed down the steps, feeling his way across the cellar. A brief shiver of fear went through Marty—Roth couldn't be playing possum, could he? No, Marty decided. Especially not after the gunshot wounds. Still, Marty was careful as he approached and, eventually, his foot thudded into something soft and lumpy—Roth.

Marty grew silent. He couldn't hear a sound. Nothing from the steps. Nothing from Roth.

Marty had a distinct feeling...

Again he squatted, feeling Roth's chest with his left hand. There was no movement. He slid his hand to Roth's neck, searching for the man's pulse.

No pulse. Felix Roth was dead.

Marty pulled his own hair in frustration. Who knew what the professor's friend, Professor Mocaata in Greece, had done to find Roth? What markers did he call in? Marty recalled the crucial passage from the note that was under his door:

```
We lucked out with this one, only because he's
too stupid to have known the precautions he
should have taken to protect his true identity.
There is no information about the rest of the
men who went missing. None. From here, you're
on your own.
```

"On my own with nothing to go on," Marty whispered through clenched teeth.

And on the verge of getting caught.

*Damn!*

Marty could hear the man's voice calling out in the castle courtyard. With Roth's pistol leading the way, Marty crept back to the flight of steps, steadying himself with his free hand as he climbed, prowling upward like a three-legged cat.

There, when he reached the upper steps, Marty saw the lemon-yellow of a hand torch sweeping the area. The man continued to speak to the darkness, asking if anyone was there. He was alone.

Marty crept higher, hoping the man stayed where he was. He was on the far side of the beer garden, well away from Roth's blood. As the man moved the hand torch, Marty was able to glimpse him. An older gentleman, he was tall and lean, wearing a bathrobe over his nightshirt.

Suddenly, the man stopped moving, the light trained on something across the beer garden. Marty followed the beam of light, seeing the green bench on its side.

Spattered across the surface of the bench was a shiny liquid.

The man hurried across the beer garden, staring down as if he couldn't believe what he was seeing. When he knelt, touching the slick liquid and bringing his hand to the light, Marty moved away from the steps.

*"Dies ist Blut,"* the man said to himself, the light beginning to tremble. He stood, the light cutting a brilliant pathway across the jagged trail of blood before focusing on the dark rectangle that led to the cellar steps.

Marty peered from the lower corner.

The man turned to the castle entrance, his eyes cutting between it and the steps. He was deciding on what to do. With a visible swallow, he began to follow the trail of blood, slowly moving toward the steps. As he walked, he swept the light all around, probably terrified that someone was lurking in the dark.

Pausing at the top of the cellar, he called out into the darkness, asking if anyone was there. Then, slowly, the man lowered his left foot, almost as if he were testing his weight. He descended another step. Then another, leaning around the curve of the steps with his light, trying to see what lay ahead. On he came, taking what seemed like hours. With the gunshots and all the blood, doing what he did must have taken terrific courage.

When the man finally reached the base of the steps, just as his light cut to Felix Roth's corpse, Marty made his move. He lurched from the left, bringing the Walther down in a hammer blow on the crown of the man's head.

He crumpled to the stone floor.

\*\*\*

Gregor Lutz awoke four minutes later. His first sensation was the splitting pain in his head. The second was the piercing light to his right, slicing an arrow through the utter darkness. The third sensation was the smell, the earthy smell. It was the same smell that Gregor associated with his own cellar.

The light moved and, as it did, Gregor tugged on his hands. They were bound behind his back and tethered to something. He was stuck. Gregor tried to speak, hearing a muffled sound, realizing he'd been gagged. As he moved his mouth, he was able to feel the texture of the gag—it was a piece of his own bathrobe.

Now, as Gregor's mind began to clear, he recalled what had happened. He blinked upward into the direct, eye-watering glare of his own hand torch.

"I'm truly sorry I had to hit you," said the voice behind the light. "I was attacked here tonight and I defended myself. Unfortunately, I don't think anyone will believe my story, so now I must leave. But, before I go, I have more to do upstairs—so I'll be there for a while. If I hear you trying to yell through that gag, I will kill you to protect myself. Do you understand me?"

"Who are you?" Gregor mumbled through the gag.

The light came close enough to Gregor's face that he could feel the heat from the bulb. "Do you understand me?" the tense voice asked.

"Yes!" Gregor said, nodding vigorously.

"Not a sound."

Gregor had been a soldier during the Great War and, near the war's end, had wound up as a prisoner of the French. He'd learned quickly to obey orders such as this. Many of Gregor's brethren had chosen not to obey such orders, and were no longer alive because of their disobedience.

The piercing light remained focused on Gregor as the man backed away. Due to the light's intensity, Gregor couldn't make out a single feature of his captor. He saw him stoop to retrieve something, then slowly back up the stairs and out of sight.

Gregor sat there for many hours before he began to yell for help.

He wouldn't be found until the following afternoon.

***

Despite his warnings to the captive man, Marty had no desire to linger at Gleiberg Castle. In fact, as he walked down the corkscrew road with two handguns, a beer stein and a darkened hand torch, he pondered what the Polizei would discover. His fast sanitization had taken only a few minutes. The binding on the captive man's hands was the extension cord from the strung lights. Marty didn't think the police could lift usable fingerprints from that. While at the beer garden, he'd only used the one beer stein and, after wetting the man's bathrobe, Marty thoroughly wiped down both tables and benches where he'd sat. He also used the water to clean the blood from his hands.

Once he'd taken care of his own fingerprints, Marty's biggest concern, aside from the resulting murder investigation, was the lack of productivity from his mission. *Damn it! All this way, all this planning, for nothing.*

While Marty felt no remorse for Roth, the incident had left Marty shaken. In fact, dealing with the older man had actually settled Marty's nerves a bit—it had given him something to focus on. But now that the man had been handled, Marty's mind came back to the problem at hand. What was the next step? He was going to have to start from scratch in his search for Nadel—but how? All three of Marty's Berlin targets had told him Roth was the key to finding Nadel, and now Roth was dead.

They'd mentioned Zeckern, too, but Professor Mocaata's note had been emphatic. Roth was the only one stupid enough to leave clues about his—

Marty stopped cold, nearly dropping the beer stein and the hand torch. *Roth's woman.*

*Why not?* Marty reasoned. *She's already a witness to the killer's possible identity. Surely she'll be questioned and recall an average-sized man, who spoke Hochdeutsch, visiting earlier in the evening. So, why shouldn't I go to her now and find out what she knows?*

*But I can't tell her what it is I'm looking for,* Marty realized. *If I do, and I leave her alive, then the Polizei will know my motive.*

*But they're going to figure out Roth's true identity. That's for certain. Surely, when they discover the massive corpse in the castle, they'll eventually learn that Michael Rüdin, alcoholic carpenter brute, is actually Felix Roth, most-wanted Schutzstaffel killer.*

Marty had read about Jewish commandos hunting and killing men like Roth. He'd also read rumors of the SS eliminating their own men—men who, for whatever reason, were high risk. Professor Mocaata had said Roth was stupid, so perhaps the Polizei would write Roth off as a criminal who got killed by another criminal.

*But if you go to the woman, and she talks, then the story changes. The Polizei will have a strong lead.*

Marty was just above Roth's house, standing below the castle on the steep, scalloped street cut into the side of the hill.

*Think...*

*The woman could be the key. She could also be your undoing.*

His decision only took a few seconds. He turned left, descending the curving road, heading back to Roth's house.

# Chapter Six

Journal Entry

After I'd been here in Germany about a week, I had an interesting encounter with a kraut kid who lives downstairs from my apartment. I didn't know how to react to him at first, but he actually seemed like a good egg. Being a kid, I guess he's innocent enough, hasn't been corrupted yet. If he'd been born in the States, he wouldn't even know he was German, would he? And maybe I'll someday get over this…this tension that hits me when dealing with the krauts. The professor warned me a thousand times about it, and showed me the percentages of the krauts that were complicit with the war, the percentage that were indifferent, and the large number who were actually against it. But, for those who were against it, you'd think they'd let me know first thing. Not that I'd believe them, but still…

Playing devil's advocate…what about black people? Do I tell every person with dark skin that, even though I wasn't alive back then, I don't agree with slavery? That I don't agree with what was done to their ancestors? Back in Oklahoma, when some poor sap was sweeping the floor at Woolworth's, did I stop him and say, "Hey pal, sorry you're on the bottom of the totem pole, but I want you to know I don't agree with what my forefathers did." Or did I just step over his dust pile and keep right on going?

But I wasn't even alive during slavery. It's not the same. And I left philosophy back at college and I don't feel like writing about that kind of stuff right now.

But it does make me think…

Anyway, that kraut kid tore his arms up but good. I remember doing the same thing dozens of times…elbows and knees. The kid's mother is my landlord. She seems like a typical kraut: a little distant and too in love with her own efficiency. She's not much of a cook, though—that much I do know. I know because they conned me into coming to dinner after I helped the kid. It was sheer misery. I had to look at pictures of that woman's husband, some Podunk transport pilot for the Nazis. Who knows how many men that bastard delivered to their deaths? He's either dead or rotting in a Russkie prison. Either is fine by me.

Eating that German woman's excuse for roast beef made me think about mama, a woman who could make a masterful meal from even the poorest ingredients. She was the most important person in my life. If I hadn't gone off and joined the Army, maybe I'd have been around when she got sick. Who knows, maybe she wouldn't have even died? I suggested that to her doctor and he told me it was hogwash.

"Cancer is cancer, son. Your mother probably had a small mass for months, maybe even years. Your being gone for a bit had nothing to do with that disease."

Still…to get that call from an ocean away…nothing I can do about it now.

My mama was the most giving lady I've ever known. I was just a toddler when my dad died and, even though I think my mom always wanted a mess of children, she vowed to never marry again. Her sisters—four of them (who all still believe I was killed in the war)—always urged her to remarry. Heck, my mama was only twenty-six years old when my dad passed away. Who knows? She might've had three or four more kids. But she didn't want to remarry. Said my dad was the man of her dreams, and there'd be no other.

While I grew up on the farm and just kind of took everything for granted, now that I'm grown it truly amazes me at what mama was able to accomplish on her own. We had over a hundred North Dakota acres that mama farmed to grow spring wheat and durum. She managed our farmhands expertly, always rotating the crops on time, anticipating weather, and negotiating sales at harvest. She did all of this while being a complete and loving mother to me.

My mama kept me clothed. She kept me fed. Helped me with my homework. Kept a roof over our heads. Jerked a knot in me when I needed it. Most of all, she loved me. And, to repay her, I acted like an ungrateful little jerk when I enlisted in the United States Army.

The day after graduating high school, I learned I was I-A for the draft. Based on the speed at which the I-A graduates from the year before had gotten drafted, we knew I'd get the notice soon. Mama had been after me for the last few months of high school to get enrolled in a university, despite the fact that she hardly had the money to afford it. She told me she'd make it work. But, for whatever reason, I didn't heed her advice. And about a week after graduation, my buddy Mike and I, both of us sporting eye-watering hangovers, staggered downtown to the recruiting station and enlisted.

I don't know exactly why we did it. Sometimes two chums get to passing the bottle back and forth and things get a bit dusky. The night before, he and I started talking about getting away from North Dakota. We spun tales about possible adventures, about seeing new places, women to meet, things to do…and, of course, duty we both owed to our country. We didn't know what the hell "duty owed to our country" meant but, being new adults, we had some sort of inkling that we were supposed to feel led in that direction.

Despite our ignorance—and hangovers—we busted into that recruiting station and made that recruiter's day. Both of us signed up on the spot and were promised by the recruiter that Uncle Sam wouldn't separate us.

Recruiters never lie, right?

And, hey, it actually wound up being the truth. They didn't separate us. We left Bismarck on the bus together, bouncing along all the way down to Camp Rapid, in South Dakota. It was there we got our heads shaved together. Got our uniforms together. Heck, we even took our first ass-chewing together. For three whole days, the Army kept us together.

Three days.

Then they split us up to attend basic training in different companies.

I learned quickly—real quickly—that Uncle Sam'll promise his soldiers all kinds of things, then change his mind as it suits him. I can still recall Mike's face when he realized we were going to be in different units. He looked over at me, his mouth hanging open in surprise. Then he grinned, realizing we'd been had by that slick recruiter. Mike always had a wry, sardonic grin about him. I swear, sometimes I think he enjoyed getting screwed over, especially when it came to his expectations—he appreciated the irony.

It was a moment when two sheltered young men learned that they weren't back in Bismarck anymore. When their mamas could no longer protect them. It was time to grow up.

Now, I realize South Dakota is pretty far north in the United States, but if there's a hotter, more miserable place on this earth in summer, I'd like someone to prove it to me. The damned buzzards, hundreds of them, would circle our huts day and night. We stunk so bad, and it was so blasted hot, that those birds probably figured we'd be dead soon. It's a miracle we weren't...

About Mike, I'd see him out on a detail every now and then and, on occasion, we had a chance to sit and chat while we scrubbed our uniforms or shined our boots. Then, on our last day of recruit training, we got to spend a few hours together before our graduation. That evening, Mike got shipped by train to Fort Benning, down in Georgia. I got an unhurried, could-have-walked-faster, twenty-two-hour bus ride to Fort Sill, in western Oklahoma.

A few months later, I saw Mike one final time. We were both in New Jersey, in the shadow of Manhattan, living in massive warehouses down at the docks, awaiting our troop transports to Europe. With tens of thousands of soldiers in those cramped warehouses, it was sheer luck that we even bumped into one another. Our time together started off somewhat strange. Mike and I had been inseparable since we were six years old—we hardly ever did anything apart. But just those few Army months with new friends and acquaintances changed us.

Once we found each other there in New Jersey, it was a tad awkward that we were no longer as close as we once were. Despite all that, after a few hours of warm-up discussion, it was just like old times again. On our last night before sailing, we were allowed a twelve-hour pass, six in the evening until six in the morning. Like most other soldiers, we hopped the first ferry over to Manhattan. Two hours into our pass, Mike and I met two girls from Brooklyn and spent the morning hours getting absolutely nowhere with them. As the sun came up behind us, Mike and I slumped on the deck of the ferry, sharing a bottle of rot-gut wine as we steamed back to New Jersey. We made our port call with only a half-hour to spare.

Mike's ship sailed to England, mine to Scotland. I got a single letter from him a few weeks later. He told me all about his training in England, and how his infantry unit was preparing to sail again for the Mediterranean. The next time I heard about Mike was in a letter from mama. She figured I'd already heard the news but told me anyway: Mike had been killed in Italy. He died on January 4th, 1944 in a battle that few people know about.

Up to that point, I wasn't very familiar with death. I snuck off by myself and curled up in a shadow, thinking about my old friend, remembering the times we shared.

Mike was the first of many of my friends who would die.

Hearing about Mike's death must have really hit close to home with mama. I'm sure she was worried sick that the same thing might happen to me. She tried not to focus on such morbidity in her future letters, but her concerns bled through with each paragraph. And she knew we were soon to deploy for Europe's mainland.

To this very day, I thank God she wasn't alive to hear about the massacre. That would have crushed her soul.

***

Felix Roth's woman opened the front door, this time making no effort to hide her battered face. And Marty had obviously woken her. She appeared disoriented and seemed to wince with every movement. The beating she'd taken was having an effect on her. After a shake of her head to clear the cobwebs, she frowned rather harshly.

"Why are you here again?" she asked.

"I want to talk."

"I told you he was up at the beer garden. Didn't you go up there?"

"Yeah, but now I want to speak to *you*."

"Mister, you're going to get us both killed," she whispered, glancing both ways on the small street. "The beer garden's probably closed by now. He'll be here any second."

"No, he won't."

"And how do you know that?" she asked, scanning the street again with wide eyes. Her tough demeanor had transformed to fear.

Marty hitched his thumb over his shoulder. "He went to Giessen with another fellow. I was sitting *right* beside him before he left."

"I thought you wanted to hire him to build cabinets?"

Marty pulled in a long, deep breath through his nose. "Once I got up there and got a beer in my hand, I couldn't stop thinking about you. About what he'd done to you."

She pulled the door all the way open. "This is nothing. You should've seen what he did to me back in March."

Marty glanced to his left, where he'd hidden his items behind a clump of bushes. "May I come in?"

Inside the door, a small lamp lit one side of her body in amber light. Her chest rose and fell as she clenched the top of her gown, pulling it shut. "Why? What is this?"

"I just want to talk to you."

"No, you *cannot* come in."

"*Just* to talk."

"But if Michael changes his mind…if he comes back." Her head shook and the words hung in her mouth, as if she couldn't verbalize the destruction he'd bring with him.

"He won't change his mind. I promise."

"You can't know that."

"Believe me, I do."

"Come inside and talk about what?"

"I swear on my life it's important."

"What is?"

"If you'll let me in, you'll see. I'm not here to hurt you."

"This is going to get us both killed," she breathed, moving aside and ushering him in.

Once inside, she led him into a small sitting area, the intimate rendezvous foreign to Marty. He'd have been lying to himself if he didn't admit that being this close to an appealing woman, meeting in the dark—in *secret*—didn't have an effect him. After all his accumulated hatred of the Germans, his biological response, his male impulse, was to do more than just talk to this woman. A tiny piece of his brain screamed at Marty to seduce her, here and now, and pleasure her. From where he sat he could even smell her, completely feminine and womanly.

Marty froze, examining his train of thought. *You just killed her boyfriend. Is this sexual weakness a denouement of that action? Is it somehow related? Are men programmed this way, somewhere deep in our subconscious? Kill the mate and take the partner?*

Marty massaged his eyes.

*Stop thinking like the professor. There's a dead man a few hundred feet away, along with another one you bound and gagged. Soon—if not already—the Polizei are going to be searching for the killer. I'd suggest you clear your mind and get down to business.*

Marty grasped her hand. "I have to tell you something…something…big." He used the word "big" because he couldn't think of a single word that would capture the moment's gravitas.

She cocked her eye at the peculiar preamble. "Okay, tell me."

Somehow he didn't think she would overreact to the news he was about to give her. There was just something about this woman. She seemed tough. Street-smart. Rather than sugarcoat it, Marty blurted it out.

"Your boyfriend, or husband, or whatever he is, isn't really named Michael Rüdin. His name is Felix Roth. He was Waffen-SS during the war, and he's a hunted killer."

Her only reaction was to swallow. Twice. Her head slowly tilted to the side, viewing Marty as if he were a mildly interesting painting.

"And the man that was once known as Felix Roth, your man…he didn't go to Giessen tonight. I was lying to you. He's up there at Schloss Gleiberg, down in the cellar." Marty paused before saying, "He's dead."

"Why are you telling me this?" she said impatiently, as if he were spinning a fantastic tale.

"Lady, I'm not bullshitting you. He's *really* dead. He pulled a gun on me after everyone left. It went bad after that and I shot him before he shot me. You can look beside your porch. My gun is hidden out there with his."

As she realized Marty wasn't lying, she covered her mouth with her hand. But for whatever reason, she didn't seem as horrified as Marty would have predicted.

"You were lying to me about the cabinets," she eventually whispered.

"Yes, I was. I went up there to confront Felix—that was my original intention. I didn't go there to kill him." Marty gestured up to the castle. "Then, after it all went bad, some other man, an older fellow, heard the gunshots and came up there. He's also—"

"Did he have a gray beard?"

"Yeah."

"That's Herr Bettenger, the caretaker. You killed him?" she shrieked, her voice pitching upward.

"No. He'll be okay. I did have to tie him up. He's also down in the cellar."

The woman began to sniffle.

"Listen to me," Marty said, remaining in front of her to prevent hasty reactions. "I didn't intend to kill your husband and—"

"Don't apologize," she said stonily, wiping her tears. "And he wasn't my husband. We live here together, against the wishes of my parents. I'm only crying because it's finally over." She deflated a bit. "Everyone always warned me that he'd eventually kill me—I never dreamed it might end with *him* dead."

Unable to resist, Marty asked why she stayed with him.

"Why does anyone stay with someone else?" She seemed to search for the words before shrugging and shaking her head.

After a brief silence, Marty spoke. "I really need to get far away from here but, before I do, I need something from you. I need to know something."

"What?"

"I need to know what *you* know." Marty leaned forward. "First, did you know he was Waffen-SS?"

"No. He never talked about the war."

"Did you know that he was using a pseudonym?"

"A what?"

Marty had used the English word because, despite being fluent, he didn't know the German equivalent. He searched his mind, finally saying, "A *Deckname*...a fake name...did you know 'Michael Rüdin' wasn't his real name?"

"No, but I always knew something was odd about his past." She reached to the side table and removed a hand-rolled cigarette from a beat-up tin, lighting it with a match.

"May I ask your name?"

"Gloria."

"Okay, Gloria, here's the important part. Did he ever speak to any men in a secretive way? Did he get letters from people you didn't know? Phone calls?"

"We don't have a phone."

"Fine…telegrams, strange visitors, odd trips. Anything like that?"

"He'd sometimes go for drinks in Giessen with his war buddies. That was all he'd say about them."

"Names?"

"He didn't tell me anything."

"You have no idea?"

She shook her head. "He didn't like me knowing his business. He'd knock me across the house if I asked."

"What else can you tell me?"

"We've only been together two years." She dragged on the cigarette so hard the tobacco crackled audibly as her eyes searched upward. "Three times since we've been together he took a trip. Called it a 'business trip.' Acted funny about it, and when he came back, he always had money. Lots of money."

Marty perked up. "Where did these trips take him?"

"He didn't tell me."

"How long?"

"Four days, each time."

"Did he drive?"

"Took the train."

"And you have no idea where he went?"

She shook her head.

"Gloria, did he have a safe, or a lock box, or anyplace he might have kept items he didn't want anyone to know about?"

She turned her head to an open door and stared for a moment.

"Is that the bedroom?"

"Yes," she answered, gnawing on her lip.

"Is there something in there?"

She turned back to Marty. "Not that I know of, but I've always wondered."

"Why?"

"He's locked himself in there before and I heard some bumping and shuffling. When I asked him what was going on he cursed me and told me to leave him alone. I left him alone. I didn't want a beating."

"How many times?"

"Several."

"Were you suspicious?"

"Yeah."

"Because of the bumping and shuffling?"

"That, and I remember him doing this just before, and just after, his business trips."

Marty walked to the bedroom.

***

While Gloria rested sleepily on the bed, Marty searched every surface he could think of in the bedroom and adjacent bathroom. During the first hour, Gloria asked him a number of questions about himself, most of which Marty ignored. Never once did she give him any indication that she thought him to be anything other than a German.

Flummoxed, Marty viewed the bedroom again. He'd searched everything, including the wooden floor, the furniture and the light fixtures on the ceiling. Gloria's head was cradled on her arm. She lifted it, rubbing her bleary eyes.

"How long did I sleep?"

"Maybe twenty minutes."

She worked her jaw and moaned.

"You should ice that."

"I should do lots of things."

"Are you sad, Gloria?" Marty asked, pausing his search for a moment. "About Michael?"

"Yes."

"No, I'm not sad."

"Not at all?"

"He was vicious. By the time I realized that, I was trapped."

"Why didn't you just leave?"

She closed her eyes and shook her head. "I can't explain. Find anything?"

Marty threw his hands up. The bedroom wasn't large at all. When entering from the sitting room, a person would see the bed situated against the outer wall and slightly to the left. On the left wall was a solitary rear window and, to the right, the entrance to the bathroom that also had a second door that led to the sitting room. The entire house had only four rooms: kitchen, sitting room, bedroom, and bathroom.

Marty scanned the room, forcing himself to view it as if it were new to him.

*Find inconsistencies.*

The ceiling was plaster and cracked in spots. Nothing unusual and, other than the small, chintzy light fixture, there was no place to hide anything.

The floor itself could have been used as a hiding spot, but Marty had checked every single floorboard. None were loose or out of place. He'd try to go under the house later, if need be.

The walls were all plaster, except for the short wall to the right, which was slat board on its lower half, probably due to the bathroom being on the far side. Marty knew that different wood had to be used around bathrooms in case of a water leak. But he'd jiggled all the wooden slats and found nothing out of the ordinary.

Minutes earlier, when he'd checked the bathroom, he'd painstakingly touched every square inch of the small room. There was nothing to be found.

Back in the bedroom there was precious little furniture. The bed was simple and contained no hiding places, other than the mattress, and Marty had run his fingers over every crease and fold of the mattress. It was clean. He'd gone through the spindly night table and removed all drawers in the chest of drawers. That was it. There was nothing else.

"You're sure he was in here when he was bumping and shuffling?" Marty asked.

Gloria opened her eyes. "Yes. He locked the door and I could hear it very clearly. I heard a loud thud at one point."

Marty moved to the bedroom door and closed it. He thought about sounds in the main sitting room—*"I could hear it very clearly."* Looking down, Marty eyed the short slat wall again. It was adjacent to the door. Dropping to his knees, he ran his fingers down its length. From right to left, the wall measured probably about six feet. Still, he could find no loose boards.

Stepping back into the bathroom, Marty viewed the other side of the wall. The old claw foot tub and sink backed up to the wall, where each fixture's pipes originated. Marty gauged the thickness of the wall, probably about ten inches. Pretty thick, but there was plumbing in there.

Again he pressed on the slat boards, trying to discern movement. He found none. Then Marty went into the bathroom and eyed the pipes that led into the wall. There were small pipes for hot and cold water, and larger drain pipes for the tub and sink. Marty grasped each one, shaking it and hearing the faint rattle of the pipes behind the walls. He viewed the sink drainpipe. The piping was cast iron and old. But up against the wall, where the pipe entered, was an escutcheon, a decorative flange for concealing rough edges. It was large and seemed newer than the rest of the plumbing. Marty eyed the tub's drainpipe. Like the sink, it had the old piping and the newer escutcheon.

*Roth was a carpenter. He'd be able to create an intricate hiding space.*

Marty tried to turn the sink escutcheon. It was too tight. He stepped through the bedroom where Gloria was again sleeping. Easing outside, Marty checked his hidden items before glancing up at the black shadow that was

Schloss Gleiberg. There were no lights and there appeared to be no activity. He wondered if the caretaker, Herr Bettenger, were still sitting quietly next to Roth's corpse. Continuing on, he walked to the dilapidated shed and retrieved the old, oil-stained toolbox he'd seen earlier. Marty walked back inside and fitted a large wrench on the outer fitting of the escutcheon.

When he'd made several turns, he realized it was closely-threaded, meaning it would take many turns to release. After a number of revolutions, the escutcheon let loose with a clunk.

"What was that?" Gloria mumbled.

Marty walked into the bedroom and found her sitting up, bewildered. "Go back to sleep." He looked at the slatted lower wall, finding the entire piece slightly off axis. The left side was especially out of alignment.

"It's a false front," he breathed. Marty tried to remove the portion of the wall but it was still being held on its right side.

*The other escutcheon.*

Back in the bathroom, lying on the floor, Marty unscrewed the tub escutcheon, the action taking at least ten minutes due to the limited motion he was able to achieve under the tight space. And the closer he came to releasing the wall, the harder it was to turn. The weight of the wall was hanging from the escutcheon. Marty guessed that Roth probably pushed the chest of drawers up against the wall when he was attaching or releasing the furtive cover.

With one final turn, there was a scrape and a loud thud.

The partial wall had fallen.

"Come look!" Gloria yelled.

In the bedroom, even without much light, Marty's eyes went wide over what he saw. The slat wall had covered a standard inner wall frame, dissected by numerous pipes. But between the framing and piping, on small wooden shelves, were numerous clues to Roth's former life. And situated in the very middle was a basic SS field cap. At its peak, the cap had a silver Waffen-SS eagle. But most menacing was the large emblem below the eagle, the dreaded SS *Totenkopf*, or death head—a skull and crossbones that defined the essence of the SS.

Kneeling before the cache, Marty carefully removed the cap, feeling it for a moment before turning it over. The cap was well used and had Felix Roth's name stamped inside. Doing his best to control his escalating rage, Marty set the cap aside.

On the lowest section of the hiding spot was a disassembled rifle of some sort. Marty lifted the receiver and studied it for a moment. It was a Sturmgewehr 44, the assault weapon of the SS. He replaced it, taking several deep breaths, aware of his own pulse. This rifle was almost certainly used to kill his fellow soldiers. In fact, it could have even been used to shoot Marty, the recipient of two gunshot wounds.

In an attempt to refocus, Marty shut his eyes, lowering his head.

"Are you okay?" Gloria asked from the bed. Marty didn't respond. He resumed his inspection.

To the right of where the cap had been were a notebook and also some jewelry. Marty decided to view those items last and, instead, turned his eyes to what rested to the left. First were three gold ingots, stacked neatly. Each one was no larger than a business card holder. Marty lifted one, surprised at its heavy weight. He turned it over, finding it stamped with a serial number and the words *Deutsche Reichsbank*. According to an etching at the bottom, each ingot weighed a kilo. A kilo was around 32 ounces and Marty remembered seeing that gold was currently worth around $35 per ounce. That meant each bar was worth around $1,100, or its German equivalent, more than 4,500 Deutsch marks. If Marty had to guess, he felt Roth probably kept the gold in the event he ever had to flee.

Next to the ingots were two short stacks of gold coins, each emblazoned with Hitler's image. Marty pressed his thumbnail into one, finding it soft. He spoke over his shoulder without turning. "You won't have to worry about money for a while, Gloria. You can braze the identifying marks off all this gold and exchange it for cash."

Gloria sounded breathless as she asked, "How much is all that worth?"

"I could be way off, but I'd guess roughly 15,000 marks."

She didn't respond. He turned his attention to the jewelry.

There were three pieces altogether, two in silver, one in gold. The first silver item was a worn ring displaying the Totenkopf as the centerpiece. Felix Roth's name was inscribed in the band. Next to the ring was some sort of locket on a chain, done in silver and depicting a German eagle backed by a sunburst. It wouldn't open and held no other clues to its owner. Adjacent to the locket rested a chunky gold ring. Marty lifted it, his eyes going wide when he realized the ring's origin. He fell backward off his haunches into a sitting position.

"What is it?" Gloria asked.

"The top light," he croaked. "Turn it on."

"Is that a ring?" she asked, coming off the bed and flipping the switch.

Marty didn't reply—his mouth was too dry. He twisted the ring in the light, viewing it from every angle. It was notable due to the bold double-T on its face. The ring was for alumni of Texas Technical University and, although there was no name inscription, Marty knew it had once belonged to one of his best friends, Kenny Martin, the former football player from Texas. He even recalled Kenny wearing the ring, proud of his school despite the fact he was kicked out for disciplinary reasons.

Felix Roth had stolen the ring from Kenny's lifeless hand.

Marty covered his eyes, feeling nauseous. Behind him, the bedsprings squeaked as Gloria resumed her position.

"Are you okay?" she asked.

"Yeah," Marty managed, taking deep breaths.

"Why did that ring upset you?"

"It belonged to my friend. Honestly, I shouldn't be all that surprised."

Regardless of the trove he'd found, Marty needed to pick up the pace. Sooner or later the Polizei were going to discover Roth's body and the bound caretaker. And there were no more trains running tonight. If he were to stay in this area till morning, the Bahnhof would probably be overflowing with Polizei searching for the murder suspect. He needed to get far away from Giessen.

Dropping the ring in his jacket pocket, Marty reached for the notebook. The first dozen pages were notes, penned almost illegibly. Not only was the penmanship horrible, but the writing itself was that of a second-grader. No huge surprise. Marty skimmed the notes—most having to do with tips for a change of identity. But after that were address entries that caused beads of sweat to erupt all over Marty's body.

This was the first address he came to:

# A.O. – Heinrich Geilen

## Junkersstrasse 12

## Zorneding, Bayern

"What's the notebook?" Gloria asked.

"Hang on," he replied. He heard the bedsprings again as he flipped the pages.

Marty studied the next few entries, finding the format exactly alike: initials, followed by a name and address. He reached into the inner lining of his coat pocket, whipping out the short-version roster the professor had created. Running his hand downward, he found one man whose family name began with an "O": Anthony Osleiger, an NCO, from Bad Tölz.

Following suit with each set of the initials from the notebook, Marty found numerous matches for the select group of men the professor believed to be in *Die Bruderschaft*.

Slowly flipping through the pages, Marty searched for R.N., the initials for his primary target, Raban Nadel. There was no match. He continued to look at each of the initials and, while there was no Raban Nadel, the last set of initials made Marty's heart rate spike. The initials read O.Z., standing for none other than Oskar Zeckern, the battalion commander. The men he'd interrogated in Berlin had all told Marty that Roth and Zeckern were the keys to finding Nadel. Roth was dead but, presumably, Marty now had Zeckern's name and address. His new name, according to the notebook, was Dieter Siegst.

But why wasn't there an entry for Raban Nadel?

*Slow down and think.*

Marty recalled his first target, Rheinsdorf, mentioning that Roth was Nadel's *Schwanzlutscher*—a much more vulgar version of "brown-noser." If Roth was so close to Nadel, he probably didn't need to record his address. He probably knew exactly where Nadel lived.

That's why there was no address for Nadel.

Marty had heard Gloria step from the bed a moment earlier. She'd been rustling around behind him, but he hadn't thought much of it. Just as he closed the notebook, something cold and hard pressed into the base of his skull. He could feel two distinct round holes, top and bottom. Now he realized what she'd been doing.

She'd retrieved a shotgun.

*Damn.*

# Chapter Seven

Journal Entry

My buddy Mike, the one from back home, was the first person I lost to the war. There would soon be more. Many more. That's not something a person thinks about, even with a huge war going on. You don't sit around talking to your pals, then start quietly thinking that they could wind up dead tomorrow. Maybe because you know that the same thing could just as easily happen to you.

So I didn't worry about it. But my mama surely did.

When I enlisted in the Army with my buddy Mike, I didn't break the news to mama in a soft manner—the way an only son should have. No…insolent jerk that I was, I showed up back at the farm with my papers, a prideful grin on my face, and smacked those papers down in front of her. I'd been so proud to tell her, as if I was declaring my independence. Oh yeah, I was a real man, alright. A big time, soon-to-be war hero. (With a terrible hangover.)

Then I watched her break down and lay her head on the kitchen table, crying, shuddering, fearful her baby boy might die. Suddenly it hit me: I was the only close family my mama had. I was her only window to my dad. And here I was gloating about leaving her. Boy, did I feel small.

While I would have probably been drafted, regardless—and while I don't regret joining independently—the way I threw my enlistment in mama's face bothers me to this very day.

It's one of my biggest regrets in life.

The woman who had always showed me nothing but love knew how many men were dying in that war. She had one man left in her life—me. And there I was, toying with her emotions for no good reason whatsoever. To this day, I still have no idea why I did it. Maybe acting that way simply comes natural to eighteen year-olds. A sign of our independence. A harsh method to make our parents angry, so they won't grieve our leaving of the nest.

The entire process was out of character for me. I realize that in the grand scheme of things, it's probably not such a big deal. I'm sure if mama were still alive she'd hug me and tell me not to regret anything. She'd say it didn't bother her at all. Yeah, that's exactly what she would do.

Even still, if I could somehow go back in time, I'd like to punch my old self right in the face.

Thank God she never had to endure the aftermath of the massacre. I think just hearing about my involvement, about all that happened to me, would have probably killed her. If there's anything good that came out of mama's death, it's that she never knew about the Massacre at Kastellaun. To mama, when she died, her son was just fine.

Now, however, I'm left thinking about all those other mamas—184 of them, assuming they were all alive at the time—who did have to hear the gruesome, horrid news of what happened to their sons.

My hands are sweaty and shaking as I write this.

What I'm here in Germany to do is in memory of all those I served with, but a piece of it's for mama, too. Mrs. Betty Clara Whiteside.

I miss you, mama. I love you so much.

And I'll see you soon.

\*\*\*

In a bleak moment of recognition, Marty knew the weapon pressed against his neck was an over-under shotgun. He was able to feel both barrels of the cold steel as Gloria gave his neck a little nudge, saying, "Drop that notebook by opening your fingers, but don't move your hands downward. This shotgun is loaded for mule deer and my finger is on the trigger."

Marty opened his fingers, allowing the notebook to fall.

"Now, do this slowly...interlace your fingers and rest them in your hair on top of your head."

Again, Marty complied.

"Okay, carefully turn and cross your legs. If you move your hands a centimeter, I'll blow you back into all that plumbing." She spoke with a coolness that told Marty she'd done this type of thing before. The highs and lows of the night took their toll on Marty, making him feel weak and almost faint.

Once he'd turned, he viewed the shotgun. It was old but well-oiled, with long over and under barrels. The twin maws seemed enormous, especially when aimed squarely at his chest. During his training, Marty had used a number of shotguns, a weapon he'd previously only used in small gauge for birds and rodents. The one she carried, a 12-gauge, loaded with deer shot from a range of only three feet, would not only kill Marty, it would probably perform as she'd warned, and blast him cleanly through the partial wall behind him.

"Lady, I don't know what—"

"Who are you? And don't even think of bullshitting me again."

Marty eyed her. Eyed the shotgun again. Eyed her. He swallowed before saying, "I'm an American."

She narrowed her eyes, head cocking slightly. "My ass, you're an American. You're a bullshitter who killed Michael over all that gold."

"I am an American," Marty repeated. He switched to English. "I'm from North Dakota. Grew up on a farm. You want to hear it all? Do you speak English?"

Her chest was rising and falling with speed. "Yes. Keep going."

"I was in an artillery unit that was massacred late in the war. Your boyfriend, Felix Roth, was in the SS Panzer unit that massacred us. I was th-the…" Marty's voice hitched so he paused. "…I was the sole survivor. The United States allowed me to change my identity to avoid all the attention that would have come from the press. I changed my name and moved to Oklahoma to convalesce. That's my story and it's true."

Gloria seemed bewildered.

Marty switched back to German. "I said what I just said in my normal accent from back home. Translated, it meant that I'm an American from—"

"I said I speak English," she whispered, in English, clearly affected. "Did you come here just to get revenge on Michael—Felix—and rob him of his gold?"

Marty shook his head. "He's not who I'm looking for and you can keep *all* this gold. I just want the notebook and the college ring. And I *don't* want them for their value."

"What's in the notebook?"

"I think it's the names of his associates, former SS, who are now members of a group called *Die Bruderschaft*. They have new identities."

"What, you want to go kill all of them?" she asked, tears welling in her eyes.

Marty made sure he had good eye contact when he said, "I wasn't going to kill your boyfriend. And I'm *not* lying about that. I just wanted to talk to him but he was suspicious when I engaged him and *he* pulled a gun on *me*. Then he tried to rob me. He's the fourth man I've targeted."

"The other three?"

"Are alive and well. I'm no savage killer."

She listened to this and didn't speak for a moment. "Then what *are* you doing?"

"There was a man in Felix's unit, the final commander. He shot their first commander right in front of all of us. Then *he* gave the order to kill us all."

"Why did he kill the first commander?"

"Because the first commander had no intention of killing us. He was going to use us to bargain his own surrender."

"And the second commander's name?"

"It was Raban Nadel. I want *him*. He's why I'm here."

"To kill him?"

"I'm here to capture him. To expose him. To make him stand trial for what he did."

"This entire story sounds like more of your bullshit," she said, tensing the gun.

"It's not bullshit," Marty retorted, her assertion angering him. "It happened in March of 1945…"

Marty spoke slowly for the better part of ten minutes. He told her everything, right down to how he'd hidden himself under the lifeless bodies of his friends as German tanks drove back and forth over the dead and near-dead, finishing the job they had no ammunition to complete.

By the time he finished, Gloria had lowered the shotgun. Marty didn't move, remaining where he was with his hands on his head. "And you can check my body for scars if you like." Marty moistened his lips. "You're only the second person who's ever heard the whole story. I even left things out when I was debriefed by my own military."

Placing the shotgun onto the bed, Gloria told him he could get up. She walked from the room, coming back with a glass of cloudy water, probably from a well. "Here."

Marty guzzled it and asked for another. After drinking the second glass, and taking a few deep breaths, he said, "I need to ask you a huge favor."

"I know what you're going to ask and you don't need to worry. I won't say a word."

"They're going to question the hell out of you when they find your boyfriend, especially after they see you've been battered."

With closed eyes she shook her head. "I'll play dumb. The best thing I can do is tell them he slapped me around, then went for beers, and that's all I know. Anyone who knows me can verify that he abused me before, many times." She touched her face. "The more I volunteer beyond that, the more I'll look like I knew something. And you said you left Herr Bettenger, the caretaker, alive...right?"

"He's fine. I had to hit him in the head to subdue him but, by the time I left, he seemed okay. I can't believe he hasn't started yelling."

"Did you threaten him?"

"Yes. I wasn't going to hurt him but I had to make him believe I would."

"He won't yell if you threatened him." She narrowed her eyes. "So he saw you? They'll know who to look for."

"He didn't see me and he only heard me speak German. Did I sound native to you?"

"Yes."

"Then I'm protected. They won't find me, Gloria. I'll be long gone." Marty glanced to the front door, feeling the urgency to get going. "I need to put this wall back up."

Gloria assisted him and, as he began threading the first escutcheon back on, she spoke from the bedroom side of the wall. "I can understand why you're doing what you're doing, but you're just one of many...you know that."

"What do you mean?" he grunted, getting the wrench in place after hand-threading the escutcheon onto the pipe.

"There are a thousand stories like yours from the German perspective."

"Well, that's what happens when you start a war."

"I didn't start a war," she snapped.

Marty paused what he was doing. "What are you getting at?"

"Do you really want to hear it?"

"Yeah."

The voice from the other side of the wall suddenly sounded like a child's. "I'd normally never tell anyone this, but since you're on your life's quest, you should hear it." She pressed against the wall. "Keep working while I talk."

Marty complied, working slowly so he could hear.

"In 1945, when your beloved General Patton stormed through here, we were overrun by American soldiers. And we were actually overjoyed at first, believe it or not. While the world was made to believe we were all willing cogs of some bloodthirsty war machine, most of us were just scraping by to survive. I can't tell you how many nights we'd boiled turnips, spindly potatoes, or even wallpaper, just to get the starch. By the end of the war I was twenty-three, working for a formerly wealthy family as a nanny in return for two cans of food a week."

Marty finished tightening the first escutcheon. He ceased movement, almost scared to hear the rest of this story. "Go on."

"After the Americans and Brits arrived—this was in May of '45—I was walking home to my grandparents' house one evening. I had to pass a checkpoint. Two of the American soldiers from that checkpoint grabbed me by my arms. They dragged me into a vacant home and they raped me. Brutally raped me." She paused for several moments. "I would have just given in to them. I wasn't stupid and many, many women, a lot of them young girls, had to drop their morals and do this type of thing just to keep the peace. Compared to our former life, it wasn't all that bad."

"Gloria…I'm not so sure you should tell me more."

"Well, I'm going to tell you more!" she shouted, her voice breaking. After a pause, she said, "The two men that night were depraved. Not only did they rape me, for hours, but they did things to me that went beyond rape. They did things to my body that I can't even begin to explain…"

Marty closed his eyes and said nothing—he had no words.

"Do you know what it's like to be tied to a bed, made to wait while they smoked and drank and recovered? I never knew when they would come back into that bedroom, ready for more…more of their deviancy."

Marty's eyes were now squeezed shut, his perspiration dripping onto the floor.

"Anyway, by the time they finally grew bored with me and let me go, I was hardly able to even walk. I was a mental wreck and I had to hide what happened from my family."

"Why?"

"I can't explain and I wouldn't expect you to understand." She sniffled a few times. "Then, weeks later, when I'd finally just about healed, I turned up pregnant. The pregnancy was from the rape, no mistaking it. My grandpa almost killed me when I told him and my grandma. He was just a superstitious old farmer and, after blaming *me* for what happened, he made me endure a savage abortion from some crazy old man who wasn't even a doctor. It nearly killed me again." Gloria began to sob. "And since then, I've never been worth a shit to anyone. In fact, the only way I can attract a man anymore is by laying down for him."

Though Marty knew such things had gone on during, and after, the war, he'd never taken the time to focus on it. His words felt greatly inadequate as he said, "I'm…I'm sorry, Gloria."

She was crying, sobbing. "So…after you find that sonofabitch who murdered your friends, maybe you can find those two stinking drunk *American* bastards who raped me and robbed me of my soul!" She screamed every syllable, the animalistic fury of her plea shaking Marty and making his efforts seem selfish and trite.

He stood, coming around the wall, finding Gloria curled up on the floor. Her body shuddered with her cries. Marty knelt, lifting her and taking her to the bed.

As he pulled the covers up to her neck, he said, "I'll finish putting the wall back together. I'm going to hide that gold for you. Once the police have closed the investigation on your boyfriend, I want you to sell the gold and get the hell away from here."

Gloria nodded although she didn't seem to care.

After Marty finished with the second escutcheon, he stashed the gold in the small backyard, burying it in the soft earth under what was once a small garden.

Once he explained exactly where it was, he made one final sweep, making certain he'd left nothing that might incriminate her, or him. He came back to the bedroom.

"So, you'll tell them—"

"I'll tell them nothing," she said, head cradled on the pillow. "He beat me up, then went drinking. Just a normal night around here. When they tell me he's dead, I'll react naturally. Don't worry. Go do what you came here to do."

Marty lingered.

"What is it?" she whispered, looking up at him.

"One last thing—his SS friends, *Die Bruderschaft*, may come when they find he's been killed."

She closed her eyes. "I'll be long gone from this hellhole."

Marty pushed her hair back over her ear. "If they suspect you...they *will* find you."

"I'm in no mood for any more abusive men," she said flatly. "If they come for me, they're getting the shotgun." A small smile overcame the pain on her face. "Go and find the man you seek, and that's enough for me."

"I'm sorry for...for what the two Americans did."

She eyed him. "There are animals everywhere."

Marty said nothing.

"Go on. I'm fine."

Five minutes later, Marty had swiped a squeaky bicycle and was a full kilometer away.

***

The last weekend of June passed with a mid-summer blast of chilly rain that crept in on Berlin and lingered like an unwelcome relative. During most of June, a month of pleasant dry weather, the citizenry had essentially forgotten how miserable Berlin weather can actually be—at any time of the year. And when the foul, mid-summer weather first arrived, people exited their homes, palms skyward, before hugging themselves due to the cold, gritting their teeth and cursing this unfair weather transformation.

*Kriminaldetektiv* Werner Eisch, however, loved it. He had no desire to endure the bitter cold of another brutal winter, but he loved the chilly, wet days of October, and that's exactly what this June day reminded him of. He paid thirty phennigs for a Monday newspaper and a cup of steaming coffee. Werner sipped the strong brew, remembering how scarce it had been just a few years before. Satisfied with the chilly weather and his accompanying drink, he hurriedly made his way to the bureau. There, more than an hour before his reporting time, Werner sat in a vacant interrogation room, enjoying his coffee as he perused the newspaper. As always, he studied the pertinent sections of the *Zeitung* before indulging himself with the *Oberligen fussball* scores.

Finished, Werner meandered the hallways, watching the various police activities as he awaited the arrival of his day-shift section. As he usually did, he wandered into the briefing of homicide detectives, a group with which Werner yearned to serve. The Homicide Division, in Werner's mind, was the pinnacle for detectives. And getting there was Werner's ultimate professional goal—his dream job.

Each year, during a short window of time, Werner was allowed to submit papers for consideration of transfer to Homicide. And each year, quite perfunctorily, his chief read him the terse rejection. Though the Homicide chief, a man named Leipziger, never came right out and said it, Werner knew it was because of his missing arm. Leipziger was an elitist and a clothes-horse. The chief clearly disapproved of Werner's sale-rack suits and prosthetic—whenever they passed each other in the halls, Leipziger curled his lip and turned away.

*Just keep putting in for it,* Werner always told himself, not allowing himself the luxury of taking it personally. *Someday they'll let me in. When they do, I'll prove I belong.*

So, on Monday mornings, though it visibly irritated Chief Leipziger to no end, Werner liked to slip into the rear of the weekly Homicide briefings and listen. What Leipziger didn't know, and probably didn't care, was Werner had an IQ far superior to any of the Homicide bulls. Werner absorbed the information like a sponge, ready to unleash his knowledge in the event he was ever promoted. But, for the moment, he dealt with a variety of less threatening activities in his own department of Burglary. Burglary primarily centered around its namesake, along with motor vehicle theft and the occasional mugging. Werner was sometimes called in to help other departments—all except Homicide. Never Homicide.

He'd just have to be patient, so he told himself.

Werner slipped into the rear of the Homicide bay, standing along the back wall, viewing the orating chief through the slow-moving haze that emanated from two-dozen cigarettes.

"...and the Amis have promised an all-expense-paid weekend at the hotel of your choosing for the man who nabs this sonofabitch. He's making a habit of robbing their soldiers first and unnecessarily stabbing them afterwards." The chief looked up from his notes and slid his glasses down his sharp nose. "Personally, I think this killer is a cold-hearted Russkie, but let's try to find him regardless."

"How many Amis are they claiming this guy's killed?" someone asked in a sleepy voice.

"Hang on," the chief muttered, pushing his glasses back up scanning his notes. "As of last week, seven American soldiers have been found dead in a period of almost one year. They've all been found near the river, all near bar districts and they were all very drunk. The stabber appears to be the same one each time. He's almost assuredly left-handed and, according to the examiner, strong as hell. He's stabbed through bone several times."

The chief looked up, snatching his glasses from his face as his mouth opened to speak. He suddenly froze, eyeing Werner. Leipziger's finely-plucked eyebrows cocked in an expression of disapproval. Then, recovering himself as he did every week, he cleared his throat and resumed. "Now, as you fine *Homicide* detectives know, left-handedness accounts for about twelve percent of the male population, so that's a big clue to start with. And the killer has taken full paydays from a number of the victims in the last six weeks, so he's flush with cash."

"Does he only attack at payday?" someone asked.

With a nod of approval, Chief Leipziger said, "Excellent question, Karl. Look into that, will you? Post that on the board when you find out."

"Yes, sir."

Leipziger glanced at Werner again before saying, "You men are in my division because you're the best, and *only* the best get to serve in my division." He let it hang for a moment, a trace of a smile showing on his face. "You're the elite, and let's show our Ami friends what the *elite* can do."

His weekly insult dealt, Leipziger prattled on for fifteen more minutes, covering a variety of topics. His deputy was up next, running down a laundry list of murders in the region and country, in the event that there was a connection to the dozens of open murders in Berlin. While mundane, the run-down sometimes led to breaks in other cases.

"...and this next one is sensitive, meaning the locals there *don't* want it leaked to the press." The deputy, Karch Buchner, an obsequious little knee-licker who followed Chief Leipziger around like a sweatered schnauzer, surveyed the room, his lips pursed as he allowed his proclamation to sink in. "I want everyone to avoid the temptation to make ten marks from your reporter friends, *ja*? So bottle this one up."

"If you leak it, I'll find out," the chief warned from his side chair. He was leaning back, arms crossed as he surveyed the room.

Rumored to be "on the take," the forty-something Buchner, his eyes probably beginning to fail him, lifted the paper close to his face as he read. "The victim, killed by two gunshot wounds, was living under a false name in the village of Krofdorf-Gleiberg, in Hessen, near Giessen." He paused for effect. "After being found dead near a castle beer garden, it was discovered that the deceased was wanted for criminal activity while serving in the Waffen-SS."

"Another one who was living in hiding and got himself killed," some detective called out. "Those boys clean up their own, don't they?"

"Maybe it was more marauding Jew-boys that did it," another one chimed in. "They've been cleaning up, too, if you believe all the rumors."

"Knock it off," Leipziger barked, eyes scanning the group as he kept order like a strict school teacher might when his prized, but largely disliked, pupil delivered his book report.

"The deceased was living under the alias of Micheal Rüdin," the deputy said. "Fingerprints and other evidence have revealed him to be Felix Heinrich Roth. As I said, he was living in the village of Krofdorf-Gleiberg, which is about fifty kilometers from his place of birth. I've got a laundry list of criminal charges here, the most important being murder." The deputy flipped the page. "Roth was formerly of the 101$^{st}$ SS Heavy Panzer Battalion and served in both the east and the west."

Upon hearing the exact Waffen-SS division, Werner straightened and nervously clicked his prosthetic.

"A few more to go," the deputy droned on. "Alfred Sepowitz in Oderberg. He was forty-one years of age and his wife is the chief suspect. He was a reputed philanderer. Report says she waited until he fell asleep and…get this…after using a kitchen knife to slice off his—"

"Excuse me," Werner called out, halting the deputy. "About Felix Roth, the dead Schutzstaffel. Would you please repeat his unit?"

The bureau's wooden chairs creaked loudly as every detective turned and glared. The chief stood, frowning, hands on his hips. Werner might as well have disrobed and yelled "look at me!" given the dirty looks thrown his way.

"Why should I repeat it, *Kriminaldetektiv?*" the deputy asked, saying the "criminal" portion of the title the same way he would say "*Durchfall*," the German word for diarrhea.

"There's a case I'm working that could be related," Werner said, feeling sweat breaking out all over his body.

"I will *not* repeat it for *you*," the deputy said primly. "You may inquire through your own chief afterward. And such information will only be released through the approval of *our* chief. This, *Kriminaldetektiv*, is why we have divisions as well as a chain of command." The deputy took a great breath afterward, massaging the bridge of his nose, as if speaking to Werner had somehow sullied him.

Werner dipped his head as he exited the bay and hurried back to his own department.

# Chapter Eight

The most important person in my "recovery" was Professor Walden, the dean of history at East Central. He instructed me in one class, History of the Modern World, during my junior year. Before that, I'd never spoken to him, but I certainly knew who he was. The professor was a peculiar-looking little man, almost always wearing a quizzical, twitchy expression. He strode across the campus studying everything in his path: trees, ants, rocks—even the clouds in the sky. He had a round face, tan skin, leonine hair and large brown eyes that suggested at least a partial Asian ancestry.

Most distinct was his German accent. When I first heard him lecture, the accent bothered me. Really bothered me. To the point of giving me anxiety attacks.

Once, during my junior year, Professor Walden was lecturing about the war. The combination of the subject and his German accent created such angst in me that I sweated droplets onto my desk and the floor. Unable to recover from the sudden anxiety, I rushed from the classroom. He'd not protested at all. In fact, he gestured with his hand as I hurried by, as if inviting me to leave. Four more of his classes passed and he never said a word about me leaving. A girl who sat next to me did ask me what happened and I just told her I had a stomach bug. By this point, Professor Walden had moved past the war and we were on to more mundane items.

It was late September of 1948 and I was preparing for tests and catching up on required reading. I was about two pages into *Paradise Lost* when I noticed an ancient pair of scuffed brogues whisper to a stop next to my chair. I felt a hand—a powerful, vise-like hand—clamp down on my shoulder. Then, in that German accent that had always thrown me for a loop, Professor Walden whispered, "Mister Elder, I would like a moment with you in private. I'd like to speak about the war."

His mention of the war was key. No one at East Central knew that I was a veteran. After the massacre, the government had created a new identity for me. They fabricated my past life and medical records, both pointing to a farm accident as the reason for my injuries. According to the records, those same injuries kept me from serving in the military. While his reasons for wanting to discuss the war might have been innocuous—after all, he was a history professor—my instinct told me there was more to the story.

"What about the war?" I asked, unable to control the tremor in my voice.

"You've heard my accent, Mister Elder," he whispered. "I lived in Germany. My father was Jewish. I had to flee."

I was too overcome with a mix of emotions to respond.

"Did you hear me, Mister Elder? My father was Jewish. I am Jewish. We share a bond."

"What bond?" I croaked.

"I don't know, but I can sense it." He patted my shoulder. "That's why I'd like to chat. Are my senses wrong?"

I shook my head.

"Fine." He leaned over my shoulder. "If you can spare the time away from..." he adjusted his spectacles, "the good Mister Milton, perhaps you and I can convince my friends in the cafeteria to brew us a small pot of coffee?"

I went with him, of course. Despite my awkwardness back then, I felt awful for the horrible things I'd assumed about the man.

He obviously had pull with the cafeteria workers because the steaming hot coffee was placed in front of us ten minutes later. It was good and strong. He curiously tossed in a dash of salt and sipped his audibly.

"Mmmm. So many little things we take for granted. A few years back, what we wouldn't have given for a cool cup of weak coffee."

I cradled the hot cup in my hands, waiting for him to speak. Finally he did.

"My father died in 1943, Mister Elder, assuming what I've been told was accurate. He was in a concentration camp known as Flossenbürg. I was told that one day he'd had enough and simply didn't cooperate with the guards." Professor Walden opened his hands and shrugged. "I needn't go on about that because I'm sure you can imagine the rest."

Each word stabbed me like a large, rusty knife.

A bubble of silence ensued. He didn't seem emotional. But when he spoke, it was deliberate.

"My mother died sometime before that," the professor said. "It was in the early days of the round-ups. When they came for my father, he cooperated so she might be spared. That's how it started, you know. They didn't always take full families. They'd come and take people like my father—influential types they deemed troublemakers. So, he went peacefully, in some perverse show of good faith." Professor Walden removed his spectacles and wiped his eyes with a handkerchief.

"I have accounts from two eyewitnesses that, even though it was strictly forbidden, a military officer violated my mother minutes after my father was hauled away. Then, other soldiers that were there joined in, en masse. They killed her, afterward, and took what was left of my family's valuables." He took a few deep breaths, smiling ironically the way people sometimes do after they've just opened a horrific closet of their mind.

There was another significant gap in the conversation. I'd have loved to have said something, but I couldn't manage any words.

Finally he said, "And I also had two sisters in Germany. I've no idea what happened to them. Supposedly they fled before the unpleasantness with my parents." He shrugged. "No one has a record of where they went."

The professor had turned his head to wipe his eyes again. I finally looked at him, studying his face as he dealt with those unthinkable memories. As I wrote before, he had unkempt gray hair, wiry, running off in all directions. His skin was tan and marked by sparse afternoon stubble. I'd guess he was about forty-five or maybe fifty years old, still holding on to a full mouth of teeth tinged a few shades from white by coffee and perhaps cigarettes. And in those amber-brown eyes I could see abject horror as he pondered the brutality of what his family endured.

The conversation turned at that moment. As did what was left of my life. The professor wiped his face a few more times, perched those spectacles back on his nose, then focused on me as he took a sip of his coffee.

"And you, my friend, young Mister Elder...you know of such horrors, don't you?"

He could have gotten less of a reaction if he'd punched me in my nose.

My fingernails left marks on the freshly waxed cafeteria table. His hands gripped mine, squeezing them, ceasing their drag. And together, our hands joined as one, we trembled.

"I'm truly sorry to do this to you, my friend, but it needs to be done. I've been watching you for some time. And I know something is terribly wrong inside you."

"Let...me...go."

"It won't matter, Mister Elder. I can let you go. I can choose to leave you unmolested for the balance of your time here. And you'll graduate and then you'll get a job in Oklahoma City or Dallas. There, your employer will soon learn that you're unreliable, too tense, unable to think clearly." His expression was sympathetic. "You might find a wife, have a few children. The marriage will be doomed before it's even begun. You know all this, Mister Elder." He held fast to my hands. "Though I might let you go, those haunting memories, whatever they are, are indelibly tattooed on the recesses of your mind. They will never release you, young man. Ever."

Then he spoke the most pivotal words my ears have ever heard. "The horrors are a part of you...*unless*...you do something to eradicate them."

One of the cafeteria workers ambled over. Professor Walden never broke eye contact with me. He simply gave a slight shake of his head. The worker turned and walked away.

"Mister Elder, while my nightmares are borne of a different tragedy, they're nightmares nevertheless. So, rather than the two of us spending the balance of our lives haunted by these horrible visions, why don't we discuss eradicating them together?"

"How can you eradicate yours?" I muttered.

"By helping you."

My chin was down to my chest. I remember the shirt I was wearing that day. It was a light blue button-down. The sweat from my chin dotted the front of the shirt, as if I'd spilled my coffee. When he said nothing else, I managed to lift my eyes from my captive hands to his face.

"What are you talking about?" I rasped.

"I'm talking about the injustice my family has endured. I'm talking about whatever happened to you, Mister Elder. You've been distant your entire time at this institution. But any mention of the Second World War...and the Nazis, in particular, sets off visible personal anguish for you." He inclined his head and spoke softly. "Certainly, I'm not the only one who's noticed."

I squeezed my eyes shut, having no idea how to react. Then I heard his words.

"And I know I'm correct about my assumptions, Mister Elder, because you've said absolutely nothing to dissuade my line of thinking." He unclamped my hands and abruptly stood. "Come see me when you're ready."

Professor Len Walden, chair of East Central's history department, shuffled away. I watched him cross the cafeteria and step outside. Then, through the glass, I saw him light a cigarette. He stood there, his chest expanding and contracting. His hand rubbed his temples before he used it to prop himself up against the stone column.

It was late afternoon and the lingering September sun seemed to set Professor Walden ablaze.

I didn't sleep for two days.

*** 

On Wednesday evening, a few hours after arriving home from work, Marty sat in his small kitchen nook, realizing he'd gotten away with murder. Well, "murder" was too strong of a word. His actions at that castle beer garden had been in self-defense. Regardless, he'd not heard a word about what had happened and didn't feel one trace of remorse. In fact, he was mildly disturbed that he wasn't at all bothered by his killing of another man. In the end, he chalked it up to all the death he'd experienced during the war, combined with his lack of sympathy for the Germans—and especially the SS. Now, with Felix Roth's notebook in his possession, Marty planned his next action. As he searched for a city on his large map, there was a faint knock at the door. Marty walked to the door, asking who it was.

"It's Josh."

Marty shut his eyes and whispered, "I should've never helped this little kraut." He unlocked the door and yanked it open, finding Josh standing there with bleary eyes and a splotchy face. It appeared he'd been crying.

"Yeah?"

"Can I come in?"

"I'm busy."

"You always say that," Josh muttered.

"Why do you want to come in?"

"I'm angry."

"About what?"

Josh showed irritation. "Can I please just come in?"

"Just wait there a minute." Marty walked to the desk and quickly put away his maps and the notebook. He then yelled for Josh to come in. Josh shuffled around the corner, his eyes down.

"What's the problem?" Marty asked, immediately admonishing himself for acting as if he cared.

"I wish I could move in with you."

"Why do want to move in with me?"

"It's my Mutti…she loves me, I know…but she's just a woman. She doesn't *understand* me."

"Well, my dad died, too, Josh and—" Marty halted himself, remembering that Josh didn't believe his father, the pilot, to be dead. "Anyway, Josh, my dad wasn't around and my mother had to finish what he'd started. So I guess I understand what you're feeling. But it's hard for her, for any parent, to play both roles."

"I'm thinking about running away."

"You're not going to do that."

Josh looked up, his eyes growing fierce. "You don't *know* that."

Trying to contain his frustration, Marty jerked two chairs from the sitting table and pushed one to Josh. Marty turned his own backward and sat down, frowning at the kid. "Okay, so you're going to run away. What did she do that's making you want to leave?"

"She pissed me off," Josh replied in pitch-perfect English.

Marty raised his eyebrows. "How?"

"I had a…a *magazine* in my room," he said, switching back to German. "She found it."

"What kind of magazine?"

Josh averted his eyes.

"What kind?"

"It had girls in it."

"Girls?"

"You know…"

Marty grunted. "And you think she was wrong to take it?"

"Papa wouldn't have."

"I think you're wrong. I think he'd have taken it, and he might have given you the belt."

Josh raised his eyes. "Did you get the belt?"

"You bet I did. But usually, my mom would make me go cut a maple switch."

"A what?"

"I'd have to go to the maple tree in the back yard and cut off a small limb, about the thickness of a pencil. I'd strip it of leaves and smaller branches, and then she'd whack me with it." Marty grinned for effect. "It could draw blood."

Josh winced. "That's not right."

"Right or not, it didn't kill me and it sure made me realize that I'd screwed up. And I still think your pop wouldn't want you looking at naked women. Your mom's just doing her best."

"My friends look at magazines like the one I had."

"Yeah, I had friends like that, too. They'll get theirs, believe me. Just try to behave like a good kid, okay?"

"I'm not a kid," he said. "You sound like *her*."

"Okay...if that's the way you see it, then be a man. And take your punishment like a man."

Josh nodded as if such a statement were acceptable. But he stayed right where he was.

"Is there anything else I can do for you?"

Josh shook his head. Stayed in place.

*Then get the hell out of here!* Marty opened his mouth to say the words but couldn't get them out. He rubbed his face vigorously. "What else do you want?"

"What do men typically do when they sit around?"

"Sit around?" Marty shrugged. "Josh, I don't have time to just—"

"How about cards?"

"Yeah, some men do play cards but I don't have—"

Josh, his face suddenly alight, whipped out a tattered pack of cards. "I've got some."

"Shit...did you plan this?"

Josh pointed. "You said 'shit' again. And it's okay if you're not good at cards." He handled the deck like a seasoned pro, methodically removing a segment of the cards and sliding them back into the pack. "I'll teach you."

"I said I don't have time."

"Don't be scared."

"Scared?" Marty asked.

"Are you?"

"Whatever...I'll play for twenty minutes," Marty said, hating himself for acquiescing.

The game was similar to pinochle, but played with only 32 cards. Like spades or hearts, the players bid on expected books before actually playing. Josh destroyed Marty in the first two games. Then he questioned Marty's intelligence.

"I just learned," Marty snapped.

Josh shrugged. "The little girl, Marta, down in two-A...she beat me in her second game."

*Smart little prick.* Marty hurriedly shuffled the cards for a third game. He'd gotten the hang of it and was going to beat this kid's ass.

"Play time's over," Marty said.

"I wasn't even trying very hard," Josh countered with a confident wink.

"We'll see."

"Yep," Josh grinned.

A sharp rap on the door halted the coming bloodbath. Marty opened the door to find Frau Schaal. She peered around Marty, seeing her son. Marty knew the look he was seeing on Frau Schaal's face—he'd seen it many times from his own mother.

"Joshua Thomas Schaal, you get downstairs to your room this very instant," she said lowly, aiming a rigid finger down the stairs. Josh pushed past both of them, mumbling his goodbyes to Marty. Frau Schaal slumped when Josh was out of sight. She closed her eyes and shook her head.

"I was only letting him stay for a few minutes," Marty said. *Why the hell do I feel the need to explain, anyway? What the hell did I do? These damned krauts are trying to pull me into their—*

"You didn't know he was in trouble," she murmured, poking a cigarette into her mouth. Then, as if she realized the inappropriateness of her action, she shook her head and tucked it back into her apron.

Marty nearly responded to her but this time he managed to keep his mouth shut.

"Did he tell you why he stormed out?" she asked.

"Yes."

With a grim expression, she said, "Some days I wish I'd been born a man just so I'd understand what goes on in those hard heads of yours." She turned and walked down the stairs.

"Wait," Marty called out, closing his eyes as he said it. *Idiot!*

She halted, staring up at him from the lower landing.

"You did the right thing," Marty said. "But, since you want to know what goes on in a man's head, what he did to get in trouble was normal, too. All boys have that kind of curiosity."

"Well, I'm glad to know you approve of *both* our actions," she snapped, her voice cynical as she disappeared down the stairs.

Marty stood there for a moment, letting her caustic remark seep in. He eventually stepped back inside, slamming the door as he unleashed a torrent of curses.

# Chapter Nine

Journal Entry

Nearly a month went by before I decided to approach the professor. It took several days to put the things he'd said to me out of my mind. After that, it took about two weeks before I began to come back to his proposition. Rather than think about my own plight, I tried to imagine his. Tried to imagine the horror of hearing that my mother had been violated and killed. Tried to imagine my father in a concentration camp, murdered for standing up for himself. Tried to imagine my sisters missing and presumed dead, and the brutalities they likely endured while on the run.

And I thought I had problems.

So, for the final two weeks in the month that passed, I began to read about the atrocities of the Second World War. It was difficult at first. I had horrible nightmares the first few nights. But I knew I'd eventually become somewhat desensitized, and able to study such horror with a clinical eye. Through it all, I continued to go to class. I didn't socialize, only spoke when spoken to, and basically just went through the motions to keep my grades at a satisfactory level. In the evenings, when my schoolwork was done, I read.

At the beginning, I stayed away from any incidents like the massacre in which I'd been involved. Then, after bolstering myself, I read about the Nanking Massacre, a multi-week slaughter of Chinese civilians and soldiers by the Japanese Army. Hundreds of thousands of people died.

I read about the Russian "destruction battalions" and their "scorched earth" policy. When they plowed forward, gobbling up chunks of soil, they deliberately destroyed everything in sight. They used murder, rape, burning and mayhem as their tools of war.

And, over my final week, I read about atrocities committed by the Allies and, yes, the United States. There isn't nearly as much information available. But when, on a Saturday, I took the bus to Oklahoma City's library, I was able to unearth a number of controversial articles that outlined numerous vile acts allegedly perpetrated by my fellow soldiers. I was stunned at how many I found. One that struck me in particular was the killing of roughly 75 Japanese soldiers who'd peacefully surrendered. This wasn't a killing in the foggy, adrenaline-soaked moments just after surrender. No, these men were slaughtered during their march to a prison camp.

If there's one thing that I found in common with all of these massacres, it's this: in each instance, the idea of killing the defenseless originated with someone. With one person. One man. Yes, soldiers then had to carry the order out, and doing so, at least in our military, is unlawful. But someone had to give that order...someone had to light the match. They had to willfully lower the match to just the right spot to fully ignite the tinderbox.

In a moment of perversity my mind conjured the old radio tagline, "Who knows what evil lurks in the heart of men?"

So, back there in Oklahoma at East Central, it was late on a Friday afternoon, almost one full month after the professor had approached me in the library. I'd been in my dorm room reading about another massacre when I snapped the book shut. I walked down the hallway, ignoring my hall mates who were revving up for a Friday night of fun and frolicking. Outside, late afternoon storm clouds had gathered, spilling oversize droplets of rain on me over the last portion of my walk across the campus. Leaves swirled all around in the growing wind and lightning struck as I grasped the door of the administration building. As I walked down that cavernous hallway, the thunder boomed, rattling glass.

Down the hall I marched—straight to the professor's office. Without knocking I flung the door open, finding the small man behind his desk. Two female students, their books open, sat in the chairs opposite his cluttered desk.

The professor eyed me for a moment, his eyes flicking to my shirt. "Mister Elder...judging by the sound outside and the dots on your shirt, I suppose it's begun to rain."

I didn't speak. My chest was heaving like I'd just run wind sprints.

He whipped open his appointment book, running his finger down the page. "Well, it appears I've double-booked this half-hour." He eyed the two coeds and removed his reading glasses.

"I think we're clear on what needs to be done, aren't we?"

They slapped their textbooks shut as they quickly agreed, eager to start their weekend.

"Ladies, hopefully another discussion won't be necessary. If so, it won't be quite so pleasant. Do know, I realize Captain George Vancouver's expeditionary achievements might not be paramount on your weekend agenda, but he better find his way into your bright minds at some point before Monday at eight in the morning. I have a powerful hunch that an unannounced assessment is imminent." He arched his unkempt brows. "Are we on the same page?"

They eagerly affirmed their understanding. The professor shooed them away. I stepped aside while the two young ladies evacuated as if the history building was ablaze.

The professor gestured to one of the chairs before propping himself on the edge of his paper-littered desk. One hand massaging the other, he stared at me, his eyes twinkling.

"How may I help you, Mister Elder?"

For several years I'd been speaking to people with my eyes diverted, as if I had something to be ashamed of. I was like some addled kid who'd been promoted a grade too far beyond his abilities. But, at that moment, something clicked in me. I guess it had been building over the balance of the month. I finally felt sure of myself.

I looked up at Professor Walden, my eyes boring into his as I spoke. "About what's been bothering me, professor."

"Yes?"

"You mentioned eradicating the problem."

"Indeed, I did."

"I'd like to know exactly what you have in mind."

"Are you willing to open up to me?" he asked. "To be honest, no matter the pain?"

"Yes, sir. I am."

The professor stood and closed the door.

We talked for hours.

\*\*\*

The statuesque man strode casually beside the Danube River, taking time to appreciate the soft, brush-kissed scenes straight from a Max Liebermann painting. The humid summer light diffused the panorama, adding a soft glow to hard edges. He paused to watch a pair of swans parenting their maturing cygnets. An older nanny passed by, pushing a double carriage containing twin babies. The man walked to the edge of the Danube, the afternoon sun behind him. He viewed the wide, spangled waters illuminating the buildings across the water in shimmering light. It was a majestic day, filling him with good cheer, giving him great hope for the future.

"Father Germany," the man said aloud. "My troubled home."

There had been no reason on earth that could have convinced Oskar Zeckern to permanently flee the bountiful splendor of his beloved fatherland. He'd have died before he fled.

In fact, he almost did.

Oskar Zeckern, his name now Dieter Siegst, paused, looking beyond the rebuilt buildings at the waterfront. Behind them, rising ten meters into the sky, were unsightly piles of rubble. Massive stacks of brick, concrete, wood and building materiel were topped only by curving fingers of rebar, jutting out like crazy hair on top of a lumpy skull. The rubble once was part of a picturesque city whose beauty went on and on for many kilometers. Then, nearly nine years before, a good deal of the Bavarian city of Regensburg had been blown to smithereens when it was mercilessly bombed one fateful August evening. The reprehensible Americans and Brits could have surgically excised the Messerschmitt factory and oil refinery—the only worthwhile targets—but, instead, they killed hundreds of innocents while brutishly leveling three-quarters of one of world's most picturesque cities.

Zeckern spat the collecting acid from his mouth and walked on.

A minute later, as he rounded the bend, he noticed two young ladies walking in his direction, their hard leather shoes crunching on the pea gravel. As they approached, he could see they were in their upper school years, probably sixteen or seventeen years of age. While tattered, their clothes were also too small, their erect bosoms straining against the taut fabric. Those young bosoms had only recently reappeared across the country, when the average caloric intake of a German had finally moved back to an acceptable level.

Seventeen was too young, he reasoned, but not by much. Zeckern felt his neck and chest flush as he passed them. He smiled warmly to see what sort of reaction he might garner. *Nothing.* They hardly cut their eyes at him, giggling about something else, perhaps a boy. Perhaps a man.

*But not me.*

*You're 43, old friend. The carnal victories you once enjoyed are now few and far between. But the wealth is there. Don't take that for granted. The young ones will now have to come to you via your affluence, distasteful as it is. You're like honey that attracts only a certain type of bee. You must learn to love that bee...*

Zeckern cursed his own mind for conjuring such ridiculous metaphors. Like many men, he enjoyed the thrill of the hunt. Store-bought girls, or even hangers-on, didn't appeal to him the way women did who desired him for his looks, for his mind. There had been a time, especially back in the 1930's, when Zeckern had enjoyed a new woman almost every night. When his youthful looks and his dashing uniform of the Schutzstaffel were irresistible to young women, many of whom were married. The married ones had always been his favorite. And Zeckern, in his opinion, had left every one of them with the healthy glow of satisfaction.

Oh, what a glorious time it had been.

He snapped open his silver case and lit a tasty American cigarette, completing his stroll at a charmingly restored hotel on the south bank of the Danube. Inside, after a discreet inquiry, Zeckern was directed to the fourth floor. Exiting the lift, he pressed the cigarette into an ashtray, adjusting the Windsor knot of his silken Italian tie. The thick wine carpet of the hallway absorbed each step as he walked to the far end, rapping on the last door.

In the span of only a second, the door was yanked open and Zeckern was jerked inside by his lapels. When the door was shut, he was unhanded, staring into the fierce eyes of the man who was once called Raban Nadel. Nadel had originally been under Zeckern's charge but, in the strange politics of the post-war brotherhood, he was now Zeckern's superior.

"Did you see those two men?"

"What two men?" Zeckern demanded.

"The two men in cheap suits. One had a wide black mustache."

"They passed me in the lobby and were discussing which colors of paint sell best," Zeckern said, adjusting his lapels. "Salesmen of some sort."

Nadel seemed relieved. "They'd been milling about in the hall a few minutes before. I thought they might be cops."

"I'd know if they were," Zeckern said flatly. "You've underestimated me again, as usual." He adjusted his jacket again. "Why are you in Regensburg?"

"The Danube reminds me of home."

Zeckern understood.

After admonishing him for being late, Nadel thrust an already-poured whiskey into Zeckern's hand, commanding him to sit. "We *must* talk."

"Why all the anxiety?" Zeckern asked, still standing.

Nadel scraped all ten fingers back through his sandy blond hair. "You honestly don't know?"

"No, I do not."

"Then do as I said and sit down."

Zeckern had never fully accepted taking orders from the power-hungry, peremptory Nadel, little shit that he was. With a reproachful stare, Zeckern crossed the Persian rug and sat in the center of the sofa. "Pray, what is the commotion?"

"Felix Roth is dead."

Zeckern felt himself flinch. It was involuntary, mainly through his right cheek, like someone with a bad tic. He cleared his throat, stuttering a few times before he got the one word query out. "How?"

"He was shot."

"What else do you know?"

Nadel explained the basic facts of the case, including the story of the caretaker who had provided most of the testimony. Nadel told Zeckern about the male suspect, a German of approximately thirty years of age, and spoke of the witnesses who saw the stranger at the beer garden before Roth was shot. When Nadel finished, Zeckern took a long sip of the drink, tightening his lips over his teeth.

"Are they certain it was this stranger who did it?"

"No, but it had to be him. He lingered after everyone had left."

"Felix Roth," Zeckern said in a velvety, whiskey-induced baritone, "was always your personal loose cannon, Raban. Who knows what he did to anger this man to the point of murder? They could have simply had an argument that devolved into violence."

"You're assuming Felix was killed on the spur of the moment. What if the killing had been carefully planned?"

Zeckern cocked an eyebrow. "Was it?"

"I have no idea. But there are a few other facts that I find disturbing."

Sipping his whiskey, Zeckern waited. Finally, edgily, he said, "Then tell me."

Nadel crossed the suite, dropping two chunks of ice into a highball glass, following them with whiskey and a splash of soda. He carefully mashed a mint leaf under a spoon and dropped it in the glass. He swirled his simple concoction as he turned, leaning against the black marble of the bar.

"Felix had been living with a woman. We discussed her at our last meeting." Sipped his drink. "They were having problems."

Zeckern placed his drink on the table. "When did Felix *not* have problems with any human being?"

"The girl is gone," Nadel said, ignoring the remark. "The Polizei are nearly positive she left on the night of his death."

"She heard he was killed and she left," Zeckern said with a shrug.

Nadel shook his head. "Wrong. No one knew Felix was dead until the next day."

"Her new lover," Zeckern surmised. "She starts screwing this new man. She tells him what a piece of shit her boyfriend is—which would have been *sheer* truth—and the new man kills Felix so he can take her unfettered. We've got millions of war veterans here, Raban. Seven, eight years ago, we were all killing. Those habits die hard."

Nadel allowed a wintry smile. He took a large swallow of his drink before placing it behind him. Then, his narrow fingers slid into the inner pocket of his tailored suit, producing a folded piece of foolscap paper. Unfolded, he clasped it with both hands. "This is an inventory sheet Felix filled out at the last gathering."

"What about it?"

"Do you remember Leonard Hutier, from the 75th?"

"Just the name."

"He's now in the BKA, the federal police."

"How on earth did he manage that?"

"He stole the identity of a well-educated corpse at the war's end. Doesn't matter," Nadel said, waving his hand. "Anyway, during the ensuing investigation, I sent him into Roth's home, to find Roth's cache."

Zeckern blew out an exasperated breath. "And the gold bars are gone, aren't they? We've been over this a dozen times with many of the men. He could have already sold them or maybe his woman took them. Hell, I would have. And you're getting too worked up over—"

Cutting him off, Nadel read the contents of the inventory in a loud, authoritative voice. "Three gold ingots, one kilo each. One Schutzstaffel NCO ring. One Schutzstaffel gorget. One gold ring from Texas Technical University, taken during the incident at Kastellaun." Nadel looked up.

"So the cops discovered he was an SS who changed his name," Zeckern said indifferently, leaning forward and lifting his drink. "Nowadays that will hardly make news other than the local newspaper. And if his woman stole all that, then so be it."

"*And*...one notebook."

"A notebook?"

Nadel nodded one time.

"What sort of notebook?"

"I don't know."

"Well, what does the inventory read?"

"One—notebook," Nadel said, drawing each word out.

Zeckern placed his drink back on the table without taking a sip. He stood, wiping his palms on his jacket as he began to walk the suite. "It could be nothing, some sort of diary of his duties in the war. The investigators would find out about all that anyway."

"He kept this notebook *hidden* in his cache," Nadel said, sounding as if he was enjoying the act of spreading his own misery. "So, yes, if he were normal, it could have been a diary."

"What are you getting at?"

"Felix Roth wasn't normal—he could barely even write."

"Then what's in it?"

"I'm fearful it's a roster."

"A roster of what?"

"You know what. A roster with original names, and *current* names. Names and addresses."

The view from Zeckern's eyes darkened slightly, marked by rings on the outer edges of his vision. It felt similar to the time he had been in an automobile accident and bloodied his head, making him feel as if he was viewing the world through binoculars. Steadying himself with his hand, he said, "My God, man! Do you know what damage that could do?"

"Indeed," Nadel replied calmly, studying his nails. "It would be your end."

"My end?" Zeckern roared. "Our end."

"I'd be willing to bet, due to my superior intelligence, I'm far more insulated than you."

Zeckern readied a retort but was cut off by Nadel.

"Nevertheless, such a roster would be catastrophic to *Die Bruderschaft.* Thus, I propose we do one of two things: The first option would be notifying everyone. We'd advise them to sanitize and run. Run *now.*" Cracking his knuckles, Nadel said, "In his coded letters to us, Walter Rauff goes on and on about the insatiable Chilean women and the weather down there."

The only sound in the suite was Zeckern's heavy breathing as he waited on the second option.

"The other alternative, which I prefer, is to find Felix Roth's little twat and get that damned notebook."

Zeckern opened his hands. "But we don't know that anything damning is in that notebook."

"He couldn't write. He hid it in his cache. Therefore, what else would it be?"

Jerking the tie from around his neck, Zeckern undid his top button and flopped back onto the couch. He guzzled the rest of the double whiskey and rolled a piece of the half-melted ice around in his mouth. Leaning all the way back, he put a hand on his forehead. "We have to try to find her before we think about running."

"Agreed."

"Will your man in the BKA tip us off if the authorities are onto us?"

"Of course," Nadel said. "I'm not concerned with the authorities. I'm concerned with whoever killed Felix. Maybe *he* has the notebook."

Zeckern lowered his head and rubbed his eyes. "The woman is the key. Either she has it, or she knows who killed Felix."

"Again, I agree."

"But how do we find her?"

"We don't have to find her."

Zeckern lifted his head.

Nadel grinned. "I already *know* where she is."

# Chapter Ten

Journal Entry

The late autumn and early winter of 1948 was one of research and learning. Yes, I was still in school, doing as was expected of a college student. But this learning was extracurricular. While the other students went to parties or played sports, I delved into prescribed research. The lead researcher was Professor Len Walden—and I was his assistant.

A person wouldn't typically expect to find a man like Len Walden in a small town like Ada, Oklahoma. Born and raised in Germany, the son of well-educated Jews, he seemed cut out for a much bigger city. I eventually learned what attracted him to Ada. The fact that he was Jewish and had few credentials recognized by our education system made a job difficult to find. He told me he inquired at more than fifty colleges and universities and East Central was his only offer (other than a newly-created position educating prisoners in Massachusetts, which he politely declined.) It obviously paid off for East Central because within three years Professor Walden was chair of his entire department.

Away from the school, the professor embraced the Oklahoma lifestyle. He lived in a small, turn-of-the-century ranch cottage out on the north side of town. The cottage was shaded by two large blackjack oaks. However, the rest of his 144 acres was mostly barren other than some scraggly seasonal grass. The only other trees of any size were out on the northern end of the property, next to the Canadian River. Don't ask me why the river is named that—it doesn't run anywhere close to Canada. A split-rail fence surrounded the living area of the professor's dusty property. Surrounding the outer perimeter was a high game fence, aimed at keeping his animals in and predators out.

Even though it wasn't a working farm, a person who didn't know better might have thought it was. The professor owned goats, pigs, chickens, four cows and a broken-down old nag named Siggi. The heavy presence of feed and slop also encouraged regular visits from raccoons, possum, rats and, inevitably, snakes. Even river otters were known to make their way over to his house, unfazed by the outer fence. The otters loved chasing the professor's chickens.

The professor welcomed all the wildlife and, in short order, so did I. A month into our burgeoning relationship, I'd become his animals' primary caretaker. In return, the professor fed me on the weekends and allowed me to use his Plymouth whenever I wanted. We became good friends.

As I mentioned, we spent the remaining balance of 1948 doing research. I worked on everything but the massacre, itself. I let the professor gather the specifics—I couldn't yet bear reading about it. It wasn't long before he had several binders full of research. He knew about my unit. He knew about the aggressors—the 101st SS Heavy Panzer Battalion. He knew which of the SS had been killed prior to the massacre. And he knew the man believed to be the leader of the massacre. The architect. The originator.

The man's name was Raban Nadel.

I recall a pivotal time in early December of 1948; the students at East Central had just finished exams. I was at Walden Ranch—the name I'd bestowed upon the professor's little zoo. We'd just finished eating several bowls of a hearty stew he called "cholent." The professor retrieved his binders and opened the largest one to a tabbed page.

"Raban Zelig Nadel," the professor pronounced.

I pushed my stew away. "What about him?" I certainly knew who Nadel was and the very mention of him made me lose my appetite.

"He's the man who gave the order."

"I know that," I mumbled.

"You know his name, but do you *know* him?"

"I don't want to know him."

"Well, you're going to know him, so listen up." The professor took a sip of water and spoke in his professorial voice. "Raban Zelig Nadel, born November 19, 1922 in Ulm, located in the south of Germany." The professor looked at me. "Ulm, by the way, was a beautiful city when I visited many years ago. It's known for having the tallest steeple in the world, and for being the birthplace of the famous physicist Albert Einstein."

Though I knew the professor was trying his best to keep me relaxed, I stared back at him. I was devoid of good humor.

"Anyway, according to my research, Nadel was an intelligent yet troubled young soul. The middle child of five, he was often disciplined at school for fighting and shenanigans."

"How did you learn that?" I asked.

"If one knows where to look, one can learn many things. Nadel did not attend traditional university, enlisting in the military in 1939 at the young age of sixteen. I found sketchy details of an assault he was accused of shortly before his enlistment. The victim was a young woman. Perhaps this gave him extra motivation to leave." The professor flipped the page. "During his training and subsequent combat action, the Nazis discovered that Nadel was a talented, yet ruthless, soldier. He'd reportedly inquired numerous times about joining the Schutzstaffel and, on his eighteenth birthday, he was awarded an appointment at the *Junkerschule* in Bad Tölz. It was there he earned his commission."

"I really don't care to know anything about this savage," I said, disgusted. My stomach was queasy and making noises.

"You should learn everything you can about him, Mister Elder. I realize it sickens you, but such facts might pay dividends at a critical moment. I'll try to be as brief as possible." The professor spent a half-hour educating me about Raban Nadel, the man who eventually led his Waffen-SS to massacre 184 American soldiers.

Then, the professor produced three photographs.

"No," I said, turning away.

"If you don't want to look now," he said softly, "then don't. But, at some point, you need to engrave his face in your mind."

"It already is," I said, staring out at the barren blackjack oak.

"While you may remember him, Mister Elder, you need to study his features with a clinical eye. Features such as his mouth, the shape of his nose, his brow line, the dimple of his chin—he will likely have changed his appearance." After a moment, he said, "Know thine enemy."

My eyes closed, I spun back around, taking the three photos. Slowly, I opened my eyes and spread those photos before me. And there he was, author of my nightmares, murderer of my friends. He wore the same expression in all three photographs, with his chin slightly upturned, an arrogant expression on his smug face.

I cannot describe the feeling of seeing him for the very first time since the massacre. Suddenly, numerous details flooded back into my mind. Little things—awful things—that I hadn't thought about since the massacre. The way Nadel had stared into my friends' eyes as he'd shot them. The way he'd whipped his SS into a frenzy after we were all covered in blood. I even recalled Nadel's order to grind and pulverize our flesh with the tracks of the Panzers. He'd given the order in English, just to strike fear into those of us who were still alive.

He was a monster in every sense of the word.

While I later memorized every feature of Raban Nadel's appearance, on that Saturday I managed to only view the pictures for a few minutes. It was only a few minutes because I soon became violently ill.

I felt as if I were staring at the devil himself.

***

It had taken *Kriminaldetektiv* Werner Eisch three hours to fill out the request form and pen the accompanying report. His chief liked such reports to be typed and free of errors or even visible corrections. Since Werner had only one hand, typed papers took quite a bit longer than they did back when he had ten fingers. Not to mention the fact that he chose to do the report after hours, since it was deemed extraneous, not a part of his regular job. Though most cops wouldn't have given a spare thought to willfully bending the rules, Werner lived his life by the book and had stayed late the night before, typing and retyping until the report was as good as he could make it.

Werner's chief, a man named Mainhardt and one of the oldest men on the Berlin force, leaned forward as he read the report through the aid of a magnifying glass. He showed little reaction and read slowly. Werner could smell the sharp tang of the chief's peppermint breath mints, which he constantly sucked to cover the smell of his booze. Like a number of men on Berlin's force, the chief of the Burglary Division was an alcoholic. Werner felt the number of alcoholics was probably higher in Germany due to the ready availability of alcohol, and the fact that many of its users probably self-medicated, tamping down residual horrors left over from the war and the Nazis' reign of terror.

Other than the booze, Chief Mainhardt was a capable policeman in Werner's eyes. The chief wasn't a political animal. Therefore, he'd been shuttled down to Burglary, widely regarded as the least important division on the force. Mainhardt was a slight man, short in stature and almost skeletal. His hair was gray and sparse, his face and hands dotted by liver spots. Yet, somewhere behind all the age and hard living, a person could see the structure of what was once a handsome man.

Years ago Chief Mainhardt, just a beat cop at the time, made a name for himself by singlehandedly taking out a pair of kidnappers who'd nabbed a wealthy German industrialist. The case had made national news and was a boon for the Berlin Polizei. Managing to take the kidnappers down on his own had cemented Mainhardt's upward trajectory on the force—until the Nazis seized power. Then the war reshuffled the force and eliminated much of the prior leadership. Werner guessed that ninety-percent of the force had no clue that, three decades before, Chief Mainhardt had been a national hero. In Werner's eyes, Mainhardt's life was somewhat of a tragedy, wrecked by sudden fame, the Nazis and, subsequently, liquor. His circumstances had left him hidden away in a dark corner of the force, sauced-up and reading reports from disliked, unwanted one-armed detectives.

Placing the magnifying glass on the report, the chief looked up, pausing for a moment as the breath mint clicked around in his mouth. When he spoke, he summarized in a reasonable tone, without tipping Werner as to his position. "So, *Kriminaldetektiv* Eisch, you worked a mugging that piqued your curiosity. The man had been in the..." he frowned, gesturing to the report, "...whichever SS Panzer division. Then, a few weeks later, you listened to the national homicide brief and heard about a murder that occurred five hundred kilometers away. The victim had been in the same SS Panzer unit as the man who was mugged." The chief crunched his peppermint and sipped from the water on his desk—at least, Werner assumed it was water. "These two incidents, through their common military thread, have set your curiosity aflame, and now you want to look into the possibility of a connection? Is that a fair summary?"

"Yes, sir. It is. But I also feel the need to say something about the mugging victim. He was very cagey about—"

The chief silenced him by showing his palm. "In this well-written report, *Kriminaldetektiv*, you've failed to mention one crucial element."

Werner frowned as his mind raced. "What's that, sir?"

"Motive."

"Because I don't know what it is, sir."

"I realize that. But if I'm to freelance one of my men, in a department that's already shorthanded, don't you think I'd best cover my narrow ass by making sure you're after something that is connected to a startling motive?"

"Er...I suppose so, sir."

"There's no supposing." Mainhardt tilted his head back, eyeing the ceiling. He spoke slowly, the way a person does as the story is coming to them. "The men that had served in this SS unit...are being sought after...no...*stalked*...by one of their own....and the stalker is after a cache of diamonds that were stolen...from a wealthy German...no...a *Belgian* family, in late 1944." Mainhardt nodded as if satisfied. "You learned this from an informant. If anyone asks whom, tell them to see me. Do you need me to repeat the motive?"

"No, sir," Werner breathed.

"You have one week from this very second. I said Belgium, but it could have been France, Poland...wherever. Find out where this SS Panzer unit was serving in December of '44 and go with that."

"Should I make it known?"

"Absolutely not. That so-called motive is only to be used in the event you get questioned by anyone of authority about working this angle." The chief's face was grave, his yellowish eyes narrowed. "I don't want this coming back on me, Eisch, and I don't want anyone knowing about it. Everything you learn, you learn privately. There will be no written orders and, if you get nabbed for doing something reckless, I'll play ignorant to all this and you'll take the fall. Is that motivation enough to not get caught?"

"It is, sir."

"Get me a list of what you're currently working and I'll cover it myself."

Werner stood. "Yes, sir."

Mainhardt placed his palms flat on his blotter, his mouth crinkling into something resembling a smile. "Nice to see someone around here actually acting like a policeman."

"Thank you, sir."

"Dismissed."

After bringing his current case files back to the chief, Werner walked from the bureau, crossing Bunsenstrasse and descending into the basement under the old administrative building. Down there, near the rear, were the military records. And near the back of the military records were five large cabinets reserved for one paramilitary organization.

The notorious Schutzstaffel—the SS.

Werner's first mission was to find a roster of all who served in the 101st SS Heavy Panzer Battalion.

He was curious if any others lived nearby.

***

With permission from his boss, Jimmy Gallotte, Marty left work in mid-afternoon. He'd used the excuse that he had to take care of some personal business at the power company—something about a mistake with his billing. While that was true—the power company had spelled Marty's name incorrectly on his account—Marty rectified the error by way of posting a letter. Gallotte, in his typical easygoing fashion, couldn't have cared less. He told Marty to take care of his problem quickly, and to enjoy his afternoon as they approached American Independence Day.

"Just won a new contract for three new S-bahn stations that are to be fast-tracked," Gallotte had said with a wink. "Gonna bring our revenue up twenty-percent next year. Better enjoy your free time while you can."

Outside, the cool snap having departed, the weather was clear and sunny and the temperature as warm as it had been since Marty's arrival in Germany. Marty had a strong feeling that Gallotte probably left shortly after he did, using his "I'm gonna go look at a few construction sites" excuse.

Marty mailed his letter to the power company, then traveled by regional train northeast to Prenzlau. Prenzlau, only a half-hour away, was in the Russian sector, which was the primary reason for Marty's traveling there. There, in the backroom of a seedy pub, Marty purchased both a Russian submachine gun and a Russian pistol. The two items cost him less than the American equivalent of five dollars.

Given the condition of Prenzlau, from what Marty saw, and the general feeling of poverty, Marty wasn't a bit surprised that the weapons were so inexpensive. Since the war, because so many millions of weapons had been produced and used on German soil, they were incredibly common. Marty had even seen German children playing with actual rifles out in the street. Hopefully the kids didn't have any corresponding ammunition. Marty had heard talk about hundreds of people dying since the war, killed when they accidentally disturbed unexploded ordnance.

The war that had brought so much misery continued to provide aftershocks, like a deadly earthquake that just refused to be forgotten.

His new weapons disassembled and slung over his back in a canvas bag, Marty had arrived back at the Steglitz S-bahn station on the 7:20 P.M. train. He purchased a quick meal from the Turkish imbiss to eat on the walk to his flat. Weaving his way between the piles of rubble on his street, he ate the tasty lamb sandwich, a close cousin to the Greek gyro. The Turk on Marty's street used a spicy red sauce on the lamb, instead of the tangy white tzatziki sauce favored by the Greek restaurants. Marty liked both styles. He trashed the wax paper in the can out front, trudging up the flights of stairs to find Frau Schaal sitting on the step in front of her door. She was smoking a cigarette and briefly viewed him through her bleary eyes.

He nodded perfunctorily and kept right on going.

"I thought Americans were supposed to be a friendly people," she said, once he'd turned to take the next flight of steps. Her voice was edgier than normal, and loud.

Marty paused, his lips parting in response. *No, don't respond.* Dipping his head, he resumed his climbing.

"Go ahead…just ignore her," Frau Schaal mocked in a low man's voice. "She probably only wants the cash in your wallet, or wants you to be a daddy to her son. She's not a human being with feelings; she only wants something out of you, doesn't she?"

Stopping again, Marty spoke into the dark upper stairwell. "Why are you saying such things?"

"I tend to get this way when I drown my misery in a full bottle of wine."

"Where's Josh?"

"Why? You worried I won't be a good Mutti *and* Papa tonight?"

"It's a simple question."

"Yes, sir!" she yelled in English, mocking the shouted elocution of a soldier. "Josh has gone to his friend's house for the night, sir! He was '*so sick of me,*' sir! His exact words, sir!"

Marty licked his lips. "He's just a kid. I said the same stuff to my mom, once."

She laughed sharply, without humor.

"Go to bed," Marty said.

She didn't respond.

"Frau Schaal…are you okay?"

"I have to be okay," she shot back. "When a woman has a child and no one else to help her…what choice does she have? It all falls on me, get it? I can't just take a weekend for myself, or pick up and move…no…good old Mutti's got to stay right here and look after my son and my tenants like some doting mother hen, held fast by her ball and chain."

Taking a few steps backward, Marty peered down through the bannister. He saw the tears streaming down her cheeks.

*Just leave her be. She's drunk.*

A different thought passed through his mind…

*What would mama want you to do?*

*Dammit!*

"Stay there. I'll be right back."

After keying the door, he carried the bag of disassembled weapons to his bedroom, hiding them in the back of his closet. Once he'd shed his coat and tie, Marty quickly brushed his teeth. He knew his breath was ripe after the spicy sandwich. He even gargled some Listerine. Mouth sufficiently clean, he walked back down to where Frau Schaal still sat, the nub of the cigarette dangling from her lips.

He passed by, stopping two steps below her and turning, having no idea what to say. She was obviously not having a good night, probably just having a stressful moment due to the pressure of being a solo parent. Finally, he broached the silence by saying, "If you've had a full bottle of wine, you might feel better to just go in and get some sleep. Otherwise, you'll probably feel—"

Her immediate sneer silenced him.

Who was this woman? Certainly not the same lady who'd fed him dinner weeks earlier. Up until now, each time he'd encountered her she'd seemed overly nice and easily approachable. He'd seen her angry with Josh, but nothing like this.

*Here you are again, dumbass, sucked into these people's lives. Don't you remember the promises you made to yourself, that you were here to do one thing and one thing only? Get on with that one thing and ignore this moody kraut…*

"Suit yourself," he said, pushing past her.

She snatched the short cigarette from her mouth and crushed it on the stairs. "Can't you just talk to me like a normal person talks to another normal person?"

"I'm *doing* that."

"No, you always have some guarded façade. It's painfully obvious and irritating as hell. Josh thinks it's just how you are but I don't. I think it's an act."

"I really don't care what you think," Marty said, annoyed at his legs for not carrying him up the stairs. Instead, he stood on the landing, right next to her, removing his cigarettes and holding them in his hand.

"And on the occasions you do let that façade down, you immediately turn into an all-knowing man, like you're my father or something."

"I don't mean to come off as deliberately rude to you, or Josh. I just don't like people…nosing into my life."

She narrowed her eyes at him, as if she were about to unload. Then she snatched the pack of cigarettes from his hand, lighting one with a match. After her first drag she held the cigarette out in front of her, twisting it. "Why is it that your American cigarettes taste so much better than the ones we get here?"

Marty shrugged. "I guess because the best tobacco growing fields are in the United States. Just the way it is. I could say the same about German beer being better than American beer."

"A man *would* know useless facts like those."

"Common knowledge."

She half-smiled. "The joke in the year or two after the war was something like, 'forget the schools, forget public works, just get the breweries back up and running,' or something like that."

"That was probably the Allied occupiers who first said that."

A chilly pause signaled to Marty that she was about to turn back to the mood she'd been in before. Instead, she lowered her head, resting her forehead in her hand. "I feel awful for what I said earlier."

"Don't apologize."

"I'm not apologizing to *you*," she said. "I'm referring to what I said about Josh. He deserves better than me."

Marty wasn't going to stand here and dole out compliments all night. Reluctantly, he said, "You're doing your best given the situation. The whole world's still recovering from the war."

"He still thinks his father's alive," she muttered, shaking her head. "Do you have any clue what that means?"

"Not exactly."

"Not only does he live with false hope—which is the worst part—but it also means I can't remarry."

"It doesn't mean that."

"Real easy for you to say, but you have no children. But sitting where I'm sitting, to know if I open my heart to another man means to break the heart of my son…" Her lips knotted up as she tripped on the words.

"That's tough."

"Yeah, it is. But it's not like men are beating down my door. Because I'm stuck, I can't even make an effort to meet anyone."

Setting aside his dislike of the krauts, Marty tried to view this microcosm of the war academically. How many millions of lives were upended by the war? What would the net effect be thirty years later? Would the population heal itself naturally, or would the ramifications be felt by generations on down the line? Would the birthrate go down to a detrimental level? Would the sudden occupation of Germany by four other world powers result in Germany's ultimate downfall? Had that already occurred, and the fact that the land was still known as Germany was nothing more than window dressing? Would there even be a German language in a hundred years, or would it go the way of Latin?

"What are you thinking?" she asked, staring up at him.

"It's staggering to think of how many people are affected by the war."

"And we're saddled with all the guilt, too."

"What do you mean by that?"

"Because of Hitler, because of his minions, because of what they did—we have to cash those societal checks from here on. Who knows how long that'll go on?"

Suddenly, all of Marty's introspection, all of his thoughtfulness, all of his academic viewing of the situation blew away as if she'd lobbed a grenade at him.

"You *should* feel guilty," Marty snapped. He stalked up the stairs.

When he slammed his door, he hissed a single phrase. "Manipulative kraut bitch."

***

At five minutes past eight, Kriminaldetektiv Werner Eisch tugged on the brim of his fedora and said hello to an elderly woman. The woman was knitting in front of a spanking new apartment building. She noticed his mechanical hand, eyeing it for a second before going back to the baby blue infant's blanket that seemed to be nearly complete. Passing by her and entering the building, Werner confirmed the apartment by the typed names affixed to the new mailboxes in the lobby. He turned, climbing the stairs, feeling the stuffiness grow with each step. By the time Werner reached the fifth floor, he was sweating profusely. The stifling conditions of the unvented stairwell were made worse by the cloying smell of tapioca.

"Hopefully he'll invite me in," Werner muttered, using his prosthetic to tap on the door.

Footfalls could be heard followed by the click of the bolt. The door was pulled open just a fraction, leaving Werner with a partial view of a bearded face, topped by a wide blue eye. "Who are you?" came the gravelly voice. The scent of fried pork wafted from the partially open door. It was a welcome smell over the sickening odor of the tapioca.

Smiling politely, Werner displayed his badge. "Sorry to bother you on this Thursday evening. I'm Kriminaldetektiv Eisch and just want to ask Herr Oberlander a few questions."

"About what?"

"Are you Herr Oberlander?"

"Maybe."

Werner stopped smiling. "Would you prefer me to radio headquarters and have them send a few men? We can take you to our station in the *Mitte* and determine your identity there."

Though Werner couldn't see much of him, the man didn't seem impressed with the threat. "I'm Oberlander. What's this about?"

"It's about your unit from the war, Herr Oberlander, the 101st SS Panzers."

Oberlander blinked several times before clearing his throat. "I was cleared. I've been living a normal—"

"Herr Oberlander, this has nothing to do with your past service record and if you will just open the door, I will speak quickly. I promise to be gone in ten minutes or less."

Oberlander turned, barking guttural German and telling someone to go to the bedroom and close the door. When an inner door could be heard clicking shut, Oberlander opened the apartment door but didn't move. "What do you want?"

"May I come in?"

Oberlander checked his watch. "Ten minutes."

Werner stepped inside as his host shut the door behind him. When Werner turned, Oberlander stared back at him with crossed arms. A well built man, his muscular upper arms made his shirt strain. He had a full head of dark hair parted severely, and his beard, while thick, was neatly trimmed and flecked with silver on both sides of his chin. The eyes were bright blue and intelligent, having quickly taken Werner in, head to toe. His eyes didn't linger on Werner's prosthetic, a rarity. Oberlander seemed the kind of man who might have a career ranging anywhere from a lumberjack to the head of a successful construction company.

"You are Marcus Oberlander, formerly a *Sturmscharführer* in the 101st SS Heavy Panzer Battalion?"

"I am."

Werner nodded, wasting no time before asking the primary question. "When was the last time anyone other than me approached you, in *any way*, about your time in the SS?"

Oberlander didn't react at all. He was completely stony, but he allowed the question to linger a tad too long. Had he frowned, or made a sour face, or reacted in some way that would dismiss it as a silly question, Werner would have felt it more natural. But to take the question in such a controlled, such a measured, way alerted Werner that he was on to something. The man was clearly willing himself not to react.

After a good five seconds Oberlander said, "I don't exactly know. So long that I can't recall when." He spoke the words neutrally, as if he was telling someone the sky is blue.

Werner took a few steps to the left. Oberlander turned his body, keeping himself facing Werner.

"Did you hear about the recent murder of one of the men who'd served with you?"

"No."

"Do you want to know who?"

"I don't care who," Oberlander said with a shrug. "That period of my life is over."

*Cool cucumber, this one is.* Though he didn't need his notes, Werner produced them. "His name was Felix Heinrich Roth, although he was living under an assumed name when he was killed." Looking up, Werner asked Oberlander if he remembered Roth.

"Of course, I do," Oberlander snorted. "Anyone who'd spent more than a day with Roth would remember him."

"Why's that?"

"Is that what this is about, Roth's murder?"

"Yes. There are three or four members of your unit in the Berlin area and the local police investigating Herr Roth's murder asked us to reach out to you and ask a few questions. Like I said, just take a few minutes."

Oberlander couldn't hide his relief.

Frowning at his notes, Werner said, "Any idea why anyone would want to kill Felix Roth?"

"Detective, I haven't seen or heard from Roth in more than seven years. I would have no idea." Oberlander, in Werner's opinion, was speaking reasonably now, less guarded and fully natural.

"Was he a member of ODESSA, or any other underground association of former Schutzstaffel?"

"Again, I have absolutely no idea. I don't associate with *anyone* in those circles. I live a very normal, very boring life and, because of the reputation attached to the SS, I've done all I can to disassociate myself with that chapter in my life. I was young and stupid and thought I was doing the right thing."

"Understandable," Werner said.

"But truly, detective, I can't help you. All I can say about Roth is he was aggressive and I found him to be extraordinarily cruel, both to our adversary and his fellow men. It doesn't surprise me that he got himself killed. Fair enough?"

"Certainly."

Oberlander extended his hand the way people do when an unwelcome meeting has run its course. He then remembered Werner's prosthetic and quickly extended his left hand.

As they shook, in a measured move, Werner cut his head to the back of the apartment and yelled, "Frau Oberlander!"

"Hey, *don't* call her out here!" Oberlander objected.

But the woman responded by opening the rear bedroom door. When she did, Herr Oberlander whipped his head in her direction, telling her to shut the door.

"Sorry," Werner said, eyeing Oberlander's scabbed ear before turning to the woman of the house. "I simply wanted to apologize for interrupting your dinner, Frau Oberlander. It smells like schnitzel, and it smells divine."

Frau Oberlander eyed both men and closed the door without response.

"Good evening, lieutenant," Oberlander said with finality, opening the apartment's front door.

"Herr Oberlander, did you hurt your ear?" Werner asked, gesturing with his mechanical hand. "There's a large scab just inside the opening. The scab is round, as if you've been poked with something sharp."

Oberlander stood there, his hand on the doorknob. His nostrils were flared wide, each of his breaths audible. "Detective, unless you plan to arrest me, I want you to leave my home this very instant."

He wasn't angry. He was scared.

Werner proffered his card. When Oberlander didn't take it, Werner placed it on the table by the door. "In case you want to talk." Werner walked out and Oberlander slammed the door behind him.

In the stairwell, his prosthetic steadying himself on the balustrade, Werner fist-pumped the heavens with his good hand.

Someone was *indeed* going after the men of the 101st SS Panzers.

***

It was 12:30 A.M. Unable to sleep, Marty pulled on his clothes and walked into the stairwell. The building was eerily quiet, the nighttime air thick with summer humidity. His sweaty hands gripped the banister as he stared downward, through the center of the tall stairwell, viewing the black and white tile floor eighty feet below him.

*Just go, before you chicken out and turn back.*

Marty got himself moving and slowly descended, his feet padding silently on the steps until he stopped in front of Frau Schaal's door.

"Josh is at his best friend's house for the night," she'd said.

*It's easy. Just knock on the door and say you're sorry storming off earlier. Tell her it kept you awake.*

*Wait…"sorry?" I refuse to say that to a kraut. Say, "I shouldn't have reacted that way." Hell, she should say she's sorry for what her people did.*

*I don't know if she should say that. She didn't do anything.*

*Well, she should say something about it.*

*Are you just gonna stand in front of her door, arguing with yourself?*

Marty lifted his hand and balled his fist. It hovered there, trembling.

*Knock! C'mon, you know you want to see her.*

Twice his fist jerked forward. Twice he halted it.

*Knock, you pussy!*

Snatching his hand away, Marty hurried back up the stairs. He stepped inside his flat and slammed the door. Just inside, to the right, was a built-in coat rack with a small inlaid mirror.

Seconds later, half of the mirror lay on the floor in pieces as Marty wrapped his knuckles in a towel.

He hardly slept a wink—and it had nothing to do with the cuts on his knuckles.

# Chapter Eleven

Journal Entry

Right around the fourth anniversary of the massacre, in late March of 1949, I fired a rifle. It was the first weapon I'd fired since the day of the massacre. The rifle was a Karabiner 98k, manufactured by Mauser and one of the most common weapons of the war. I purchased the rifle at a flea market on a Saturday morning, along with five boxes of 7.92 ammunition. Most surprising to me was how much foreign and enemy equipment was available at that roadside flea market. There were Japanese knives. Nazi uniforms. Russian rifles. One vendor even furtively showed me a full crate of live American grenades. I couldn't believe it. "Five bucks apiece or four sawbucks for the whole crate." Imagine some moron walking around the streets with a live grenade...

Anyway, when I decided I wanted to go with the Mauser, the old codger who was selling it cocked his silver eyebrows at me. I'd been standing there, leaning against his plywood stand for support, proffering my money while sweating bullets.

"You okay, boy? White as a ghost."

"Oh, yeah," I replied, offering up a weak smile. "Just getting over a bug."

"You sure you want 'ese here bullets, too?"

"Y-y-yessir."

"You ain't gone do nuthin' squirrely now, are ya? I'm a 'sponsible dealer, ya know."

"Just want to shoot some cans, sir." The truth.

I conveniently left out the part about going back to Germany to seek revenge against a battalion of evil Schutzstaffel. I felt that was need-to-know type information. And I wasn't confident "Schutzstaffel" was in the flea market gun dealer's vocabulary.

Ninety minutes later, the professor and I were out in the scrubby hills of Walden Ranch as I was pranging soup cans from a low spine of reddish rocks. The professor sat behind me in a folding chair. He knew nothing about firearms and watched quietly.

This was the first day of my physical training. Compared to the sophistication of what we would later come up with, the first day was primitive. But that initial day wasn't about getting better. No. That day was all about breaking through—smashing more than just cans. It was about facing many of the fears that I'd developed. The fear of firearms. The fear of German equipment. The fear of the tamped-down horrors that might come rushing back. But once I snapped that bolt shut and fired the first shot, the shooting anxiety quickly melted away.

We stayed out in those hills until sundown. By the day's end I'd figured out my zero on the iron sights of the rifle and was drilling the cans from 300 yards.

When we got back to the house, I broke that old Mauser down, cleaning every piece of that weapon before reassembling it, good as new.

I remember how good I felt. I'd broken through a wall.

Later that night, as we sat outside by the fire pit, with the professor's myriad animals lounging around us, the professor asked me a key question.

"What exactly do you aim to achieve?" He leaned forward, eyeing me over the dancing fire.

"What do you mean?"

"All this time we've been learning about your enemy. Now, we've moved on to weapons, and training. You mustn't be simply a dilettante about such things. You must become a true expert."

"I understand."

"So what is your goal? How do we make progress without knowing the goal?"

I recall being very confused. It was the professor who first approached me about confronting my demons. And, until now, he'd always seemed to drive whatever it was we were doing. It was his idea to do research on the SS and Raban Nadel. And it was his idea to purchase the rifle. And I thought my mission—whatever it was—would come from him, too.

"I don't know what my goal is," I said.

He leaned back, the light from the flames fluttering over his face. "Good. I'm glad you don't."

"What do you mean?"

"I'll help you with your plan, Mister Elder. It will take time. We will be circumspect." The professor raised his index finger. "And, perhaps most importantly, you will be prepared."

"Okay," I said, processing what he'd said. But I was still puzzled. "Making a plan is fine, but what's the main goal of the plan?"

I remember how he eyed me for a long, uncomfortable moment as his faint smile faded away. Finally he licked his lips and said, "That, Mister Elder, can only come from you."

It took a full month to finalize my goal.

\*\*\*

The two former SS officers had arrived in Frankfurt at 5 A.M. Friday morning. While they'd fitfully dozed on the boneshaker pre-war train, once they were in the city, Nadel had immediately checked them into two rooms of the city's finest hotel. Both men slumbered for four hours before meeting in the hotel restaurant and enjoying a sumptuous brunch feast of the type that was just now becoming available again. Now, their skin pink from their hot showers, and their stomachs satisfyingly full, they strode through the street-side piles of rubble, making their way to the Main River. Zeckern halted when the river came into view, lighting a cigarette as he viewed the scene.

The Main is wide and picturesque, and usually appears brown unless the sky is crystalline, as it was on this day. From where they stood, the old village of Sachsenhausen provided the backdrop on the opposite bank. Though Frankfurt had been almost completely destroyed by Allied bombing, Sachenhausen had survived quite well, and was one of the few riverside areas not dotted with mounded piles of debris. Zeckern took in the panorama before him, taking a drag on his cigarette as he leaned against the steel railing on the north side of the river.

"What is it?" Nadel asked.

"That's where I cut and ran," Zeckern whispered, pointing his cigarette at Sachsenhausen.

Nadel snorted. "Look at you, all misty over it, like a woman."

Zeckern glared at Nadel.

"We all had to cut and run someplace…no need to memorialize the exact spot," Nadel chided. "It's a piece of earth. You lived. Forget about it and look forward."

"I spent thirteen years getting to where I was, unlike *you*, with only five years under your belt while you sucked at the power teat. Walk in a man's shoes before you open your damned mouth…"

Nadel showed his palms in repentance. But Zeckern could see that the smirk remained. *Smart prick.*

Zeckern dragged deeply on his cigarette, turning away, wanting to talk about the moment, wanting to reason it out in his mind with someone who truly cared. Back in '45, the battalion leadership had been hiding in Sachsenhausen, trapped in the village by Patton's Third Army military police who had no idea of the leadership's presence. On the third morning, Zeckern had sneaked out the back of the hotel in pilfered civilian clothes, showing his hands to the two American sergeants holding their Tommy guns on him. Using charm and a gold brick, Zeckern bribed the men, telling them he was a local banker and had been trapped in the hotel after an illicit liaison with his mistress.

Without a care for his fellow SS still in the hotel, Oskar Zeckern had walked from Sachsenhausen and made it all the way to Switzerland, spending four large diamonds in the process. That's where he'd become Dieter Siegst. Nearly a year later, when he reconnected with Raban Nadel, Felix Roth and the others, he'd learned that the remainder of the battalion leadership had been killed by the Americans upon being found in Sachsenhausen.

"They came out in surrender and got gunned down right there in the street," Felix Roth had said, pounding his fist into his palm. Zeckern recalled the irony of the moment. Had the roles been reversed, had it been American soldiers coming out in surrender, Roth would have wounded each of them first, making sure they died an agonizing death.

After he was told about the killings, Zeckern had displayed the requisite outward remorse. Inwardly, he'd cursed his men for fools. What did they expect? Did they think Patton's men were going to give Waffen-SS a pat on the back, followed by a cot and three hot meals each day?

"How'd you make it out of Sachsenhausen, anyway?" Nadel asked, shattering Zeckern's recollection.

Zeckern turned back to Nadel. "I've already told you."

"I don't remember. Tell me again."

Zeckern tugged at his starchy collar. "Battalion leadership had holed up in a hotel, in the basement. We were there for several days. On the third day, in the morning, I donned civilian clothes I'd scrounged and I reconnoitered the American positions around Sachsenhausen. The fighting had ceased days before and they'd finally begun to relax. Just as the sun came up, I saw two American guards sleeping."

"And?"

"You know this part."

"I don't remember," Nadel said innocently.

"I slit their throats."

"Hmm."

"What do you mean '*hmm*?'" Zeckern asked testily.

"If you slit their throats, I'm just curious why no one else left."

"Those two Americans weren't the only guards. They were all around the village."

"But *you* were able to leave after you killed them?"

"I got lucky enough to slip through."

Nadel's eyebrows were cocked. "Where did you go?"

"I walked in the refugee parade. Getting to Switzerland was as simple as soiling my face and clothes with grime and acting like a D.P. I walked my feet bloody in the midst of hundreds of thousands, many of them probably acting the part just like me."

"Hard to believe."

"Why?" Zeckern snapped.

"I just find it a rather fantastic story, that's all," Nadel said, wearing the full smirk again.

Zeckern squared his body in front of Nadel, pointing his hand and cigarette in Nadel's face. "Let me make something perfectly clear: I don't like your imperious attitude. You'll recall that it was *me* who recommended your promotions and *me* who signed off on your ruthless power grab. And now—"

"Wait," Nadel said, cutting Zeckern off as a U.S. Army Jeep rounded the nearest corner. It roared down the riverside lane and squeaked to a stop behind them.

Nadel waved to the passenger, a soldier whose rank Zeckern could not see. He watched as Nadel walked around the Jeep, smiling as if he were meeting an old friend. Nadel shook the uniformed man's hand as he discreetly passed an envelope he'd taken from his coat. Zeckern side-stepped, adjusting his view so he could see the silver oak leaf on the Army fatigues—a U.S. lieutenant colonel. The colonel brazenly opened the envelope and thumbed through the money, appraising the wad with his lower lip poked out. He then smiled and handed Nadel a manila envelope before the Jeep roared away.

"Who the hell was that?" Zeckern demanded.

"Lieutenant Colonel Samuel Frost," Nadel replied. "He's based over in the Farben Building."

"What did you just pay him for?"

"Information."

"How did you find him?"

"We're natural friends, *Dieter*. Like magnet and steel, the pull to a natural friend just occurs. Frost and I have been working together for five years now. Believe me, he's pulling every string he can to remain in Germany. He'd be an idiot not to…getting rich the easy way."

Zeckern felt the familiar stab of jealousy. While he had no right to complain—Zeckern's own net worth was sufficient to support him till death—he'd often wondered how Nadel was creating such immense wealth for himself. In the past few years, it hadn't been uncommon for Nadel to disappear to New York for the summer, coming back a full-fledged bon vivant, carrying with him tales of glitzy parties, dinners at the finest restaurants and, of course, high-priced whores.

"What sort of collaboration do you have with him?" Zeckern asked, knowing the answer would only increase his envy.

"Among other things, we run an import business together." Nadel opened the clasp envelope, removing a sheet of yellow paper. He glanced at the paper before refolding it. "I import hashish from Turkey. The good colonel distributes it through a surreptitious distribution network. Then, after it's mixed with weeds and hay and cow shit, it's eventually sold to American soldiers who smoke it, fiends they are." Nadel smiled as he pulled in a mighty breath. "There's nothing like hash-head soldiers who get paid regular as clockwork."

"Running a big risk, isn't he?" Zeckern asked sourly.

"I don't care," Nadel replied. "If he gets caught, I'll just find someone else."

"How'd you find him in the first place?"

"Like I said, magnet and steel," Zeckern said dismissively. He reopened the paper and read the following: "Gloria Riddenger, officially of Wetzlar, was logged in the American Zone three days ago, entering the secure U.S. Army Zone-Frankfurt by checkpoint on the zone's north side. She has not been logged out since and is thought to be shacked up in the home of an American Sergeant Major."

"Did you get the address, too?"

"Indeed," Nadel said. "Nine Böhmerstrasse."

"But we can't get inside the U.S. Army zone."

Nadel reached into the manila envelope and produced two pink slips, handing one over. "Two passes, old friend, signed by a major general."

Zeckern stared wide-eyed at his pass, realizing he'd been underestimating Raban Nadel for too long. Despite his ruthlessness, he might be the most resourceful man Zeckern had ever known.

"You ready?" Nadel asked.

"What about the sergeant major she's shacked up with?"

Nadel's eyes went back to the white paper. "According to the colonel, the sergeant major's division is on red cycle…and the sergeant major in question will be tied up today until no earlier than 1800 hours." He slid the note back in the manila envelope and tucked it into his inner pocket. Then, from his outer pocket, he removed a straight razor, flicking the razor open, running his finger along the glinting blade. "Shall we go pay Frauleine Riddenger a visit? I'd enjoy hearing her tale of Felix Roth's final night."

Still amazed at Nadel's orchestration, Zeckern followed him across the rebuilt Eiserner Steg footbridge into the village of Sachsenhausen.

\*\*\*

Like two ravenous foxes sneaking into a henhouse, the former SS officers had crept into the sergeant major's home through the unlocked back door. Zeckern followed Nadel's lead, both men removing their shoes once inside. Zeckern surveyed the shadowy space as he wiped his sweaty hands on his trousers. After passing through a small utility room, they found themselves in a cluttered sitting room that stank of mildew and cigar smoke. In the center of the sitting room was a low square table, littered with beer bottles and a teeming ashtray. Also on the table was a worn deck of playing cards and a cigar cutter. Both men stood at the room's rear entrance, attuned to the silence for any trace of their quarry.

As the stillness evolved to the slight sounds that take time for a person to hear, Zeckern thought he heard something recurrent. Nadel's blue eyes focused on Zeckern as Zeckern raised his eyes to the ceiling. After focusing on the recurrent sound, Zeckern pointed upward. Nadel nodded. There was no sound of movement, but only the distant sighing that might, or might not, be the rhythmic snoring of a person in a deep slumber.

Zeckern lifted the silenced Beretta, the balance of the fine pistol spoiled by the heavy silencer screwed to its barrel. Though he'd done it twice already, he tugged on the slide and peered inside, confirming that a shiny bullet rested in the chamber. Wiping his sleeve over his forehead, Zeckern looked at Nadel as he mouthed the command that Zeckern go first.

"Why me?" Zeckern mouthed.

"Well…you've got the gun!" Nadel mouthed animatedly, grinning maniacally afterward.

*This prick is actually enjoying himself!* Zeckern swallowed thickly, cursing the sweat that poured from his body. *What in bloody hell am I doing here? I could have been in Brazil or Argentina, sitting on a beach, planning a raucous evening with a cocoa-skinned beauty.*

Nadel gave him a nudge, earning a frosty glare from Zeckern.

Something about this entire scheme seemed wrong, but now was not the time for hesitation. *Just go on and be done with it.*

Pistol leading the way, Zeckern crept toward the stairs.

\*\*\*

Gloria Riddenger awoke naturally, her eyes fluttering mechanically as she regained her bearings. She saw the rich light of late morning, the sun illuminating the cluttered bedroom in slanted shadows. It took ten more seconds before she recalled where she was. Frankfurt—the lusty American soldier—his quarters—safety. Twisting her head to the adjacent window, she watched the high clouds scudding across the blue sky. If it was warm today, maybe she could find a park and take in some sun. Something about tanning always made her feel better.

Gloria ran her hands over her face, mildly miffed with herself for having slept so long. But she and the American had made love until, what, maybe three in the morning? Though the man was at least 45 years old, it had been easy for her to tell that he was sex-starved, craving the pleasures that she so skillfully doled out. She'd be lying if she said she hadn't enjoyed it. While her motive was to develop him as someone to support her—at least for a time—sex always cleared her mind. Even after what the Americans had done to her at the war's end, Gloria liked Americans. For the most part, they were open and giving—and, best of all, predictable.

This one, in return for her giving him wonderful sex, now provided her quarter, and hopefully it would burgeon into something permanent. Who knew how long the Americans were going to be in charge? And under the secure umbrella of a senior U.S. Army soldier, Gloria would be in good stead as long as the relationship lasted. She stretched luxuriously, grunting slightly as she congratulated herself for such a nice soft landing after the debacle with the man she now knew was named Felix Roth.

*Craaack.*

Eyes whipping to the open bedroom door, Gloria's pulse spiked. In her few days here, she'd memorized the sound of the creaking stairs. When she and Bo—that was her new man's name—had gone up and down the stairs with great frequency, the sounds mostly ceased. But when the stairs had settled for any period of time, they would groan and creak whenever a person eventually did use them.

Had she heard it right? The four middle stairs were the culprits. If someone were coming up those stairs, she'd hear it again when they added weight to the following steps.

Gloria waited, her right hand slithering down behind the mattress, probing.

Still no sound.

Her fingers wrapped around the barrel of her shotgun, tugging at it to pull it from under the folds. *Slowly…slowly…don't want to make a bumping sound.*

The shotgun's girth hung on the cheap headboard. She twisted it, trying to bring it through the void. It wouldn't quite fit.

*Dammit!* She coaxed the weapon, careful to remain silent.

Then, from the open door…

*Craaaaaaack.*

There it went again, longer this time. Someone was on the stairs! Knuckles white, Gloria tugged on the shotgun with greater force, the gun finally releasing with a clunking sound.

Trying to hurry but remain silent, she eased herself to the edge of the bed. The bedroom was square, with the door in one corner and the bed shoved up against the diagonal corner, next to the window. The sheets and blanket breathed as she moved. The telltale sign would come when she slipped off the mattress, whether or not the box springs would squeak.

They did.

Knowing she couldn't do anything about that now, Gloria situated herself in the inner corner of the room, blind to anyone in the short hallway. Her shotgun was trained just inside the door.

Finger on the trigger from a hip-shot grip, she thought about the American man that had killed Felix Roth. He'd warned her that, once they realized it was a murder, Felix's friends from the SS would come for her. Though she truly hadn't believed they would, the possibility had remained in her mind.

"But how would they know?" one part of her mind screamed. "They couldn't know where I am!"

"They *do* know because the devious *always* find a way," another portion of her brain calmly reasoned.

Settled into her corner, Gloria remembered her box of shells was under the bed inside her suitcase. When she'd made her way into the American sector, she'd hidden the shotgun in her suitcase, having broken the weapon down. But there were two shells in the gun. Hazarding a glance at the suitcase, she cursed herself inwardly. If someone were coming up the stairs, she'd expose herself if she went for the rest of the shells.

*Nope...don't move. Make do with what you have.*

Gloria trained her eyes on the open doorway, waiting for a person to pass through.

Waiting.

Waiting...

A flash of blue in the doorway made her jump. Instinctively, she pulled the forward trigger, the shotgun blast deafening in the confined space. She watched in horror as her shot demolished the cheap lampshade from the tall hallway lamp. The mangled lamp clattered to the floor as bits of plaster fell from the apple-sized hole in the wall.

Gloria already had her finger on the second trigger. As her ears rang, she again silently cursed herself. Whoever was out there in the hallway was a wily sonofabitch. He'd shoved the lamp through the doorway to bait her into shooting. Now she had only one shell remaining.

Hesitantly, she removed her finger from the trigger. If someone comes through that door, she would have time to react. If they push another object through, she would scream instead, making them think the shotgun was only single shot.

*Two can play your little game, asshole.*

Finger on the trigger guard, willing herself not to shoot, Gloria waited.

# Chapter Twelve

Journal Entry

By the fall of 1949, my training techniques had rapidly improved. Although I was limited to the geography of Walden Ranch, I was able to create challenges for myself that pushed my meager skills to their limit. Even the professor, who had no experience in warfare, applied academic techniques to my training, finding a number of creative ideas in military manuals. He obsessed over it, often reading ideas aloud to me as we ate.

My favorite was a contraption he came up with that we called "Take Your Pick." Essentially, Take Your Pick was similar to the active gun ranges that some big-city police departments had developed. Ours, while primitive, worked just as well.

Using plywood and a few struts, we created a pop-up barrier, held by a few hinges. When the professor yanked out the stops, the barrier would fall. Once it fell, I could see behind it and was faced with a number of adversaries, as well as friendlies. These were painted plywood silhouettes. Despite my objections, the professor painted the bad guys like SS in their uniforms. He even added blond hair and snarling mouths. I wasn't nearly as amused by this as he was.

The catch to the exercise was the ability to switch out the silhouettes. You see, many of them were the so-called "good guys." Women with babies. Businessmen. Teenagers. The elderly. When the wall fell, I had to quickly discern friend from foe before pulling my trigger. The professor kept time with a stopwatch.

When I'd perfected the exercise, we even added rails below the silhouettes. Using a small, single-cylinder engine from the professor's farm, we added pulleys to the contraption. Depending on the size of the pulley, we were able to create varied movement in the silhouettes, making the activity far more difficult and unpredictable.

After a while, the training became enjoyable. It was like a game. But, whenever I found myself on the cusp of fun, I reminded myself of the massacre. While sobering, the memory always helped me refocus.

Hopefully, I was improving.

Before long, my bedroom at Walden Ranch was loaded with guns, ammo and training manuals. Most of the manuals were from the American military. But we also had an old, turn-of-the-century British manual. We had one from Australia. Once, on a trip to Oklahoma City, I even found a mercenary's guide to firearm training, penned by a Dutchman and, according to the foreword, translated into eight different languages. It was a helpful guide.

Although the professor tried to fund my little exercise, I wouldn't hear of it. I was receiving a full disability from the Army, and I also had a nest egg from a private "settlement" they'd insisted on giving me. While I've never cared for charity, I finally came to grips with the money that, until then, had just been sitting in the bank. Now it could be used solely for my mission.

When the new decade arrived, I informed the professor that I felt I'd done all I could to improve my weapons prowess. Concurrent to my training, when I wasn't studying for school, I read about espionage techniques. Things like blending in. How to spot a tail. How to shake a tail. Covert communications. Building a false identity. And the area I focused on the most: interrogation techniques. While I learned many methods of interrogation, my favorites originated in Asia.

As I mentioned, I informed the professor that I felt tactically prepared.

"How's your German coming?" he asked. I'd had three courses thus far.

*"Es geht,"* I responded.

He shook his head. "You must be fluent. You must have a native tongue. You must be so good that every single German believes you to be just like them: German. One slip-up will ruin all you've done."

"I agree."

"So, from this moment forward, we only speak German."

"But what if I can't under—"

"Du musst lernen."

I nodded resignedly. Boy, he wasn't kidding, either. Other than when we were at the university, we spoke German exclusively. Not once did we revert to English.

We went on this way until the professor's death.

***

On the small landing at the American sergeant major's home, Zeckern backed away from the door. He clutched his chest, feeling his heart pounding as if he'd run sprints. It had been Nadel's idea to push the lamp through, and what an idea it had been. The lamp lay mangled on the floor as bits of plaster from the hole in the wall continued to tumble down. Zeckern worked his mouth to clear his ears. Then he chanced a quick look at Nadel, who mouthed, "Told you." Nadel treated this as if this were an advanced game of childhood hide-and-seek.

*He's enjoying this. What a sick man.*

The threat of another shotgun blast made Zeckern lose his nerve. He motioned Nadel forward, trying to hand him the silenced Beretta. Nadel forcefully shook his head. "You go," he mouthed.

Just as Zeckern turned back to the door, he felt Nadel tap him. Zeckern turned again, watching as Nadel silently articulated his words, also miming the motions of a person pumping a shotgun. "That was a shotgun," he mouthed.

Zeckern nodded animatedly and mouthed back, "No shit!"

Nadel mouthed, "Single? Double? Pump?"

Zeckern shrugged.

Nadel tapped his ear, then made the pumping motion again, then shrugged.

"No pump," Zeckern mouthed back.

Slipping his suit coat off, Nadel handed it to Zeckern. "Use this," he mouthed.

Zeckern took the coat, holding it in his hand as he took steadying breaths. His mouth was parched. Fearing he might get his hand blown off, he gripped one sleeve of the charcoal gray suit, glancing back one last time.

"Do it!" Nadel silently urged.

Zeckern mopped his face with the suit coat before taking a step forward.

***

Gloria was just able to see a hint of a shadow coming to the threshold. *Don't shoot till you see! Don't shoot till you see!*

Suddenly, something gray whipped through the air, flagging inside the doorframe several times, flopping as someone moved it up and down. It was a coat. Rather than pull the trigger, she screamed, and it was deliberate.

*They'll think I'm out of shells.*

She moved her finger back to the trigger.

***

Once they'd heard the scream, Nadel ceased being quiet and, instead, yelled to Zeckern to rush her. Zeckern dropped the coat and, feeling the shove from Nadel, burst into the room, whipping the silenced Beretta to the left.

Just as he began to turn, he saw several things all at once. Crouched in the corner of the room was a woman, a shotgun at her hip. He saw the twin black orifices of the over-under barrels for maybe a half-second before they were obscured by a dragon's spit of fire and smoke.

The next sensation was unlike anything Zeckern had ever experienced. While not painful—not yet, anyway—it felt as if he were being jerked by something with ferocious animal strength. Probably the way a person feels when tossed about in the jaws of a crocodile. It felt as if this crocodile had clamped on his right leg and snatched Zeckern backward, violently spinning him. And when Zeckern hit the wall he seemed to stick there, hanging till, after a moment, he slid slowly downward. He felt like the butt of one of those cartoon reels at the beginning of movies.

When Zeckern's movement ceased he saw Nadel rush in. Though Zeckern was partially deafened from the two blasts, he did hear the high-pitched staccato of the woman's screams.

Then as things seemed to calm somewhat, the pain enveloped him. Eyes on the ceiling, Zeckern probed downward with his hands. *Cloth. Cloth. Cloth. Belt. Cloth. Ohhhhh....*

There it was, mid-thigh. His first sensation was the warm, slick blood. The second thing he felt, other than the stringy pieces of mangled flesh, was the void in his leg. It felt as if someone took a razor sharp ice cream scoop, a big one, and shoveled out a dollop on the outer side of his quadriceps.

Zeckern felt faint. He slowly twisted his head to the left, watching as Nadel lifted the girl, her arm wrenched behind her bare back. As he held her there, Nadel leered at Zeckern—still playing that twisted game of hide-and-seek. Nadel's eyes moved down to the wound before coming up. Through that broad smile, he gleefully yelled only one word.

"Ouch!"

***

Nadel unbuttoned his tailored shirt and hung it on the post at the end of the bed. He opened a drawer from the chest, removing a U.S. Army-issue undershirt, slowly mopping his face as he caught his breath. Turning his head, he looked at Zeckern. "How's the leg?"

Zeckern was sitting in a corner chair, his leg straight out in front of him on another chair. He was smoking, holding a cigarette with a shaky, bloodstained hand. His face was pale and sweaty. Over the injury were several towels and, holding the towels, a clamp-style belt courtesy of the American sergeant major's closet.

"She's told you everything," Zeckern said through chattering teeth. "Now will you make the damned call so we can go? I need a doctor!"

Nadel chuckled before turning back to the girl. Her arms and legs were bound, tied to each of the bedposts, leaving her spread-eagled on the mattress. He'd covered her initially and only removed portions of the blanket when threatening, or performing, torture.

"The man who killed Felix Roth claimed to be an American, you say? He came to Gleiberg specifically to speak to Felix, but you say the American said he was never originally intending to kill Felix?"

"Yes," she said. "How many times do I have to tell you that?"

"And this man pretended to need a carpenter and you sent him up to the Biergarten to find Felix. Then, later, the man came back and informed you he'd killed Felix?"

She nodded.

"So, how did he discover Felix's hiding spot for the gold?"

"It...it took him some time, but eventually—"

"That's not what I mean," Nadel snapped, lifting a hand to stop her. "How was he so free to search Felix's home?"

"I..I..I…"

"You let him," Nadel said with a tight grin. "He didn't force you. No…you *let* him do it." Nadel turned to Zeckern and winked, then turned back. "You screwed him, too, didn't you?"

She glared, both of her nostrils flared wide.

Nadel walked back to the chest of drawers, removing the items from the old felt bag she'd guided him to. "Three gold ingots, an SS ring, and an SS gorget." His eyes turned to her briefly. "And what of Felix's pistol and rifle?"

"I left them behind. Brought my shotgun instead."

"Yes, well, my wounded friend here knows all about your shotgun," Nadel said, chuckling again. He produced a small black notebook from his pocket. "Just a few more things, my dear, then we'll be done." Slowly, the way a person does when they're not at all concerned about the time needs of those around them, he thumbed the pages, humming to himself as he searched. Finally, he touched a spot on the page and looked up.

"Here it is. There were a few other items you didn't account for." Nadel's free hand touched Gloria's bound foot, tickling it like he might if she were his lover. "Darling, are you listening to me?"

She stared out the window, mouthing the word "yes."

"The first missing item is a ring from Texas Technical University, in the United States. The second item is…" he waited, "…a notebook, not unlike this one."

Gloria didn't budge.

"Your American friend took the two items, didn't he, dear?"

"Yes," she said in a clear voice.

"Did he say why?"

"No."

He held the knife under her nose.

"He didn't say why!" she screamed.

Nadel took a deep, chest-expanding breath, accepting her answer. "Once more, darling, please describe him in great detail. After that, we will be through."

She just stared out the window.

"I have cut you five times, dear. I honestly don't want to add another. His description…please."

"He's just average. Normal height. Sandy hair. Blue eyes. Not really handsome but not ugly, either. No features that stand out other than scars on one of his hands."

"Which one?"

"I don't remember."

Nadel then said, "You told me you thought he was German at first."

"I did. He spoke perfect German."

"Did you hear him speak English?"

"Yeah."

"You're sure he's American?"

"He said he was."

"Did he say where he was from in the U.S.?"

"I don't think so."

"Was there an accent to his German?"

"Not really."

Gripping her foot, Nadel slid the razor under the tip of the toenail of her big toe. He slowly began to push. "You're not telling me the truth about something."

She hissed as the razor made its way several millimeters in. "*Berlin!* He sounded like he might be from Berlin, or that area. Please stop!"

"Good, dear." Holding the razor under the toenail, Nadel gave it a small twist, making her cry out again. "Where did he say he was from in the U.S.?"

"He didn't!"

"I'm going to take this razor and split both of your feet from the bottom. I'm going to saw through that thick skin on the pads of your feet then pull the incisions wide with both hands, as if I'm cracking open lobsters. Or you can just tell me and this will all be over."

Her mouth was open but no noise came out. A string of saliva hung down. In his own mind, Nadel wasn't enjoying this. While ruthless, he didn't fancy himself as savage. And, thus far, each of the cuts he'd given her could be mended with only a finger bandage. What he'd just threatened her with was mental torture—he wouldn't really go through with it.

*Well*, he thought to himself, *I probably wouldn't...*

He slid the razor from under her toenail and touched it to the thick skin at her heel. "Time to crack open the first lobster."

"Dakota!" she screamed. "Dakota!"

Nadel smiled at Zeckern before turning back to her, making his expression severe. "You're confused, dear. Is it North or South Dakota?"

"North Dakota."

He nodded. Then he paused, cocking his head. "You seem like you want to say more."

"That's all."

With no hesitation at all, Nadel punctured the skin of her heel.

When she ceased her scream she mouthed a word as she cried and struggled against her bonds.

"Calm down, dear. What are you saying?"

"Oklahoma," she breathed, her arms going slack. "That's where he lived after the war."

Nadel knew from many previous experiences with interrogation that she'd just told him the truth. When a person under duress lets the truth out, they relax in the finality of the act, thinking somehow that their ordeal is over. Just as she'd done.

*If only she knew…*

"Very good, precious," Nadel said soothingly. "I knew I liked you." He used the blanket to dab the pinheads of scarlet blood that emerged from the two wounds of her foot. "I appreciate your forthrightness." Narrowed his eyes. "But what else might you have held back?"

Flicking his cigarette and striking Nadel in the back, Zeckern roared, "Just finish, damn it!"

Ignoring his wounded comrade, Nadel massaged Gloria's leg. "Three times you've told me you don't know this American's motive…three times. But the fact that he took the notebook, to me, seems that he's seeking members, or *an individual*, from our Schutzstaffel unit."

"I've told you everything. I don't know anything else." She cried for a moment before turning her bleary eyes to Nadel. "You can cut me more but I'll just be making things up to get you to stop."

Nadel nodded. "Very well, then. I respect your candor." He used the undershirt he'd wiped his sweat with and methodically stuffed as much as he could into her mouth. Her yells were immediately stifled. Nadel produced a silver cigarette box. He opened the box and removed a syringe, not much bigger than a small cigar. "It's over now, my dear. I must end your life. Because you were forthright with me, I'm injecting you with a hyper-dose of a pleasant drug. Your end will be painless."

Her screams turned to indistinct speaking sounds. He lifted the sheet, running his hand up her smooth, shapely leg, sliding his hand all the way to her inner thigh. "Be glad I'm a gentleman, dear. The men who will come to retrieve you would have *had* you for the balance of the day." Without hesitation, he jabbed the needle into the faint blue line that led to her groin, the femoral artery. He began to slowly depress the plunger. "There now, your slow descent shall soon begin."

She was still trying to speak.

"What's she saying?" Zeckern demanded.

"What does it matter?"

"She's not screaming. Let her talk," Zeckern said, leaning forward.

Shrugging, Nadel eased the shirt out of her mouth. She took a few quick breaths before asking, "Are either of you Nadel or Zeckern?"

"Shit! I knew it!" Zeckern bellowed.

At the mention of his name—because they'd not once used names—Nadel gaped at her with wide eyes. "How the hell did you know that?"

"He's looking for you," she said with a faint smile, her breaths quick and shallow.

"For both of us?" Nadel asked.

"No," she whispered.

"Which one?" Zeckern yelled.

Her voice was very weak. "The massacre…"

"What are you talking about?" Nadel roared.

"She's talking about Kastellaun!" Zeckern hissed.

"Yes…Kastellaun." Her words seemed to come with great struggle. "He knows…knows where Zeckern lives…but…but he's coming for…"

Nadel shook her. "Who? Say it, you damned bitch!"

"He's coming for you…*Nadel*."

Eyeing Nadel, the woman seemed satisfied with his expression. Her eyes were unwavering.

Behind Nadel, Zeckern spewed curses.

Then, after several more labored breaths, the woman convulsed briefly. She died soon thereafter.

Rubbing his freshly-shaven face, Nadel walked around the bed, leaning against the window frame. He stared at the top floors of the Farben Building behind the homes across the street. While he wasn't stunned at her revelation, it had taken him off guard. He'd done a piss-poor job of interrogation, today. He'd lost his edge.

Suppose he was to believe everything she'd said: an American was here hunting him because of the Massacre at Kastellaun. If true, Nadel wouldn't typically be all that concerned. But if this American were smart enough to find Felix Roth, a man who had taken the same precautions as Nadel, what else was he capable of?

And now he had Felix's notebook.

Nadel removed a cigarette from the same case that held the syringe of phenobarbital. He tapped one end of the cigarette on his fingernail, reflecting on all he'd learned.

"That was a horrible interrogation," Zeckern admonished.

"Agreed."

"You shouldn't be surprised at what she said. After all you did in that damned war, it's a wonder this hasn't happened before." Zeckern sounded quite smug despite his condition.

"No, I shouldn't," Nadel allowed, lighting the cigarette. After a few drags he walked around the bed again, lifting the bedside phone and twirling in a five-digit number.

Once he'd given the address of the sergeant major's home, Nadel asked, "You've got your passes to get in the zone? Good. Pull up in front, cover the refrigerator, bring it inside, then take her body back out inside the shell. Then do the same with his body. Just cover it each time you come and go and it will just look like you're just making appliance deliveries. When you're done, set the thermite bomb in the center of the house and give yourself long enough to get out of the inner zone. By the time anyone puts two and two together, we'll all be long gone and there will be no useful evidence." Nadel listened for a moment before replacing the phone on the receiver.

"You're going to kill the sergeant major, too?" Zeckern asked.

Nadel pulled hard on the French cigarette, making the tobacco crackle. Smoke escaped his mouth as he said, "I'd thought about it."

"Look at my damned leg! I can't stay here with you waiting for him to get home. You've got to get me over to Dagmar's place," Zeckern said, referencing a medical doctor who did contract work for *Die Bruderschaft*.

Nadel dropped his cigarette, grinding it under his polished shoe. Then he lifted the Beretta from the bedside table, twisting the silencer for tightness. "You won't have to wait on the sergeant major, old friend. In fact, you'll no longer be a burden to me or anyone else." Nadel aimed the pistol at Zeckern's head.

Zeckern's mouth hung open briefly but, ever the noble, he closed it. He tilted his chin upward as he spoke without alarm. "You always were the worst sort of bastard, Raban. I rue the day I ever allowed you in my unit."

Nadel brayed laughter, feeling the merriment flush his cheeks as he taunted the man he loved to hate. "You were a terrible commander, Oskar. Indecisive. Soft. Weak."

"You don't know a thing about leadership."

Touching a finger to his lips, Nadel said, "Oh, there's one other thing I should tell you before I kill you." He paused for effect. "Back in '43, when we were in Munich...you remember...when we received the new tanks?...I screwed your first wife at the Hotel Torbräu. She was easily convinced and, unfortunately for me, lousy in bed."

Zeckern's eyes cut to the side as he thought back to that time. Then, probably trying to seem indifferent, he said, "We weren't in love anymore by then."

Nadel grinned, as if he were verbally sparring with a child. "*Everyone* knew I tapped her, Oskar...just another of your pathetic, ignominious moments." He waited a moment. "Oh, and before I kill your new wife, I will enjoy fucking her as well."

This was obviously too much for Zeckern, and his nobility, to take. Spittle flew from his mouth as he yelled, "You miserable, sick son of a—!"

Zeckern's vulgar insult was cut off by the lead bullet that burrowed two-thirds of the way through his brain.

# Chapter Thirteen

By the summer of 1950, I was speaking German with ease. Although I felt I could pass as a native, the professor assured me I was nowhere near ready. In fact, he told me, if I approached him as a stranger, he'd know I was American before the first sentence was out of my mouth. Because we had no idea where I would base myself in Germany—nor had we created the plan—the professor began to teach me about the different dialects. He soon became frustrated, claiming even he, a native German speaker, didn't know enough about the subject to teach it. Then, on a blisteringly hot June day, a cardboard box arrived by post. I watched as the professor opened it, grinning with satisfaction as he removed hundreds of discs—they were reel-to-reel tape recordings.

"These," he said, touching the stacks reverently, "contain recordings of the common dialects in Germany."

"Good," I replied. "Very good. Once I know where I'm headed, I can learn the correct one."

He shook his head.

"What?"

"Mister Elder, I'm an academic. If I've learned anything in my forty-seven years, it's that one can never know too much. You'll learn them *all*."

"That's impossible."

"Is it? Or is that just something that people say? What truly is impossible, Mister Elder?"

We drove to the school and retrieved a playback machine. That evening, as the sun lingered in the western sky, I listened to the Swabian dialect of German, common to inhabitants of western Bavaria. Then I changed the tapes, comparing Swabian to North Low Saxon, the dialect spoken by Hamburgers.

"Do you hear the difference?" the professor asked. I didn't realize he'd been standing behind me.

"Hell no," I muttered. "They sound just alike."

"Then you have much to learn," he said, stepping outside.

And learn I did. By summer's end, I knew eleven German accents, and could roughly mimic them in my speech. It was then, on Labor Day weekend, just before I was to start my last semester of college, that we hatched the true plan that would send me back to Germany.

"What do you want to achieve?" the professor asked me over breakfast. It was the same question he'd been asking.

I'd been thinking about this for many months. And now, finally, after much deliberation, I had my answer. "I want to go to Germany and determine if Raban Nadel is still alive. If he is, I want to find him." I paused and swallowed a few times. I'd never spoken words like I was about to speak. Finally, I said it. "When I find him, I will kill him. And I'll kill him slowly. That's my plan."

The professor's face showed surprise. "So...now you're a killer?"

"I'm not a killer. But I will kill him. There's a difference."

"And doing that will solve everything? That will complete your life? An eye for an eye?"

"Yeah," I snapped.

The professor stood and carried our plates to the sink. He stood there, staring out the window at the sun-splashed eastern panorama of his ranch. The scraggly grass was green due to the unusual amount of rainfall we'd had in July and August. Finally, he turned to me.

"Fine, Mister Elder. The plan is to find a way to send you to Germany. There, you will somehow learn whether or not Raban Nadel is alive. If he is, then you'll find him and kill him. And you'll make certain he suffers."

Coming from the professor, my plan sounded oddly foreign and foolhardy. Most importantly, it didn't sound satisfying. We were both quiet for several minutes.

"Professor..."

"Yes?"

"If I can do all that...up until the part about killing him..."

"Yes?"

"If somehow I could capture him..."

"Go on."

"Would the government...theirs, ours, whichever...would they recognize...no...would they allow the manner in which I tracked him down? What I'm saying is, would they prosecute?"

The professor came back to his chair and sat. "Oh, I'm almost certain the new German government would allow for great latitude in the apprehension of Raban Nadel. Even if they don't, Nadel's capture would be his undoing."

"Do you think he's alive?"

"I do."

"Because of your research?"

"That, and other inquiries I've made."

"Inquiries with whom?"

"Doesn't matter."

I remember wringing my hands. "Do you also think he's in Germany?"

"Probably. Or, possibly, Austria or Switzerland."

"Is that from the same source?"

"It is."

"Is this source of yours hunting him, also?"

"No, Mister Elder. My source is a professor, just like me. But he has the ear of men with influence."

I later learned that the other professor was Professor Mocaata, in Greece, the one who'd helped me find Felix Roth. To this day, I don't know whose ear he has. I have suspicions, but I doubt I will ever know.

From that day forward, my mission was clear. I would go to Germany and, assuming he was alive, hunt down Raban Nadel. And I'd do it in the name of justice. After that, everything else fell into place.

\*\*\*

On Saturday morning, Marty awoke early, anxious to proceed with the next phase of his plan. His train was scheduled to depart the Hauptbahnhof in an hour. Even with no train connections, it would take most of the day to reach Bayreuth. He was going to Bayreuth to find Oskar Zeckern, courtesy of Felix Roth's notebook.

As the first streaks of apricot light kissed the eastern sky, Marty had gone outside and done calisthenics before buying a breakfast sandwich and newspaper from the street vendor up at the S-bahn station. The activity having cleared his mind, he finalized preparations for his trip.

Marty packed his duffel, first placing his ammo in the bottom of the bag, stacking two pairs of trousers on top. Over the trousers he placed the disassembled pieces of the TT-30 pistol and PPD-40 submachine gun, nestling the rest of his clothes over the weapons. Marty made a mental note to add his toiletries after he'd showered. Rather than carry Roth's notebook, he transcribed Zeckern's alleged address—making two copies. He placed one copy in his wallet and the other in the duffel. Now all Marty had to do was—

A clicking sound made him whip his head to the front door.

It had just clicked shut.

The wind, maybe? But all the windows were closed. There was no breeze or change in air pressure. *Damn!*

Marty reached under his mattress, jerking the Sauer-38 from its hiding place. He ran to the front door and pulled it open, leaning out over the rail. Though he didn't see anything, he heard a door close down below him. Standing there, mind racing, Marty thought back to when he'd come inside this morning. He'd been carrying his breakfast and a newspaper.

*Did I close the door?*

Once inside with his food, Marty had munched the sandwich in the kitchen while practicing assembly of the two Russian weapons. He'd never walked back into the short entry hall so, yes; it was entirely possible that he'd not latched the door upon entry.

*Of all the stupid, careless things to do.*

He leaned over the railing again, peering downward. He had a feeling he knew which door it was that he'd heard shut. Marty placed his pistol on the table inside the door and pulled his own door closed. He used his hand to comb his unkempt hair to the side and walked down to Frau Schaal's apartment, rapping loudly.

No answer.

He repeated the action and waited. Then he knocked a third time.

Josh answered the door, opening it very slowly. He was visibly shaken.

*Knew it.* Marty also knew his expression was grim. He couldn't fake it. "Morning, Josh."

"Hi," Josh said weakly.

"What are you doing?"

Gnawing on his bottom lip, Josh shrugged. "Nothing, really."

"Tell me the truth, Josh. Were you in my apartment a minute ago?"

Adam's apple bobbing twice, Josh nodded. "Y-y-yes, sir. Your door was open. I was...I was just coming to say hello."

"What did you see?"

Surprising Marty, Josh didn't hesitate as he asked, "Why were you packing guns in your bag?"

Marty looked beyond him. "Where's your mother?"

"Down at the Saturday market."

Marty let out a relieved breath. *Okay...now to contain the leak...play it off smoothly.* "Can you come back upstairs for a minute?"

Josh took a step backward. "I'd...I'd better stay here."

"C'mon, Josh...nothing to be afraid of. I just want to show you what I was doing so you don't have the wrong idea."

Josh followed, reluctantly, as if he were headed to face a firing squad. Marty remembered his Sauer was sitting just inside the door on the key table. He asked Josh to wait just a moment and ducked inside, cursing himself for his carelessness. Rushing in, Marty hid the pistol back in its place before opening the front door, telling Josh to come in.

"Right in here, Josh," Marty said, smiling disarmingly. He lifted the top layer of clothes from his bag, removing the grip and receiver of the Tokarev pistol. Josh took a cautious step backward.

"No need to be scared; it's harmless in this state," Marty said. "This is a Tokarev TT-33 pistol, manufactured back in the thirties. It's Russian, from the war. I collect things like this." Lifting the long, one-piece receiver and barrel from the bag, Marty hefted it a few times as if he were gauging its weight. "And this is the PPS submachine gun. Not a very valuable or handsome weapon, but I know a collector who's looking for one from this production batch—collectors like me know that type of thing from the serial number that's stamped on the side. I'm taking these two items to the collector today and trading them for an old German rifle I've been after for years."

"Aren't those guns illegal?" Josh asked.

Marty shrugged and offered up an unsure smile. "I honestly don't know, buddy. Back where I come from, we don't ask permission to do a lot of things, we just do 'em. Gun collecting is a hobby for lots of people. I keep the weapons disassembled so, in case someone asks, they'll know I'm not planning something illegal." He put a hand on Josh's shoulder. "But, please, don't tell your mom. I'm afraid if she hears about this, she won't let you come around me anymore."

"If you're a collector, where are your other weapons?"

"Great question. They're back home in the States. When I get that rifle I've been looking for, I'll ship it back."

Josh eyed each of the pieces before gingerly taking the pistol grip from Marty. He got the feel for it before aiming it at the wall and making shooting sounds. Grinning, he handed it back. "I won't tell my Mutti…if you'll take me shooting sometime."

"Uh—well…"

"My papa would have taken me by now."

"Yeah, Josh, but—"

"I know of some woods that stretch on for many kilometers. We can just shoot at a tree."

"We'll see."

"Promise."

Eager to get rid of him, Marty nodded and they shook hands. "I need to hurry. I'm catching a train shortly so I don't want to be late, okay?"

"When will you be back?"

"Either tomorrow or early Monday."

"We can go shoot next week?" Josh asked.

"Maybe. I'll have to see how work goes."

"It stays light till ten, now." A seasoned negotiator, Josh crooked a finger at Marty. "And we *did* just make a deal."

"Yeah, Josh, we did."

With a satisfied smile, Josh turned and started for the front door. He stopped, pointing to the coat rack above the key table. "Where's the mirror that was in here?"

Marty casually moved his scabbed right hand behind his back. "It was cracked so I pulled it out."

With a nod, Josh waved and walked out. Marty hurried to the front door, calling after him. "Remember, Josh, don't say—"

"A word to my mother. Don't worry," he said from the landing below. "Just remember our deal."

Marty walked inside and slammed the door. Once the shower was running, he eyed himself in the bathroom mirror, baring his teeth and saying, "You stupid, careless sonofabitch."

That little slip-up could have been a disaster.

*** 

As Marty's train was chugging from Zoo Station toward Bavaria, and as Raban Nadel fled after murdering Gloria Riddenger and Oskar Zeckern,

*Kriminaldetektiv* Werner Eisch sat at his corner desk peering at the final roster list of the 101st SS Heavy Panzer Division. The department was quiet this Saturday morning. The gorgeous weather outside, with mild temperatures and clear blue skies, must have tempted all of the other duty detectives away from their desks, out to do "field work." But Werner, as he'd always done when he found himself at a dead end, went back to his available data. He'd stare at it like he might study a word search, turning the page, viewing it from odd angles.

One never knew what sort of inspiration a fresh view might provide.

But it was Chief Mainhardt who provided the inspiration on this morning. Werner heard the slight man approaching, shuffling his bad leg along with him, his cross to bear from the kidnapping incident so long ago. Werner turned, watching the chief come around the corner. Boy, did he look worse than normal today. Last night must have been a doozy for the old toper. The chief's skin, which was perpetually sallow, had turned a greenish-yellow tint. His face drooped badly, as if the tiny muscles behind the skin had no remaining will to pull the skin taut. Mainhardt was hunched forward and appeared ready to topple over at any moment.

"Mornin' chief. In on a Saturday?" Werner asked cheerily.

The chief barely wagged a finger as if to say, "Don't ask." He was carrying a sheet of paper, which he handed to Werner.

"What's this, sir?" Werner asked, glancing at the sheet of paper written in English and roughly translated to German at the bottom. Werner was familiar with these bulletins, sent out by USAREUR, United States Army Europe, to the Germans and the other occupying forces. Many Polizei felt the Americans were self-serving, demanding help only when one of their own happened to be the victim. But Werner didn't see it that way. Did the Americans zealously protect their interests? Sure, they did. But they were also good about sharing information. And information, in Werner's opinion, was a policeman's most powerful weapon. More than guns, or equipment, or manpower—information was the key to halting crime.

"That's a rather innocuous report from the American MPs down in Frankfurt," Mainhardt said, suffering a brief coughing fit. He dabbed his mouth with a handkerchief as he continued. "Long story short, one of their senior soldiers had shacked up with a German gal for a few days. He went to work yesterday morning and returned home to find his house burned to the ground. The gal was nowhere to be found." Mainhardt took the paper and glanced at it, holding it away from his face as he searched for the optimum, sans-glasses, viewing distance. "Initial thoughts were that maybe *she* set the fire, on purpose or accidentally, and scrammed."

"Okay?"

"But when they started interviewing neighbors, one reported hearing several loud bangs, like gunshots, from inside the house. The witness heard these sounds around noon, or a little before. Since the sounds came from inside, she said they wrote it off as the soldier doing handiwork. He's supposedly the type of man who tinkers all the time."

Fighting the urge to read the paper, Werner said, "I'm following you, chief."

"Then, later, the same neighbor said she saw a number of men come and go, two that appeared to be delivering, and removing, appliances to and from a big panel van. The third man was nattily dressed and barked orders, in German, to the deliverymen."

Werner's impatience was getting to him. "Chief, I appreciate the visit, really, but where are you going with this?"

The chief nodded with closed eyes before continuing. "Then, about three hours into his investigation, the German fire marshal pronounced that the fire was professionally set—thermite, or something of the sort. The fire bomb burned a crater into the earth below the basement." The chief handed the paper back to Werner. "You want to know why I brought this to you?"

"Yes, sir."

"The woman who'd been staying in the home, and is now *missing*, was the former girlfriend of Felix Roth—the dead man, the former Waffen-SS in Gleiberg, that first set you off on this goose chase."

"You're kidding!" Werner uncharacteristically yelled, turning and flattening the paper on his desk.

"She went through a few checkpoints to get into the inner American zone. The sergeant major whose house it was confirmed her first name and several other identifying features of her person."

Werner took a sip of water, his mind racing as he glanced all around the quiet room. *Slow down.* He eyed the chief again. "So, it's possible she knew something, and the man who killed Felix Roth tracked her down and rubbed her out."

"Could be," the chief said, using the tone he used when he didn't wholly agree with a person's suppositions.

"Wait a second." Werner scratched his face with his prosthetic as his mind raced. "Since I'm suspecting a lone wolf hunting some of the men of the 101st Panzers, then this could have actually been the work of someone *from* the 101st, or even ODESSA, in the event *they* wanted to silence her."

"Mmm-hmm."

"Or maybe Roth was the primary target. He was known to be violent and was disliked by many." Werner shrugged. "The lone wolf rubbed Roth out, then took care of the girl since she knew something."

"Possibly," the chief said. "But consider what you know about your hunter."

Werner was silent for a full minute as his mind whirred with the speed of an engine at redline. At the end of his rumination he asked, "Mind if I summarize the entire case for you?"

"Please," Mainhardt said, pulling a chair from the adjacent desk.

"We get a former Waffen-SS in here, claiming he'd been mugged. His story stinks, so you have the patrol officer bring me in. I agree that the victim is full of beans, then I notice the big scab in his ear. I'm versed on interrogation techniques and there's an excellent, yet rare, method that recommends holding a punch knife in a person's ear in order to get complete cooperation."

"Duly noted," Mainhardt said academically. Werner knew the old man was humoring him and probably not paying as close attention as he could. But repeating the facts of a story was sometimes as helpful to the primary detective as it was to those who were listening. Oftentimes more helpful.

"So, I filed the strange report away in my mind and forgot about it."

"Go on."

"So, then we learn about that murder in Gleiberg, over in Hessen. I got lucky that I even got wind of it," Werner said. "The victim, Roth, had been in the same SS unit as my mugging victim. But, unlike the mugging victim, Roth had been living under a different name, definitely in hiding. By all accounts he was not a savory individual. I checked with the attending M.E. and there was *no* punch hole in Roth's ear."

"What else did the investigating locals tell you?"

"Roth had fired a pistol. There were powder burns on his hand and empty casings around him. They found one bullet that they presume was from his gun embedded in a nearby post—can't be sure, yet, since it flattened on impact. They found another slug on the road outside the castle that they also think was his." Werner motioned his finger above his head and back down. "They think it went up in the air before falling back to the road."

"How many times was Roth shot?"

"Twice, .32 caliber. Big man like that, he'd still be functional."

"So they think he was shooting as he fell?"

"Probably."

"Then what?"

"The shooter dragged Roth to the cellar."

"What about the caretaker?"

Werner was about to speak but stopped, his mouth open before it transformed into a smile. "Right...good memory, chief. The shooter disabled the castle caretaker, a man named Bettenger—well-respected fellow, by all reports. The shooter knocked him cold and tied him up."

"What did the caretaker give us?"

"Hardly a thing because he never saw our man. Got hit over the head and then listened to our suspect warn him not to make a peep. Had a bright light in his eyes the whole time."

"Anything else from the caretaker?"

"He said our suspect spoke indistinct, perfect German. Said he was *very* polite and didn't seem the violent type."

The chief screwed up his face. "Other than slaying Felix Roth."

Werner shrugged. "I'm just telling you what he said."

"So, just guessing, it sounds like a standoff that the former SS lost," Mainhardt said.

"Sounds that way." Werner stood. "Once I learned all that, I found a unit roster of the 101st Heavy Panzers, and I located two other members living in Berlin. I went to see them."

"You told me, but tell me again. My old mind…"

"Both men had the same hole in their ear as the mugging victim. Neither of them would tell me anything but were both clearly nervous." Werner tapped his index finger on his lip. "In fact, I'd say both men were quite scared. All three of the Berlin former SS appeared to be living normal lives now."

"What did you learn about Felix Roth's woman?"

Werner shook his head. "This is where I get puzzled. So, some guy interrogates three SS here. He finds what he wants, then goes to Gleiberg and kills Felix Roth. But Felix Roth's girlfriend, who by all accounts had been living with him up until the day of his death, is gone."

"So, when they found his body, his girlfriend wasn't around for questioning?"

"Correct. And there was no evidence of foul play at Roth's home." Werner's snapped his prosthetic twice. "And now you bring me an American report that Roth's girlfriend was staying in a house that was professionally burned."

"Do you think she's the killer?" the chief asked.

"No," Werner replied firmly. "I read the Polizei report on her. She was nomadic and seemingly a tortured soul, but why would she have been in Berlin interrogating ex-SS when Felix was right under her nose?"

"Think she knew something was going down with Felix and scrammed?"

"Quite possibly. And—I'm theorizing here—but, because she scrammed, she might have known something about Roth's killer."

"So, the thermite-bombed house was our killer tying up loose ends?"

"That's the first assumption," Werner said.

"You don't agree?"

"After talking it through, my instinct says no. You don't agree, either, do you?"

The chief replied with a grim smile.

"Assuming the interrogator from Berlin is indeed a lone wolf, he left those men here virtually unharmed. Then, the evidence indicates that he and Roth had a showdown of some sort, and Roth got killed. But the lone wolf then leaves the caretaker virtually unharmed, too." Werner rifled through his papers, perching his spectacles on his nose as he read the passage in question. "See, he even told the caretaker he was *sorry* for hitting him, and to remain quiet until sunup." Werner repeated it incredulously. "Sorry!"

"What else did he say to the caretaker?"

"Just a few words. Said he was attacked by Roth. Said he'd defended himself but was afraid no one would believe him. Said he'd kill the caretaker if he started yelling, but also apologized for what he'd done."

"Well, if Roth attacked *him*, then why was he compelled to run away?"

Werner arched his eyebrows. "You see what I mean? One big puzzle. And a guy who leaves a caretaker and three SS in Berlin mostly unharmed, probably doesn't track down a woman to Frankfurt, kill her, then firebomb the house she'd been in."

"Maybe this lone wolf wasn't looking for Felix Roth...not ultimately," Chief Mainhardt said, leaning back, crossing his arms and eyeing Werner. "Maybe this lone wolf had gotten Roth's name...his new name...from one of the three here in Berlin. But maybe Roth isn't his ultimate goal and things just went bad that night. You said you learned from the others that this Roth character had a history of violence. Maybe the lone wolf showed up to interrogate Roth, but Roth was armed and didn't acquiesce. At that point, someone had to die."

"I agree, chief, with every single thing you've said." Werner lifted the American bulletin. "But what about this...the girl?"

"How many men from that SS unit are missing?" the chief asked. "Not *confirmed* dead, but missing in action?"

"I've got it in my notes somewhere, but I think it's thirteen or fourteen," Werner answered.

"And Roth was one of them?"

"Yes, he was."

"But the three here in Berlin weren't?"

"Correct. They were...excuse me—they *are* all living seemingly normal lives."

Old Chief Mainhardt's hangover seemed to be temporarily gone. His previously sallow face was flushed, his eyes twinkling. He pointed to the sheet of paper. "Your lone wolf is looking for one of those hidden SS men...one of that thirteen or fourteen. When he was mugging the former SS here in Berlin, he wasn't a threat. Not yet. But now he's taken down one of the men living in hiding, and now the others who are in hiding are springing into action."

"They killed the girl."

"I was theorizing."

Werner squeezed his eyes shut, frustrated by the chief's indecision. "What's your gut tell you, chief?"

"Okay, son…my gut says one or more of the SS in hiding is hiding the lone wolf's target. And the target found out Roth's girl was alive, that she knew something about them…or maybe about the lone wolf. They located her—probably through some bent American soldier who's on the take and gave them her identity from the Zone checkpoint—then the SS-in-hiding questioned her and killed her." The chief shook his head. "Sure as shit, that's what my gut tells me."

"I agree," Werner whispered, his eyes going back to his papers. The two men were quiet for a few moments.

"Werner?"

"Yes, sir?"

"Don't breathe a word of this to *anyone* else. If these men are ODESSA, or something of the sort, they won't think a thing about killing some one-armed detective from Berlin."

"Understood."

"Good."

Werner took a step closer. "Permission to make a trip, sir?"

"Frankfurt?"

"Not yet. I want to go to Gleiberg, first."

"If you go, I wouldn't spout off too much to the locals."

Werner nodded. "I'll be careful, sir."

"Come get a travel chit from my secretary."

"Thank you, chief."

"You can thank me by solving this." Whistling, Chief Mainhardt shuffled away.

# Chapter Fourteen

Journal Entry

By the time this journal is found, my plan will be easy to piece together. Put simply, I used my fluency in German, and a few flattering letters of recommendation from the professor and his acquaintances, to secure a job that would take me to Germany. The professor helped me gather together the information on the 101st SS Panzers, as well as dossiers on numerous SS personnel.

To this day, I have no idea how he got that information. Again, I have my suspicions, but it wouldn't be fair to speculate.

In January of this year, shortly after I was hired by Day Construction down in Dallas, I received a phone call from a hospital in Oklahoma City. While lecturing at school, the professor had suffered a major heart attack and was in critical condition. He'd managed to tell the attending nurse to call me. It took her a few days to figure out how to reach me. Although I was in training, my new boss was fine with me leaving for a few days. I arrived three days after the professor had been rushed to the hospital. By the time I arrived, he'd improved enough to transition to a regular room. When I entered, he was flat on his back, reading a book that he held above him.

"Ahh, Mister Elder," he said, sounding as if nothing happened.

"Are you okay?" I asked, for lack of anything better to say.

"I'm fine as long as I lie here perfectly still. Reading helps me pass the time."

"Are you going to be alright?"

"That remains to be seen. My heart doctor, a fine young man from Oregon, seems quite concerned with my symptoms. Though he's not yet leveled with me, I've a sneaking suspicion that I have a ticking time bomb in my chest." He said this in the same tone he would use to tell me what he planned on cooking for dinner.

"Why do you think that?"

"It doesn't matter, Mister Elder. What's a hundred more days? What's ten thousand more days? All of us must rejoin the basic elements of this sphere at some point. It's as natural as childbirth and completely unavoidable, unless I've missed something along the way."

I hated it when the professor contemplated such weighty matters academically. He was a history professor, not a damned philosopher. "You're going to get better, professor."

"Perhaps. Perhaps not. How's the training in Dallas?"

I shrugged. "Lots of civil regulations to learn."

"Sounds exhilarating."

"Yeah," I snorted. "A real gas."

"Have they told you when you will depart for Germany?"

"Probably early summer."

He nodded then shut the book, placing it beside him. Just that simple movement winded him, making him wheeze.

When he recovered, he turned his head as he spoke. "Mister Elder, I just want you to know I've enjoyed our time together. After this visit, I want you to return to your training and not concern yourself about me." The professor saw me opening my mouth to speak. He silenced me with a shake of his head. "Other than our study and preparations, we've had a fine time together. I'll always treasure it." The faint smile on his face disappeared. "But, as of today, you're on your own. I wish you good luck in your hunt...and I think you will need it. If you happen to get close to the dishonorable Raban Nadel, have no illusions about his reaction. He will attempt to destroy you. He will react with ferocity. That's the type of man he is."

"I get all that. But, when you're better, why can't we just—"

"I'm not going to get better, Mister Elder. I shall be frank. If I sit up, I black out. My doctor has proposed several radical invasive maneuvers but no procedure has been perfected for my condition."

"You're not going to let him try?"

"No."

"Why not?" I asked, my voice quite loud.

He eyed me for a moment. "Why don't you give up this ridiculous mission of yours, Mister Elder? Why don't you move to a small town and find your peace in feeding pigeons and baking cakes?"

I was about to retort when I realized what he'd just done. "Touché," I whispered.

"Growing up, my rabbi had a wonderfully simple saying that he used often, especially in regard to those of us who didn't worship regularly." The professor licked his lips. "The saying was, 'We do what we want to do.'"

I was looking away, the gravity of the moment sinking in. "Yes, we do."

"Listen to me," he commanded. I turned my eyes back to his.

"Mister Elder, what you're seeking has elements of nobility. Going back and serving justice, even vigilante style, can be admired through some lenses. But it's how you go about your mission that will define your walk on this earth." He cleared his throat. "You've expressed hatred for the Germans. I understand this. Just promise me, as you go on this search, that you'll carry yourself in a way that even your mother would approve of."

"My mother?"

"Yes," he replied in a firm voice, "your mother. And remember your mission. You're going there to bring Raban Nadel, and him only, to justice."

I let his words sink in for a moment. "Okay, professor, I'll do everything you said. But, while we're at it, what's been your motivation in all this? I've asked you this question a dozen times. If you're going to make me go along with all your rules and regulations, then I at least want to know why. Why did you approach me? Why have you helped me?"

His eyes crinkled as he smiled. "My impetus. Yes, that's a fair question, especially at this juncture. In my view, Mister Elder, each of us are but one being. We can go along through life and never help a soul. Or we can kill ourselves trying to help a million. But no matter who a person is, even if they're serving Thanksgiving dinner to a hundred hungry souls, they can only serve one person at a time. And here, in my waning days, you've been that one person." He held his hand out for mine. I took it, listening as he continued.

"And by helping you, my son, I've helped myself. My family isn't suffering anymore. They were ripped from this earth, yes. But will my avenging them bring them back? No. And, in the bitter end, would it even make me feel better? Doubtful."

I was still holding his hand. "Are you suggesting I shouldn't go?"

"No, Mister Elder. I think, in the event you find Raban Nadel, it will be a glorious moment. But it could also be your undoing."

After a moment, I asked him something I'd always wanted to ask him. "Do you think I'll be successful?"

"Whether you are or aren't isn't of importance."

"C'mon, professor. Don't feed me that line."

He pulled his hand away and faced the ceiling. "It will be very difficult." His eyes cut to mine. "But I'm envious. Your chase will be Saturday matinee, white-knuckle fun." The professor laughed uproariously.

He died eight days later.

The same nurse called me, in tears, and said he suffered another massive heart attack during rehabilitation, while trying to walk with a walker. They attempted to revive him but were unsuccessful.

My mother. My best friend. The men of my unit. And now the professor.

I'd never felt so alone.

After that, my mission had never seemed so clear. I was going to bring the weight of the world down on that bastard Raban Nadel.

\*\*\*

Chief Mainhardt had insisted that Werner play the entire situation by the book, meaning he had to check in with the local Polizei upon his arrival in the Gleiberg area. Werner had benefited from an express train to Frankfurt. There, he connected to Giessen, the entire trip taking less than seven hours.

Werner did just as he was told, checking in with the Polizei in Giessen. They oversaw a number of nearby villages and towns, including Krofdorf-Gleiberg. After an obligatory meeting with the duty officer, Werner received a frigid reception from the officer in charge of the Felix Roth murder investigation. The policeman, a lieutenant, was the one and only detective in the entire bureau. Werner's first order of business had been questioning the caretaker, Herr Bettenger, which they did at the small hospital. An older gentleman, the caretaker had been kept for observation due to a concussion he received from the blow to his head. By the time Werner and the detective arrived, Bettenger was dressed and in the process of checking out. Werner questioned the caretaker for an hour, learning hardly anything new. There simply wasn't much to go on from the caretaker's limited interaction with the assailant. But, like he had before, the caretaker insisted that the assailant had seemed remorseful.

"Even made sure he hadn't tied my wrists too tightly," the caretaker said, sitting on the edge of the hospital bed. "My head was fuzzy from getting hit, but I stand by my assertion that the young fellow was telling the truth about not having started the dustup. He sounded more scared than anything."

"*Young?*"

"Well, I don't know his age for certain, but he sounded youngish. Twenties…maybe thirties."

"I asked you his age the other day and you said you had no idea," the Giessen detective scolded.

"I don't recall you asking me that," Herr Bettenger said without anger.

That had been the limit of the revelations.

Afterward, Werner and the Giessen detective drove in silence to Gleiberg Castle. The detective's name was Maier. He was tall, thin and prematurely gray, although his face was handsome and unlined. Werner glanced over at his counterpart, noting the sour expression as he drove. He did not seem pleased by Werner's presence, though Werner felt Maier's displeasure ran deeper than his own visit.

"How long on the force?" Werner asked, breaking the silence in an effort to build rapport.

Maier spoke flatly. "Eighteen years, not counting the time I was in the military."

"You from here?"

The detective wrenched his hands on the wheel as he waited for the traffic light. "Nearby."

"I've never been here before," Werner commented. He looked off to the north, able to see the structure and jutting tower of a castle, stark against the solid gray of the cloudy sky. "I guess that's Gleiberg I can see up on—"

"Let's cut out all the chitchat, how about it?" Maier snapped.

"Sure, we can cut out the chitchat." Werner waited a moment and asked, "Other than the chitchat, is there a problem?"

"You mean, other than the dead man in the cooler down in Frankfurt whose toe tag leads back to an unsolved investigation sitting on my desk?"

"Yes. Other than that."

"Well, let's see," Maier said, his voice changing to a different pitch as he jammed the old BMW into third gear. "My wife of sixteen years turned out to be less of an angel than I'd previously thought, especially when she told me she was leaving me for my own *cousin.* Then my two children announced to me that they wanted to go with her. And now the lawyer I hired told me, since I don't have any concrete evidence of the affair I know she's been having, that I'm going to have to live off scraps for the rest of my life while I'm putting food on my deadbeat cousin's table." He rolled down the window and spat, as if the words had made his saliva suddenly acidic.

Werner made no response.

"And on top of all that, Mister-Fancy-Berlin-Detective, now my detective rating is in jeopardy due to my inability to solve this case. We don't get many murders here and, when we do, my bosses expect them to be solved, *tout de suite*, especially when they involve ex-Schutzstaffel." He turned and glared at Werner. "Thus far, I haven't produced a damn thing and your being here will do nothing but make me look more clueless."

Werner nervously clicked his prosthetic and nestled back into the seat, his eyes straight ahead. "I appreciate your honesty and I sincerely hope your family situation improves."

All he earned from Maier was a disgusted grunt.

\*\*\*

Gleiberg Castle, despite its age, was quite impressive. According to a tarnished brass plate at its entrance, the castle was more than 1,000 years old, dating back to the Holy Roman Empire. Upon entry, a person would find themselves in a broad courtyard with the *Biergarten* to the right and the looming tower straight ahead. Werner craned his neck, guessing the stone tower to be at least twenty meters tall. And with the castle perched on the high hilltop, the tower would probably offer the best view of the nearby countryside available. Werner walked to the tower, peering inside, finding a rickety spiral staircase of wooden stairs.

*No, thanks.*

To the left of the tower were the soaring gable ruins of some sort of inner building, perhaps the residence and kitchen. Below that, a dark opening led downward to what must have been the cellar or keep. There were two lines of red string stretched across the opening with a *"Polizeiabsperrung"* tag hanging from one of the lines.

Werner pointed to the opening. "Is that where Roth was found?"

Maier, a newspaper wedged under his arm, was struggling to get a cigarette lit in the stiff breeze. When he finally set it aflame, he took a drag before motioning at Werner with the cigarette. "I'm gonna do this one time, got it? Get out those photos I gave you and pay attention because, after I point all this out, I'm sitting my butt on one of those benches and reading my newspaper."

"That's fine, detective. I will listen attentively."

It took Maier about five minutes to laconically relay the facts of the case. From inside his newspaper he produced a sheet of graph paper on which was drawn a rough diagram of the castle floor plan. Pertinent items were represented on the diagram, such as bullet casings, blood trails and Felix Roth's dead body. All of this matched everything Maier had just told Werner.

"That's it," Maier said with finality, sweeping his hands around the courtyard as if to say, "Get on with it." He turned and walked to the corner table, sitting with his back to the wall, spreading the paper out and lighting a fresh cigarette. He weighted the corners of the paper with salt and pepper shakers and did not look up. Werner was on his own.

With the aid of a battery-powered hand torch, Werner went into the cellar and eyed the scene. Felix Roth's bloodstains were easily found on the far side. They had blackened and tarnished the ancient cobblestones, making Werner briefly wonder how many people had spilt blood in the medieval castle over the centuries. Numerous scuff marks could be found around the area where Roth's big body had lain. According to the diagram, to the right of that spot was where the caretaker had sat. The only evidence Werner could find was a slightly cleaner spot on the dirty cobblestones, probably where the man's rump had occasionally shifted, wiping the accumulated grime with each movement. There was nothing else to see so Werner went back into the daylight, what there was of it. The cloudy day had turned darker, and a steady cool wind that smelled of rain began to blow from the south.

Crossing the courtyard near to where Maier sat, Werner eyed the area where Roth had probably been shot. Though the blood had been cleaned, he still could see the dark remnants and match them to Maier's photographs. The shell casings from Roth's gun had fallen in that general area, to the right. Werner turned, holding the photograph that showed where one of Roth's slugs was found. It had been embedded in one of the four thick corner posts of the *Biergarten's* heavy pergola. Werner stood where he assumed Roth had stood, aiming and mock-firing at the post. As he did, it began to rain.

"Aw, shit!" Maier barked, squinting up into the sky. "Aren't you done yet?"

"Not even close," Werner murmured without looking at his counterpart.

From his pocket he produced a roll of yellow string and an envelope of small tacks. He pinned the string at the bullet entry point in the thick post, walking back to where Roth had stood. There, he stood a bench upright. He pinned the taut string twenty centimeters higher than where his own right hand would likely fire from, doing so to simulate Roth's height.

"Th'hell are you doing?" Maier asked in disgust. "All that fancy shit ain't gonna tell you anything."

"Perhaps not," Werner remarked. He walked around the bench, trying to gauge where the killer had stood as he'd fatally wounded Roth. Had the killer fired first? Probably. Since Roth was hit on his left side, he would have almost certainly twisted left, meaning the killer was standing to the left of the bullet's path when facing Roth. Werner moved just inside his taut string, mock-firing in the direction where Roth had stood.

There had been no shell casings from the deadly weapon, leaving Werner to reimagine this little scene. He stared downward at his feet, looking for any sort of clue.

The cobblestones were gray and rounded from centuries of feet, horseshoes, carts and whatever else might have been moved over the old stones. Now they were shiny smooth from the pattering rain that was growing harder by the minute. Werner slid the wet photos back into his coat and dropped to his knees, scrutinizing the wet castle floor.

"Come on!" Maier protested. "I'm getting soaked and you're staring at wet rocks!"

"Please, go to the car if you'd like." Werner ran his hand over the cobblestones, poking his prosthetic down into the natural grout and scraping out a small pile of dirt and fragments of refuse. He ran his fingers through the debris, finding bent bottle caps, cigarette butts and matchsticks. Werner looked up at Maier, who was frowning back from the temporary umbrella of his rapidly saturating newspaper.

"Did you search these grout lines for shell casings?"

"Think we're stupid? Of course we did. The shooter policed up his brass."

Werner nodded, letting out a long breath as he stood. *Slow down. Maier's hurrying you, as is the rain. Circumspection is key.*

Turning slowly, he began to examine each and every item in and around the *Biergarten*. The wooden bar and rough-hewn storage shed backed up to the stone wall of the castle. Two large planters bounded the shed, both planted with sickly-looking petunias, wilting under the weight of the rain. Above the planter was a green and gold Licher Pils sign, crafted from tin and dented at its right edge. Werner's eyes slid slowly down and left, studying the cobblestones at the base of the outer wall. A line of wet leaves ran the length of the wall, probably blown there by the perpetually swirling winds inside the castle.

Werner walked to the leaves, crouching as he began to sift through them. Many of them were old leaves, left over from last fall. Some were new and still green, probably blown in during storms and high wind. Interspersed through the leaves were scraps of trash: napkins, slips of paper, bits of beer labels peeled by nervous hands.

"C'mon pal," Maier griped. "The place has been gone over half a dozen times."

Ignoring him, Werner produced his pen, doing a slow shuffle down the length of the wall, poking through the slick leaves. A third of the way down the wall's length, a lighter shade of color caught his eye, protruding from under a deep green leaf. Probably just another peeled beer label. Using his pen, he flipped the leaf over, finding a small piece of tattered cloth; it was slightly soiled and seemed to have an amber stain on one end.

Werner lifted the cloth with his prosthetic, using his good hand to turn it over. It was a clothing tag of some sort. He carefully wiped it clean, lifting it close to his eyes to read the small, indistinct words…

## Jepson's Markdown Menswear
## Ada, Oklahoma

Detective Maier had tossed his soaked newspaper and now walked beside Werner, narrowing his eyes at the tag. Werner allowed him to read it before producing a small envelope from his jacket pocket, depositing the item.

Maier stood there dumbfounded.

Meanwhile, Werner kept scouring.

***

Late that afternoon, Werner sipped a cup of hot tea in the basement of the Giessen Polizei Bureau. They'd been inside for a few hours now but Werner's old suit, the one he'd privately dubbed "Hound Dog" due to its small hound's-tooth pattern, was still quite wet. He'd brushed the loose soil from the knees of the suit; however, he knew when the fabric dried, it would be heavily stained. Maier was sitting across the room, quietly filling out contact sheets, a cigarette burning in an ashtray beside him. He hadn't said much after Werner found the tag, and he had definitely ceased his protests. Both men knew the tag could amount to nothing, could have belonged to anyone, could have been there for months. There were thousands of American GIs stationed nearby, and GIs love *Biergartens*.

Finishing his hot tea, Werner resumed a study of his case notes. This went on for ten more minutes.

The door finally banged open, startling Werner. Through its opening came a tall, gangly man in a lab coat, the bureau's lab chief. His face was long and thin, a perfect match for his elongated body. The lab chief's skin was pale and he had dark rings under his eyes. Werner wondered if he ever went outside. Trained as a chemist, something Werner had learned earlier, the lab chief was carrying a polyethylene bag containing the clothing tag. In his other hand he carried a typed piece of paper along with close-up photos of the tag. He placed the photos and evidence bag on the table, glancing at both detectives.

"Listening?" the lab chief asked perfunctorily, reminding Werner of many a university professor he'd once endured.

"Yeah," Maier said.

"Intently," Werner added.

"The primary elements found on the tag are aluminum-silicate; sand consisting primarily of quartz; elemental grime; and other organic matter. Dirt, in other words. The dirt is very likely local, especially since the grime is high in potassium and magnesium. Secondarily is the liquid mixture that created the large stain on the right side, as the tag is read by the human eye. When I tested the stain I learned that it consists primarily of D-5 emollient with suspended PTFE."

"D-5 what?" Maier asked, standing and holding the clear bag in front of his eyes.

"I'll get to that. I also found trace elements of nitrocellulose along with bits of nitrate and diphenylamine. In other words—"

"Spent gunpowder," both detectives answered in unison.

The chemist smiled primly, as if they'd passed his most elementary of tests.

"What's the D-5 stuff?" Maier asked.

"D-5 emollient with suspended PTFE. PTFE is more commonly known in my circles by its trade name of Teflon. D-5 is an oil and Teflon is a high-viscosity compound. Mixed together with other trademark ingredients, they create a common series of products sold under numerous trade names." The lab chief gestured to the tag. "And, as I'm sure you already know, based on the robust golden thread that was found dangling from one side of the tag, I'd hazard the tag came from a pair of sturdy pants. Care to theorize?"

The two detectives shared a look.

"A jerked handgun caused the tag to rip from its clothing," Werner said. "That's what added the trace gunpowder. Would gunpowder residue exist on a handgun even after a good cleaning?"

The lab chief nodded with closed eyes. "Such residue is very difficult to fully remove, as it chemically bonds to the resident metal."

"And if the handgun had been freshly cleaned, could one assume that the tag absorbed some of the oil as the handgun resided in a person's waistband?" Maier asked.

"One could certainly assume that, yes," the chemist responded. "And given what would likely be a barrel-down position, especially when in close contact with a warm body, a handgun whose parts had not been wiped exceptionally clean could certainly weep a quantity of oil as the body temperature warmed the oil. To your assumption, detective…" The chemist lifted the polyethylene bag and pointed his tweezers at a small split. "Notice the tear marks on the bottom of the tag. They're found directly over the oily stain."

"Anything else about the tag?" Maier asked.

"Nothing pertinent regarding its properties," the lab chief answered. "While you're certainly making assumptions about the weapon, from my limited point of view, I think they're plausible." With a polite nod, the gangly lab chief departed.

The lab chief's presence was almost immediately replaced by the deputy commander, the top policeman in the Giessen Bureau and one of eight divisional chiefs who reported directly to the Hessen chief located down in Frankfurt. Werner had met the deputy earlier and found the man to be helpful, if a tad harsh. He wore an eye patch over his left eye and stared at Maier, his good eye cocked as he spoke.

"Am I to understand our Berlin counterpart here found something that could be helpful?"

Before Maier could respond, Werner took a step forward and spoke quickly. "Detective Maier was amazing, sir. I've never seen more of a bloodhound detective. He'd already scoured the scene a dozen times but, when the rain began it must've allowed him to see things in a fresh light. We had pouring rain and he was down on his knees searching. Wasn't twenty minutes before he found a clothing tag that could possibly belong to the shooter."

Maier gaped at Werner. The deputy nodded thoughtfully, taking the evidence bag and scrutinizing the writing. "Is the man you're seeking an Ami?"

"Not that I was aware of, but it's possible, especially now that I've had a chance to ponder it a bit."

"You realize we've got to keep the tag here."

"Yes, sir. I have the photographs."

"What did you learn from the caretaker?"

"Nothing helpful, sir. Maier had already gotten all he could out of the man."

The deputy nodded. "Then what else can we assist you with?"

"Nothing, sir. Your man Maier, here, gave me all the help I needed. I'll make sure my chief sends a commendation."

The deputy's chest swelled with pride. "Maier's a good man and, thus far, this is a tough case. Please keep us copied on any progress by Telex and we'll do the same."

Werner gathered his things, including the photographs of the clothing label.

"I'll walk you out," Maier murmured.

In the small, plain lobby Maier jammed his hands in his pockets and stared at the ground. It took him a moment before he said, "Detective, I feel pretty small for the way I acted. Especially after you told the—"

"Say no more," Werner said, cutting him off. "Just do the same for someone else someday, fair enough?"

Maier took Werner's left hand and pumped it vigorously. "I will do *just* that."

"Let me know if you learn anything else," Werner said, winking and clicking his prosthetic. With that, he turned and exited the building. During the five-minute walk to the train station, Werner decided he would still take the regional train to Frankfurt. But instead of quickly connecting to his Berlin express train, he would stay in Frankfurt for a bit.

He planned to visit the headquarters of the United States Army European Command.

# Chapter Fifteen

Journal Entry

It's time.

I feel like I've made progress.

I'm finally going to write about the incident...the massacre.

This is the very first time I've ever committed to tell *every* single detail I can recall. In fact, I held back during the resulting investigations and I didn't even share everything with the professor. My mind just couldn't open those doors. But, being here in Germany, getting closer, and doing some of the things I've done...I feel better. I'm not sweating. I don't feel sick. Other than slightly shaky hands, I feel ready to recount all I can recall about the massacre.

Yes. It's time, indeed.

The Massacre at Kastellaun occurred in late March of 1945. I don't recall the exact date. I suppose I could look it up but the date doesn't matter. As I think I indicated on an earlier page, the warmish weather seemed drastic after what we'd endured over the balance of the previous months. Words can't describe how utterly cold and miserable the winter of '44-'45 had been. Perhaps someday history books will recall the brutality of that winter, not only brought on by man, but also by the weather. I can distinctly remember passing German soldiers who'd frozen to death between battles. Our medics inspected the bodies of several of them, finding no injuries other than those brought about by the vicious cold.

By late March, it was probably nearing fifty degrees and, on the day in question, it was sunny. I'm not talking about the sunny that's slightly buffered by haze or occasional clouds. I'm referring to a crystalline sky and powerful sunlight that warms a man's face and clothing, filling him with optimism. To us it felt like joyous summer.

We'd just rotated off the front line after helping the Allied forces plow into Germany with the goal of crossing the fabled Rhine River. On the day in question, we heard reports that the leading edge of American and British forces were doing just that.

Since the frontline Germans had nearly lost the will to fight and were pulling back with such pace, we were unable to keep up and were held back for resupply and a half a day of maintenance.

I remember seeing on the map that we were west of the small village of Kastellaun. Some of our guys had walked there for water and had come back telling of the celebration that was going on in town.

Why were the Germans celebrating? Well, despite the fact that their country was losing the war, they were overjoyed at our presence. I guess when a large portion of your village is in smoldering ruins, half of your citizenry is dead, your children are starving, and many of your women have been violated...well, you get the picture. But they were, indeed, celebrating. Just take it in context.

Often when we would proceed through a town, be it French, Dutch, Belgian, whatever...the villagers would greet us with cheers, tears of joy, and whatever paltry peace offerings they could muster.

On the day of the massacre, my crew and I stayed with our gun. It needed work and, being as tired as we were, we didn't feel like cavorting with the locals. We had no clue what lay ahead. Around noon, our maintenance work done, we sacked out in the sunshine and took peaceful naps.

We were awoken just after two and were informed that our unit had been told to stand by for movement orders. Our XO said we'd follow the advance over the Rhine and needed to be in range of the frontline in case the commanders called for artillery support.

Obviously the charge forward, and the Rhine crossing, had gone well. No one was surprised. For weeks the German resistance we'd encountered had been tepid. Regardless, the charge was on, so we were headed back to the front line, or near it. Optimism reigned as rumors of a cease-fire continued to build.

At the movement briefing, we were informed that Captain Rook, our battery commander, had fallen ill. I didn't think much of it. Stomach flus were rampant, especially given the filthy conditions, our weakened bodies, and the warming weather. The XO said Rook was in the back of the deuce-and-a-half. He'd finally stopped retching and was fighting off his remaining fever.

"He'll be back on his feet in a snap, gents," the XO said crisply, sounding like he was speaking to a group of Ivy League graduates. I didn't know much about the XO. His name was Breston, one of the new arrivals, and honestly I didn't view him positively or negatively. He was just there. By this point, half of our men were replacements, guys we'd not gone through initial training with. It got to where a person just grew numb to the new faces. And with all the talk of the war ending soon, our minds were occupied with the desire to just go the heck home.

So, as the briefing droned on, me, John Vincent, Kenny Martin and Danny Elder didn't think a damned thing about it when the XO warned us of a new intel report of left-behind German soldiers and units. Any time we'd made fast advances forward, this type of thing was brought up. The only instance I can recall that had turned out bad for us was when the battery clerk got himself killed by a wounded German sniper who had remained behind while his fellow krauts retreated.

The sniper had hidden in the attic of a house and, after he killed our clerk, I'd hazard that we put a thousand rounds and a dozen grenades into that house. There was little left of that sniper's body by the time we were done.

But that had been six months before. Six months is an eternity during wartime. Breston's briefing and subsequent warnings fell on deaf ears. I remember turning to John. He rolled his eyes and said, "Same shit, different day."

He was wrong. We all were. And off we went.

If we'd have had any clue what awaited us, we'd have turned north and sped away.

***

Stretching luxuriously for five full minutes, Marty began to feel human again. Eight hours on an old train was not only mind-numbing, it numbed the body as well. *Especially my butt.* Thankfully, the daylight lingered this time of year. Marty still had two good hours of light, allowing him enough time to get his bearings and reconnoiter Zeckern's address, assuming the address from Roth's journal was correct. Hopefully the bastard would be home—and alone. If anyone else were there, Marty would probably have to wait until Zeckern went out. Marty might even have to facilitate such action.

Most pressing at the moment was Marty's need of a map. Not an easy acquisition on a Saturday evening. He'd thought about the need of a local map days before but had been unsuccessful in finding a Bayreuth city map all the way up in Berlin. Now that he was here, Marty doubted any petrol stations would be open at this hour. Maybe out by the autobahn, but probably not in the *Stadtmitte*. He lit a cigarette, ambling down a shady street that, due to the leaf cover, was essentially dark at this hour. Though the skies above were still deep blue, the low sun was behind the buildings, creating a night-like effect on the street.

Pausing beside an elegant older Mercedes, Marty tested the passenger door, finding it unlocked. He casually slipped into the car, checking the glove box and finding numerous papers but no map. He repeated this with several other cars, none of which were locked, eventually locating a Bayreuth road map in an old Opel cabriolet. After exiting the car, Marty walked back to the main thoroughfare, sitting on a bench as he spread the map on his lap. Using the legend, he intersected his fingers at the grid square containing the electric company's address. Thankfully, it was only a few blocks away.

The driveway gate at the rear of the Bayreuthwerk Electric Utility Company was open. Using a technique he'd learned long ago, Marty simply strode into the parking lot as if he belonged there. One worker stared quizzically at Marty. Marty waved and said, "I'm Hans's brother. He left something for me." The worker smiled and nodded and went about his business.

"Works every time," Marty whispered to himself. He opened a panel van, finding what he needed in the rear. Afterward, Marty consulted the map for Zeckern's address, finding it to be about two kilometers east of town. A quick check of his watch told Marty that he had about another hour before darkness would fall. Hitching his pack up on his back, he began heading east. It was then that a strange sensation fell upon Marty.

Stopping suddenly, Marty turned and looked behind him. A person's foot and pants leg could be seen stepping behind a tobacconist's shop. Marty continued to face that direction, watching as other people walked behind the shop. It only took a moment to realize that it was a busy alleyway, probably a cut-through to another street. Just because he saw someone walking away doesn't mean that person was following him. Tapping out another cigarette, Marty lit it and turned to continue his walk.

Going straight through the handsome old city, Marty passed two teeming *Biergartens*, the smell of fresh beer assaulting his nose each time. At both *Biergartens* he heard more English than he did German. Seeing the white scalp on the sides of many young men's heads, Marty reasoned that there must be an Army post somewhere nearby. In his planning he did learn that Bayreuth was inside the American Zone, as well as a former stronghold of right-wing ideology.

Marty eyed one of the American soldiers as he passed. The soldier was a brash kid of about twenty, yelling foul curses to his friends in an obnoxious effort to stand out from the crowd. Marty wanted to jerk the skinny punk over the ivy wall that separated the *Biergarten* from the sidewalk. Marty would have liked to have pinned the punk down on the sidewalk and make him listen to what the soldiers from the war had been through. To remind him of the blood that was spilt on this land so the punk and his friends could play soldier and get drunk and laid without ever offering up one little bit of their soul.

*Listen to yourself,* Marty admonished. *You're a hateful, mean-spirited man. All the more reason to despise those Nazi sons of bitches for doing this to you.*

Dragging on his cigarette, Marty continued on. Up ahead, a store sported an angled window at its entry. Marty slowed his walk just a tad, prepared to use the window to check behind him. He approached the window as casually as he could. As he reached the window's reflection, Marty was able to see five people walking close behind him. Young people, they were walking shoulder to shoulder, jostling and occasionally turning backward to view their friends the way teenagers often do.

Marty halted just past the store, pretending to read the menu at an adjacent restaurant. He glanced to his right, confirming what he'd seen in the window. It was just a group of boys, probably no more than 15 years old. As they approached, he overheard them. They were talking about *High Noon*, the American movie they'd probably just watched at the downtown theater. Flicking his cigarette into a drain, Marty pronounced his tail clear and marched on.

By his estimation, he'd reach Zeckern's street in ten minutes. And there, Marty was going to bring his own brand of high noon to Oskar Zeckern.

*** 

Hours earlier, Raban Nadel had arrived at Oskar Zeckern's home. Nadel found the home to be quite charming, probably built in the early 1800s and designed in the Rococo style of Sanssouci. Zeckern's cover as a wealthy investment banker had most likely influenced the purchase of such a stately home. His new wife, a seductive Austrian with long legs and a languorous, indifferent air about her, fit Zeckern well, also. Nadel had arrived just after lunch, stationing his men on the main avenue of approach. The men wore Polizei uniforms and carried new, state-of-the-art radios concealed under their clothing with earpieces and wrist microphones. Nadel himself wore a vibrating apparatus on his hip, radio-activated by the push of a button from each of his sentries.

"I have to sanitize our friend's home," Nadel had told them gravely, as they'd mustered a few blocks away. "The wife might get suspicious if she sees me with an earpiece. So, if there is a problem, you'll buzz me and I'll react accordingly."

The two sentries had been briefed about who they were looking for. According to Raban Nadel, the American was the murderer of Felix Roth *and* Oskar Zeckern. Though no accurate description was available—other than he looked "average"—they also knew the man was fully fluent in German. For that reason, the sentries, both former SS, had been given a very American phrase to yell at anyone who might fit the bill. If the person reacted with alarm, the SS had been instructed to kill him on sight. Armed with machine guns and pistols, each of the men, renowned for their weapons prowess, gave Nadel the assurance that they could take the American down cleanly.

Nadel had stationed them there an hour before, beginning his little ruse in a pleasant manner, just in case anyone else happened to be home. He'd arrived at the large home on Atzlerstrasse just a few minutes after 2:00 P.M. Pressing the doorbell with a rigid finger, Nadel listened to the deep chimes reverberating inside the large home.

There had been no answer.

The Austrian wife, as Nadel recalled, was quite independent, and owned a sporty British MG with a supercharger. The car, along with Zeckern's silver Mercedes, was parked in the back—Nadel had checked. Perhaps she was napping. He rang the bell again, following it with several sharp raps from the heavy doorknocker. Then, faintly, he heard thud of feet from one of the upper floors. Nadel slipped a breath mint into his mouth, knowing his plan involved unnecessary self-indulgence, but also knowing that he wouldn't be Raban Nadel if it didn't.

From the corner of his eye, Nadel could see through a sliver of beveled glass that framed the doorway. He pretended not to notice Zeckern's wife peer over the bannister of the stairwell. Nadel turned his head, aware that his profile was his best angle, and also so she might recognize him with such a limited perspective. When she continued her descent and turned onto the runner in the entrance hall, Nadel's manhood twitched when he realized she was wearing only a thin bathrobe. He heard the turn of the bolt, the click of handle, and turned to watch as the door was pulled halfway open. The wife, whose name was Katharina, tilted her head at Nadel, offering a polite smile that contained little warmth before she said his name—his cover name.

Nadel quickly removed his fedora, smiling back at this woman whose beauty he hadn't properly remembered. She must have been in the tub, judging by the beads of water on her upper chest and the sheen of perspiration about her forehead. Her sandy brown hair was pinned up behind her and he caught a faint whiff of lilac.

"Katharina, I'm very sorry to disturb you."

"I thought Dieter was with you," she said, referencing Zeckern's pseudonym. Per organizational rules, Katharina, like all wives and mistresses, knew nothing of the group's former service as Waffen-SS.

"Yes, well, he was with me. We had business together. But..." Nadel chewed the inside of his lip and made his face troubled, "...there's a small problem. That's why I'm here. Might I come inside?"

Katharina didn't move for a moment. She simply frowned. But the mention of trouble must have done the trick as she eventually opened the door wide. "Is he okay?"

Nadel stepped inside and placed his hat on the table in the entry hall. "He is, but I think you'll be disappointed by what I'm about to say. And, if I may be so bold as to surmise, I doubt you'll even be surprised."

She made no move to go any further. She stood right there, leaning against what was probably a closet or bathroom door, pinching the top of her robe shut while her other hand resided over her midsection. It was a protective stance.

Though he hid it well, he lustily drank in her form. This seduction was going to take all of his skill. He took a deep breath, trying to hide his attraction.

"My dear, this is difficult to say..."

"Out with it," she said brusquely, made all the more coarse by her Austrian accent.

"Dieter's been having an affair for quite some time." He chanced a look at Katharina, watching as the hand that had been holding the robe shut elevated to cover her mouth. "Normally I wouldn't get involved in such matters but, as you're surely aware, Dieter and I have many business interests together. His careless, thoughtless actions could jeopardize all of them."

He watched her carefully. As Nadel had suspected, especially dealing with a May-December romance, she wasn't hurt. No, not at all. Instead, she was pissed. Angry. Livid over that old buzzard thinking he could somehow do better than her. Nadel watched as she surely calculated the financial windfall that might soon come her way, but *only* if she could prove the affair.

Now, on to the second phase. He took a step closer.

"My dear, I want you to understand something."

"What?" she snapped, clearly distracted by her sudden anger.

"Dear, focus on what I'm about to say. There now, that's my girl," he said soothingly. "I'll give you more than sufficient evidence to get *all* that's coming to you in a divorce..." he let it hang. The phrase had done the trick.

"I'd appreciate that."

"I have everything you need. I have photos of him and a recording. I know the woman's address and even know where they prefer to go for overnight trips."

"That sneaky, duplicitous..." her voice trailed away.

*Here comes the close.*

Nadel bridged the gap, gently touching her shoulder. "My dear, bringing him down to earth by helping you successfully divorce him won't harm my financial dealings with him. In fact, I think it will refocus him. So, selfishly, it'll help protect my positions."

"Good," she said through clenched teeth. "I knew it...I knew something was going on and...well, things just haven't been right for a while."

*Perfect!*

"Katharina," Nadel said, swallowing the remainder of the nearly dissolved breath mint, "I'm unashamed to say that my personal motivations are also a bit selfish." He looked away briefly, for dramatic effect. "Katharina, forgive me for saying it, but I've always desired you."

Again this woman, this chilly gorgeous creature, pondered his inappropriate suggestion. She knew him to be married, but she also certainly knew that his net worth was ten times that of her aged husband. Nadel was also thirteen years younger than "Dieter," more handsome and, of course, far wealthier. She'd just been presented with the ability to take half of her husband's assets, along with the chance to begin an affair with a man who would be a significant upgrade in several key areas.

As he'd hoped it would, Nadel's indecent proposal had scored a direct hit. She showed a hint of a smile so he pulled her to him, giving her a passionate kiss while his hands roamed her body, drawing no protest at all. He embraced her, resting his chin on her shoulder, her womanly scent inflaming him as his mind screamed the question, "Does she live or die?"

"My dear," he said, pulling back from her. "Please, pack a bag. Dieter will be home later and I do *not* want you here. I will confront him then and come to you later."

"No, I want to tell that bastard that—"

He touched a finger to her lips. "You *will* have that chance. But first I have to confront him to protect my business interests." Nadel reached into his pocket, retrieving a key and pressing it in the palm of her hand. "The top suite at the Blume Hotel. I shall be there this evening, when I've secured both our futures." He lifted her chin with his finger. "And at that time, gorgeous, if you'll allow me, I want to make beautiful love to you."

She looked down at the key before clasping her fingers around it. "I need twenty minutes." A half-hour later, when she came back down with a fashionable Rimowa overnight case, Katharina said, "I'm trusting you, Dieter. But, thus far, you've shown me no proof."

Nadel crushed out his cigarette and reached into his jacket, producing a small photograph. It displayed Zeckern entering a hotel with a young woman, his hand perched just above her derriere.

"That slimy geezer," she seethed.

"He's a devil, alright." The photo had been taken at the organization's last meeting. The woman was simply a high-priced call girl. All of the men from the organization had taken one, but Zeckern—idiot he always was—had no idea he was being set up. Though Nadel certainly couldn't have seen all this coming, he'd planned to blackmail Zeckern at some point. It was all he could do not to chuckle over his keen prescience.

"Run along now, dear. I'll be there this evening, and what an evening it shall be." He lifted her hand, kissing it.

After staring back at him with a lusty gaze, she roared away in her MG. Even when she'd reached the top of the street, the overpowered car was still audible, screeching its tires up through the gears, well after it was out of sight.

Nadel stood in the doorway, having watched her go. His only true regret was his inability to tell Oskar Zeckern that, after tonight, he'd banged both of his wives.

"Well, old boy, you can't *always* get what you want." He closed the door and began his preparations for the American.

\*\*\*

As Marty neared a violent confrontation 270 kilometers away in Bayreuth, Werner Eisch reviewed the information shared with him by the U.S. Army's Criminal Investigations Division down in Frankfurt. Sitting in a quiet basement room, with waning light filtering in through a narrow window high on the outer wall, Werner eyed the stacks of files in front of him. He'd skimmed each of the files, finding nothing helpful on his first go-round. Now, having been through the personnel files a bit more carefully—and still finding nothing—Werner leaned back and tapped his prosthetic on his forehead. He was missing something, and he had a strong feeling it was right in front of him. Since he was alone, he spoke to himself.

"I've confirmed the identities of the men from the 101st SS Heavy Panzer Battalion who are alive and paying taxes. I've also found the certified death certificates of the members who were confirmed dead." He paused, thinking that through. "Some of those men could still be alive, as their death could have been faked in the war's final days. Despite all that, more than a dozen men are presumed dead, but were never found. Felix Roth was in that group." He lifted his notes. "As are these individuals, most of them former officers."

Werner turned his notepad back to the war-era roster he'd stapled to the page. Confirming what he'd read a dozen times, he continued to speak aloud, hoping it would help order his thoughts. "Of the officers who are missing, Raban Nadel was a company-level commander who took his position by brute force. And Oskar Zeckern was the battalion commander. By all accounts he was a pragmatist. According to intelligence, he's also thought to still be alive." Something occurred to Werner as he retrieved the thick stack of personnel files, locating the detailed file on the man named Oskar Zeckern. Born in 1909, he'd have been 36 years old at war's end. That's the right age for a battalion commander during wartime.

He turned to Raban Nadel's file, eyeing the picture taken in 1944. At 22 years of age, Nadel had been quite young, especially for a Waffen-SS company commander. Werner referenced Nadel's date of command, noticing that it was only a few months before the end of the war. In the picture, the handsome young man's chin was tilted up slightly and his eyes were narrowed. It made him appear egotistical. He reminded Werner of the star athlete/bully at many high schools—the fellow who couldn't let his accomplishments speak for themselves—the fellow who still had to prey on the weaklings in the hallway.

Nadel's death was presumed in May of 1945, the note stating that Nadel refused to take part in the organized surrender. He was one of a large group of SS believed to have been killed during the Battle of Berlin. Werner lifted the file containing information on numerous clashes during the battle, the Red Army's intelligence describing much of the SS portion of the battle as a "milk run," especially since the defiant SS had quickly run out of ammunition.

"Idiots," Werner breathed, wondering how any man could have still felt righteous by that point in the war. But, these weren't just "any men." These were the Schutzstaffel, chosen for their Aryan blood, for their willingness to fight and, in some cases, for their refusal to ever give up.

Though he'd done so before, Werner ran down the list of crimes attached to the 101st SS Heavy Panzer Battalion. Shaking his head, he skimmed the list, the content sickening him. There were at least three-dozen rapes, with names, places, dates, and ages. One line relayed the rape of four sisters in Belgium—it stated that the sisters' ages were 19, 16, 13 and 10. The girls had been left alive, although the 13-year-old succumbed to her injuries a week later.

"Vile savages."

In France, a farmer shot and killed a young SS from 3rd Company, claiming he'd caught the SS man in his home in the early hours of the morning. The file alleged that the farmer was drawn and quartered in front of

Charlie Company, but not before he was made to watch his wife and two daughters be violated by members of the company. Though the file didn't go into specifics, it said the wife and daughters were killed later that day.

Baker Company was accused of burning three French towns to the ground, the commander claiming that they were angered that each town had no food. Able Company was accused of pillaging a Dutch textile factory staffed mostly by women. They stole, raped and killed before burning the factory to the ground.

The list went on and on, with crimes in Russia, Poland, Germany, France, Belgium, the Netherlands and even a few in Luxembourg. There were multiple crimes associated with Americans, all occurring after June of 1944. One that briefly caught Werner's eye occurred in December of 1944, when the battalion XO killed five American POWs by execution. According to the succinct paragraph, the five Americans were pulled from a makeshift prison camp solely due to their large stature. The entry stated that the Schutzstaffel XO, a man later confirmed dead, was quite short and "despised big men." Because of their towering height, each American received a bullet in the forehead.

Werner went back to Nadel's file, staring at each of the pictures of the man. He burned the man's image into his mind—and it sickened him.

Nearly ready to wrap up, Werner flipped to the last page, eyeing several long entries that were listed from the war's final months. One entry he'd passed over several times before now caught his eye. The entry was from March 1945, titled "Massacre at Kastellaun." Next to the entry were three asterisks, then the words "see file ACF-SS-MK-345." Werner searched his stack of files, unable to find the file in question. He exited the room, walking to the records room at the end of the hallway. The heavy sergeant first class who'd so helpfully assisted him before pressed his cigarette into the glass ashtray's notch and stood.

"All done, detective? Been a long Saturday and I'm 'bout ready to get the heck outta here."

"Almost. Sergeant, might I see this file?" Werner asked, tapping the contracted title.

Probably in need of reading glasses, the sergeant held the paper away and at an angle. "Oh...that's a classified file."

"I can look at it right here if that helps."

The sergeant rubbed his chin. "Wait one." He ambled away, disappearing into the rows of files. A few minutes passed before he returned with a gangly major who looked like the type of man who'd be in charge of a basement full of files. With pale skin, dark eye sockets and an uninterested mien, the major barely arched his eyebrow.

"This here's the Berlin detective, major."

"So, I see."

"Good afternoon, major," Werner said, making his tone polite. "I was hoping to see this file, ACF-SS-MK-345."

"That's classified," the major said monotone.

"Ah, yes," Werner said, producing his travel orders, as well as the permissions he'd received from the civil section upon his arrival at the USAREUR headquarters.

"That's his orders I told you about," the sergeant first class offered.

The major briefly eyed the sheet of paper. Without a word, he walked away.

"I think he's gonna show you," the sergeant offered with a wink.

A moment passed before the major returned with the file. He unclasped the pages, removing several sheets of paper from the back of the file, reattaching the main set of pages and handing the remaining file to Werner. "You've got ten minutes and you must stand right here."

"May I ask what you removed?" Werner asked, gesturing his prosthetic to the pages in the major's hand.

"That portion of the file is for certain eyes only."

"Not my eyes, I take it?"

The major gave Werner a warmth-free, mouth-only smile.

After retrieving his notepad and pen, Werner began to read about the Massacre at Kastellaun. As he read, he became conscious of his breaths—they were coming quickly. Werner scribbled as fast as he could, getting as many of the salient points as he dared under the strict timetable.

"That's ten minutes," the major finally said, holding his hand out for the file.

Werner lifted his head, nudging his reading glasses down his nose. "Major, I need more time."

"You need more time to read about *your* countrymen slaughtering several hundred of mine?"

"It was a horrid, despicable incident for which I make no excuse. But I'm trying to solve a crime, here."

The major snatched the file away, carefully replacing the pages he'd held in his hand. "Solve away, detective, but you'll not see those pages again without a written order from the USAREUR commander. And you won't get that on a Saturday."

Werner eyed the major before turning to the helpful sergeant, who shrugged and gave Werner a regretful expression. Werner turned back to the major.

"Then may I ask one more thing of you?"

The major arched his eyebrows.

"Major, all of the men from the American 32nd Field Artillery, Able Battery, were killed, correct?"

"*Massacred.*"

"Yes, massacred." Werner cleared his throat. "I'm interested in seeing the roster of that battery."

"Your orders again," the major said, snapping his fingers. He eyed them before disappearing into the rows of files.

"Sorry he's down here, detective. But just think about my job," the sergeant whispered with a sour expression. "I have to live with him six days a week."

Werner shrugged. "He's not all that bad."

"Sheeeeit," the sergeant replied. "Word is that the major's birth certificate is a letter of apology from the prophylactic factory."

Werner allowed a small smile at the clever joke. Moments later, the major returned with two sheets of paper. There were punched holes in the top indicating that he'd taken them from a file. Werner scanned the roster, finding two men hailing from Oklahoma.

"Major, I'd like to see two personnel files."

"Nope. Not with the orders you were issued. Personnel files, of the living or dead, are of a higher classification."

Werner scribbled the names of the two Oklahomans. "Very well, sir. Thank you for your time."

The sergeant wished Werner luck. The major walked away without a word.

Moments later, Werner ran from the building into the waning light of the Frankfurt summer evening. He needed a pay phone because he desperately needed to speak with Lieutenant Mainhardt.

# Chapter Sixteen

Journal Entry

There's no other feeling in the world, at least none that I've ever experienced, like advancing in military vehicles. Maybe it's because a soldier spends so much damned time advancing, and retreating, by use of his LPC's. (LPC is a derogatory acronym for the dreaded, blister-inducing Army boot—the "Leather Personnel Carrier.") So, whenever a soldier gets to ride with a fresh cigarette dangling from his lips, and there's sun blazing down on his wind-chapped face, and the wisps of his hair that's gotten too long flutter above his ears, and the vibrations of the rough road and the coarse vehicle flow through his body, a soldier gets the treat of a sensation like none other. It's a feeling he'll almost certainly take for granted later in life. It's akin to the comfort of a warm and cozy bed. We all climb in bed each night and don't think a thing about it. But when you've slept in a pile of wet leaves for a week, that bed feels altogether different.

So, to us, riding—instead of walking—was sheer bliss.

Off we went in a convoy, unable to proceed tactically due to the narrow forest roads of Rheinprovinz. At first we were surrounded by lowlands, wet from all the snow melt. Soon, however, we motored into a hilly forest.

Having grown up in North Dakota, I quickly learned that the forests of Europe are much different than what I was used to. Back home, the only place a person can find a thick stand of trees is by a river or a pond. And even then, most of our wooded areas are scrubby and knotty. The forests of Western Europe, however, are deep, dark places that go on and on and on. The canopy of trees is so thick it's not uncommon to be unable to find a single ray of sunlight peeking through. And the forest floor, often covered in a carpet of pine needles, is so soft it buffers sound, making the forest eerily quiet.

But this particular forest was a bit different. While still pristine in spots, it was battle-scarred in others. Some of the forest's towering trees had been splintered by artillery and mortars. For all we knew, our own battery could have been to blame for the shelling. Friendly area one day might have been in enemy hands a week before. The blasted-out areas of the canopy bled light down on the destruction that lay below. We went through one section, finding the charred remains of a German Panzer unit. Thankfully, all the bodies had been cleared away. Nobody in their right mind likes seeing corpses—even enemy corpses.

We'd been lumbering slowly through the forest, our crew sitting atop our old M5 tracked vehicle while some newbie private drove. A Howitzer section is supposed to have seven soldiers, but I'd yet to see a single tube with that many. The most we'd ever had was six, and that was way back when we'd first gotten to Scotland. Uncle Sam moves men from unit to unit and, as casualties and sickness mounted, our number soon fell to four. About a month before the massacre, when Lieutenant Breston first arrived, we got a load of newbies along with him, including the kid driving our track. With the war all but done, us "old timers" found it was easier to do the skilled jobs ourselves.

The kid—his name was Pollack—was our driver and ammo handler. When we were shooting the gun, his job was to "stack the bricks," meaning to keep the rounds staged and nearby for fast loading. Despite some of the razzing we gave him, he was a good kid and took orders well.

As we drove through that bombed-out forest, we suddenly stopped. Whenever a convoy halts, it's extremely vulnerable. We'd been trained long before, during any stoppage, to provide cover. John Vincent, the crack-shot of our bunch, jumped up on the mounted fifty-cal, aiming opposite of the crew in front of us. Pollack, the newbie, aimed his rifle from his seat. Kenny, Danny and I piled out, taking up positions around the track, aiming at nothing while the whole battery cursed our new XO who was probably lost.

Again.

After a few minutes, we saddled up and started moving again. Creeping. At one point, when the road curved, I could see Breston in the Jeep out front. He and his driver were pointing all around with Breston's map spread all about the Jeep.

Yep. Lost.

We stopped two more times, executing the same cover drill as soldiers broke regulations by openly cursing the XO.

On the third stop, the grumbling had turned to shouts in the direction of XO Breston. I'd gotten out and walked to the left, keeping my rifle at the ready but joining in the chorus of bitching. I could see that Breston was out of the Jeep, trying to get his bearings with his map and compass. Then the canvas of the deuce-and-a-half whipped up and out tumbled a ghostly white Captain Rook. Though he definitely looked sick, I could tell he was mad as hell. He stalked up to the new XO and began yelling.

I took up a position behind a stump, about twenty feet off the road. The forest here was the pristine variety I'd remarked on earlier. There was no evidence that there was a war going on. In fact, from where I'd provided cover, it was one of the most peaceful spots I'd ever seen. Just below us, a brook could be heard trickling with snow runoff. To my left, a gentle rise led to the high point, and a small shed could be seen at the top.

Since this was our third time dismounting, we probably were guilty of not being on our highest alert. We were irritated. Adding to our frustration, the sun was westering and, unlike when it was high above, it actually did penetrate the thick forest. From its afternoon angle, it beamed in low and blinding. I remember turning to look behind me, at our towed gun, and seeing Kenny Martin on the other side, smoking a cigarette and shaking his head at me. But when I looked to the west, behind the gun, I was blinded from the sun.

I became aware of a faint noise, coming off and on, that continued to draw my attention. It was a squeaking sound.

"You hear that?" I hissed at Kenny. He shrugged. Kenny had been slightly injured by a mortar a few months back and his hearing still hadn't fully recovered.

"John?"

"Yeah, I hear it," he answered. "Sounds like tracks moving. Probably Baker Battery."

"Where's it coming from?" I asked.

He pointed behind us, to the sun. That was the direction I heard, too.

"Can you see anything?" I asked.

"Sun's too damned bright."

No one seemed incredibly concerned about the sounds. I guess what I now know colors my memories, but I still recall finding those sounds unsettling. The words from the movement briefing continued to echo through my mind. The XO had been reading from his notes when he told us about the possibility of left-behind German soldiers or units.

Units...

I don't recall that word ever having been used before. Unfortunately, whoever wrote that intel report had been spot-on. Boy, I wish we'd have taken it seriously.

***

By the time Marty closed in on Oskar Zeckern's street, the day's long twilight had cast flattering, roseate light on the handsome homes. As he'd left the center of Bayreuth, the *Stadtmitte*, he'd walked through a tony business district that had obviously been untouched by the war. He'd seen numerous law offices, fine clothing boutiques, ritzy restaurants and high-end jewelers. And now, just past the business district loomed the towering green trees, the colossal homes and the hushed exclusivity that typically represented the affluent area of a city. Just one glance told Marty that this was the correct postal code, the "blue" side of town, the place where the bourgeois resided. The type of money these people had, generational money, ran deep enough to survive even the most catastrophic of wars. Long, curving brick driveways supported big Mercedes and BMWs. The homes all had artfully landscaped lawns, decorative windows and exceptional architectural features—the neighborhood hit all the right notes to easily set it apart as the quintessential place to live in Bayreuth.

After making a left and a right, Marty found Zeckern's street, passing by where it intersected the much busier Regensburgstrasse. He'd done this deliberately, wanting to view Zeckern's street from several blocks away. The street itself was straight, and ran slightly downhill from where he stood. Only a few cars were parked on the sides of the street and there was no through traffic. This was good. Marty wanted as few witnesses as possible.

He continued on, searching for an isolated spot, finding it in the form of a creek two blocks ahead. Marty crossed the road over the creek, turning right and quickly navigating the drainage runoff that led down from the street. Below the road, he stood in a broad culvert, careful to keep his feet dry. Then he waited, his eyes scanning all around for other people. After Marty was satisfied that no one was nearby, he began his preparations.

As the creek trickled lazily by, Marty opened his bag, donning the pilfered brown and red jumpsuit that represented the Bayreuthwerk Electric Utility Company. Marty clipped the tool belt around his waist, adjusting it so it hung loose. He then chambered a round in the Russian TT-30 pistol and placed it in his large cargo pocket. Next, Marty assembled the PPS submachine gun, keeping the curved magazine of rounds in his pocket. After hiding the rifle and his bag in some creek-side brush, he glanced up at the road, still struck with the unsettling feeling that he was being watched. He saw no one.

*You've been paranoid all day long. Take a few deep breaths and get on with things—it's time.*

But Marty knew this time was different. Much different. The first three interrogations had all been targeted at law-abiding men. Yes, they were former SS, but now they seemed to be trying to toe the line. Though any number of things could have gone wrong, Marty had felt reasonably comfortable with the results of each interrogation. Then came the Felix Roth debacle. Roth hadn't known who Marty was and, even with the element of surprise on Marty's side, Marty considered himself lucky for not getting killed.

But now that Roth had died, now that Marty had left a witness alive and even spilled his guts to Roth's lover, the stakes were most certainly going up.

Marty knew very well that Zeckern could have somehow found out that he was being hunted. Whoever this organization was, be they ODESSA, or the Legion of Former Schutzstaffel, or even the mythical organization Werewolves...whoever they were, they surely knew that one of their own, Felix Roth, had been killed. Perhaps they were now simply more vigilant. Or, maybe they, or the Polizei, had learned more about Marty from evidence left at the scene in Gleiberg. Or, God forbid, perhaps they'd found Roth's girl, Gloria, and forced her to talk. She may have even sought them out—there was no way to know and Marty had to consider all possibilities.

Therefore, Marty knew he could be walking into a hornet's nest...

There was only one way to find out.

Purposefully leaving the machine gun behind, he climbed the dry runoff from the culvert and headed toward Oskar Zeckern's home.

***

The ashtray overflowed. Nadel lifted it from the Victorian table, carrying the ashtray to the toilet and dumping the contents. He flushed the toilet, moodily watching the butts and ash get whisked away, mildly curious if the entire clump of refuse would disappear. It did, making him fleetingly proud that the toilet was a German brand, pre-war, of course. A fastidiously neat man, he rinsed the ashtray, wiping the white porcelain clean before carrying it back to the table by the window.

"What the hell am I doing here?" he asked the empty house, taking up Rodin's Thinker-pose once again. "I should leave those men out there and get my ass over to the Blume Hotel. I could enjoy a fine meal, alone, finishing with several cups of strong, laced coffee. The meal and coffee will give me energy and the brandy will settle my nerves. I could then go to the suite, disrobe, and take the hottest of showers. Then, sufficiently clean once again, I should push that delicious *Östi*, Katharina, down to the floor and command her to—"

Nadel's ribald aside was cut off by the buzzing on his thigh. It startled him, making him jump. He snatched the handset from the table and hissed, "What is it?"

"Wait one," came the whispered reply.

Nadel shoved the chair out of the way, peering out the window and up the street, searching for anything out of the ordinary. The panel van, where his two men currently resided, was parked up the road on the right side. If his man was whispering, then whoever they were calling about must be close. But Nadel could see no one. Finally the radio clicked.

"We've got one man, on foot."

"Okay. A man on foot. We've had that five times today, four of them walking their dog."

"You probably can't see him yet because he's in front of the van."

"What about him?" Nadel asked.

"He's wearing a utility worker's overalls…electric company. Thomas says it's the correct uniform. The guy's got tools and is checking the junction boxes on the base of the lines."

Nadel blinked as he pondered this. "Could be a cover."

"Agree," chimed in his man hidden midway up the street. "We picked him up as soon as he turned down the street off of Regensburgstrasse."

"Did you see a work truck?"

"No."

"Then we just watch and wait," Nadel said.

Just then, Nadel saw him. He lifted his binoculars, watching the man in the canvas jumpsuit crossing the street opposite the van. He walked to the power pole, looking at something at its base and writing on his clipboard. To Nadel, the scene seemed quite innocuous.

"Do you see him yet?" Nadel's man asked.

"Yeah, checking poles."

"There's someone following him."

"Who?"

"Keep watching behind him, once he starts moving."

The utility worker began walking again, moving diagonally to the next pole across the street. "I don't see anyone else," Nadel said testily, peering all around with the binoculars.

"The other guy is ducking for cover then moving. He's in front of the van right now but you should pick him up in just a second."

Nadel could barely swallow. "Who is it?"

"See him?"

"No, damn it!" Nadel snapped. "That's why I asked. Who is it?"

"Just some kid."

"A kid?"

"Yeah. Here he comes now."

Just then, Raban Nadel saw a young man flash from in front of the van. He sprinted across the street, ducking behind a manicured hedgerow. Even at a distance, with the aid of the binoculars, Nadel could tell he was probably no more than 13 years old.

*A kid. Why would a kid be following a utility worker?* Nadel touched the walnut stock of his rifle as he chewed on the inside of his cheek. *Maybe the utility worker is genuine and the kid's just amusing himself, playing cops and robbers at the worker's expense. Or, maybe this is part of the murdering sonofabitch's ruse—throwing us off by having a kid trailing him.*

Nadel lifted his radio. "Train your rifles on them *both* and just be ready for my order to fire." From beside him, the former SS commander slid the tall tripod over. He lifted the old, trusty Mauser 98, clipping the screwed-in base into the top of the rigid tripod. Shoving the chair aside, Nadel took up a firing position behind the rifle, adjusting it so he'd be firing through the empty pane where the glass had been earlier. He lifted a shiny 7.92 millimeter hyper-velocity round from the box on the table. After fingering the round for a moment, Nadel patiently inserted it into the breach. He slid the bolt forward, snapping the handle down once the round was satisfyingly seated. With a deep breath he settled behind the stock of the legendary rifle, eyeing the utility man in his scope.

His target was currently about 300 meters away. Nadel swiveled the rifle to the left, seeing the kid. Holding the radio in his left hand, Nadel's right finger rested on the trigger. He continued to watch.

\*\*\*

Marty was halfway down the street, doing all he could not to stare at the Zeckern house. He'd just passed a panel van, trying to see inside as he'd passed the rear windows. The van seemed to belong to a handyman of some sort as the glass was obscured by work racks with hanging tools. Given the high income of the street's inhabitants, he wrote the van off—somebody was probably having work done on their house.

*At this hour?* He turned and looked at the van again. Dark and silent. After a moment's thought, Marty chose to ignore it. Just a van...

Although he'd studied several pictures of Oskar Zeckern, Marty knew the man might have changed his appearance. Therefore, his plan would require thinking on the fly. Once Marty reached the end of the street he'd be directly in front of the Zeckern mansion. At that time he planned to check the junction box in front of the house, then approach the home and knock on the door. If whomever answered the door wasn't Zeckern—a woman or a teenager, for instance—Marty would ask about flickering power, power spikes, and things of that nature.

If a man remotely fitting Zeckern's description answered, Marty would consult his clipboard and say, "Herr Dieter Siegst?" Dieter Siegst was Zeckern's pseudonym. He'd then inform the man that there had been reports of flickering power on the street. He'd ask "Herr Siegst" if he or his family had noticed the flickering. The "family" portion was intended to get Zeckern to divulge if anyone else was home. If there were others there, Marty would initiate his backup plan. He'd wait for darkness and kill the power to the Zeckern home—after he'd retrieved his rifle. Then he'd wait for his moment because, eventually, he felt the family would leave and he'd get an opportunity to create a solo encounter with Zeckern. Marty hoped he didn't have to use this plan because it was fraught with holes.

But if Zeckern were home alone, Marty planned to quickly pull the pistol and go inside. Then he planned to have a nice long talk with Herr Zeckern about Raban Nadel. Despite all the angles, Marty felt good about this plan. At the next power pole, he eyed the mansion, seeing nothing out of the ordinary. He decided to let this be his last pole before he walked up to—

A scraping sound, behind him...

Marty whipped his head around, stunned to see a young man running and ducking behind a stone-built, ivy-covered mailbox on the far side of the street. *Was that Josh?* Unable to reconcile what his eyes had witnessed, Marty stalked to the mailbox, leaning around and grabbing Josh's shirt, lifting him from his crouch.

"Josh, what in the hell are you doing here?" Marty thundered.

Mouth hanging open, Josh was momentarily dumbstruck.

\*\*\*

"What's going on?" Nadel hissed into the handset.

"The electric worker is yelling at the kid. We're going to roll down the window and try to hear," the former SS replied.

Using the rifle scope, Nadel watched the scene playing out 250 meters away. The utility man had discovered the kid following him and had snatched him up by his scruff. Something about the exchange seemed wrong. If some kid decided to have fun by playing a little game of cops and robbers, why should that worker be so pissed?

*Maybe that's the utility worker's own child,* Nadel reasoned. *He certainly seems familiar with him. Maybe he's angry that he's so far from home, or not doing his homework, or who knows what?*

*Stay ready,* Nadel told himself. *But don't be hasty with your hostility. Cleaning up an unnecessary bloodbath out on the street, even with your connections, could be a serious problem.*

He readjusted his position on the sturdy Gewehr rifle and awaited word from his men.

***

"I asked you a question!" Marty bellowed. "What in the hell are you doing here?"

"I...I..."

Marty released Josh's shirt, closing his own eyes as he summoned patience. "Okay, Josh," Marty said, voice quavering as he tried to sound reasonable. "I'm not mad at you. I want you to take a deep breath and relax."

Josh did.

"Now, tell me why you're here."

"I didn't believe you this morning," Josh said. "About selling the Russian guns."

***

"Can you hear anything?" Nadel hissed.

"We're trying to, dammit!" came the reply. "I can't hear if you keep calling."

Nadel released the radio and spat in anger.

***

"You didn't believe me, so you *followed* me?" Marty asked, his voice rising again.

"I've known for a week that you don't always tell me the truth."

*Outed by a damned kid!* "Well, how the hell did you get here?"

"I took the train."

"My train?"

"Yes. I was in the car behind you," Josh said, smiling weakly.

"Where did you get the money for a ticket?"

"I took it from my bank."

"Did you tell your mother?"

175

"Sort of."

"Sort of? She's probably going nuts," Marty barked.

Head drooping, Josh nodded.

"Dammit, Josh, it'll be tomorrow before I can even get you back to Berlin. There's not another train tonight."

\*\*\*

Nadel's radio crackled before his man's voice came through loud and clear. "It's him! The kid followed him from Berlin."

"What?"

"He just said they both came from Berlin," Nadel's man said, his tone adamant. "Isn't that where Felix's killer was from?"

"Shoot them both," Nadel said, the realization coming to him. "Do it now!"

"Out on the street? The kid, too?"

"Do it!" Nadel roared.

The former SS commander adjusted the rifle slightly to the left, sighting the man in the utility worker's jumpsuit.

"Got you now, *Wichser*."

# Chapter Seventeen

Journal Entry

I kept hearing the noise from the west.

Our column of vehicles had been stationary for at least ten minutes. I was away from our track, providing cover to the left. As I looked back to the west, the only thing I could see was the ammo carrier and the first sergeant's Jeep, both of them in the rear of the column. The first sergeant, we called him "Top," had gotten out and walked by us, just as he had at every stop. His driver was out of the Jeep now, standing with the ammo drivers, all of them "smoking and joking" with their helmets off.

creak—creak--creak

There it went again. Squeaking and a slight rumble. "Danny," I called out, unable to see him but knowing he was mirroring me on the other side.

"Yeah?"

"You hear that?"

"Yeah. Somebody said it's probably Baker or Charlie."

"Sounds and seems heavier," I said. "Feel the rumble?"

That made everyone grow quiet for a moment. John was up on top of the track and broke the silence. "Damned if it doesn't. The M-fives make a clicking sound. What I'm hearing sounds kinda like our new Pershing tanks. And I can feel the shake of the ground, too, even up here."

"But heavy armor shouldn't be this far back, unless the XO screwed up and took us past the front line," Kenny added.

"Oh shit," John muttered. "That'd be just great."

"We didn't go far enough," Danny added. "We'd have come to the Rhine. Maybe some unit was down for a bit and now they're heading back to the front."

"Hey!" I called out to the first sergeant's driver and the two privates in the ammo carrier. "Get your gear on and provide cover back there! You think this is your uncle's yearly camping trip? Can't you hear that movement behind us?"

Grumbling, the trio donned their helmets and staggered to positions at the rear of the convoy.

Aside from the mechanical sounds of a moving unit and the chatter and cursing of the dismounted battery, I could hear the argument between Captain Rook and the new XO, who had been navigationally challenged since his arrival.

I walked to them.

"I'm tellin' ya, this crossroads here doesn't exist," Breston said, frantically poking the map.

Rook was green with sickness. Sweat beaded from every pore on his face. His voice was weak. "It doesn't exist, Phil, because we're nowhere near that spot."

Breston moved the map in front of Rook. "Then where are we?"

"If you'll shut the hell up for a minute, maybe I can figure it out."

Breston turned as I approached. "What do you want?" he snapped.

What I wanted was to punch the new XO in his face. Twice. Instead, I made my tone respectable. "Begging both your pardons, but is Baker or Charlie, or one of the heavy armor troops, bringing up our rear?"

Breston grimaced as if I'd just asked the stupidest question imaginable. Rook, however, slowed by sickness, swallowed thickly and cocked his head, taking longer to respond. "Baker and Charlie should be abreast of us but, since we're a *little* out of position…" he yelled that part, "…it's entirely possible that they're behind us. And all armor units are supposed to be out front, leading this Rhine charge. Why?"

"We're hearing mechanized sounds to the west," I said, thumbing that direction. "Sounds heavy."

Rook looked west, shading his eyes. "Sun's blinding."

My track was about fifty yards behind us. None of us were acting tactically, so I called out to John since he was sitting up top. "John, you still hear it?"

"Nah. Gone all quiet, now."

Breston put his hands on his hips, speaking academically. "Sounds can be deceiving, sergeant. Especially with the sound waves bouncing all around these hills. This is the Hunsrück mountain range, you know."

"Mountains?" I asked, unable to stop myself. "You know the names of these piss-ant hills but can't follow the roads on the map?"

My insolence earned me an ass-chewing.

While the XO ripped into me—and he was right to do it, despite the fact that he couldn't read a map—Captain Rook trudged over to his Jeep. He lifted the radio, asking Baker and Charlie to call in their positions. As the positions came back, Breston, at least able to mark coordinates, noted them with a grease pencil.

"They're here," the XO said, proudly holding his fingers on the map as if he'd just done something remarkably difficult.

"Now we need to know where *we* are," Rook said.

"May I?" I asked. The two officers stepped aside, though Breston was hesitant.

"Okay," I said, finding Kastellaun. "We started well to the west of town, went around it, then crept due east. We picked up this brook to our north and then we took the left here, keeping the brook off to our left."

"You took the left?" Rook asked incredulously. "You should have taken a right."

I stabbed the map. "My guess is we're about right here."

"With Able and Baker damn near two miles to the east," Rook added, his rheumy eyes glaring at Breston. "Where's the tac-map?"

Breston removed his helmet, rubbing his hair as his pale cheeks flushed. He let out a few loud breaths and trudged to the passenger side of the Jeep, coming back with the rolled tactical map. When he unrolled it, showing the positions of units that were updated only a few hours ago, Rook covered his eyes with his hand.

"Great job, Phil. Can't you see the defined salient here? Our division pushed forward like an arrow and we were supposed to move forward inside the protection of the salient. But somehow, you walked us clear off the left flank, leaving us naked as a jaybird."

"It's easy to get turned around," Breston griped, gesturing behind the convoy. "Dickhead here just said all these hills look the same."

"I didn't say that." Then I turned, gesturing down to the valley. "A good navigator reads terrain features, sir…things like a well-defined brook."

The XO reddened, his eyes blazing fury, as he opened his mouth to lay into me again.

And that's when, at the rear of our convoy, the first sergeant's Jeep and the ammo carrier both exploded.

***

Marty had calmed down and slowed his questioning. Josh explained that he'd left a note for his mother telling her the truth that he was traveling with Marty today and would be back when Marty came back. That, in itself, was flabbergasting enough. He didn't tell his mother that he was following Marty—just that he was traveling *with* him. So, of course, he gave her no indication of when he'd be home.

As Marty was pondering this, a glint of a reflection in the dusky evening caught his eye as the door to the panel van swung open. Marty looked over, seeing that actually both front doors were swinging open.

The doors were being pushed open by two serious-looking men—men with machine guns at the ready.

Josh pointed. "Hey, what are those men doi—"

Marty grabbed him and thrust him toward the driveway where he'd been hiding earlier. Josh sprawled on the concrete, tripped by the slight rise between the driveway and the road. Marty followed, leaning forward as he reached down to lift Josh from the ground.

Somewhere in the blaring cacophony of klaxons in Marty's mind, he heard the gunshots.

His training taking over, Marty had but one current mission: RUN!

***

Nadel saw the spark and puff of smoke where his first 7.92 millimeter round had impacted the macadam just behind where the American sonofabitch had stood. He'd been spooked by the men emerging from the van and moved just as Nadel had squeezed off what would have surely been a fatal chest shot.

"*Scheisse!*" Nadel shouted to the heavens, his hand snatching another round as his jerky movements sent the box of bullets clattering from the Victorian table down to the hardwood floor. Ignoring the racket, Nadel yanked the bolt backward, seating another round as the two figures began to run to the left.

*Two more seconds and they're gone.*

Moving the rifle smoothly on the tripod and adding just a hint of a lead to his aim—as if he were in the Schwarzwald shooting fast-flying pheasant—Nadel gingerly pulled the trigger and watched the results with satisfaction.

A burst of pink spray signified to him that he'd made a clean hit on the man just before the twosome disappeared behind a home.

Nadel lifted the radio, feeling like an all-powerful deity as he said, "Got him. Get over there and finish them both. Then take their bodies, and get to the rally point."

Checking his watch, Nadel knew he had about five minutes more than he normally would. He'd made arrangements for any reports of gunshots, or other suspicious activities, to be delayed at the Bayreuth Polizei dispatch. But, prudent man that he was, he also knew there were other problematic possibilities. What if a Polizei lived on this street? Doubtful, given the income needed to own a home here, but it was still a possibility. Or what if someone had a direct line to the BKA or the American military? All of these, and more, potential stumbling blocks flashed through his mind.

Despite the mitigated risk, Nadel decided to keep the rifle mounted on the tripod for another minute. He wanted the warm assurance that both humans had been dispatched. Then he could clean up this little disturbance before sinking himself into Zeckern's wife—a woman he would regretfully have to dispose of soon thereafter.

Lighting a Gitane, Nadel watched his men rush across the street and into the driveway, machine guns at the ready. And thankfully, no one else could be seen.

Nadel breathed deeply, the fine cigarette mixing nicely with the smell of cordite, taking him back to the heady days of the war. The accuracy of his shot, the adrenaline of the situation, and the pungent smells painted a satisfied grin on his face.

There was a burst of static from the radio. Then silence.

"Report in," Nadel barked.

"They're gone."

"What?" Nadel shouted.

"There's some blood here, but the man and the kid are gone."

"Find them, dammit!"

\*\*\*

Moments before, Marty had tripped as he'd been shot, rolling forward before scampering through the occupied carport where he'd hidden behind a trellis.

He'd yanked the TT pistol from his pocket, spying Josh further back in the lush yard, flat on the ground behind a raised flowerbed.

"Don't move," Marty whispered, covering his lips with his finger. Josh nodded eagerly. To his credit, he seemed alive with energy but unafraid.

As Marty's shoulder burned, the voices were clear through the carport. He pulled a stem of the flowering vine aside, seeing the two men. One was providing cover, sweeping a machine gun in an arc in Marty's general direction. The other was staring down the street as he spoke on a handheld radio, probably talking to whoever had shot Marty in the shoulder.

Suddenly, a woman's voice joined the conversation. Marty watched as the man on the radio told her to go back inside and lock her doors. "This is Polizei business, ma'am," the man said authoritatively. Marty heard a door slam.

As the man went back to his radio, Marty became keenly aware of the intensity of his injury. Hissing from the searing pain, it was all Marty could do not to eye his shoulder. Having been shot before, he knew it was best not to look.

Listening to the radio exchange but unable to clearly hear the man on the other end of the radio, Marty could tell the men were about to give chase. He was torn on whether to shoot through the trellis, or allow them to reach the backyard. Then he remembered Josh, thirty feet away, and that cemented Marty's decision.

Don't hesitate.

"...well he sure kept on running!" the man yelled into the radio. "I'm telling you, he's not here." The man listened before turning to his partner.

"Let's clear the area behind those cars and then head through the backyard. Boss said he couldn't have gotten far."

*Boss.*

The 116 millimeter barrel slid through the flowering vine like a hungry snake. The weapon felt quite similar to an M1911 and, in a brief moment of fear, Marty hoped it worked like one.

Radio slung on his belt, the talker joined his fellow man. Marty studied them, both wearing the uniform of the Bayern Polizei. They moved with efficiency, clearing the space between the cars like seasoned pros.

*Polizei...am I getting ready to shoot two cops?*

Twenty feet remained between Marty and his pursuers.

"Careful," one of the men said to the other. They were on the outside of the two cars, coming Marty's way. Once they cleared the space in front of the cars, they would have to walk to Marty's right to pass through to the backyard. That was the kill zone.

"All clear here," the one on the outside said.

"Tiny blood drops leading to the backyard. Nadel's estimation of his shooting prowess exceeds his skill," the other man remarked sourly.

*Nadel! Nadel is here!*

"Hey, no names," the radio talker hissed.

They'd almost moved into the kill zone.

Marty chanced another look back. Josh was *gone.* Keeping the pistol in place, Marty whipped his head all around.

"He's not in the carport," came the radioman's voice, just as he'd walked to the front of one of the cars.

It was time.

A faint hissing sound caught Marty's attention. He looked to his left, seeing Josh standing in the adjacent yard, screened by a row of spruce trees. The boy was peering through, silently motioning to Marty. Glancing back, the two men were standing just feet away, murmuring about the danger of walking into the back yard.

"You cover left and I'll cover right. Even though he's hit, the guy could start shooting."

"Let's go."

Marty looked back to Josh. He was signaling for Marty to come.

***

"Careful," the senior man whispered. "Wait for my count."

"Got it. You-left, me-right."

The men nodded their agreement. Just inside the trellis' threshold, the senior man mouthed the countdown, *"Drei...Zwei...Eins...Gehe!"*

Machine guns leading the way, the two men burst into the backyard.

Just a well-manicured lawn.

After clearing the space and communicating their negative findings, the senior man lifted the radio. "No sign of him back here."

"I hit that sonofabitch!" Nadel growled. "He's either hiding or he didn't make it far."

"We saw the blood, but not much. Maybe you just nipped him."

"It was a clean hit," Nadel's voice roared over the radio. "Find them!"

After a brief consultation, the two men continued on through the back yard, headed to the rear of the homes on the adjacent street.

***

Marty and Josh watched the two men go, racing through the yards and disappearing around the large homes on the next street. They were already hundreds of meters away. Rather than wait, Marty urged Josh to run parallel to their street, telling him to stay in the back of the homes, running behind the cover of the row of spruces.

When they'd gone through three back yards, a tall ivy-covered wall halted them. Marty told Josh to stop. He grasped his shoulders as he spoke

182

through heaving breaths. "Did you see me when I went into the culvert down at the creek?" Marty asked.

"Yes."

"Good. Run as fast as you can, okay? Cross the street, get behind the next row of homes, then turn left and make your way to the creek. When you get there, go towards the road and meet me down in the culvert, okay?"

Josh reached up and touched the crimson stain at Marty's shoulder. "Are you okay?"

"Yes. Just haul ass and if I don't make it, stay there until it's fully dark, then pound on the doors of one of those houses till someone helps you, got it?"

"You *will* make it."

"I agree. But, just in case." Marty gave Josh's shoulders a shake. "I want you to run as fast as you ever have when you cross the street."

"Because they will shoot?"

"Yes."

Josh gritted his teeth but managed a smile. "I'll run faster than I ever have."

"Good. Get to it."

Marty watched him go. He jogged until he was out in the open. Then he sprinted with his feet hardly touching the ground. Wincing, Marty waited on the gunshot that never came. When Josh reached the safety of the homes on the other side of the street he turned, beckoning Marty.

*The men in the van were on my right. But I was shot from the left.*

*And they'd said "Nadel" was a poor shot.*

*Nadel…*

*He's still up there in Zeckern's house.*

*Raban Nadel…*

Knowing what was coming, Marty dug deep for the energy to endure this dash. He unbuckled the tool belt, flinging it upward and lodging it unseen in a dense conifer. Pistol in hand, Marty would jog while he was behind the cover of the hedgerow, saving his sprint for the crossing of the street.

"Hurry!" Josh yelled.

\*\*\*

Once his men had given chase to the west, Nadel had known that his target, assuming he was still mobile, might double back. Spitting his Gitane to the floor, Nadel grasped another bullet, reloading the rifle. Now he stayed focused on the road, watching it without the aid of the scope. When the boy sprinted from behind the hedgerow, it was all Nadel could do not to aim and shoot. But the boy wasn't the prize.

"Come on," the ex-SS urged through clenched teeth. "I got you once and I'll get you again."

Five seconds. Ten seconds. As he waited, he allowed his left hand to slide forward, caressing the warm rifle barrel the way he might touch the smooth skin of a woman's inner thigh. Again he smelled the cordite. He felt the welcome sweat on his palms. The adrenaline coursed through his body.

It was 1944 all over again.

***

Each jarring movement sent stabs of electricity through Marty's shoulder. As he jogged behind the long hedgerow, the pain became quite localized, hurting the most at the rear edge of his left shoulder. Marty could feel the blood oozing all the way to the small of his back, making him wonder how long he had before he fell unconscious. He looked up, watching Josh, his face splotchy and red, urging Marty on.

When Marty reached the end of the driveway, he sprinted forward, running as fast as he could. His legs and arms pumped with renewed vigor, propelling him into the street. There was a slight drop between the driveway and the street. Coupled with the gait-altering wound on Marty's shoulder, the sudden descent, even though minuscule in height, was enough to send Marty sprawling. He fell forward, splayed on the ground, barely managing to hold onto the Russian pistol as the rough macadam shredded his left hand and chin.

Just as he'd come to a halt, a spark and a puff of dust to Marty's left signified a gunshot, quickly followed by the report to Marty's right. Marty looked to the origin of the sound, to Zeckern's house at the end of the street. He hadn't seen it before, but now, with dusk upon the neighborhood, each of the windows of the Zeckern home shone with mirror-like reflectivity. But on one upstairs window, on the left side of the home, one single pane didn't shimmer. It was a dull black.

The glass of that single pane had been removed.

Though he was faintly aware of Josh's yells, Marty got to his feet, turning and staring at the black rectangle. The longer he looked, he was able to make out the frontal silhouette of the rifle, perched just inside. It was mounted on a tripod. Five full seconds had passed, and Marty knew he was leaving himself open for the kill shot. He was able to discern motion inside the window...

A man.

***

Nadel knew his shot would have killed the running man but, clumsy sonofabitch, the man had fallen flat on his damned face, unknowingly saving his life. Then, in one of the brassier displays Nadel had ever witnessed, the man got up and faced Nadel. Stood there, dumbly, as if he were in a trance.

*This'll be your undoing, smart bastard!*

Nadel greedily thrust his hand down to the box of rounds, suddenly remembering that he'd spilt them on the floor.

*Damn!*

When Nadel stooped down for another bullet, glass shattered and fell all around him. Then came the report.

The sonofabitch was shooting!

\*\*\*

"Marty, come on!" Josh pleaded.

Marty heard him but, at the same time, he didn't. One part of his brain registered the request, and wanted to act on it. But another section of Marty's brain, that icy cold wretchedness reserved only for the deeply scorned, overrode the request. The wretchedness urged Marty forward, despite the risk, challenging him to end the years of misery, here and now.

Despite the war in two areas of his mind, the cognitive side of Marty's brain worked the shooting problem as the simple physics and geometry calculation it was. Few people realize the true range of a powerful handgun. In the military, handgun training is designed for close-quarters and short-range combat only. And it's true; handguns aren't typically effective over long ranges.

A handgun can fire a bullet a great distance. During his own Army training, Marty witnessed a handgun, a .45 revolver, sturdily mounted in a machine rest, that fired a three shot grouping of less than six inches—from a range of 150 yards. It's doubtful that a human being could achieve such accuracy due to the difficulty of accurately sighting such an extremely short barrel. But if a person could create such a steady platform, long shots from the right type of pistol could theoretically be successfully achieved.

In this current problem, Marty was firing at a large window, probably around six feet high and three feet wide. Nadel—or whoever the shooter was—probably didn't believe Marty could kill him over such range, not with a handgun. Now Marty wondered if the bastard would risk standing at the window, shooting back with the rifle while Marty fired the pistol.

Had they been playing head-to-head poker, Marty's odds would have stood at less than two percent.

But occasionally, even poker players with a powerful hand get "backdoored." And Marty hoped to backdoor Nadel right here.

The former American soldier began to fire the pistol, slowly pulling the trigger after carefully aiming each shot above the top edge of the tall window.

\*\*\*

Nadel risked a glance at the man, slowly walking in his direction, the pistol aimed at the window. *A pistol! Ha! Try to match me with your little popgun!* With a maniacal cackle, Nadel reached back down and grasped three of the shiny 7.92 millimeter rounds. Grabbing the bolt and jerking it open, Nadel heard another round thud into the wooden window frame a half-meter from the open windowpane. He looked up, seeing the shattered pane at the top of the window from the American's first shot.

*That's two rounds inside of two meters. From such range, the prick's doing a pretty damned good job of shooting.*

*But I only need one chance…*

Nadel jammed the bolt forward, whipping it down with a satisfying click. He sighted the man with the scope, able to see the detail of his snarling face, the blood of his chin, the blue of his livid eyes, as he aimed another circus shot.

"Got you now, *Arshloch*," Nadel whispered.

Just as he began to apply pressure to the trigger, Raban Nadel saw the flash and puff of smoke from the man's pistol. A millisecond later, Nadel was thrown to the floor, sending the Victorian table smashing down, too. Grasping his throat, choking, unable to get a breath, Nadel was incredulous that the brazen American bastard had shot him.

With a pistol!

\*\*\*

Just as Marty saw a spark and a flash of movement inside the dull black rectangle, he felt a frenzied tugging at his jumpsuit. Slowly emerging from his trance, he looked behind to see Josh, pulling and urging him to come. Marty blinked several times, lowering the pistol as he began to return to the gravity of the situation.

Looking around the dark residential street, Marty saw several residents, cautiously peering from their front doors. Though Marty's ears were ringing from the Russian TT's cannon fire, he was able to hear one man, just inside his door, describing Marty's appearance to what must have been a Polizei dispatcher.

"Please, come on!" Josh yelled.

Touching the boy's sweaty hair, Marty nodded.

The two men began to run.

***

Inside the Zeckern mansion, Raban Nadel was flat on his back. He continued to hold his throat, struggling to breathe. When he finally managed to suck in a harsh, dry breath, he realized the rifle and tripod had fallen over his legs. Scrambling backward, Nadel sat up, probing all around his neck with both fingers.

No blood.

After what seemed minutes, he managed to gasp a few times before he was racked with dry coughing.

He crawled to the corner of the room, switching on a lamp with a shaky hand. Shiny bullets covered the hardwood floor and, in their midst, the rifle. It had become disconnected from the tripod, the entire assembly on the floor. Nadel lifted the rifle, eyeing it as he continued to cough. Then he studied the steel tripod, finding a massive gouge of sharp and twisted metal at the crown, just below the male connector. That's where the American's round had struck. The force of the large bullet had thrust the tripod and rifle backward, the bulk of the force being spent on Nadel's searing throat.

The table, and its contents, had fallen. The porcelain ashtray was shattered. Nadel lifted the radio from the floor. He keyed it, calling to his men.

Silence.

Nadel turned the radio around. The rear was broken, displaying busted vacuum tubes and a leaking battery.

"Damn it!" he yelled, hurling the radio against the wall.

Now on his feet, Nadel staggered into the hallway. He had to get downstairs to the telephone.

***

Situated just over a kilometer away, on the western edge of Bayreuth's Mitte, was the Polizei Bureau. And in the basement of the unattractive three-story building were the switchboard and dispatch. The dispatcher who was supposed to be working at this hour had been relieved by one of the bureau's three lieutenants. His name was Tiller. Though it was widely whispered throughout the Bayreuth Polizei that Tiller was a dirty cop on the take, nothing had ever been proven against him. And few dared cross Tiller, a man who was extremely well connected on the force as well as politically.

Tiller had locked himself in the switchboard room, patiently fielding calls, most of which—for the past five minutes—dealt with a sudden flurry of gunfire on one of Bayreuth's most exclusive streets. As the dispatcher would have done, Tiller scribbled every description he received, all of them describing a man in an electric utility jumpsuit armed with a pistol. Several of the callers also described an adolescent who was yelling for the man to come with him.

A bizarre scene for certain.

One caller described two other men that had fled through several yards, both of them Polizei, armed with machine guns. Tiller told that caller, "Yes, we have Polizei on your street right now. Lock your doors and stay inside. The Bayreuth Polizei have the situation under control."

Finishing another call, Tiller decided to let a few of the lines continue to ring. He'd been paid a thousand marks to delay police reaction for fifteen minutes. Normally Tiller would be afraid of this ruse somehow coming back to haunt him. But he happened to know that the dispatcher he'd relieved was having a torrid affair with the evening captain. So, as he'd slipped the dispatcher a fifty-mark bill, Tiller had quietly leveled his threat that, if she mentioned this to her lover, he would expose her little tryst to the high chief *and* the evening captain's wife.

"Or you can just take this fifty and go have a nice break," Tiller had said, winking and popping the average-looking lady on her derriere. She'd agreed without reservation. As she'd sashayed away, Tiller had admired her form. Though her face wasn't much to look at, the woman was built like Tiger Tank. He could see why the evening captain had begun the affair— poor *Scheisskerl*.

Now, ten minutes into the fifteen-minute delay, Tiller plugged the receiver cord into another flashing line, sounding tired and speaking with his cigarette bouncing in the corner of his mouth. "Bayreuth Polizei, what is the nature of your call?"

"This is Dieter Siegst," the voice said, enunciating the name clearly. "A man just shot up my home! He's running to the north."

Tiller spit the cigarette into the switchboard in a mini hail of sparks. Any calls from Dieter Siegst were his signal to act. "This is a secure line, Herr Siegst. Are you referring to the man in the utility jumpsuit?"

"Yes! He's got some punk teenager with him. They should be shot on sight."

"Is the kid armed?"

"I don't know."

"Then, I *can't* give that order."

"Then give it for the one in the jumpsuit. I already shot him."

"Is he down?"

"Didn't you hear me?" the man pretending to be Dieter Siegst growled. "They're *running* to the north."

"Okay, Herr Siegst, hold the line." Cursing, Tiller pressed the button that would place that call on hold. He lifted the handset to the police radio, calling his three field units with the bureau's "mayday" call. After giving the location, he set the scene.

"We have reports of multiple gunshots. Several residents have described the shooter as a man of average height with sandy blond hair, wearing an electric utility jumpsuit. He was last seen on foot, heading north on the eastern side of Regensburger. The man is believed to have been shot by a resident and he's accompanied by a smaller man. Both men are armed and very dangerous, having unloaded dozens of rounds on the homes. All deadly force is authorized," Tiller said, squeezing his eyes shut. This was as close as he could come to recommending the kid be shot. "Field units, report your positions."

He relit his cigarette as he listened to the Polizei relay their locations. The closest was five minutes away by car. Tiller ordered the units to stay in radio contact before he pressed the button on the switchboard, going back to Nadel.

"You've got three minutes to clear out. I've done my job."

Tiller clicked off and departed the room, finding the dispatcher in the small break area. He briefed her quickly, making her agree that she'd taken all the calls before summoning him.

Satisfied that his job was done and his money earned, Tiller went back upstairs to the bay to listen to the resulting action on the radio.

The wad of cash in his right pants pocket rubbed his leg as he walked. And it felt good.

# Chapter Eighteen

Journal Entry

There in those woods at the German-Dutch border, we'd been arguing over a wrong turn made by our XO, First Lieutenant Breston. To this day, I don't fault the man for his mistake. He'd been thrust into action due to Captain Rook's stomach flu and, despite the fact that I wasn't crazy about Breston, I blamed the people who allowed him to graduate from training without the ability to read a map. Regardless, he couldn't have imagined what would have happened because of his shortcoming.

No one could.

So we'd been standing there arguing. Captain Rook had just bent over, his hands on his knees, retching saliva and what little bile he had left into that loamy German soil. Breston had just chastised me for my fresh mouth when, at the rear of our convoy, the ammo carrier and Top's Jeep exploded.

We didn't even hear the incoming round. Didn't hear a thing, other than the explosions. And, of course, we couldn't hear the resulting yells due to the ammo carrier's artillery rounds that began to cook off. Before then, I'd only seen one ammo carrier go up, and that one had been damned near empty. This one, since we'd just come from resupply, was loaded to the hilt. A person couldn't stare at the brilliance of the explosions for the risk of the brightness blinding him.

Instinctively, we all hit the deck, scrambling for cover. I was hoping that the explosion was an accident. Maybe something went wrong with the engine and started a fire. Or maybe one of the rounds had a faulty trigger. I was hoping for something like that—but, after the sounds we'd heard before, I didn't believe it.

Not for a second. I knew we were under attack. So much for the coming ceasefire.

I'd found the cover of a thick tree trunk and, when I peered around, I saw John Vincent on top of our track, going to town with the .50 cal. He was aiming west, straight into the sun. The tracers were zipping out with every fifth bullet, helping me to see who he was shooting at. Despite the blinding sun and explosions that were beginning to die down, I squinted my eyes and was able to see hulking silhouettes on the distant ridge.

Tanks.

Large. Menacing. Sitting there in our blind spot, savoring the moment—they were like a hungry, yet patient, snake viewing a defenseless mouse.

I saw a puff of smoke emerge from one of the tanks.

I heard the rip of the round. I saw the resulting explosion.

I watched as my own M5 track flipped over.

Yelling, I was on my feet and heading that direction.

John Vincent, agile as always, had managed to survive the impact. The tank round struck the M5 at the right rear, pitching it up and over. As the track flipped,

John leapt off, his legs running in midair. Despite his agility, it was a long way down and he hit the ground unnaturally, tumbling away as he scrambled behind the cover of a tree. As I closed in on him, I could see his boots had been unlaced and now one of his feet was pointing 90 degrees in the wrong direction.

Aside from the incoming tank rounds, the area was blanketed by small arms fire—ours and probably our enemy's—making my run difficult. I finally reached John, maybe thirty seconds after the round hit our track. I don't even remember what I asked him, probably something stupid like, "You okay?"

John was cursing, but it wasn't his broken ankle or all the cuts on his face from the ammo carrier's shrapnel. He was cursing because he had no weapon and he probably knew what sitting ducks we were.

I grabbed him, shaking him. "What did you see?"

Gritting his teeth he wiped blood from his eyes. "There's armor all on that ridge. Probably a dozen tanks. Bastards hid in the sun and waited. That first round hit the ammo carrier and the explosion killed O'Malley, Eppes, and that new kid," he said, referencing the ammo dogs and the first sergeant's new driver. "I saw 'em all cartwheeling away like rag dolls."

John and I were now as close to the enemy armor as anyone. I turned, seeing my own unit reacting predictably. Per our training, some of the tracked vehicles had moved, opening the column to prevent multiple vehicles from being taken out with a single shot. Soldiers had taken cover all around. Behind me, about twenty yards away, two privates fumbled with a bazooka.

"Get that stovepipe up here!" I yelled.

John Vincent, broken ankle or not, was the crackshot of the unit. He was our best chance.

Both privates tumbled into our makeshift position, bewildered, asking what was happening.

Though John was wounded, he knew what I had in mind. As he positioned himself for the bazooka, I told the two privates that we were in some deep shit and they'd better get ready to fight.

"Who's attacking us?" one of them yelled.

I'd learned long before that such crazy questions were the norm in a time of duress. In fact, I'd seen all sorts of irrational things during battle. One time, back in '44, we'd been under heavy attack from German artillery. We were dug in pretty good, hiding in foxholes covered by heavy timber. Well, some poor bastard got himself blown up and, consequently, scattered all over the snow were dozens of his Chesterfield cigarettes (along with his body parts.) We'd been having supply issues and damn near everyone was out of smokes—this guy had obviously saved his. I couldn't believe my eyes when I saw three of our guys out there, with shrapnel slicing the air, scrambling around and collecting the dead man's broken cigarettes.

That was just one instance of lunacy. It happened again and again.

So, rather than be a smart aleck, I responded to the private's question with the truth. "I'd have to guess the tanks are German. Go find yourself some cover and dig in because they'll be coming soon." The two privates low-crawled to another nearby tree as I armed the bazooka.

With the bazooka on his shoulder, John aimed it by instinct. "Not yet," he muttered. "They're too far."

"They're not moving," I noted.

"Help's twenty minutes away!" Breston yelled from behind us, as if this were somehow good news.

I turned to the rear, opening my hands wide. "Twenty frigging minutes! These krauts'll turn us into mincemeat in two minutes."

"We got movement," John said.

By this time, the ammo carrier had finally stopped cooking off. The valley grew quiet. Just as I heard John's frightening phrase, I heard the squeaking of the tracks. When I turned back to the ridge, I could now clearly see the numerous ominous tank silhouettes as the tip of the sun's flame was all that remained to illuminate them.

"I've got a good bead on the center tank," John said. "It's a German Tiger-Two." The Tiger II was Germany's newest Panzer, greatly feared for its firepower and durability. John's shot would have to be perfect to damage it.

Again I turned. I saw Captain Rook, his pot crooked on his head, taking cover behind the stump where I'd been. I made a shooting signal before gesturing to the ridge. He shook his head, and yelled, "Not yet!" Rook was an experienced tactician and wore the distinctive blue Ranger lozenge patch. He knew the tanks were out of effective range.

But Lieutenant Breston, who was right next to him, shouted, "Hell, yes! Shoot those bastards!"

John had never ceased his aim. Crooked, broken ankle and all, he'd stayed true on target the entire time. Before I could say a word, he yelled his warning and fired the bazooka.

Feeling helpless, I watched that projectile streak right at that center Panzer, catching it in the sweet spot just below the turret. Just to give John all the credit he deserves, he struck that moving tank in a four-inch weak spot. Captain Rook had been correct in telling us to wait—but he'd not factored in John's shooting prowess. Had the round hit that Panzer anywhere else it would have been impotent. But John nailed it. The tank's rounds began to cook before the real explosion took place, sending the turret flipping through the air like a hot flapjack.

The oncoming tanks began to turn, moving laterally.

John dropped down behind the tree, giving me that sideways grin of his. "Do me a favor? Have those privates get us some more rounds. While they do, turn my ankle the right way and lace my boot real tight. It's throbbin'."

I sent the privates for more rounds and yelled for the rest of the stovepipes to spread out. Then I went to work on John's ankle. He'd been perched in the track with his boots unlaced—something we all did this late in the war. After all the marching we'd done, and the winter conditions we'd lived through, most of us had some sort of foot or cold weather injury. Had his boots been tight when he jumped, he might not have broken that ankle.

A splintered bone was protruding against the top of his foot but it wasn't sticking through the skin. I situated his boot in my two hands. "Ready?"

"Just do it," he growled, holding the warm bazooka to his face.

I twisted John's foot straight, hearing his yelp followed by his ever-present humor. "Oh man...better than a strong cup of coffee! Now lace it up, quick."

As I did, three things happened. The privates shuttled back to us, dropping to their bellies and telling me they couldn't find the M6 rockets for the bazookas. Then, from behind us, Captain Rook and Lieutenant Breston began to yell something about securing our perimeter.

But that was all quickly drowned out by the rumble of approaching armor.

The Germans had ceased their flanking and, probably sensing that no more bazooka shots were imminent, now roared right at us. From the other side of our column, I watched with hope as a bazooka round streaked out—but it missed an oncoming tank by six feet. Then an explosion shook the ground as whoever had been manning the bazooka was vaporized by a high explosive round from that tank's main gun.

Damn.

Seconds later, our vehicles began to explode. To my left, one of the tracks was hit and, in the resulting explosion, I was struck in the face by a piece of hot metal. It stuck to my cheek, sizzling. By the time I'd knocked it off, leaving me with a scorched facial brand the size of a stick of chewing gum, we were being overrun.

A Panzer unit, like the one that was thundering into our position, was far too powerful an opponent for a lightly armed artillery unit. Yes, the artillery unit can defend itself, to a degree, with bazookas and .50 cals. But for us to hold them off, even for a few minutes, we'd have had to have been prepared. We weren't.

More vehicles exploded. Rounds began to strike trees behind which our soldiers were concealed. Bodies, torn and mangled, were flung through the air. Blood was everywhere. We returned what fire we could. We fought with all our might.

As the first Panzer rumbled by my position, I eyed its markings. On its turret was painted a crest displaying massive hands, like those belonging to Thor or Zeus. In one hand was a hammer, in the other a sword. The crest oozed strength and power.

But making my blood run cold as ice was the insignia next to the crest.

Painted stark white were the lightning runes we'd all come to despise and, at times, fear.

These were the Panzers of the Schutzstaffel—the dreaded Waffen-SS.

\*\*\*

In the culvert, Marty stripped off the electric company's jumpsuit. He eyed the crimson stain on the left sleeve of his undershirt. Carefully lifting the sleeve, making himself hiss, Marty eyed the neat entry wound on the outside of his upper arm.

"Can you see where the bullet came out?" he asked, keeping the sleeve pulled up.

"Yes. It came out of the back of your arm." Wincing, Josh said, "It has strings of skin hanging out...it looks like a tiny squid."

Marty flexed his hand and moved his arm up and down. "I think I got lucky...didn't hit the bone. Help me get this undershirt off, then rip the bloody parts off the shirt using the knife from my pocket. Do it fast." Marty watched Josh work. "Good, now take the white portion and cut it in two. Make one piece smaller." A moment later he said, "Okay, take that long strip and wrap my arm, then use the strap from my bag to go around my arm and the bandage. Hopefully that'll stop the bleeding."

Marty leaned against the inside of the concrete pipe as Josh diligently worked. Once he'd retrieved the canvas strap and adjusted the buckle, he pressed the folded white cloth over the two wounds.

"Are you okay?" Marty asked, noticing that Josh was slightly pale.

"Yeah. Are you?"

"I can't believe you followed me."

Josh cinched the strap. Marty gritted his teeth. "You okay?" Josh asked.

"I'll live."

Sirens.

Marty's eyes looked up to the road as the Polizei car raced over the culvert. "Listen to me, Josh. We've got to get moving. There can't be too many cops in Bayreuth, so the farther we get from where all that shooting went down, the better."

"Is there a train tonight?"

"No. And we couldn't use the train station, anyway."

Josh frowned. "How will we get back?"

"I made a few contingency plans before we left, none that I feel very good about at the moment."

"What were they?"

"One involved stealing a car, but I don't like my chances of pulling that off right now."

"What else?"

"I've got another idea, but I wasn't exactly planning on a travel companion."

"Will it still work?" Josh asked.

"Maybe...if you're willing to help."

"What would I need to do?"

"You can start by going into my bag. Feel around on the inside. There's a false seam. Reach inside the seam and pull out the wad of money."

It took a moment for Josh to find the money; it was too dark in the culvert to see the bills. He held them up in what little light there was. "It feels funny."

"That's American money, Josh...a thousand bucks."

194

"Wow," Josh said reverently, rubbing the currency. "What am I going to do with it?"

"Do you feel like using that English you've been practicing?"

Even in the dark, Marty could see Josh's smile.

The two men headed to the north, wading through the creek, masked by the numerous summertime saplings and bushes on each bank. When they eventually came to the next road, Josh broke off through the woods. Marty told Josh to follow the rising moon and not to divert his course. After about a kilometer, he would find his destination, probably in the form of a high, barbed wire fence. He was to follow that around to the east.

***

The blood red rectangle rose majestically above the foursome, hanging there in the fog of smoke like an executioner's blade. The three others watched it intently. Over the five seconds that the red rectangle lingered above their heads, the only movement in the room came from descending beads of sweat on the collective faces. With their mouths open, each of the men trembled with anticipation. Like a seasoned performer knowing precisely what the audience wanted, the man wielding the rectangle made them wait. Three seconds. Five seconds. Then, theatrically knifing downward, the rectangle made a satisfying splat on the other three rectangles. The top card displayed the regal king of spades that everyone had known still lurked somewhere in the dwindling deck. Just below the king of spades was his mate, the queen of spades, crushed by her suited superior.

"Get that old ho' off my streets!" roared Leotis Blassingame, smacking the hand of his spades partner as the twosome broke into contented, infuriating laughter.

"Damn!" the soldier to Leotis' right griped. "Yall's some cheatin' bassards! How you gone have bof' jokers and king o'spades fo' three straight muh-fuggin hands?"

"Skill, brother, skiiiiiill!" Leotis jabbed an unlit Kool into the corner of his mouth as his partner scribbled the score onto the paper sack. "That got it?"

His partner did the arithmetic stunningly fast, carrying his numbers and circling the product. "519 to 488. That's the ol' ballgame, boys."

"Dat's some bullshit what dat is!" yelled one of the defeated partners, a buck sergeant. "Blassingame, get your loudmouth butt outside and relieve Smithson. You're already ten damned minutes late."

"Yes, sergeant!" Leotis Blassingame responded, taking his split of $3.85 from his grinning partner. "That'll buy my smokes for the ho' month." He grabbed his M-1 and pulled on his utility cap, dancing his way outside the guard shack at Christensen Barracks.

"Damn, boy, can't you tell time?" asked PFC Smithson, one of Leotis' platoon mates. "They don't teach you coloreds how to read a clock?"

Leotis was feeling far too good to let Smithson's demeaning talk get to him. He scratched a match on the stone wall, lighting his cigarette and puffing luxuriously. "Sorry ah'm late, K? Now take yo grumpy ol'self in there and fill out yo contact sheet, how 'bout it? I'll work ten past my shift to make up for it."

"I cannot believe that idiot president integrated this man's Army," Smithson mumbled, cursing as he yanked the door open.

Leotis simply smiled, having just won a day's pay despite being partnered with one of the platoon's lousiest spades players. "Some nights a man jus' gets lucky," he sang to the starry sky. Just then, a rattle from the nearby bushes made Leotis jump. The wild boar in this area were known to attack without provocation. The boar didn't usually wander all the way up to the main gate, but their mere presence was enough to keep him on constant vigil. Though he had no rounds in his M-1, Leotis brandished the weapon as if he was ready to unleash a flurry of hip shots.

"Who 'dere?" he hissed.

He heard more shakes from the bushes.

"I said, who the hell 'dere?"

A person emerged, relieving Leotis beyond measure. He straightened, squinting his eyes at the silhouette—it was just some kid.

"Damn, boy! Th'hell you doin' out here sneakin' around in the night like some ol' alley cat?"

"Hello," the kid whispered, glancing around. "You are alone?"

"Squad's in the guard shack there," Leotis said, taking a mighty pull on his cigarette. "This here's my guard shift and I s'posed to do it *alone*."

The kid looked away, as if he was trying to process what he'd heard. "Al alone, yes?"

"Yeah. I'm alone, and you ain't s'posed to be near this here main gate, got it? Now take yo little schnitzel-eatin' ass on back home 'fore yo mama tans it for bein' out too late."

The kid cocked his head as if he had no idea what Leotis had said. He shrugged and said, "Uh, I have problem, yes? I make ask want help."

Leotis took another drag, speaking through his smoky exhalation. "I can't help you none, kid. Fo' serious, get th'heck outta here. 'Fore long, both of us'll be in up the creek."

"Yes! I came from creek."

"What?"

The kid shrugged then pointed to the Jeep with the mounted utility canvas. "You drive American Jeep?"

"Naw. That's the duty Jeep. Stays here all night."

"You learn drive?"

"Do I know *how* to drive?"

"Yes," the kid smiled. "Know how?"

"Yeah, I know how, but that don't matter none. My sarge sees you out here, he's gonna call the MPs. And I don't like them cracker boss dogs, and they sho' don't like fellas like me none. You get me?"

The German kid seemed confused. Leotis could tell he didn't understand the last sentence. Just as he was about to clarify, the kid did something that made Leotis drop his cigarette. There, under the yellowish sodium-vapor lights of the front gate, the kid dug into his pocket and retrieved a wad of money, fanning it out like a tom turkey on the rut.

"Boy! Where you get all that cash?"

"I make idea, yes?"

Entranced, Leotis and the kid counted the money together, all of it. Ten minutes later, after a good bit of basic English from the kid, Leotis asked his sergeant of the guard to come outside. When he did, Leotis made the finest sales pitch of his 22 years. By the time the negotiation was over, Leotis was $500 richer, having split the take with the sergeant and the rest of the guards. Leotis also had to agree that, if he got caught, he was taking the entire fall.

"According to the map, Blassingame, Berlin's four hours away," his sergeant said, waving four fingers all around. "You know that means it'll be at least eight hours round trip?"

"I can do 'rithmatic, b'lieve it or not, sarge."

"Relief'll be here at zero-eight-hundred, meanin' you got about nine hours to get there and back. That gives you just enough time to fill up a couple of times and take a leak."

"I can do it, sarge. Jus' make sure them jerry cans is full and that Willys'll get me there and back with a nice knot in ma' pocket."

"What are you gonna do if you get stopped? Any idiot can look at the bumper number and see that Jeep's from down south."

"Ain't gon' get stopped, sarge."

"My friend is smart man, yes?" the kid said, reaching up and patting Leotis' shoulder at the 2nd Cavalry Regiment patch. "He help we."

The sergeant eyed the bills in his hand before turning his eyes to Leotis. "They call here, I'm sayin' I sent you for evenin' chow and coffee and you *never* came back. The MPs won't be shocked once they find out you're colored."

Leotis frowned. "Y'all always gotta bring that into it, doncha?"

The sergeant shrugged. Then he ran the money under his nose, smelling it before bee-bopping back inside the guard shack.

"Come on, kid. We gots to haul ass. You know where yo pardner is?"

Less than ten minutes later, Marty was resting in the back of the Willys Jeep as Leotis roared onto the autobahn. As Leotis predicted, they encountered no trouble at all on their drive to Berlin.

*** 

Marty dozed on the long ride home while Josh practiced speaking with Leotis. Because Leotis spoke with a slow southern drawl, Josh claimed he was much easier to understand. Though the ride in the Jeep was rough and very loud, they made it to Berlin slightly earlier than they thought they might. Fearing that Frau Schaal might have called the Polizei after Josh had been gone so long, Marty instructed Leotis to stop half a kilometer down the street from the flat.

His arm hurting much worse than before, Marty struggled to get out of the Jeep. Once he was out, he handed $240 more over to Leotis with his good hand. The soldier rubbed the bills together, his toothy grin gleaming with the aid of the lights from the nearby Steglitz S-bahn station.

"Best night'o guard I ever done had," Leotis laughed. He shook hands with Josh and asked Marty if he was okay to walk.

Marty was gingerly working his left arm when he said, "Yeah, I'm good, Leotis. Just remember, if anyone asks about us—"

"Didn't never happen, my friend. Just 'nuther borin' night of gate guard."

"Be safe."

Josh slapped hands with his new friend and, after a grind of the gears on the Willys Jeep, the American soldier whipped the vehicle into a U-turn before racing back to the south. It was not even 3 A.M. yet, leaving Leotis plenty of time to make it back before changing of the guard.

"How's your arm?" Josh asked, having switched back to his native tongue.

"It tightened up when I slept. Hurts worse, but your bandage stopped all the bleeding."

"You were really snoring," Josh said, putting Marty's good arm around his shoulder. "Where did you put the guns and other stuff?"

"When you went for Leotis, I buried them in the creek under rocks. I put the ammo in a trash can when you guys picked me up."

"Ready to go home?"

"Josh, about your mom, I don't think either of us can envision how upset she probably is. If there are Polizei waiting—"

"I followed you on the train," Josh said. "You didn't know I was in Bayreuth until sundown—"

"Stop," Marty commanded. "Where were we, Josh?"

"Oh, yes! *Hannover*. We were in Hannover."

"And you're sure you've been there before?"

"Many times," Josh said with confidence. "Our cousins used to live there."

"Good. Don't slip up again."

Continuing his ruse, Josh said, "And when you realized I was there, you paid a taxi to drive us all the way home."

"She's going to wonder what took me so long to realize you were following me," Marty murmured.

"It's a long train ride to Hannover," Josh said. "And…the train was delayed. Yes…delayed. By the time you realized I was there, it was night. You bought me dinner because I was hungry, then there were no more trains."

Marty rubbed his face. "I guess it'll have to do." He was angry with himself that he was making the kid be dishonest. He pulled his arm away from Josh, took a great breath, and began walking on his own. "Watch me walk under the street lamp. Can you see the outline of the belt and bandage under my blazer?"

Josh halted and watched. "Nope. Can't see it."

Marty turned. "Josh, if you don't want to lie, if you're upset about what you saw, I'll understand."

"It was like watching a movie," he said with a smile. "I'm fine."

"Yeah, but you might end up with nightmares later."

"I'm okay, Marty."

Marty tousled his young friend's hair.

Earlier, when they'd first gotten into the Jeep, Marty had a chance to reflect on what had happened—and all that Josh had seen. Marty had sat in the back of the Jeep, watching Josh excitedly interact with Leotis, as if the gunfight had never even happened. Then Marty realized that, despite his youth, Josh probably recalled the war. Heck, he'd been in Berlin, the scene of horrific fighting in the war's final weeks. Who knew how this generation of adolescents in Germany might turn out, given all the horrible and violent exposure they'd received?

The two men walked in silence as Marty continued to think.

Assuming he could get away with the Frau Schaal encounter tonight, Marty would have to get creative in finding medical care. He'd probably be best suited to use some of his cash reserve and find an immigrant doctor in the Turkish community down in Steglitz. Given the Turks' poor economic conditions, he might luck into someone who would patch up Marty's arm for cash under the table.

Frau Schaal's building came into view. There were no Polizei cars visible. The two men went through their story once again. As they approached the stoop, the front door clicked open. Frau Schaal stepped outside.

Aided by the light of the stoop, Marty could see that she was pale and her eyes were puffy. Like any mother would, she looked at her son and, speaking in a voice bordering on hysterical, said, "My God, are you alright?"

"I'm fine, Mutti," Josh said, using the reassuring tone of a seasoned actor. "I know you're mad. I...I guess I didn't know we'd be gone so long."

"Gone so long, *where*?"

"All I did was take a train ride and follow Mister Marty around Hannover. But when he caught me following him, he got angry because he knew you'd be worried." Josh looked up at Marty. "He paid hundreds of marks for a taxi to drive us all the way home."

"A taxi? From Hannover?"

"Yes, Mutti. By that time, there were no trains coming back."

"So, where's this taxi?"

"Uh, he dropped us off up in Steglitz," Marty said, gesturing with his right arm. "Something about rules against taxis driving down residential streets late at night."

Frau Schaal processed this, her nostrils flaring as she sucked in an audible breath. Her eyes cut to Marty. "Could you not at *least* have found a phone and called me?" Her words were the sharp scalpel wielded by infuriated mothers the world over.

"You're right," Marty said contritely. "I'm sorry. My main focus was getting him home as quickly as possible."

She considered both men for a moment before opening the door wide. "We will talk in detail about this tomorrow, young man." As Marty passed through the door, she glared at him through narrow eyes.

"I'm surprised you didn't call the Polizei," Marty said.

"I did call the Polizei. They wouldn't do anything until he'd been gone for a full day."

"I honestly didn't know he was following me. This wasn't my fault."

She eyed Marty for a moment before coming inside. The three people marched up the flights of stairs. Marty was terribly weak but doing all he could to walk naturally. At the Schaal's landing, he tried to appear normal as he bade them goodnight. Josh returned the farewell, smiling triumphantly behind his mother's field of vision. Frau Schaal said nothing.

Upstairs, Marty went into his medical kit and took two Erythromycin tablets, washing them down with three large glasses of tap water. Before he'd departed the U.S., he'd been told Erythromycin was the newest antibiotic available. Then, leaving his clothes on, he lay on his bed and closed his eyes. He was asleep in mere seconds.

# Chapter Nineteen

There's no way I can describe the terror of being overrun by an SS Panzer unit. Being overrun is bad enough, but knowing you're about to come face-to-face with an enemy renowned for their ruthlessness is sobering, indeed. I'm sure plenty of others knew a similar dread long before me. The Lakota Sioux—men, women, and children—overtaken and slaughtered by American cavalry at Wounded Knee. The Waxhaw Massacre in South Carolina, when, after the defeated American force raised the white flag, British soldiers butchered them, man by man. I've read about countless more...

I remember when I was a teen, watching a fight one day on my walk home from school. Billy Shanklin bested Nab Holloway that afternoon. It had been a pretty even fight, but Billy was bigger and a year older. He eventually won and to all of us the fight was over. Nab had been knocked nearly unconscious and fallen to the ground. He was just beginning to move again. But, rather than leave well enough alone, Billy jumped on Nab's chest and began to punch him in the face. Nab's head was bouncing on the asphalt. It was vicious. It was disturbing. We pulled Billy off, thankfully saving Nab from any serious damage. But I never understood why a man would want to continue hurting an opponent that was already beaten.

And before those German Panzers had even roared into our position, we were already beaten.

Oh, we defended ourselves as best we could. From what I can recollect, I remember seeing six or seven dead from the Panzer unit. John killed at least three with the initial shot from the stovepipe, and the rest were shot by small arms when the SS first peered from their tanks.

But by the time all the Panzers had surrounded us, Rook and Breston had begun to yell to us to surrender.

Writing this, and I would imagine reading it, doesn't do justice to the act of surrender. It sounds cowardly. It sounds despicable. But good men have surrendered. The old saying that discretion is the better part of valor holds much truth.

We had almost two hundred men in our unit. Men with families. Men with futures. The war was nearly over. And though it still makes some small piece of me wilt to admit it, surrender was our best option. What were we going to do? Kill five, maybe ten more SS? All we'd accomplish by doing that would be to piss them off. And that would just get more of us killed.

At least, that was our thinking. How little did we know...

Obeying the orders of our commanders, the soldiers of the 2$^{nd}$ Battalion 32$^{nd}$ Field Artillery's Able Battery threw up their hands. Some waved white handkerchiefs. I remember John whispering to me that he didn't think things would end well.

"Why?" I asked, trying not to move my lips.

"I just have a feeling," he whispered.

After that, I recall seeing several of our men get shot by top-mounted machine guns. Their hands were up; they weren't a threat to anyone. Seeing a man killed just after a battle is an awful sight but a reality of war. Until a unit's collective blood cools, such killings occur. Had the boots been on the other feet, I'm sure a handful of German soldiers would have died in the same manner. I'd seen it before, more times than I care to recall.

So, our surrender went up and, other than a few late shots from their machine guns, the SS Panzer division halted its assault against us. When those massive Maybach engines had lowered to idle, English-speaking Germans yelled for us to lower our weapons, turn off our vehicles, and move to the middle of the perimeter.

"You're being taken prisoner!" one of them yelled.

"By the SS," John added.

***

*Boom! Boom! Boom!*

Marty opened his eyes, lurching upward, the movement making him yelp in pain. He realized he was at home and fell back on the bed, gingerly touching his arm. Grim reality came back to him in only a few seconds—he'd been dreaming he was back in North Dakota, but as an adult. The dream had seemed so real, as if the massacre had never happened. But it *had* happened, and here he was, smack dab in the middle of his own personal vengeance. Sitting up again, he tested his arm. The pain radiated from the wound all the way to his fingertips. It also ran the other direction, flowing through his shoulder and into his neck and chest.

*Boom! Boom! Boom!*

That's what had woken him—a knock. Had to be Frau Schaal. *Oh, Josh…please tell me you didn't cave in. Please…*

Marty slung his legs over the side of the bed. "Let me put some clothes on!" he yelled, his dry voice cracking as he spoke. He glanced at his arm, satisfied that there was no visible blood through the bandage. Using his good arm, Marty hurriedly unbuckled his belt and trousers, pushing them down. Then he retrieved his bathrobe, slipping it on, doing all he could not to yell out as he worked his left arm through the sleeve.

Another knock, then Frau Schaal's voice. "Herr Marty, please hurry!" She sounded angry.

"Damn," Marty mumbled. "Alright! I was sleeping! Be right there!" Despite the big hurry, Marty staggered into the kitchen and poured two of his aspirin powders into his glass. He held the glass under the sink before guzzling the cloudy water, some of it running from the corners of his mouth and down his neck. Despite the need to urgently relieve his bladder, Marty shuffled to the door, ready to face Frau Schaal's firing line. Realizing he'd not even locked the door last night, Marty pulled it open, surprised to see a short man standing slightly in front of Frau Schaal.

The man was approximately 5'6" and weighed no more than 140 pounds. He had a kindly, round face under a balding head. Expressive green eyes looked Marty up and down with keen interest, the way a collector might view a rare painting discovered in some old woman's attic. Marty noted the man's tattered suit and, most notably, he saw the man's right hand was missing. It had been replaced by a metal prosthetic, pinching a fedora in its grip. Due to the shape of the man's sleeve, Marty guessed the prosthetic ran all the way to the shoulder.

Marty's eyes moved from the curious man to Frau Schaal. Her face was splotchy—she appeared distressed.

"Herr Marty, I'm sorry to disturb you but this is Detective...I'm sorry, detective, but I've already forgotten your name."

He smiled back at her before turning back to Marty. "Not a concern at all, madam. I'm *Kriminaldetektiv* Werner Eisch of the Berlin Polizei." The detective turned back to Marty and offered his *left* hand in greeting.

The action made Marty want to instantly vomit.

Not knowing if he could complete the gesture, Marty gritted his teeth and lifted his left hand, surprised that it still moved. The small detective gripped his burning hand in a surprisingly strong grip. Marty stifled a scream as the man pumped it in the vigorous and hearty German style. Lightning bolts of pain bounced around in Marty's body.

The detective cocked his head. "Are you well, Herr Elder?"

Realizing his eyes were watering and he'd broken out in a cold sweat, Marty used his right hand to wipe his face. He forced a smile as he allowed his arm to fall back to his side and said, "Yes, sir, I'm fine. I was in a pretty bad farming accident as a teenager. And when I first wake up, it takes me a while to get my left arm going. Left knee's the same way."

The detective nodded amiably, as if this somehow jibed with what he expected. Marty glanced at Frau Schaal, who appeared skeptical. The threesome grew quiet.

"What can I do for you?" Marty grunted.

"Might we come in?" the detective responded.

"Uh...okay." The detective stepped by Marty and, as she'd done the night before, Frau Schaal glared at Marty through gun-slit eyes as she passed.

In the rectangular center of the apartment, a foyer-like room that each of the rooms branched from, the detective did a full circle, eyeing the space. "You were *still* sleeping?" he asked with surprise.

Marty glanced at the clock, seeing that it was a few minutes after noon. "Yes, sir, I was. I was up late last night…too late."

"We all need our rest," the detective said.

"What's this visit about, detective?" Marty asked.

"Well, we're speaking to a section of people, Americans, who fit the profile of someone we believe might be involved in an activity of interest to us."

*Does he know? If he does, it wouldn't seem wise to open that way. Sounds like he's fishing. No…he doesn't know, but you've left a clue somewhere, idiot. Well, no point in worrying about it this very second. Simply be helpful, to allay his suspicions…but play stupid.*

Marty cleared his throat. "What activity, sir, and what profile?"

The detective smiled again; Marty had already determined that the natural, soft smile was the man's disarming mechanism. "Herr Elder, someone has committed a number of crimes. We believe it to be a single person, and we also think that person is a male, an American, and originating from Oklahoma."

*Sonofabitch! How'd he get Oklahoma?*

"I see," Marty responded, managing a light chuckle. "Well, I'm a man. I'm certainly American. And I'm from Oklahoma. Also, please call me Marty."

"Fine, thank you."

As the detective consulted his notes, Marty glanced at Frau Schaal. She shook her head, her expression a mixture of anger and disappointment. The detective looked up.

"Herr Elder, where were you last weekend?"

Marty blinked several times. "Last weekend?" He looked up at the ceiling. *Don't delay too long!* "Sorry, I haven't been in Germany all that long and the days have kind of run together—especially the weekends. Let's see, last weekend I—"

"We," Frau Schaal interjected.

Werner took a step back and turned his head to her.

"Yes, we…" Marty agreed, careful not to make it a question but not knowing what else to say.

Clasping her hands in front of her and lowering her face contritely, Frau Schaal said, "Herr Marty is trying to protect my virtue." She looked up, first joining eyes with him before turning to the detective. "I'm a widow, detective. I've come to…to *know* Herr Marty, and we took an overnight trip together to Bad Freienwald."

"Bad Freienwald," the detective repeated, making a notation in his notebook.

"That's personal information, detective," Frau Schaal said demurely. "I'd appreciate it if you keep it to yourself."

Though stunned at this unexpected assistance, Marty knew he wasn't out of the woods yet. He watched the detective's expression as his eyes came back up to Frau Schaal. Unless the man had a world-class poker face, Marty felt the detective believed her.

"Bad Freienwald is a beautiful spa town," the detective said, probably embarrassed by the revelation. "And where did you stay?"

"At my cottage," she responded.

"You have a place there?"

"It was my father's hunting retreat. Now it's hardly ever used and, with the real estate market the way it is, I probably couldn't sell if I tried."

"I see," the detective said, still smiling but sounding crestfallen. "And did you see anyone while you were there?"

"See anyone?" she asked.

"Someone who could verify your presence in Bad Freienwald?"

Frau Schaal's cheeks flushed. "We didn't go out, detective."

"Oh," the detective said awkwardly, making another notation.

Marty cleared his throat. "Detective, I feel because I just happen to be American and Oklahoman that it's putting Frau Schaal in an uncomfortable spot. It's not fair to her. Were there other questions you had for *me*?"

"Yes," he replied. "Marty, did you serve in the U.S. military?"

"No, sir. The injuries I told you about prevented my service."

"Farm injuries?"

"Yes, sir."

"Very well. And you're in Germany because…"

"I'm with Day Construction. We're a building contractor in the reconstruction effort."

"I see their signs everywhere." There was a long pause as the detective consulted his notes. He tucked them away, frowning importantly. "One other thing…did you have any relatives or close friends who served in the war?"

Marty widened his eyes, the way a person does when asked a ridiculous question. "No relatives, no. But dozens of friends…maybe hundreds. I'd guess that seventy percent of the boys from my town, my age or probably up to ten years older, served."

The detective nodded as if this made sense. "Any close friends?"

"Sure, a couple."

"Were any of them in the 32nd Field Artillery, Able Battery?"

Marty felt as if he'd just been jolted by 220 volts. Though he struggled to appear impassive, he wondered if he was giving off cues to how he felt. Fighting not to swallow, Marty shrugged, shaking his head. "I don't know much about military units. My best friend Mike served in the infantry and died in Italy. My only other close friend who served, Billy, fought in the Pacific. He survived the war and settled in Washington State. We write each other around Christmas, each year."

The detective exhaled, his entire body deflating, as if everything Marty had said wasn't what he wanted to hear. "I appreciate your time, Herr Elder." The detective moved to shake hands before pulling his good hand back. "I won't make you do that again." He eyed Marty's hand. "That old injury looks red."

"Yeah," Marty replied, turning slightly. "It does that when I wake up. Circulation issues. I have to keep it moving."

The detective lifted his prosthetic and clicked it a few times. "Take care of yourself, Herr Elder, lest you end up like me."

Marty smiled politely and nodded before the detective turned back to Frau Schaal.

"I'll show you out, detective," she offered.

"No need, madam. Good day to you both." The little detective exited the flat, pulling the door shut. His footsteps could be heard descending before silence enveloped the twosome.

"I just saved you," Frau Schaal whispered through clenched teeth.

Acknowledging what she said would only be an admission of guilt, and could further complicate things for Marty. "Look, I'm sorry about what happened yesterday. But I can't control what Josh does. If he decides to follow me, how am I to—"

"*Where* did you go yesterday?"

"Excuse me?"

"Where—did—you—go?" she asked, switching to English for emphasis.

"Like Josh said last night: Hannover," Marty lied.

"Hannover?"

"Yes."

"Traveling to Hannover from here isn't all that difficult. It's a well-traveled rail line."

"Sure," Marty said, unsure of why she would say something so obvious.

"I know this because my sister lived there for ten years."

"Josh mentioned that he knew the city from visiting his cousins."

"And the morning train to Hannover that you two would have taken is an express, meaning it doesn't stop at the small stations."

"What's your point?" Marty asked.

"It goes directly to the main station."

"Yeah. So?"

"Describe the Hannover Hauptbahnhof," she demanded, referencing the central train station.

"I don't pay attention to that kind of stuff," Marty said dismissively.

"Is it new, or old?"

"What?"

"You might have noticed that there was a recent war here, Marty. Many things were destroyed, but *some* things weren't." Her expression was one of great intensity. "So, I ask again, is Hannover Hauptbahnhof new or old?"

Marty licked his lips, knowing that giving an answer was the wrong move. "I honestly didn't notice."

"Well, Josh knew the Hauptbahnhof was rebuilt...but he failed my follow-up questions. Failed miserably." She pointed to Marty's hand. "Coupled with the misleading story you told that detective about your arm, now I'm extremely curious."

"You've seen my scars."

"Yes, but your arm has always worked fine. So, take it off."

"Take what off?"

"Take off your robe. I want to see your arm."

"This is ridiculous. I'm not showing you an old wound."

"I just saved you from a Berlin Polizei detective," she said sharply. "And stop your pretending—it's absurd. Now, take it off."

Closing his eyes, Marty resignedly said, "I can't."

"Why not?"

"Hurts too much."

She walked behind him, carefully tugging at the robe.

"Hey...I don't have on my trousers."

"I'm a grown woman," she replied in a clinical tone. She gently worked the robe down and back. Marty didn't resist. When the robe was off, her fingers floated above the slight bulge at his shirtsleeve, not touching it. "That's a bandage under there."

Marty didn't respond.

She moved in front of him, unbuttoning two of his buttons.

"Frau Schaal, don't do this."

"You just stay quiet," she said in a voice not to be trifled with.

One by one she undid each button of the untucked shirt. When it was fully unbuttoned, she opened it, her eyes focused on his arm. Then, as she'd done with the robe, she walked behind him and lightly pulled the shirt from his body. Marty heard her suck in a sharp breath when his back was revealed.

"My God, are those scars from bullets?"

He nodded.

"And what are the other scars?"

"I'm not really sure what caused them," he said in a low voice. "Maybe from a chain swung like a whip."

She walked around him, viewing his chest and stomach, her hand motioning to the two round scars at his abdomen.

"Exit wounds," he said. "I'm pretty sure I was face-down."

"What happened?" she asked, her hand covering her mouth as soon as the query was out.

"You'll pardon me for not going into it right now. I just can't do it."

The hand that had covered Frau Schaal's mouth eased up her face, with the thumb and middle finger massaging her temples for a moment. When she looked up, she nodded as if she had some measure of understanding—though Marty could see no way that she did. Without a word, she gingerly touched the strap around Marty's arm, easing pressure from the buckle even as Marty hissed.

"I'm taking this off. Can you handle it."

"I'm a little dizzy."

"Let's go in the bedroom."

She had Marty lie on the bed in the opposite direction than he normally slept. She covered him with the sheet and moved the pillow under his head, instructing him to close his eyes. When Frau Schaal fully released the strap, she handed him the clean end of the strap and told him to wad it and bite down.

"Don't pull that off," Marty mumbled. "It's clotted to the wound."

"Just close your eyes and bite down."

Marty did as he was told, his back spasmodically arching as the makeshift bandage pulled large, gluey clots from the entry and exit wounds. It took a moment for her to get the bandage all the way off; when she did, she told him to relax.

"This is another gunshot wound," she said. "A fresh one."

He opened his eyes and looked at her. Her fingernail tapped on her front teeth as she looked away, eventually talking to herself. "We're going to need an antibiotic, a strong one. Need antiseptic, too, and my suturing kit. We'll also need a proper sterile dressing and medical tape."

"I've already got an antibiotic."

The t-shirt bandage was lying below his arm. She lifted it, pressing it back against the wound with light pressure. "You're not going to pass out, are you?"

"I don't think so."

"Hold this on. I'll be back in a few minutes."

Marty did as he was told. When she returned, she went into his small kitchen, boiling two pots of water. The next hour was one of the most painful, sweat-inducing hours of his life.

\*\*\*

Around the time Frau Schaal had been removing Marty's robe and shirt, Kriminaldetektiv Werner Eisch ambled down the concrete steps of the Steglitz S-Bahn station. He'd purchased a mustard-slathered sandwich and a cola at the kiosk upstairs, munching away as he awaited the train that would take him back to Berlin's *Mitte*. As he'd crossed the bridge a few minutes before, he'd seen the previous train pulling away from the station, meaning he had twenty minutes before the next train. This was good; it would allow him time to eat while he processed all he'd learned.

According to the Federal Foreign Office in Bonn, there were a total of 3,137 American men in Germany whose home of record was in Oklahoma. More than two-thirds of those men were currently serving in the U.S. military. The remainder consisted of civilian employees, students, or the occasional miscellaneous artist or random person who warranted a visa for a long-term stay.

The total number did not include vacationers—regardless, there were few in that category. Much of Germany still lay in ruin, and the war was still fresh on people's minds. Germany wasn't exactly a popular vacation destination. As of yesterday, 71 Oklahomans were currently visiting Germany on passport, most of them on what they described as "business." The visitors weren't required to divulge their planned whereabouts and, after perusing the small list of citizens traveling on passport, Werner dismissed them all. Not a one of them had been close in age or description to the man he was looking for. Therefore, Werner focused on the large number of resident military and civilians on work visas.

Taking his first stab at whittling down the 3,137, Werner immediately eliminated anyone too young to have served in the war. This wiped out a significant portion, reducing the number to 993. Next, he made the assumption that whoever had accosted the three former SS had started in Berlin for a reason. Unless there were others Werner didn't know about, the three Berliners were taken down in relatively short order. Werner felt it natural that a man bent on some sort of revenge would begin close to home. Why not? You start close and then work your way out. It's the way a policeman would go about things, so why wouldn't Werner's assailant work in the same manner?

When he'd scrutinized the remaining 993, he'd narrowed the list down to an even 80 men who were listed as living in the Berlin metro area. 61 of those men were currently serving in the American military, all but one of them in the Army and the Air Force. The one remaining happened to be a Marine on special assignment. The Marine, however, was quickly eliminated due to the fact that he'd arrived in country just last week. That left 60 potential military suspects.

Over the past day, Werner had phoned each of their units. He further narrowed his list due to each man's iron-clad unavailability on certain dates from guard duty, military maneuvers and the like. Additionally, although many of the men could have served during the war, Werner eliminated those who hadn't served in Europe, as many of the men had been in the Pacific or elsewhere.

Finished narrowing down the list of military suspects, Werner had wound up with 12 men worthy of questioning. All but one had airtight alibis for each of the dates in question. And Werner had a strong suspicion that the one who couldn't give an alibi was innocent. According to the duty officer, the man was a frail little orderly room clerk and didn't possess enough strength to hold down an adolescent, much less a strapping former SS. The duty officer described the sergeant as hermit-like, staying in his bunk and devouring books when he wasn't on duty. Werner felt comfortable enough to scratch him from his list. All military Oklahomans were cleared as far as Werner was concerned.

That left Werner with 19 civilians in Berlin on work visas. Just as his assailant had done, Werner had started in the city center and worked outward. The man he'd just met, Martin Elder, was fourteenth on the list. It had been a strange meeting, what with the risqué alibi provided by the landlord, a war widow. Werner had also found the young American man to be a peculiar sort, especially having just woken up with the injured arm and all. As he'd left the apartment building, Werner made a mental note to add Martin Elder to his small list of suspects that might require a bit more scrutiny.

Now, finishing the tasty sandwich of *Bratwurst mit Brötchen*, Werner balled the wax paper with his good hand, tossing it into the nearby trash as his train clacked into the station. His next stop was a visit with a 54-year-old Oklahoman who worked American cargo at nearby Tempelhof. After that, he would head back to the station and plan tomorrow's activities.

\*\*\*

Marty awoke around 4 P.M. The western sun beamed into the flat, overheating his body as he lay partially under the sheet. He kicked the sheet away, the sudden movement revealing the stiffness and pain of his left arm. Looking at the neat bandage, everything came back to him. He recalled Frau Schaal patiently irrigating the wound. She'd snipped away the ragged bits of flesh, irrigating the wound further before spritzing an iodine solution liberally over both holes. Then, with the skill of an accomplished surgeon, she'd sutured both wounds, gnawing on her bottom lip as she painstakingly worked to neatly close both holes.

"You're going to have scars," she'd said as she worked. "Not much I can do about that."

Marty had watched the entire process, amazed by her skill. As she'd snipped the final ends of filament, he asked, "How did you learn to do this?"

"This is Berlin, Herr Marty," she'd said, almost smiling. "We were all doctors back in '45. I'm amazed you didn't pass out."

"I've had some practice."

She'd pulled the quilt up over him, patting his leg. "Rest now. I'll be back." That had been a few hours ago.

Marty eased his legs over the side of the bed. He actually felt decent—he was intensely hungry, and he smelled food. After slowly making his way to the kitchen, he noticed the large pot on the stove. There was a note next to the pot, folded like a tent over the rim of a thick bowl with a silver spoon. The note instructed Marty to eat the soup and to drink plenty of water.

The pot contained chicken soup, loaded with meat and vegetables. Heaven sent. Marty ladled the bowl nearly full, adding plenty of black pepper and allowing it to cool on the table. He placed a packet of soda crackers on the table, along with a large glass of water. Before eating, he went to the bathroom and donned the robe after splashing cold water on his face. Then he sat in the kitchen, blowing on each spoonful before enjoying the fine meal. He ate two full bowls.

When he finished, there was a knock at the door. Marty rubbed his eyes. Here we go.

"Come in," he said, surprised that his voice no longer sounded weak.

As he suspected, it was Frau Schaal. She walked to the kitchen, surveying the empty bowl and the half-eaten sleeve of crackers. "How much water have you had?"

"Two full glasses."

She took the glass and refilled it. "Drink two more now and at least two more tonight."

Marty dutifully guzzled.

"Josh continues to lie to me," she said.

Lowering the glass, Marty nodded. "He's protecting me."

"That much is obvious. I know my son." She crossed her arms. "And after that curious visit from the detective, well…"

"Is Josh okay?"

She shrugged. "Seems fine. He slept well." There was a long pause. "I'm struggling to be polite," Frau Schaal said in a sharp tone. "Now, enough games. What exactly happened?"

"He saw something he shouldn't have seen."

"He saw you get shot."

"Yes," Marty breathed.

"And what in God's name were you doing to get shot?"

"We were in Bayreuth," Marty answered directly, facing her. "Josh followed me there, though I didn't know it until just before I was shot."

"Bayreuth," she said flatly.

"Yes."

Her lips pressed together as her nostrils flared. "Why were you in Bayreuth?"

211

"I was trying to find a man…Oskar Zeckern."

She opened her hands impatiently. "Who?"

"Zeckern was Schutzstaffel, a battalion commander."

"Schutzstaffel?" she asked. "As in SS?" Her dubious tone was that of a person who'd just been given the most ridiculous answer imaginable.

"I'm telling you the truth," Marty said. "Oskar Zeckern was a battalion commander in the Waffen-SS."

"What on earth do you want with a Waffen-SS battalion commander?"

"You really want to know?"

"Yes, dammit, I *really* want to know."

Marty paused a moment before blurting it out. "I was looking for Zeckern because I believe that he knows the location of another former Waffen-SS. That man's name was Raban Nadel. Nadel was responsible for the massacre of 184 American men…185 if you believe the history books. Many of them were my close friends. He also killed twelve of his own SS for resisting his order."

She didn't flinch, didn't even blink. After a moment she said, "So, you *were* in the military?"

"Yes, I was."

"Your scars…"

"I…" Marty swallowed, struggling to wet his mouth despite the quantity of water he'd just ingested. She refilled the glass and handed it to him, but he placed it on the table. "I was the only survivor in my unit. I don't know how I survived. I can remember some of it before I passed out. Then I woke up a week later in a British Army tent. They didn't think I'd live, much less recover fully." He pulled in a deep breath. "That's why I'm here, Frau Schaal. I'm here to find the man responsible for that day…for the Massacre at Kastellaun."

Again she took the news impassively. Marty was trembling and she must have noticed it. She walked around him, pulling his chair back. "Please sit." Marty did, and she sat opposite him. "Sip that water."

"Already feel like my stomach's going to burst."

"It won't. Drink."

Marty drank.

Frau Schaal's fingernails clicked on the Formica tabletop. "I'm sorry for what happened to you. I mean that. But by living in my building and doing what you've been doing, you've endangered our lives."

Surprised at her tack, especially after baring his soul, Marty frowned. "Hey…I tried to keep to myself. You and Josh *pushed* yourselves on me."

"That doesn't matter. What if these enemies of yours decide it's easiest to just blow up the building? Rather than act like John Wayne in some revenge movie, why didn't you just work with the authorities to catch this man, this SS, who was responsible?"

"I don't expect you to understand," he whispered as he looked away.

"You're correct, I *don't* understand." She stood, seeming to struggle with the words. "Again, I'm sorry for what you endured. But we've all suffered, along with so many Americans, Brits, French, Russians, Netherlanders, Danes, Italians—"

"Alright!" he yelled, slapping the table with his right hand.

"But you're different?"

He glared at her.

"The war is over for everyone else but Martin Elder. No...your war goes on."

"Don't you judge me. And you're twisting the facts. This was a...an unfathomable incident."

"And the Holocaust wasn't? Should the remaining Jewish people be here killing every man and woman who had a hand in the camps?"

"That's an unfair comparison."

She waited a moment before asking, "Is it? They were slaughtered and they weren't even soldiers, like you."

"The Germans..."

"What?" she asked. "The Germans caused all of this? Murdered the Jews, slaughtered your friends? That gives you the right to potentially ruin *any* German's life in the name of your own quest?"

Marty didn't respond. He lowered his eyes to the floor.

"I'd like you out of this apartment by the end of the week, at the *latest*. In the meantime, I'd appreciate it if you'd remain within the bounds of the law. If you do feel that these...*people*," she spat the word, "...may seek revenge on you, then I'd like you to vacate immediately. I've already risked enough by lying to the Polizei for you."

Frau Schaal stormed out of the kitchen and slammed the front door.

***

Having finished the futile questioning of the cargo contractor out at Tempelhof—the American had an impeccable alibi (he'd been hospitalized for gout)—Werner removed his fedora as he walked back into the precinct. It had been a long and tiresome day. He didn't even make it through the lobby before he was halted by the desk sergeant.

"Hey detective...c'mere," the desk sergeant said furtively, urgently beckoning Werner.

"Yes?"

"Some VIP from the BKA is waiting for you."

"For me? You're sure he's BKA?"

"Yes, he's BKA," the desk sergeant replied, slowly enunciating "BKA," pausing between each of the initials for effect. BKA stood for

*Bundeskriminalamt,* a federal police organization that had recently been created and modeled after the American FBI.

"Okay, sergeant, but are you certain you have the correct detective? I'm Werner Eisch, from Burglary and Theft."

"I know who you are," the sergeant said somewhat defensively. "Your chief, Mainhardt, talked to him and asked him to wait down in meeting room number one. We tried reaching you but couldn't raise you on radio."

"I was on foot, working a special case."

"Well, the BKA man didn't care how long you'd be—said he'd wait."

"Any idea what he does in the BKA?"

The desk sergeant looked down at a piece of paper. "Didn't get his name, but his title is director, international operations division."

Werner whistled and clicked his prosthetic. "A division director?"

"Apparently."

"Where's Chief Mainhardt?"

"He stepped out right after your VIP arrived and hasn't been back. Said he was on something hot."

"Oh boy," Werner mumbled. "Well, thanks for the heads up." He hurried down the hallway, seeing the BKA man sitting there behind the two-way glass in meeting room number one. Someone had strung a phone into the room for him. The man was talking to someone, a cigarette burning in an ashtray beside his right hand. Next to the ashtray was a notepad, open, the top page scribbled full of notes.

*What in the world would he want with me?*

Rather than rush in, Werner eyed the BKA man for a moment. He was strikingly handsome, as so many of the new organization's men seemed to be. The man had blond hair that was severely slicked back, pairing nicely with his bronzed face. His hazel eyes glanced coolly around the room as he spoke, the low tones of his voice reverberating through the wall. His suit jacket hung on the chair next to him, revealing a crisp white shirt that covered a tall, lean body. He seemed the type of man that might have starred in one of Goebbel's wartime film shorts, piloting the newest fighter aircraft and flashing dazzling smiles at the wing-mounted camera.

Werner clicked the solid state switch to the left of the door, turning the volume knob low as he leaned close to listen to the wall-mounted speaker.

"*...money is more than satisfactory. But, that's not the only consideration. Well, how about the considerable risk I'm running? If we're going to keep this relationship going, it's got to be about more than just money. You need to respect my position, and my profile, by giving me more notice for a fool's errand like this.*" The man closed his eyes, nodding but showing frustration. "*I know all that and, no, I'm not levying threats. Next time give me more notice, will you? Good. Hopefully I'll have something soon.*" He hung up the phone and tapped his cigarette in the ashtray, showing little affectation after the call.

In his mind, Werner replayed the puzzling snippet he'd just heard. *What was all that? Money. Risk. A fool's errand?* He shrugged and rapped on the door. The man stood and smoothed his tie and trousers. He crushed out the cigarette and, with a broad grin, said, "Come in!"

Werner stepped inside, wondering what he'd done to rate such an obsequious smile from a man who far outranked him.

"*Kriminaldetektiv* Werner Eisch?"

"Yes, sir."

"I'm Director of International Operations, Klaus Loeffler, of the *Bundeskriminalamt*." He extended his hand. When he noticed Werner's prosthetic, he smoothly retracted his right and instead offered his left. "Thank you, detective, for seeing me on short notice."

"But, of course, *Mein Herr*. If I may be so bold as to get right to the point, what's this about?"

"A fantastic coincidence, detective."

"Oh?"

"And I must say I'm impressed."

"Well…thank you, sir."

"*Very* impressed."

Werner, feeling quite uncomfortable, nodded. "Impressed with what, sir?"

"I understand, detective, that you're seeking a person of interest, an American from Oklahoma, in a special investigation you've authored?" Again the smile.

"Well, that's…that's classified, sir."

Loeffler made a shooing motion. "Your own Chief Mainhardt briefed me, detective. There are no secrets between him and me."

"I see."

"But it displays what a committed bloodhound you are, detective. I've had the full might of the BKA behind me and here you are, one man, just as far along as me." Director Loeffler came around the table, placing his arm around Werner's shoulders and giving him a hearty shake. "From here on, Eisch, you and I will be working together."

"From here on?"

"Starting right now." The director pulled a chair out for Werner, then sat opposite him. After rolling up his sleeves, the director leaned forward, clasping his hands in front of him. "Let's get right down to business, shall we?"

For some unknown reason, Kriminaldetektiv Werner Eisch suddenly felt nauseous.

# Chapter Twenty

Journal Entry

In all the confusion that occurred as part of our surrender, I managed to push some leaves and pine needles over the stovepipe. The SS weren't stupid. They certainly knew the general area that the deadly bazooka round had come from. I was afraid if they found out John had fired the lethal round, they'd have killed him. After concealing the stovepipe, I helped John up. With his arm around my neck, we trudged to the clearing where our soldiers began to congregate at gunpoint.

From the other side of the road, Danny Elder and Kenny Martin appeared. I breathed a sigh of relief. Thank God.

We stood next to each other, whispering about what had happened, despite the chorus of Germans telling us to be quiet in two languages. It took at least five minutes to round everyone up. Many of our guys were wounded. They made us toss our helmets aside and lace our hands on our heads. When just about everyone was gathered there, we heard yelling behind us followed by the cracking of a gunshot.

"Harris," I heard a few people whisper. That would be PFC Limon Harris. Formerly Corporal Limon Harris. Formerly Sergeant Limon Harris. Hailing from Jacksonville, Florida, Harris had been in trouble the entire time I'd known him. I wasn't at all surprised that he resisted. And I wasn't surprised that the SS killed him for it.

Then an authoritative German-accented voice could be heard echoing through the valley.

"That, gentlemen, is what happens to someone who tries to resist our might." Though I couldn't see the man, he spoke precise English despite his accent. "Where is your commander?" the voice yelled.

"Here," Captain Rook said weakly.

"Did you authorize the surrender?" the man asked, stepping around to where I could see him.

"I did."

"Fine. Come with me, please."

We watched as the two men walked to Rook's Jeep. The German gestured to Captain Rook's hands. Rook lowered them. The two men spoke for a moment while looking at the map. They spoke a little longer. Then Rook talked into the radio. Several minutes later, they were back, with Rook joining us again. The SS commander climbed up on the lower rung of a Panzer's side ladder, peering over us.

"There will be no rescue, gentlemen. Not yet, anyway. If an American unit attempted to intervene at this point, such action would be deadly, and would probably result in all of us dying. The good Captain Rook understands your predicament, has no desire for further loss of life, and has called in erroneous coordinates to your battalion." The German smiled thinly. "Therefore, your brethren think you are many kilometers from this location."

Several groans could be heard.

The SS commander's face was tanned and chapped, certainly from all the time he'd spent perched in his tank's cupola. Even with a crooked scar over his prominent nose, he had an aristocratic look about him. His eyes were icy blue and lively and, despite the fact that he was the enemy, I could see why men would choose to follow him. He continued to speak, sounding as if he might be talking to his own men.

"My name is Sturmbannführer Peter Weber of the 101st Schutzstaffel Panzer Battalion. As I'm sure you gentlemen are aware, our German brethren are not faring all too well in this war. Had the United States stayed out of the war, as they should have, we could have been eventual allies. But, because our esteemed Führer couldn't help himself and chose to fight on two fronts, we will now succumb to your forces, probably before summer is upon us."

Despite my racing heart, I joined eyes with my friends, shrugging at this curious preamble.

"Gentlemen, at this stage in the war, it gives me no pleasure to have killed your fellow soldiers. It saddens me to have lost more of my own men. Know this: despite your American and British propaganda, the Schutzstaffel are not savages." Weber paused, his eyes sparkling. "But, like it or not, you're now my bargaining chip. If you behave, you will be rescued in short order. Your rescue, of course, will occur in exchange for fair treatment of my own men." He nodded. "Yes...we will surrender. We've no more desire to fight in this lost cause. Why kill more of you, and lose our own, when the outcome has already been cast?"

Despite the casualties we'd just endured, the men of our unit looked optimistically at one another. This was about as good as anyone could have hoped for. Now I could understand why Captain Rook called in the erroneous coordinates.

"My men will now search you," Weber said. "And I'd advise you not to resist or more unpleasantness will occur. When the search is done, you will sit in this perimeter while we determine how to negotiate our own surrender. To ensure your safety, you must ask if you need to relieve yourself. If you require urgent medical attention, let us know and we'll see that you're looked after. Questions?" There were none. Then Weber spoke German to his men before the SS began searching us for weapons. I remember many of the SS seemed quite disgruntled as they handled us roughly.

Minutes later, after they'd relieved us of knives, grenades, and a handful of German pistols, we sat shoulder to shoulder, chatting in a murmur. Approximately twenty SS Panzer troops guarded us at gunpoint. Others, having pilfered cigarettes from us, smoked and rifled our vehicles. We watched as our valuable items, primarily candy and cigarettes, were stacked nearby and ogled by the Germans.

John even chatted with a young SS, the two of them having a discussion in German that seemed quite amiable. The SS held up a finger at one point, walking away before coming back with a powder. He gave it to John who dumped it in his canteen and chugged the water.

"For my ankle," John told us.

"Like the guy said, I'd always been told the SS were savages," I whispered to John.

"This guy seems just like us," John whispered back to me before resuming his conversation.

During this time the German commander had been in deep conversation near Captain Rook's Jeep. He was speaking to an SS wearing a different uniform, a type of brown camouflage. In fact, roughly half of the SS were wearing this uniform. Such a lack of uniformity, even on our side, wasn't uncommon. During a long war, soldiers do their best to maintain their uniforms and, oftentimes, standardization is impossible. But these two uniforms were distinctly different.

"Ask your friend why they're wearing two uniforms," I whispered to John. John, in turn, asked his friend. After hearing the SS's response, he turned back to me, his diction already somewhat slack after the fast-acting pain medicine had hit his bloodstream.

"Those are both standard SS uniforms. The camo is newer. Most of the men in camo are from another unit. Due to losses the two units were combined just a few weeks ago."

I turned my attention back to their commander, Weber, and the other, younger man. Their conversation seemed to be growing somewhat heated as their voices escalated. Everyone watched them, including John and his chatty SS buddy.

"This isn't good," John whispered.

"What isn't?" Kenny asked.

"That's got to be the unit XO, or whatever their equivalent is. Seems pretty obvious he and the commander don't like each other." John turned to his buddy and asked a quick question. After hearing the answer, he said, "The other officer used to be the commander of the unit that was combined with this one."

"It's a 'who has the biggest cock' argument," Danny said knowingly. "Seen it on our side too many times."

"What are they saying?" I asked.

"The XO doesn't want to surrender," John said. "He's telling Weber that most of the men don't want to surrender either."

The argument intensified. It wasn't one of those collegial arguments between officers. It wasn't even like one of the arguments between the enlisted members—the fiery type that might result with someone throwing a punch. No, even though I couldn't speak German, it was obvious that this argument went much deeper than a standard disagreement. The two men were so angry they were trembling with rage. They began pointing fingers at each other's face. As they shouted, I heard many German curse words I'd learned during the war. Even their own men began fidgeting and acting nervous.

Somehow I knew this wasn't going to end well.

\*\*\*

When he'd first moved in to the Steglitz flat, Marty had found a half-roll of plastic sheeting in the back of a closet. It had probably been used by the painters to protect the floor and the balance of the roll left behind. With some creative scissoring, he'd managed to create a partial sleeve that, when held tightly against his skin, would create a moisture barrier over his bandage. Marty needed a shower, desperately—he could smell himself.

Knowing his right hand would be occupied with soap or a washcloth, he threaded a pull-string through the plastic, using his wounded left hand to tug down on the string in order to hold the barrier tight against his shoulder and upper arm. This sounded good, in theory. When he exited the shower, however, he realized his efforts had been in vain. Water had leaked through the faulty seal and left his neat bandaging thoroughly soaked.

Thankfully, the water that had seeped through didn't add any noticeable pain to his wounds. The only time he hurt was when he flexed his arm straight, requiring usage of his triceps muscle. Significant gripping activities hurt as well. But no longer did he ache when sitting still, a nod to Frau Schaal's fine sewing work.

Using the scissors, he cut the wet bandage away, eyeing the two wounds in the bathroom mirror. They'd both stopped bleeding, even after getting wet, and would be covered by his undershirt tomorrow when he went back to work—assuming he went back tomorrow. Despite the fact that the stitches had halted the bleeding, Marty felt he needed to wear a bandage for a few more days. The risk of infection was too great. He unsuccessfully tried to replace the gauze one-handed, eventually throwing the white tape in disgust. Then, after slipping on pajama pants and his robe, Marty made his way down the flight of stairs.

Standing in front of the door of the Schaal flat, he admonished himself.

*You just want to talk to her. You don't like how things went earlier, so you fouled up that bandage on purpose.*

*Preposterous,* the sensible side of his brain countered. *I've never wanted a damned thing from these people. I'm only here because I need something. I won't even chat with her.*

*Yeah, right.*

*Yeah…right.*

*Shut up.*

Using his right hand, Marty rapped on the door.

***

Werner had listened to the BKA man prattle on for the better part of fifteen minutes. While relaying several basic but salient facts about Werner's case, the remainder of what the man had spoken about was inconsequential. He also levied far too many compliments to Werner and the Polizei. In Werner's experience, and based on all he'd heard, this was out of character coming from someone in the BKA. But, perhaps the man was so far behind in his investigations that he was doing this in order to help himself. This wouldn't be the first time a federal agency played nice with the locals just to catch up. Still, based on the elementary facts the man had relayed, Werner felt the man was missing a number of critical facts. And he was a *director*. Why would he even be involved? Werner was concerned about the man's intentions until the man dropped the following bomb:

"It wasn't until last night, in Bayreuth, that we made the Oklahoma connection that led us to you."

"Really," Werner said, fighting not to look surprised. He made sure he said "really" with no tonal increase at the end—to keep it from sounding like a question. But he wanted to scream, "Bayreuth? What happened in Bayreuth?" Instead, he calmly asked, "And what about the Bayreuth incident tipped you?"

"After the shooting, our investigation revealed that the resident whose home was damaged was living under a pseudonym. He'd previously served in the *Schutzstaffel* as a battalion commander."

*Mein Gott! Another shooting?* Werner nodded as if he knew all this. "And how is the Bayreuth man?"

"He's dead."

"Oh? I didn't realize that he'd perished."

"So, you knew about the shooting?" Loeffler asked, arching his eyebrows.

"Well," Werner said, clearing his throat. "What I'm more curious about is how you made the Oklahoma connection."

"Physical evidence, detective." The man smiled. "I can't go farther than that, at the moment. But once we made the Oklahoma connection, we found out about a bloodhound detective in Berlin who'd made the same connection."

Werner didn't want to say this, but he couldn't help himself. "How? We were keeping this quiet."

The BKA man smiled. "You visited the Americans in Frankfurt. They told us."

"I see."

"We need your full cooperation, Eisch. And *if* you choose to cooperate..."

"Then you'll turn everything over to me, provided I do the same."

"Correct. But please understand, we have to be the lead, detective." He must have sensed Werner's next comment because he stabbed a finger to the sky and said, "And rest assured, you can have *all* the credit when we break the case public. In fact, all BKA involvement should remain a secret."

Now that was a surprise. Werner couldn't help but view the man with wide eyes as he processed this. "Assuming we don't cooperate?"

"Well," the director said gravely, "if you make such an unwise decision, I've already been assured by your Chief Mainhardt that *he* will turn everything over to us. And after he's gotten all relevant information from you, you will likely be censured, or worse. It would be nothing more than a waste of time and a sterling career."

Werner automatically clicked his prosthetic.

"However, *Kriminaldetektiv* Eisch, I've come to understand you have the worthwhile dream of transitioning to homicide."

"How did you learn that?"

The man opened his hands in a show of innocence. "What good detective wouldn't? Regardless, if you cooperate today, right now, I will see to it that you're a member of Homicide by next week. And I'll also see to it that the Homicide chief welcomes you with open arms—and that the move is permanent." The smile was very wide now, opening slightly as he slid the Lucky into a corner of his mouth. He scratched a match under the table, lighting the short cigarette and puffing grandly. "Now, detective, why don't you go get your case file along with your list of possible suspects? We can view the list as I tell you what I know. I have a piece of information that, combined with what you know, may lead us to our man *this* afternoon."

Werner finally managed to swallow. "You're serious about this?"

As if giving an oath, the man covered his heart with one hand and, cigarette in his other hand, raised it while showing his palm.

Temporarily blinded, Werner hurried from the conference room, two words blaring in his mind: Homicide Detective!

*\*\*\**

The door opened and Frau Schaal gave a shake of her head, her annoyance quite obvious. "What do you want?" she asked. Behind her, Josh made a waving motion with a large smile on his face.

"Hi…can I, uh, speak with you out here for a moment?"

"I'd really rather not speak with you at all."

"Please."

"Why not speak right here?" she said. "Thanks to you, Josh knows about much of this."

"You won't want him to hear this."

She turned. "Josh, read one of your summer books. I'll be back in a moment." Frau Schaal stepped into the hallway, pulling the door shut. "What is it?"

"I needed a shower and tried to cover the bandage with some plastic but—"

"It got wet," she said, frowning.

"I was filthy," he replied in defense. "I tried to re-bandage it but…"

"And what about this did Josh not need to hear?"

"Well, I wasn't sure if he knew you patched me up."

She snapped her fingers. "Give me the tape and bandage."

"It's upstairs."

"Then go get it."

"Can you just come up? All this up and down is making me dizzy."

She crossed her arms. "Before I do, will you agree that tomorrow you will seek a place to live? There shouldn't be any problem for an American with money to find an apartment."

"I'm supposed to work tomorrow, but I can get the newspaper and look during my lunch hour."

"You actually do have a job?" she asked, still using her displeased tone.

"Yes."

Frau Schaal motioned up the stairs. "Then hurry. I don't have long."

Marty led the way. She left his front door open, impatiently tapping her shoe while he retrieved the items.

"Thanks for coming up," Marty said.

Without responding, Frau Schaal accepted the gauze and tape, snatching them from his hand. "Where's the iodine?" He handed it to her, watching as she wiped the wounds. Then, as efficiently as she had done earlier, she wrapped his arm neatly and covered the gauze with two snug bands of tape.

"The next time you bathe, use the bathtub," she said, her words quick and sharp.

"I will."

She turned to leave. Marty grabbed her arm with his good arm. When she turned, her face flashed red with anger. "Let me go."

Marty's hand moved behind her neck, pulling her to him as his mouth pressed against hers. For a moment, she acquiesced, allowing his tongue to touch hers as her mouth opened. He took a half step closer to her, feeling the glory of her hips push against his, creating a welcome amount of friction. A tiny and satisfied hum could be heard from her throat. Her tongue began to move with Marty's, welcoming his before she suddenly went rigid. Then she pulled backward, staring at him with round eyes as her chest rose and fell. He watched her mouth close, able to hear the slight grinding of her teeth.

Frau Schaal slapped Marty, the sound reverberating in the small space with a sharp crack.

Eyes glistening, her face a kaleidoscope of emotions, she rushed from the apartment and down the stairs. He listened for her door to open and shut but heard nothing. Padding on his bare feet, Marty crept to his own threshold, feeling the bitter sting on his cheek. He could hear her sniffling one level down. After about a minute he was able to hear her taking a great breath, then opening the door.

"Are you still reading?" she asked cheerily, just before her door clicked shut.

Marty closed his own door, resting his head against the jamb. He muttered a single curse word, four times in a row.

*** 

Werner had been gone for more than fifteen minutes. Though he assumed the BKA man's identity would have been verified by Chief Mainhardt, he had no way of knowing that for certain. So, after retrieving his file and list, Werner found the phone number and called the governmental affairs section for the Polizei in Spandau, confirming the identity of Director Klaus Loeffler. When he received the verification, including the man's height, eye and hair color, and weight, Werner's mind lurched into high gear.

If all Werner needed to do was cooperate to gain a promotion, then his ship had finally come in! After all the years of patience, of loyalty, of duty—finally, his steadfastness was about to be rewarded.

Werner's mind went back to the case, to what the director had told him. The shooting in Bayreuth fit nicely as the keystone in the complicated puzzle. Werner had always been taught to start with the basics of police work: *The who*—an American man from Oklahoma, seemingly bent on revenge against former Schutzstaffel members. *The when*—it all started less than a month ago. *The how*—it began with violent interrogations and had devolved into several killings. But what Werner had been stuck on was "The Why."

Why was this American doing this? What was his motive? Simple conjecture would indicate that he desired revenge for something left over from the war. But what puzzled Werner the most were the interrogations. His suspect had left those Berliners virtually unharmed. Then, at the Castle Gleiberg, his suspect had shot and killed Felix Roth, but evidence indicated that Roth may have initiated the deadly exchange. And the caretaker who'd been left behind claimed that the American was actually gentle.

*Gentle!*

Now the BKA director had informed Werner that there had been a shooting in Bayreuth, killing the cloaked battalion commander of the Schutzstaffel unit.

So, was the battalion commander the man the American was after? The men who'd been interrogated in Berlin did say their captor wanted information about the battalion commander, Zeckern, and the one named Nadel, a company commander.

So, where's Nadel?

Werner checked his watch: 20 minutes. Snatching his phone, he rang the desk sergeant, asking him to tell Loeffler that he'd be up in a few more minutes. After consulting his police phone book again, Werner dialed the Polizei bureau in Bayreuth. It took five minutes to get anyone of authority on the phone, a sergeant from Vice.

"This is *Kriminaldetektiv* Werner Eisch from Berlin. My verification is 67590-*Gustav-Otto-Ypsilon*," he said, the last part representing letters from the German phonetic alphabet.

"Hang on," the sergeant grunted as he audibly rummaged for his authentication tablet that was seldom used by Polizei. "Okay, got it. What do you need, Eisch?"

"I'm working a case that may be related to action in Bayreuth. I can't add more than that, yet."

"Understood. What else?"

"You had a shooting last night?"

A snort. "I'll say. Been a damned unlocked zoo around here for the last twenty hours."

"The man was learned to be former SS?"

"News travels fast," the cop said flatly. "Yeah, the homeowner was a regular tax-paying wealthy type. Well-respected in the community, no suspicion...all that. Turns out he was the former Oskar Zeckern, a battalion commander in the Waffen-SS Panzers."

Werner exhaled in relief, his promotion to homicide mere minutes away. "Did this Zeckern display any signs of torture?"

"What do you mean?"

"On his person, did it appear that he'd been beaten, burned, stabbed...tortured in a manner consistent with interrogation or pent-up anger?"

"You lost me there, pal."

"He didn't appear tortured?"

The phone squelched as the officer exhaled into the receiver. "No, he didn't, because we don't have a body."

"You don't have a body?" Werner asked, standing so quickly his chair shot backward.

"Shit, no. All we've got out there at his fancy house are bullet holes on the exterior. Witnesses saw a man come and go from inside, but no one could give us much more than that. There's nothing inside, as of yet, to indicate who the man was, but he *was* shooting out from an upstairs window."

The room began to spin. Werner leaned on the desk with his prosthetic. "What else?"

"Hang on...got the brief here somewhere." The detective could be heard riffling papers. "Okay, multiple witnesses have a man on the street, shooting a pistol at the house, exchanging fire with someone from the corner window. The guy outside got shot, *supposedly*, and blood on a driveway and the street indicates that to be correct. Some kid, a teenager, was seen shouting at the guy on the street, telling him to hurry up. Witnesses also claim two other men in Polizei garb ran through the yards with guns moments before all the shooting started. They were seen speeding away not long after all the commotion."

"Were they Polizei?"

"Hell no. Costumes."

"And you're sure—absolutely certain—there's no body of this Zeckern fellow?"

"I think I'd know if there was."

"Right. What else can you tell me?"

"Here's the kicker, Eisch," the detective said. "Zeckern's wife, a real looker who was only in her late twenties, was found this morning in a hotel room, dead of an overdose."

"The wife?"

"Damn straight—maybe that's the body you heard about?" Cleared his throat. "They're still looking at her but the preliminary report indicates that she had intercourse shortly before she died. Whoever nailed her wore a rubber, too."

"Witnesses?"

"None yet."

Werner closed his eyes, his mind racing. "When was the last time anyone saw Zeckern?"

"That's what the fellas are out working on. Even me. They called in all swinging dicks for this one."

"Anything yet?"

"Nothing concrete. Neighbors think they saw him a few days back."

"The man at Zeckern's house...could he have been Zeckern?"

"Two neighbors say no. They didn't get a good look at the man from yesterday, but they said he was younger, taller and more handsome."

"No physical evidence inside?"

"We're working on it. You know all I know."

"The two men outside, dressed as Polizei..."

"They were driving a new model panel van, white. It had been parked there all day."

"They could have been street surveillance."

"Could've been," the Bayreuth detective said in an open tone that indicated the men could have been any number of things.

"The teenager."

"Only one eyewitness. She said he was twelve to fourteen, sandy blond." The detective described his clothing. "The witness heard him yelling for the shooter on the street to hurry up and saw them running away together."

"Anything else?"

"Nope. You got anything that could help me?"

"Wish I did." Werner exchanged information with the detective who promised to update him if he learned more. After hanging up, Werner gathered his files, his mind racing over what he'd just heard.

Why wasn't the BKA director being truthful? Or, perhaps, he knew more than the Bayreuth Polizei? Was this need-to-know type information that he was keeping compartmentalized? He had insisted that the BKA's name or involvement not be revealed.

As he placed his only hand on the doorknob, Werner halted, an idea occurring to him. He shook his head, quickly decided that it would have to wait because he couldn't keep this director waiting any longer. Preparing his mind, Werner readied the questions he would use to test this Director Loeffler from the BKA.

Because, something about his visit stunk…

***

Earlier in the day, Marty had been able to lightly clench his left hand. Now, however, just wiggling his fingers caused lightning pain that reached well into his chest. So, Marty did what he'd been taught back in the Army to do when he was in pain—he started drinking. The German beer was excellent and lubricated his senses enough for him to make a diary entry. He relayed the Bayreuth episode in a clinical fashion, sticking to the basics and leaving Josh out of it. Then, as the alcohol really went to work, he flipped the page and started a new section, drinking two more beers as he filled several pages with his thoughts, the entries unlike any of the others. Up until now, Marty had been relaying the facts of the past and present. He'd not delved into his own feelings. And doing so felt quite therapeutic.

Marty had just popped the top on his fifth beer when he heard the knock on the door. It was very light, almost like whoever it was didn't want him to hear the knocking. Placing the beer on the table next to the door, Marty opened the door to find Frau Schaal standing there. She appeared apprehensive, her eyes going to the floor before coming back up.

"I'm very sorry about earlier, Herr Marty," she said without hesitation. "While I'm still upset that you…you *elevated* our risk by bringing your personal agenda here to our home, I've behaved rudely. The way you looked out for Josh's safety means a great deal to me." She paused, appearing to search for something else to say. Then she knotted her lips tightly, lowering her hands to her side.

"Thank you, Frau Schaal, but you don't have to apologize. I'm the one who should say I'm sorry. Though I'll not apologize for why I'm in Germany, I should have found some small cottage or house in a remote area. It honestly never crossed my mind that I could endanger those around me. And, as we discussed, I will honor your wish and leave this week."

She raised her finger. "I've actually been thinking about that and—"

"I insist."

"Well…" She nodded and took a step backward.

"Frau Schaal, may I make a suggestion that you'll probably think is a bad one?"

"I'm not sure I understand."

"Um…" *Just say it!* "…could the three of us have dinner tonight?"

She shook her head. "No, Herr Marty…that's not a good idea."

"You may be right, but I think it might go a long way towards helping Josh…helping *all* of us…cope with what's happened."

"What if people are looking for you? We might be thought to be guilty by association. According to the law, I should call the Polizei right now since I *know* you've committed a crime."

"The Polizei aren't going to be interested in you."

"I sewed up a gunshot wound. I lied to a policeman for you," she said, her voice rising. "They will charge me with aiding you."

"No one knows who I am, or where I am. If that cop knew, he'd have arrested me." Marty massaged his eyes with his right hand. "Please, Frau Schaal…I'm about to be gone from here for good. Just one meal."

"It's already almost dinnertime."

"I'll eat anything."

There was a long gap of silence as she looked away, clearly in thought. A door down below opened and closed, the sound of someone shuffling down several flights of stairs the only sound. Finally, she nodded, speaking in a whisper. "We can do this under one very strict condition."

"Sure. Name it."

"It's Josh. He seems fine…too well, in fact. But somewhere in that twelve year-old brain of his is the horror of what he saw. I want you to get him to talk about it."

"In front of you?"

"In front of me."

"Okay. I'll try."

"Trying isn't good enough. You must do this."

"Understood," Marty replied.

"We'll expect you in one hour, Herr Marty." She turned to walk down the stairs before stopping and turning. "You might want to slow down on the beers. In your condition you may pass out before we eat." Marty thought he saw the hint of a smile before she disappeared around the landing.

\*\*\*

"So sorry to have kept you waiting, director," Werner said, rushing in and placing his files on the table.

The director, his face no longer affable, crushed out a cigarette as he frowned at Werner. "That was damn near thirty minutes."

Werner separated the files into several stacks before stopping what he was doing and looking up. "Sorry, but I've had an upset stomach today, sir. Not sure what I ate. Been to the toilet five or six times. I hope it's not a bug."

Curling his upper lip, the director slid his chair backward.

*Works every time*, Werner thought as he attempted to contain a satisfied grin.

"Anyway…here are my files." Placing his hand and prosthetic over the two outer stacks, Werner eyed the director. "Before I get to that, did anything else happen in Bayreuth?"

"What do you mean?"

"Any other crimes that may be related?"

"Related? No. None that I'm aware of."

"Nothing else, sir?" Werner asked, puzzled why the director didn't mention Oskar Zeckern's wife.

"No, detective, and why are you quizzing me in this manner?"

"I apologize," Werner said. "I just wanted to rule out anything else."

"Get back to your investigation," the director said authoritatively.

*He's definitely lying to me.* Werner hid his apprehension and pressed on.

"Well, in summary, what initially tipped me to this investigation was when I became aware of several illegal interrogations that had taken place in Berlin. The men who were interrogated were taken down on the street. I soon learned that each of them was former Waffen-SS."

"Go on," the director said, settling into his chair, his hardened expression softening now that he realized they were finally getting somewhere.

"It didn't take long for me to figure out that the men were all in the same unit, the 101st SS Heavy Panzer Battalion."

"Very good," the director said, tapping another cigarette from his pack. "And how long ago was this?"

"About three weeks. That initial period went on for the first week. And luckily, I just happened to hear about a man who was murdered over in Hessen, in Krofdorf-Gleiberg. He was living under an assumed name, but—"

"His name was actually Felix Roth," the director said, clamping the cigarette between his teeth and lighting it. He took a deep drag, speaking through the smoke as he said, "You were there a day before we were. A fine piece of work, detective."

"Well, I'll believe that when we arrest our suspect."

"Amen." After another drag the director asked, "You found physical evidence there, correct? A clothing tag?"

"Yes, sir," Werner breathed, shaking his head. "But that may have led me on a wild goose chase. It made me think the killer could be from Oklahoma. Right away I visited the U.S. Army's headquarters in Frankfurt and narrowed the list to Oklahomans in Germany—military and civilian—and since then have spent my time whittling that list down."

"Found anyone promising?"

"Nope," Werner lied. "That's why I was beginning to think the Oklahoma angle might be a red herring."

"It's not. Remember, that clothing tag had gun oil on it."

"Yes."

"Making it a strong lead."

"Certainly, sir, but circumstantial. If it belonged to the perpetrator, he could have purchased that clothing while traveling or, if he's military, while he was *stationed* in Oklahoma. But his home of record could be anywhere."

"Did you check American soldiers whose last duty station was in Oklahoma?"

"I asked, but USAREUR said I wasn't cleared for that information."

"Pricks," the director breathed. "I can get that information."

Continuing on, Werner said, "Maybe our perp is here under an assumed identity that lists his home as someplace other than Oklahoma?" Werner lifted his prosthetic, clicking it for emphasis. "Or perhaps, director, that tag belonged to someone else altogether. Tens of thousands of Americans are stationed in the Giessen area. Any one of them could have lost that tag, and could have gotten gun oil on it any number of ways."

Tobacco crackled as the director sucked mightily on his cigarette. "How many of those Oklahomans have you ruled out?"

"All but about ten. They're on my list to see in the coming week."

"You're sure about the ones you already ruled out?"

"I'd stake my life that they're not our man," Werner replied.

"Damn."

Werner leaned forward, ready to gently turn the tables. "What makes the BKA think our man is from Oklahoma?"

"Evidence we found in Bayreuth."

"What was it?"

"I can't say."

"So, you want everything from me, but you won't reciprocate?"

Loeffler shrugged. "To be honest, I don't know what it is. As soon as we made the connection, I hurried to Berlin because we knew you were working the same angle."

"Back to Oskar Zeckern, sir...where did your men find his body?" Werner watched the director very closely. These sudden changes in direction were obviously throwing him off. He seemed to attempt to hide his frustration.

"Uh, you know, it was there, in the house. The shooter on the street shot Zeckern and Zeckern bled out a short distance from where he'd been shooting through the window."

"Did it appear he'd been expecting this shooter on the street?" Werner asked.

"That's hard to say."

"And where was the shooter on the street hit?"

"According to the witness, he was hit in the arm."

"Which arm?"

The director rolled his eyes, quickly consulting his notes. "Left upper arm."

The words hit Werner like a thunderbolt as he recalled the man from earlier—the man who was in great pain due to an "old farming accident." He gnawed on his tongue to maintain his serious expression.

"Did you have Zeckern's body taken to the local morgue?"

"We'll come back to that," the director said with irritation, tugging at his collar. "For the moment, I'd like to see your full list of Oklahomans."

"The remaining list?"

"No. The *full* list."

Crestfallen, Werner handed over the multi-page list, replete with hundreds of scratched-out names and handwritten notes.

"I'm guessing the ones not marked off are your remaining suspects?"

"Yes, sir."

The director puffed thoughtfully as he flipped the pages, skimming the list and pointing to a column of numbers. "These are the dates that you ruled each man out?"

Werner nodded.

"How many did you actually speak with?"

"It's noted, sir. Perhaps twenty?"

The director grunted, flipping back to the first page and eyeing each name line by line.

"Sir, the man on the street who was shot. You said there was blood. Did the Polizei get a blood type?"

"O-neg," the director said absently, turning to page two.

"Thanks," Werner replied, scribbling that on his pad.

The director lowered the list and crushed out the remaining nub of his cigarette. He squared himself with the table, flattening both hands over the list. "I'll scan this later. What else of importance do you have for me?"

"That's it. I convinced Chief Mainhardt to allow me to work the interrogations. That led to Felix Roth, which led to the clothing tag, which led me to searching for Oklahomans in Germany. I whittled the list down to men, and to those who would have served in the war. And until you walked in today, sir, all I had to go on was the list."

The director narrowed his eyes. "You seem eager to do something, detective."

"I am, sir. I want to take the *remaining* names on that list and somehow find out who has O-negative blood."

The director nodded his approval. "Go on."

"Additionally, I think we should focus on the testimonies of witnesses, and any evidence you might find in Bayreuth. We should cross that with evidence from Gleiberg, and proceed from there."

"I especially like the blood type line of thought," the director said, using the tone of a doting uncle.

"And I'd like a list of all current U.S. service members who were recently stationed in Oklahoma."

"I can get all these things."

"Before we do that, sir, might I call Bayreuth?"

"Call Bayreuth?" Loeffler snapped, his tone changing markedly.

"Yes, sir…to speak to their detective in charge about updates on things they've likely found since you—"

"You will not call *anyone*, detective! Do you understand me?" the director said, slapping his hand down on the list. He lifted the hand, rigidly pointing his finger into his own chest. "I am a high director in the BKA, detective. The entire Berlin Polizei answers to me. I've spoken to your chief and you belong to *me* until I say otherwise."

Werner made sure he looked shocked. "I didn't realize that calling them would be a problem." He lowered his eyes to the floor.

The director's voice changed pitch. "Listen…I apologize for such an outburst, but you have no idea of the pressure being applied on me. This case has *grave* national implications and we can't drag in too many other parties. There could be leaks in these local Polizei bureaus."

"With all due respect, sir," Werner said as gently as he could manage, "might I ask why the case is so dire?"

The director transformed into the kind uncle again, his tone and facial expression softening. "Imagine it, detective, if the international press gets wind of a crusader over here killing former Schutzstaffel. The war is still fresh in millions of minds. Hell, over in the United States, in Britain, France…the man would be a damned folk hero. The world is still lusting for German blood, make no mistake about it. The Americans would throw him a parade."

"I see, sir."

The director lit another cigarette, a true chain smoker. "No, detective…" he breathed, the cigarette perched in the corner of his mouth, making him look like a contemplative cowboy, "…we'll take care of this quietly, on our own." He showed his palms. "No one is saying anything on the behalf of those SS animals…the balance of them can rot for all I care. But as far as this American goes…we must contain him, and soon."

"I understand, sir."

The director lifted the telephone, going through several people before he asked for the blood type and Oklahoma duty of record information. As he talked, Werner's mind raced.

*Why is this man deceiving me? Why would he lie to me about Oskar Zeckern's body? And why wouldn't he tell me about the murdered wife? What's his angle? Is he lying about his Oklahoma evidence, too?*

*And he won't let me speak to anyone other than him…*

Werner's mind changed gears to the thunderbolt he'd been setting aside until he had a moment to himself. The man from earlier, Martin Elder in Steglitz. His arm was wounded, red and hot.

His left—upper—arm!

# Chapter Twenty-One

Journal Entry

The argument continued between the SS commander and his XO. Several of the SS soldiers had moved behind each of the two belligerents. It was clear they were taking sides. More men stood behind the younger one than stood behind Weber, the commander.

"What are they saying now?" I asked John. He was listening so intently, his lips were moving as he silently translated.

"Boy, they really hate each other," John whispered. "They're arguing about things that have occurred since the younger one joined the unit. It's hard to even keep up."

"What about the one not wanting to surrender?"

John shook his head. "The younger one is calling Weber some really nasty names. Telling him he's a coward. Saying he's a disgrace to his family, to his father. Telling him what he's proposing is punishable by death."

Suddenly, a nearby SS soldier in camouflage screamed "Schnauze!" at John, jabbing the barrel of his MP-40 inches from John's face. John stopped talking.

The argument between the two officers had escalated to shoving and chest bumping. Then, in a moment that's forever etched in my mind, the XO quickly drew his pistol and shot Weber in his chest. It happened incredibly fast. Weber, upon seeing his subordinate drawing his pistol, had tried to do the same. But the XO had too much of a head start. The XO's bullet didn't pack the wallop our .45s did and Weber sat down roughly, his free hand covering the seeping wound.

I can still see Weber's expression as he looked up from his gunshot wound. He looked at the XO then looked around at all of his men. His face wore an expression of great sadness.

The XO leaned down and disentangled Weber's pistol from his hand. He said something to Weber—obviously another insult—then he spat on him. In the growing twilight, we watched as the XO fired his pistol a second time, striking Weber in the face.

Weber fell backward, dead.

Many of the assembled SS gasped. A few shouted protests. We remained quiet. Stunned.

Stunned because we knew we were in big, big trouble.

The XO turned to us, and to his men, and began shouting orders in German. Risking his life, John translated for us in a whisper.

"He said, 'I will not surrender, nor will I lead my men to such a cowardly end. If you disagree with what I just did, speak now, so you can join these spineless American pigs in their fate.'"

"Oh, shit," Danny muttered.

The leather of weapon straps could be heard tensing among the SS. Many looked at each other, seemingly puzzled about what to do. Then, an older SS, a large man in the camo uniform, smiled and walked behind his new commander, clapping him on his shoulder. Another followed. And another. After a few tense moments, all but six SS stood behind their mutinous commander. With us unarmed and grouped so tightly, I guess they weren't concerned about us going anywhere.

Still standing nearby was John's "buddy," taking great breaths as his eyes darted nervously around. Then the XO spoke again, his voice low and cold.

"What'd he say?" I whispered to John.

"He said, 'If you're not with me, you're against me.'"

No sooner had John gotten the words out of his mouth than did the XO fire at the closest abstainer. With him, a number of other SS fired, many striking the same abstainers, killing all of them in a three-second hail of gunfire.

One of our own men, a crusty old sergeant first class named Grantham, stood up. Almost certainly knowing he was going to die, he shouted his objections as he pointed at the German XO, cursing him for his actions. The big SS standing next to the XO laughed as he riddled Grantham's body with bullets. Grantham literally danced as his body was ravaged with lead. Our soldiers caught his lifeless frame as it tumbled backward, dripping blood like a sieve.

Then, with a cruel smile on his face, the XO holstered his pistol and stepped forward. It was obvious to me that he was relishing this moment as only a true psychopath could.

I'm not a talented enough writer to describe just how terrifying this moment was.

I knew—we all knew—that our lives would soon be over.

***

Long before he ever went off to war, Marty's mother taught him to always bring something when invited to dinner. As fate would have it, he'd purchased a bottle of inexpensive French wine when he'd first arrived, and now he handed it to Frau Schaal as he walked into her flat. She wore an apron and carefully gripped the neck of the wine bottle, as it appeared she had food on her fingers.

"Sorry I forgot to bring something last time," Marty said.

"Bringing something this time wasn't necessary. We'll eat in about fifteen minutes," Frau Schaal replied. "Please make yourself comfortable."

Josh quickly steered Marty into the sitting area where he had a chessboard set up and waiting. "You do play?" he asked in English.

"A little."

"I win I believe," Josh said.

"Do you want to speak English while we play?"

"Yes."

"Okay," Marty said, sitting on the floor behind the black pieces. "Your move."

"Move?"

"You go first," Marty clarified.

Josh opened play as they made several quick moves with pawns before Marty brought a knight out onto the battlefield.

"How you arm?"

"*Your* arm."

"Yes. Your arm."

"Thanks, Josh. My arm is fine."

"Not fine."

"You know what I mean," Marty said with a smile.

"Still blood?"

"Still *bleeding*. No, the two holes are not bleeding, thanks to your mother." Marty cocked his eye as Josh quickly castled. The kid knew what he was doing.

"Play fast before eat, yes?"

"Sure." Marty decided to go for the jugular and bring his queen out into the fray. As Josh studied the board, Marty lowered his voice and said, "Are you okay, Josh?"

"Yes," Josh replied distantly, his hand hovering over his rook. He pulled his hand back and touched his mouth, obviously deep in thought.

"About yesterday," Marty clarified, switching to German. "Are you sure you're okay? That was a lot for anyone to see."

Josh looked up. "No English?"

"Just stop playing for a minute. Your mom wants me to talk to you after dinner about what happened. Before I do that in front of her, I just want to know that you're okay."

Josh nodded.

"Seriously, Josh. I never wanted you to see what you saw. I'm sorry you got mixed up in it."

"You told me the man you were shooting at killed all your friends. I understand, Mister Marty. I can remember a little bit about the war and I've been hearing about it ever since." He crossed his arms and leaned back. "Even if you would have gotten killed yesterday, I can tell you believe in what you're doing."

Josh's words struck Marty like a speeding truck. Marty looked to his right, seeing Frau Schaal in the kitchen. She'd been buttering bread but had stopped, staring at the two men. She apparently could hear what they were saying and gave Marty a slight nod. Marty turned back to Josh.

"I just don't want you thinking that violence is the way to solve your problems."

Josh stared at Marty intently. "So you're wrong for being here, doing what you're doing?"

"Well…" Marty's hand rubbed the stubble on his face as he thought back to Gloria, telling him about the American soldiers violating her. He thought of Frau Schaal's tale of suffering—she hadn't wanted her country to go to war. He thought of the millions who'd been wronged with no chance at eventual justice. Marty lowered his hand from his face. "Yeah, Josh…I *am* wrong. Despite what happened, coming back to find Raban Nadel—that's his name—as a vigilante, is not the way I should have done things."

"What should you have done?"

Marty glanced at Frau Schaal. Her mouth didn't smile, but her eyes did. Marty turned back to Josh, pausing a moment to order his words.

"Thinking back on things, Josh, I should have worked within the bounds of the law to try to bring Nadel to justice. I don't know exactly how I could have done that, but there are ways to *legally* fight in situations like this."

Josh nodded thoughtfully before he turned his eyes back to the board. "I move?"

"Sure."

Josh's bishop knifed diagonally across the board, defeating Marty's queen. Josh wagged the queen a few times before setting her aside. "Your eyes not see that, Mister Marty."

Marty frowned. "Damn."

Smiling, Josh pointed at Marty's mouth. "Bad word."

"Appropriate word." Since it was his move, Marty turned his attention back to Josh, switching back to German. "You're sure you're not bothered by what happened? I don't want you to have nightmares."

"You'll live, so I'm okay. I promise."

"Good," Marty replied. He looked at Frau Schaal—she was beaming. Feeling much better, Marty's eyes slid back to the board as he pondered a last ditch offensive with his depleted troops. He moved one of his pawns forward, hoping he might spring him all the way and reclaim his queen.

"So, you will stop searching for Herr Nadel illegally?" Josh asked in German.

Marty's head whipped up. "What?"

"You just said it's wrong."

"I know what I said."

"Good. Then you will stop."

Marty again turned to Frau Schaal. She was staring intently but made no expression. He turned back to Josh. "You want me to stop what I've planned for five years—think about how long that is, Josh—even though I've already come this far?"

"You said it's wrong," Josh said with a shrug. "Stop while you can, and find Nadel the legal way you spoke about."

"It's not that easy, Josh."

"Why not?"

Marty's right hand went to his left shoulder, gently touching the wounds through the shirt and bandaging. He thought about his pursuit of Raban Nadel, assuming that his world had probably been turned upside down, especially after the assault on Oskar Zeckern's home. The two men might even be fleeing the country. From here on, it would be much more difficult to hunt them.

But, aside from the difficulties, Josh was right. Marty thought about what he'd journaled earlier, about the things he'd learned since arriving. Was all that bullshit, or were his true feelings bleeding through with the aid of today's alcohol?

Josh leaned forward. "You can stop, Mister Marty. You can stop and your life will be still okay. You have spent seven years looking backward. Turn around and look ahead."

Marty stared back at his wise-beyond-his-years young friend while thinking of the friends he'd lost. Would they want all this? Would they want revenge? Or would they want Marty—Tommy—to live his life *for* them?

"Just think, Mister Marty, after yesterday, I bet those men are very scared of you. They're probably gone."

Josh's words struck Marty like frenzied bullets. Marty arched his neck backward, staring at the ceiling as he took several great breaths. Again he envisioned his friends.

There was a period of silence in the home before Marty eventually spoke, hearing himself as if someone else were speaking.

"Okay, Josh...from here on, *everything* I do in pursuit of Raban Nadel, or anyone from that SS unit, will be legal, done within the bounds of the law."

"You must promise."

Marty brought his glistening eyes back to Josh. "I promise."

"Tell my Mutti, too."

Marty turned. "Frau Schaal, I won't go after those men anymore. If I do, it'll be done legally."

Josh clapped and let out a cheer. Frau Schaal joined in.

"Thank you, Mister Marty," Josh said.

"Thank you, Josh."

"Now that the important things are done, shall we eat?" Frau Schaal asked, carrying two serving plates to the dining room table.

Feeling oddly relieved, Marty waved his hand over the board. "I guess we can finish this game after dinner?"

"Not need," Josh replied in English, bringing his queen out from the back row. "English word is checkmate, yes? I've seen it in movies."

"Heard it."

"Yes. Heard it."

Marty eyed all his available moves. Shaking his head, he whispered, "Damn."

"Again!" Josh laughed, pointing at Marty's mouth. "Bad word."

"Appropriate word," Marty answered, tousling his young friend's hair. Then they ate.

*** 

A driving summer rain soaked Berlin, creating a mess in the streets as the remaining rubble piles released bits of sediment into the swiftly running water. With only half of the city's streetlights repaired, the urban night was dark and gloomy. Since it was a Sunday, the automobile traffic was light, other than taxis and public transit. The wipers beat steadily on the windshield of the BKA Mercedes as the Hotel Adlon slid into view.

"You wait in the lobby," the director said, parking his vehicle under the portico and telling the doorman that he was BKA and to leave the Mercedes exactly where the hell it sat. Werner noticed that the director had brought his attaché case with him.

Inside the lobby of the hotel, the director pointed to an empty grouping of chairs. "Wait there and don't think about calling anyone. You see another cop, you tell them you're just waiting on a friend. Got it?"

"I remember your instructions to the letter," Werner replied. "I'm at the pleasure of your command, sir."

"Very good," the director replied, seeming satisfied. Then his expression changed to one of irritation. "The reason I dragged you here is my wife accompanied me on this trip. Her sister lives here." Loeffler glanced around. "We may have a long night, Eisch, so I'm going to run upstairs and make sure she's taken care of. I may be up there for a little bit so just relax, order a sandwich or a coffee if you like."

"Right-o, sir." Werner sat and watched the director hurry to the elevators. As he sat there, Werner's mind warred between two distinct thoughts. The first was Martin Elder, the man who Werner had a strong feeling was the vigilante. The second thought involved the director. Because of his lies about Bayreuth, Werner was almost certain that he was dirty.

A waiter appeared so Werner ordered a soft drink. When it arrived, he sipped it, pondering his plan of action.

*** 

"What the hell took you so damned long?" Nadel hissed when Director Loeffler entered the suite.

Loeffler frowned, removing a cigarette and lighting it. After a deliberate pause, he said, "I was busy putting a lid on this loose cannon detective and trying to contain *your* mess. That's what took me so long."

"How close is he to finding that sonofabitch who shot at me?"

"That's the good and the bad." Loeffler walked to the bar as he spoke, pouring two shots of whiskey. "He knew about everything up through Felix Roth. But I put the clamps on him and now he reports only through me."

"Does he know about me?"

Facing the mirror of the bar, Loeffler swigged half of the drink, trumpeting his cheeks as he blew out a cooling breath. "He knows about Raban Nadel, the former Waffen-SS. He doesn't know about your new identity, nor will he."

"Are you certain he doesn't know?" Nadel shot back.

"Yes." Loeffler eyed Nadel in the mirror. "And it doesn't matter anyway since he won't be alive to see the sunrise, Raban."

"Who else knows what he knows?"

Loeffler gave a dismissive wave of his hand. "That's the best part. His division commander, Mainhardt, knew. But he knew this would be a wild goose chase and could land his ass in a sling, so he kept a lid on the whole case."

"You just said Mainhardt *knew*? You mean, 'he knows?'"

Finishing his drink in one more gulp, Loeffler bared his teeth as the liquor seared his throat and stomach. "Whew...the Irish aren't good for much, but thank God for their whiskey."

"I don't pay you what I pay you to listen to you rate spirits," Nadel said in a low tone. "What about this Mainhardt?"

Loeffler dragged his cigarette, making Nadel wait for a few more moments. "I played Mainhardt like a violin. Made him feel important, just as I've done with this detective. After I learned what he knew, I sent him on a very important errand out near Potsdam."

"And?"

Loeffler turned, crossing his arms, ruefully shaking his head as he created a tone of pity. "The poor old man met with an accident."

"Won't that send shockwaves that we don't need yet?"

"You underestimate me, Raban. You always have and, I must say, it's always been a tad irritating. Dating back to the war, you thought if a man wasn't Schutzstaffel, he wasn't a man at all. My *Fallschirmjäger* unit was as elite as any unit in your Waffen-SS."

"Just tell me about Mainhardt."

"I have a trap team I use on occasion. They're the best men in the world for this type of thing. Believe me, no one will ever find Mainhardt's body or effects." Loeffler touched all ten of his fingers together, then made a magician's flourish outward. "Poof. The man is gone...forever." He smiled. "Now, do you want to know what our little armless detective knows?"

"You know I do."

Loeffler explained.

***

Downstairs, Werner whipped the slick Electrofax papers from his pocket, silently praying that the ink wouldn't be so smudged that it was illegible. As he gingerly unfolded the pages, he realized the new technology was better than he thought.

Werner located the third page, where the name Martin Vincent Elder was listed. There was a scratch mark through the name, along with his notes out beside the name, including the alibi from the landlady and the notation about Elder's pre-war injuries that had kept him from serving. Thinking back to earlier in the day, Werner recalled the meeting with Martin Elder. He could barely use his left arm, and winced when doing so.

And his hand was pink—and hot.

*Could that be him? Could he somehow be the man, the vigilante, seeking these former SS?*

Werner remembered his own arm injury, when a sniper's bullet had sliced through his elbow, leaving the arm attached only by muscle and skin. But even back in those desperate times, the German field doctors had tried to save the arm—amputation was always the last resort. They'd waited three days, till Werner's hand and wrist were rife with infection. At the beginning of that three-day wait, Werner's hand looked much like the American's from earlier today.

So, if this Martin Vincent Elder was indeed the vigilante, then who was he? Why was he here? Why was he hunting members of the 101st SS Heavy Panzer Battalion, specifically Oskar Zeckern and Raban Nadel?

Werner thought back to his bit of research at USAREUR headquarters, when he'd gotten the file regarding the Massacre at Kastellaun. The major had removed the back section of the file. But why? Many men had been tragically slaughtered, but the massacre was over and done with. A horrific incident for certain, but what was there left to hide? Was there some sort of after-action, as it's known in the military? Did the massacre not occur in the way it was recorded in history books? Was there some incident on the American side that the Allies didn't want getting out?

"What am I missing?" Werner whispered, massaging his tired eyes.

***

After hearing Director Loeffler's précis of the situation, Nadel received a call from his American on the take, Lieutenant Colonel Samuel Frost. Frost was the man who'd given up Felix Roth's ex-girlfriend, Gloria Riddenger, in Frankfurt. Earlier today, after agreeing to his exorbitant fee of $5,000, Frost had done some investigating about who might have had a grudge with the senior leadership of the 101st SS Heavy Panzer Battalion. Rather than color Frost's thoughts, Nadel left the task open-ended, curious about what the resourceful American might come back with.

When the hotel operator informed Nadel that he had a call from his uncle, Nadel told her to put it through.

"This is Uncle Sam," Frost said, triumph evident in his voice.

"And?"

"I've found the man you're looking for."

"You're sure you haven't found the person you *believe* to be him?"

"It's him," Frost said with certainty. "But before I give him to you, you're going to change the terms of our agreement."

"To what?"

"I want ten grand, not five. And I want it *before* I tell you."

Nadel eyed Loeffler, who was standing over by the window, shrugging. Nadel covered the mouthpiece and whispered, "The American colonel says he found him, but wants me to double my fee."

"Typical," Loeffler said with an acerbic smile. "The Americans…such greedy people—changing deals after handshakes."

Nadel uncovered the mouthpiece. "There is no way for me to pay you at this moment. But I want you to consider the fact that we've done business now for three years. You've gotten rich off me. Now, in my hour of need, I think a little trust is in order. And despite the crassness of your doubling the fee like this, I agree to your terms, and you'll have your money within three days."

The American could be heard sucking on his teeth. "Just don't ever get tempted to make me disappear because I've taken extreme precautions. If you do something to me, I can guarantee you that you, *and* your little empire, will go up in flames."

"You're an asset, Uncle Sam," Nadel said, using the silky voice that had gotten him through many sticky situations. "I have no intention of harming you in any way. The deal is ten grand. You'll have the money in no more than three days' time. Now—please—dispense."

"Alright…the break came when you pointed me to the Massacre at Kastellaun which, by the way, is utterly disgusting…how the hell can you sleep at night knowing you killed a couple hundred innocent artillerymen?"

"Innocent," Nadel snorted. "Innocent? Were you there, colonel? Do you think your *American* files tell the *true* tale? Do you really, honestly believe that? Revisionist history, colonel, *always* belongs with the victor. You don't know what happened in those woods and, though we can discuss this later, in person, I'd appreciate your not levying judgment without all the facts."

"Yeah, whatever," Frost replied in a patently unconvinced tone of voice. "The file also says, according to the testimony of *your* own men, that you gunned down your commander and assumed control of your tank troop, then carried out the massacre yourself."

"Are you going to earn your fee or not? I'm tantalizingly close to finding this vigilante myself and now, due to your criticism, I'm actively considering hanging up the phone and ignoring whatever it is that you've found."

There was a bit of silence before Frost said, "The records available to *most* eyes claim that every person in Able Battery, 32nd Field Artillery was killed in the Massacre at Kastellaun." He cleared his throat. "Truth is, however, that you boys left a couple of fellas alive. The Brits were the first on the scene, finding three breathing bodies in all that blood and mud. Two of them died soon thereafter, but one made it. One survivor out of 185 men. Imagine that," he said, his last two words dripping with anger.

Nadel's eyes darted all around the hotel room. "That can't be true. We...we..."

"You shot them till you ran out of ammo, then you stacked the ones that were still breathing and ran your Panzers back and forth over them." The colonel's breath could be heard, coming in snorts. "Is that what you're remembering?"

Knowing there was no profit to be gained by arguing with this asshole, Nadel refocused. As he did, he reconciled himself to killing Colonel Frost as soon as possible—and promising himself to make the man's demise quite unpleasant. *'Taken extreme precautions,' my ass. We'll find out about each of those precautions when I clamp a car battery to your balls, colonel.*

Nadel said, "I knew of no American survivors from the skirmish."

"Skirmish?" Frost yelled.

"Call it what you want."

"Well...this *lone* survivor had no immediate relatives back home, so the feds stepped in and gave him a new life. New name, new residence, tuition for school—the works. Can't say I blame the kid for taking it, either. Imagine the way the press would've hounded him."

Loeffler caught Nadel's eye by waving his hands. *'What is it?'* Loeffler mouthed, reading Nadel's disturbed face.

Nadel sank into a chair and shook his head at Loeffler while placing a quieting finger over his lips. After managing to wet his mouth, he again spoke into the telephone.

"Do you have this survivor's new information?"

"Do you agree about my ten grand?" Frost asked in a steely voice.

"Yes, ten grand."

"Kid was from North Dakota originally. When you guys shot him up, his name was Thomas Whiteside. He moved to Oklahoma after the massacre. They gave him a new name that I'm guessing he chose because it honored each of his best friends—friends that you and your unit *murdered*."

Despite having calmed himself, Nadel couldn't keep ignoring the taunts. "Murdered? It was wartime, you imbecile. They were soldiers."

"It ain't known as the *Battle* at Kastellaun. It's called the Massacre. Need me to read you the definition of 'massacre?'"

"Well, what about the Massacre at Bingen?" Nadel retorted. "Sixty-one German POWs—harmless, emaciated men—all shot to death in their holding pen?"

"That was in response to the Massacre at Kastellaun!" the colonel bellowed. "You expected our men to just sit on their hands after hearing what *you* did?"

Loeffler had moved in front of Nadel and was making a slashing motion across his throat. Nadel clamped his eyes shut and nodded. "I don't expect you to understand, colonel. Now, as per our deal, will you please provide this young man's information?"

"I will. But this better not ever come back on me."

"Trust me," Nadel said, tilting his head back as he indulgently envisioned Colonel Frost's body contorting in pain while high amperage pushed electricity into his scrotum.

"The kid's name is now Martin Vincent Elder. They changed his birthday but kept the same year—born in 1925. Last known address, according to the top-secret file, was at Eastern State University, in Ada, Oklahoma. I expect, if the kid had been in federal witness protection, they wouldn't have noted where he went. But he didn't do anything wrong, nor was anyone *thought* to be after him, hence the info. They simply changed his identity so he could avoid all the hubbub."

Nadel scribbled the information after making him repeat it. "What else?"

"Nothing else."

"So, how do you know he's the one?"

The colonel could be heard chuckling. "Imagine for just a second you were him. Imagine your entire unit, your best friends, were unjustly killed before your very eyes. Imagine you'd gotten all shot up, too, but somehow lived, even while they pivoted steel tanks over your body, grinding bone and flesh into hamburger." The colonel's voice changed pitch. "Now imagine you somehow survived, and you've gotta live with what happened for the rest of your days." He paused for a moment. "Now, tell me you wouldn't do the same damned thing."

Nadel didn't respond. The Oklahoma coincidence was too great. Martin Vincent Elder had to be the man who was after him.

"You got seventy-two hours to get me my ten grand, you sick sonofabitch." The line clicked dead.

Loeffler took the pad of paper from Nadel's hand. He knelt by the bed, flattening the marked-up sheets of paper provided to him by Detective Eisch. It only took a moment to scan the remaining names. There was no match.

"Nothing?" Nadel asked.

"No, but I'm going to run through all the ones he ruled out, just in case."

In a matter of seconds, Loeffler stabbed his finger on the crossed-out name of Martin Vincent Elder. "Sonofabitch! Here it is. He's right here in Berlin, in Steglitz."

Nadel stared at the name and the handwritten notes. Colonel Frost, dead man walking, had been correct.

"Tell me what your American said," Loeffler commanded.

When he was finished relaying Frost's revelations, Nadel said, "This Detective Eisch that's downstairs, do we need him anymore?"

Loeffler's hands were behind his back, his eyes narrowed as he pondered all he'd just heard. "We may still need him."

"Why? He could complicate things."

"Think about it," Loeffler said. "The American already demonstrated that he's willing to exchange fire out in the open. Wouldn't you rather this little armless putz take the brunt of his fire before we move in?"

"But we can't afford to have this go wrong."

"Then let's just leave now, if you're going to be a pussy. You can run to Argentina," Loeffler countered.

Nadel ignored the barb. "Not before I kill this American."

"Fine. And to do so, I want Kriminaldetektiv Eisch out front. Besides, he'll be our stooge." Loeffler's chin tilted upward. "I'm a director in the BKA, Raban. I can explain everything away without question."

"Except my presence."

"Then do yourself a favor and *don't* get shot." Loeffler sat in the high-back Victorian chair, quickly affixing his ankle holster he'd taken from his briefcase. He removed the snub-nose pistol, making sure it was loaded before he replaced it. Then, after glancing at his trousers in the full-length mirror, he grabbed his fedora and motioned to the door. "Get your things, and make sure your pistol is locked and loaded."

As the two men padded down the side stairs, Loeffler told Nadel to go outside and come around the building to the portico.

"Why?"

"Just follow my lead and make sure you're good and wet when you arrive."

Nadel agreed, but he had a bad feeling about the entire affair.

***

After his second cola arrived, Werner again stared at the names of the victims from the 32nd Field Artillery Roster. His eye went straight to Daniel Nehemiah Elder, age twenty-two, a sergeant. One of Werner's first actions, after getting the list of Oklahomans, was cross-referencing the last names to the last names of the men in Able Battery, 32nd Field Artillery. There had been eight matches, and Daniel Elder had been one of them. Werner called USAREUR and learned that Daniel Elder only had sisters. He had no brothers, so Werner ruled him out.

So who exactly was Martin Vincent Elder? Could he be Daniel Elder's cousin?

Werner nestled back into the chair and eyed the Able Battery roster, staring at Daniel Elder's name. He flipped to the second page, starting with the G's, his eyes scanning slowly downward. He flipped to the next page. Halfway down, he noticed one soldier with the last name of Martin—Martin was Elder's first name. Werner read the limited information aloud.

"Kenneth Wayne Martin, of Stanton, Texas. He was born in 1922 and served in second platoon." Werner flipped back to Daniel Elder. "Elder was also in second platoon."

Werner wiped his sweaty palms on his jacket. Martin and Elder. Werner knew Martin was a common name, very prevalent in England. Werner wasn't familiar with the name Elder, and couldn't imagine it being as common as Martin. But Werner could easily envision such a coincidence occurring in 185 American names.

His full name is Martin *Vincent* Elder.

*Surely there's not a Vincent listed. There can't be.*

Werner slowly flipped the pages, scrutinizing the page that started with the T's. His prosthetic edged down the side of the sheet. Taylor. Theriault. Thompson. Thompson, again. Vazquez.

*Sonofagun...Vincent.*

Using his prosthetic as a shield, Werner slowly slid it to the right, revealing the words one-by-one: John Sloan Vincent, born in Anderson, South Carolina, in 1925.

Werner swallowed, edging the steel further to the right. Then he saw the clincher...

Vincent had been in 2nd platoon.

Leaning his head back and staring at the gilt ceiling, Werner took a series of deep breaths as the reality settled in on him. Had he done a better job of cross-referencing names when he'd first gotten the roster, perhaps he'd have noticed it. Regardless, Werner was sure of himself now. The wounded man he'd met earlier had been shot in the arm in the Bayreuth gunfight. He'd been shot by whoever had been in the second floor window of the Zeckern home. According to the director, it had been Oskar Zeckern. Werner wasn't so sure about that. But what he was sure of was Martin Vincent Elder's name honored the three slain men from 2nd platoon. Werner would bet his life on it.

Using his good hand, Werner carefully refolded the pages, tucking them into his coat. Then he stood, the reality of the situation bearing down on him like lead weights.

BKA Director Loeffler was dirty. He'd lied about Zeckern and his wife. And, for some strange reason, Werner didn't believe—not for a second—that he was upstairs visiting with his own wife.

Feeling a hand on his shoulder, Werner turned, startled to see Director Loeffler.

"All done here, detective," Loeffler said affably. "Let's step outside."

Werner's words hung in his throat.

"Everything alright?" Loeffler asked.

"Er…yes, sir." Werner left some money beside his chair.

"I want you to meet an associate of mine," the director said, guiding Werner into the revolving door. As they stepped outside, under the portico, Loeffler pulled his fedora down tight against the wind. "While I was upstairs, I received a call. We just received an enormous break in the case."

"Oh?" Werner croaked.

"Indeed." Loeffler managed to light a cigarette, dragging deeply as was his habit. "Don't let this hurt your feelings, detective, but, even though you were on the right track, you had already eliminated the killer from your list."

"I did?"

"Yes. You spoke to him today, if your notes are correct. He's right here in Berlin. Goes by Martin Vincent Elder," Loeffler said. "The man who called me had a key piece of information." Loeffler pointed past Werner's shoulder. "Here comes my man now."

Werner turned, watching a figure approaching through the heavy rain. When the man stepped under the portico, he removed his hat, shaking it off. The man's face was chiseled and handsome, with an out-of-place suntan. He smiled at Werner, displaying a mouth of squared-off teeth.

It was all Werner could do to keep his own mouth from falling open. He'd studied this man's picture at least a dozen times. Kriminaldetektiv Werner Eisch was standing face-to-face with one of the most-wanted criminals from the Second World War, the perpetrator of the Massacre at Kastellaun, the man who was once known as SS Hauptsturmführer Raban Nadel.

*Mein Gott!*

# Chapter Twenty-Two

Journal Entry

The Waffen-SS commander, Weber, who by first impressions was a reasonable man, was dead. The new SS commander had ordered Weber's followers killed. Now, all that remained were the new commander's own men. Men who wanted us dead. Though I was petrified, I forced myself to study the new commander.

The first thing that I recall was how impressive his uniform was compared to the others. Like ours, their unit was a fighting unit. After time, a person loses gear, or it becomes tattered. As I mentioned earlier, in wartime, a soldier does with what he has and what he can scrounge. It wasn't at all uncommon to see Germans wearing pieces of pilfered Allied clothing, or vice-versa. But this man's uniform was immaculate. And, unlike the rest of the Germans and Americans in that clearing, his face was clean-shaven, pink, and freshly-scrubbed.

The face itself was chiseled but had enough puffiness that a person could see he was well-fed. His eyes were green and lively. So lively that it appeared he purposefully kept them wide open, like a person trying to stay awake. He'd traded his tanker's helmet for his officer's cap, fronted by the notorious SS death head, and even that seemed to have gotten an extra bit of polish.

Every strip of leather on that man's uniform gleamed. And despite all of the melting snow and sloppy conditions, not a speck of mud dotted his glossy tanker's boots.

Finally, I remember thinking how young he appeared. Some of that could have been his clean-shaven appearance—our beard growth and lack of sleep added ten years to all of us—but I'd still have guessed his age at no more than thirty. Maybe only twenty-five. He was at least ten or twelve years the junior of Weber, his commander that he'd murdered in cold blood.

After briefly congratulating his men, in English, he calmly informed us that we were about to die.

"The coward that I disposed of a short time ago believed we were going to lose this war. Well, unfortunately for you, I don't give up so easily. Put simply, my Führer has charged me with killing enemies of the Thousand Year Reich. And I intend to follow his orders to the letter."

This next portion will be very difficult for me to write. I apologize if my recollections are unclear or disjointed.

The first thing about the massacre that I remember is the abrupt end of his speech. He told us that he would follow Hitler's orders, then he unholstered that pistol and aimed it at the nearest American, a new arrival from Indiana, and shot him in the head. Before we could even react, the new commander turned his pistol to Lieutenant Breston and shot him in the groin.

Captain Rook, despite his sickness, sprang to his feet and managed to punch a nearby SS in the side of his face. It was a really nice straight right. The punch put the stunned SS on the deck and earned Rook a bevy of bullets, killing him instantly. I have to give Rook credit—he knew he was going to die and he literally went down swinging.

During that incident, Lieutenant Breston was squirming and yelling in pain. The SS commander laughed heartily as he encouraged his soldiers to join in. John Vincent, broken ankle and all, continued to translate as gunfire rang out all around us.

"He's telling them to wound us first, to make our death as miserable as possible," John yelled as we all scrabbled down in the mud, as if we might somehow burrow ourselves to safety. "He's telling them that we've raped their women and children and that we don't deserve to die a humane death."

I was flat on my belly when I saw tanker's boots stop in front of my face. I looked up, seeing a large man looming over me and John. He used his boot to lift John's chin from the ground. "Stand," the man commanded. John did as he was told, though it was a struggle due to his ankle. The gunshots ceased. The other SS watched the scene, as did we—morbidly. While we watched, many of our brethren moaned from their injuries. I was yet unscathed.

John Vincent stood there in front of the SS, putting all his weight on his good leg. To John's credit, he wasn't even shaking. If you'll recall, John was my friend who shammed that general into thinking he was from Alabama. Good old John, with his silver tongue, the guy who everyone liked.

"You speak German," the SS said.

John replied with several sentences, harshly spoken in an accusatory tone. To this day, I have no idea what John said. But it must have been a terrific insult because the smile quickly evaporated from that big SS's face. He unsheathed his knife and stabbed John in the center of his gut. I won't describe how John died. But it was loud and slow.

I've also made the decision not to go into gory detail about the remainder of the massacre. There's nothing to be gained by doing so. I'll describe it in as general of terms as I can manage; then I will be done with this journal.

Within ten minutes of that first gunshot, I'd hazard that every man in our unit took at least one bullet. Per the new commander's orders, few of those shots were immediately fatal. Soon after John was stabbed, I was shot in my leg and my abdomen. The shot to my abdomen, I later learned, missed my organs. It passed cleanly through me, other than shattering a rib on its way out. I was conscious the entire time.

It wasn't long before the SS ran out of ammo. When they did, they began to shoot us with our own weapons. As I lay there in a pile of writhing American bodies, I recall watching a few SS discussing one of our rifles. They could have been good friends out on a leisurely hunt. They worked the mechanism, probably discussing the benefits or drawbacks of the design. One of them hefted it, aiming up into the trees and taking a shot. He said something and they all laughed again.

To me it was profane. Blasphemy. Human beings writhed at their feet, begging for quick death. And these assholes could only discuss the trigger mechanism of a foreign rifle.

In time, the SS grew bored with those of us who were still alive. I have no clue how long I'd been on the ground, bleeding, watching my friends die. To my right was John Vincent's body. His eyes were wide open, as was his mouth. I remember sliding my hand to his face and generating what little peace I could by closing his eyes and his mouth.

I looked to my left, beyond several corpses, to see Danny Elder, clawing forward through the mud. Somewhere, at that very moment, Danny Elder's son had no idea what his real father was going through. The father who had cried to us that he'd never gotten to hold his son. The father who so desperately wanted to heap love on his boy. I don't know why Danny was up and crawling like that. It didn't last, as a hand came smashing down on Danny's back. In that hand was a long stiletto knife.

For as long as I live, I'll never forget Danny's scream.

Before it all ended, as we were being shoved into a much smaller circle of bodies, I recall a tugging at my boots. I looked behind me to see Kenny Martin. You remember Kenny, the football player from Texas Technical. The one who'd taught that vicious little supply sergeant a lesson. Though Kenny had been shot, his face was alive with excitement.

"Found a pistol," he hissed.

I have no idea how the pistol made it through the search. He'd pushed it down in the bloody mud and was covering it with his left hand, but lifted his hand long enough to show me.

Despite all that we were going through, I couldn't help but grin at Kenny. If I had to pick which of my friends would go out in a ball of fire, it definitely would've been him. For the balance of my days, I'll never forget Kenny's last words to me. And, based on what he said, he must've seen what happened to Danny.

Kenny whispered, "This one's for Danny's son."

Suddenly, with no other warning, Kenny lifted that pistol and squinted his left eye shut, aiming carefully. One of the SS saw him and yelled a warning, but it was too late. The stiletto-toting SS that had stabbed Danny Elder was Kenny's target, and Kenny's aim was true. He fired the pistol at the SS and I turned to watch the man die. Kenny had shot him in the throat and, well, all I can say is Kenny got his money's worth.

As a bevy of SS pounced on Kenny, beating him and stabbing him to death, I watched Kenny's victim fall to his knees as his life leaked out all around him. While I'd like to tell you that Kenny's retribution somehow made me feel better, it didn't. The entire situation was grotesque. Sub-human. I know why Kenny did what he did, and I don't blame him, but in retrospect I believe there were no victories that day.

None.

In the end, after the SS created a pile of bodies, they revved up their tanks and drove over us. They ground our flesh into mincemeat. As it happened, primarily through instinct, I burrowed down deep in the pile and tugged my friends on top of me. Somehow, some way, I survived. My friends' corpses provided me with shelter.

Even though my physical body survived that black day, I was never the same again, nor will I ever be. Somewhere in that pile of corpses, my soul perished.

I've been dead now for seven years.

*** 

The breaded pork cutlets had been lightly sautéed before Frau Schaal liberally doused them with lemon juice. Paired with baby potatoes, green beans and fresh bread, the meal had been medicinal to Marty's soul—as well as his injury. After dinner, Frau Schaal had given Josh and Marty each a bowl of chocolate pudding, though she'd had none herself. The three of them sat there talking and laughing, getting to know each other by telling funny stories from their past.

It turned out that Frau Schaal's father, a man Josh called "Opa," might have been the biggest character in all of Germany. Josh was able to produce story after story about the man. The most memorable story about Opa involved a tree that had fallen in his yard. Apparently, Josh and Opa had been discussing sawing the tree into firewood when a nosy neighbor interrupted them, asking when Opa was going to remove the tree. According to Josh, Opa let the neighbor have it, saying, "How about you just don't worry about it, you nosy bastard?" Marty quickly learned that, not only was Opa a character, he was also an artisan with German curse words. After a half-hour of the hilarious Opa tales, Frau Schaal had informed Josh that it was his bedtime.

"I'll go now," Marty had said, standing.

"Might you wait a moment?" she'd asked. "I want to discuss things a bit more."

That had been ten minutes ago. Marty smoked a cigarette while he listened to Josh prepare for bedtime under the watchful eye of his mother. After brushing his teeth and washing his face, Marty listened as Josh dutifully said his prayers, listing at least two dozen family members. At the end of his prayer, he asked God to look over his papa, wherever he might be. Marty crushed out his cigarette as he thought about the kid's old man, wondering if Josh would ever give up hope. In a surprising realization, Marty now had a great deal of sympathy for the boy.

Frau Schaal breezed back in, waving her hand in front of her face and frowning. "You should not be smoking after being wounded. It makes the injuries heal slower."

"I've never heard that," Marty remarked.

"The tobacco companies don't want you to know that, but I saw it firsthand. People who smoked during the war healed much more slowly than those who didn't."

"Well, I won't argue with your experience," Marty said, handing her his pack of cigarettes. She crumpled the pack and tossed it into the wastebasket.

"How's the arm?"

"It actually feels a little better. If I sit perfectly still, it doesn't hurt."

Frau Schaal sat in the chair opposite Marty, smoothing her skirt and placing her hands on her knees. "Thank you for what you said to Josh. I feel fortunate that he doesn't seem bothered by what he saw."

"It could still come on later."

"I honestly don't think it will," she said thoughtfully. "And about what you promised, thank you. The fact that Josh believes you're going to stop your hunt will stay with him and hopefully do some good." She smiled. "Sometimes a lie is a good thing."

Marty averted his eyes, feeling the cold stab of her words. "Well," he said, standing. "Thanks for the meal and thank you for patching me up. I'm going up to pack my things and, as I said, I'll try to be gone by tomorrow night."

"You're leaving?"

"Yes," Marty said, walking to the door. "Thanks again."

"Herr Marty, wait," she said, catching up to him and gently putting her hand on the door. "What's wrong?"

"Nothing," he said, his eyes on the door.

"You're upset."

Marty was silent.

"Herr Marty, something's bothering you. Please, what is it?"

He turned. "You thought I was lying to Josh?"

She blinked. "Weren't you?"

"I wasn't lying, Frau Schaal. Your son was right...*he* taught *me* a lesson. I thought I could come over here to Germany and do all this without ruining any other lives. If I'd found the man I was looking for right away, maybe I could have. But that massacre just keeps on killing more and more people. And now it's my fault." Marty pulled the door open. "Josh made me see that. In fact, you both did. If something had happened to either of you because of me..." He was unable to complete the sentence. "Thanks again for tonight."

Frau Schaal grasped Marty's good hand, stopping him. He turned, viewing her sparkling green eyes. She put both hands behind his neck, pulling him to her and kissing his mouth. The kiss lingered as Marty placed his hand on her lower back, pulling their bodies together.

When the glorious kiss was over, the two people stared at one another for a lingering moment.

"I'm sorry I thought you were lying," she finally whispered.

"It's okay. After all I've done, you had reason to think that way."

Frau Schaal tugged Marty back inside and gently shut the door. She placed a quieting finger over her lips. Marty watched as she slid out of her shoes, padding barefoot down the hall and peeking into Josh's room before carefully closing the door. When she returned, she nodded once, a soft smile on her face.

On that Sunday night, July 6th, 1952, two very lonely, very sad souls made beautiful love together and, for the briefest of moments, they were both quite happy. While the act was slightly complicated due to Marty's injury, they managed quite well.

It was a fine evening.

A fine evening that would soon be shattered by terror.

\*\*\*

As if he'd known Werner might be a threat, Raban Nadel insisted Werner ride in the front seat. Nadel sat directly behind him, audibly loading and cocking his Beretta pistol. Though Nadel didn't act threatening, Werner felt the sounds were certainly deliberate, the unspoken promise of a bullet to Werner's head in case of any shenanigans. Of course, Werner had played dumb about who Nadel really was. Still, Werner was perspiring all over, his mind racing through the entire scenario as a despicable, ruthless killer sat mere centimeters behind him.

Werner pondered Director Loeffler of the BKA. Between his lies about Bayreuth and the lies about Nadel's being in the BKA, perhaps he was more dangerous than even Nadel. So, this Martin Vincent Elder fellow, who was in some way associated with the 32nd Field Artillery, had come here for revenge. And, because he was on the take, Loeffler used his BKA pull and somehow learned that Werner was very close to finding the hell-bent American. Using a heap of false information to fool Lieutenant Mainhardt, Loeffler combined what he knew with Werner's evidence, and now they were headed to kill the American.

*And kill me, too!* Werner suddenly realized. There was no way they were going to leave a witness.

"You okay, detective?" Loeffler asked, a cigarette bouncing in the corner of his mouth as he shifted gears. "Awful quiet over there."

"Just wondering about Chief Mainhardt," Werner said, watching for a reaction. Loeffler stared straight ahead.

"What about him?"

"He usually likes me to report in."

"I took care of it," Loeffler said casually. "We handle things a bit differently than the Polizei. You guys use strength in numbers. We operate in silos, limiting communications for a reason. Like you, he's to report to me directly."

"You just worry about this Ami," Nadel chimed in while patting Werner's shoulder. "He's dangerous enough for all of us."

"Yeah," Loeffler agreed. "And let's talk about how we're going to play this. After you already braced him this morning, he's gonna be on edge when you come back."

"Right," Nadel said. "So the director here wants you to get that tart of his, the landlady, to knock on the Ami's door for you. She gave an alibi for him that we all know is complete bullshit. You said she's downstairs from him, correct?" Nadel asked.

Werner's mind raced. "Yes, sir."

"So we'll threaten her with jail, et cetera, and tell her the only way to avoid it is by going up to her lover's flat and coaxing him outside. When she does, we'll take him down."

"We don't know they're lovers," Werner said.

"He's tapping her," Loeffler chuckled. "Believe me."

"And what if one of them isn't home?" Werner asked.

"They'll be there," Loeffler said. "The Ami's been shot and it's a Sunday night...where the hell would they be?" Loeffler turned, eyeing Werner. "You sure you're okay? You look like hell."

"I'm fine. Just a tad nervous."

"Well, you'd better buck up," Nadel said, squeezing Werner's shoulder where it connected to his prosthetic. "Because dicking this up isn't an option."

"No, it's not," Werner breathed. "No, it's not."

\*\*\*

The pattering of the rain had ceased, replaced by the sounds of the cicadas in the young trees that lined the street. Their emergence signified to Marty that it was getting late. The evening had been far too fleeting. He had to work tomorrow and needed to get back up to his flat to attempt to sleep with this arm injury. While this night might have changed things about his reason for being here, he still needed to move away, just in case there might be some blowback from all he'd already done. And tonight, Marty didn't need to linger in the event Josh had a bad dream and wandered into his mama's bedroom. That would be bad. Very bad.

Probably thinking the same thing, Frau Schaal had gone to check on Josh and to retrieve two glasses of water. She'd shut the bedroom door when she'd left. Now Marty lay back, pushing his sweaty hair back with his good hand. Boy, he wished he hadn't given up smoking earlier because a cigarette would taste damn good right now.

What had just occurred already seemed like a dream. Marty closed his eyes, recalling Frau Schaal's expression as she moved on top of him. Once during their intimate union she'd leaned down and kissed him, whispering that she'd been attracted to him from the moment they'd met.

"And I never thought I'd be close to another man," she'd then said, arching her neck so he could no longer see her face. When the moment had passed, they'd continued to enjoy one another, setting aside their past and living for the moment.

Now, in his own little afterglow, Marty pondered the promise he'd made the Schaals. His quest was over—his illegal quest. He didn't even want to think about how he might continue down a legal path. For now, unwinding everything illegal he'd done would be his first priority. But there was no reason Marty couldn't stay here in Berlin. He had a good job and now he had a relationship with a wonderful lady and her son. What might these coming months bring? And he could still pursue that sonofabitch Nadel. He'd simply have to create a new plan—one within the bounds of the law.

*No…my determination isn't gone. It's simply replaced by—*

The soft murmur of an engine touched Marty's ears, interrupting his train of thought.

Marty propped up on his elbows. It was probably around 11 P.M. and the sound was made clear by the two open bedroom windows. While Marty was always vigilant, the sound of an engine this time of night wasn't too unusual. Although few Germans operated cars these days, primarily due to the cost and the fact that public transportation was running again, the occasional German did drive, especially when taking trips to remote areas. And on a Sunday, it was feasible that someone on the block had made a day trip and was just now getting back home. Marty sat up, gathering his clothes. As he pulled on his trousers, he heard the gentle shutting of multiple car doors. There was a light click, followed by a hollow thud, the way people close a car door when they're trying to be quiet. They push the door to the click before putting their hip into the shutting action.

Marty walked to the windows, carefully peering out. He was able to see a tall man pulling on his hat, speaking softly to someone who was obscured by the small portico. Marty attuned his ears, trying to hear the man's German.

"…stay a level down just in case…when she goes to him…we'll rush him and take him without incident…"

Marty heard a second voice, one belonging to an unseen man and difficult to distinguish. Though he couldn't be certain, Marty thought he heard something about "the noise of a handgun in the stairwell."

Hearing only those snippets was enough. He watched as the man sucked on a cigarette before flicking it into the street, tumbling in a hail of sparks.

Marty ran from the bedroom.

*\*\*\**

"Are you sure you know what to do?" Loeffler asked Werner as they reached the landing one floor below Frau Schaal's flat.

"Indeed," Werner replied, his nervousness apparent.

"His anxiety is concerning," Nadel said flatly, as if Werner wasn't even there.

"I'll be fine," Werner replied. "Once I speak with the woman, everything will occur naturally."

"You better get her to agree," Nadel hissed. "Get her to agree then follow her up to that Ami's flat and stand just to the left. When he comes out, you use your good hand and you pistol-whip the shit out of him, you got that?"

"I told you," Werner said deliberately, "I know what to do."

"Then we'll cuff him and take him in," Loeffler added, nodding at Werner as if he was trying to instill confidence.

"Wait till I nod," Nadel said, giving Werner a nudge and sending him on his way. When Werner was up the stairs, Nadel turned to Loeffler, speaking privately.

"I say we kill the woman, too," he whispered. "Too much risk if they're not all dead."

Loeffler rubbed his own face, tugging it downward into a hideous mask. "You realize how hard it will be to sell that?" he hissed. "They're going to check forensics, powder burns...the whole bit. The Amis will be crawling all over the investigation, too. This asshole Elder will be a damned hero to them and I'll end up in the frying pan. We can't be reckless, here."

Nadel leaned around the bannister, showing his palm to Werner who was standing at the landlady's door. Werner nodded.

"Just follow my lead," Nadel whispered to Loeffler. "We kill Elder and the woman and, on the way back down, anyone else who happens to come out of their apartment. We get back in the car, then you radio in with disinformation. That buys us time. Then we casually drive down to Leipzig and we fly out to Copenhagen on my comrade's Spartan Executive."

"But I didn't plan on walking away from my life tonight," Loeffler lamely protested.

"Your kids are grown and gone. What, that wide-assed wife of yours is enough to keep you here?" Nadel's scorn turned to a knowing grin. "I've got four million sterling awaiting us in an English bank down in Jamaica. I've got a pristine estate on the white sands of Sugar Loaf beach. We'll enjoy brown women and fruity drinks for the balance of our days."

"Then why don't we just walk right now?" Loeffler whispered. "Why elevate our risk?"

"Because this American came after me," Nadel answered without a second's hesitation. "And when he did, he sealed his fate. Now it's *you* that's being a pussy. Get your mind right and be ready."

Raban Nadel checked that his round was seated and his hammer cocked. He leaned out and nodded one time, watching with satisfaction as Kriminaldetektiv Werner Eisch rapped on Frau Schaal's door.

*** 

"They've come for me," Marty said, grasping Frau Schaal's arms in the small kitchen.

"What are you talking about?" she whispered.

"They just drove up. It's the Polizei, or maybe the federal police. Or…"

"Could it be those men, the former SS?" she asked, her hand nervously clawing at her upper chest.

"I can't be sure. I only saw them for a brief moment down on the street."

"We'll hear them when they're up at your apartment."

"I heard a little bit of their plan. They're going to come here first. That means it's probably the Polizei, because of the alibi you helped me with."

Frau Schaal stepped away, her eyes going wide. "What will we do?"

"Nothing to do. If it's the cops, I'll go with them."

"Just like that?"

Marty touched his finger to his lips. "Not so loud. I don't want Josh to have to see this."

"You can't go, Marty. You'll go to jail."

He gnawed on his lip. "If we try to deceive them further, then *you* might get in trouble. If I'm honest about everything, who knows what might happen? They'll probably classify me as crazy and maybe it'll somehow bring Raban Nadel to justice."

Frau Schaal began to cry. "Marty…no."

"There's no other option," he replied, hugging her. She immediately pulled away.

"They don't have to know you're here. I can pretend I was asleep and let them in upstairs. When they see you're not home…"

"They'll camp out in the stairwell and find out eventually. Then you'll go to jail for harboring me. No…the only way to do this is for me to give myself up," Marty said soberly. "And the alibi you provided earlier will need to be explained. Just tell them you were scared of me, okay?"

"Marty—"

"You tell them that," he said, pointing a finger at her. "I won't have you in trouble for my transgressions. Please."

"But what if it's *them?*"

"Who?"

"You know who," she said, her lip trembling.

There was a knock at the door.

Marty touched her arm. "Then I'll go with them to keep you safe."

"No…"

"Look at me," he whispered sternly. "You and Josh have lives ahead of you. I don't…"

"Wait." She tip-toed to the door, looking through the peep hole. "It's the detective with only one arm."

Marty sagged in relief.

"Will you at least stand out of sight so we can hear what he says?"

"It's pointless."

"Please, Marty," she said, eyes glistening.

Relenting due to the passion of her plea, Marty nodded. "I'll stand just out of sight and listen, but only for a few moments. If he knows that Martin Elder is his man, I'm coming out."

There was another knock, this one louder. Frau Schaal placed her hand on the lock.

***

"I hear footsteps," Nadel whispered to Werner. "Be ready."

"Don't spook her," Loeffler said to Nadel. "Back up."

Nadel complied, easing backward and peering through a small gap in the bannister. He could barely hear the exchange.

"Kriminaldetektiv, you again?" the woman asked. "What on earth is the emergency that this couldn't wait till tomorrow?"

"*Guten Abend, Frau Schaal*," the detective said kindly, removing his fedora with his prosthetic. "I'm sorry to disturb you this evening but additional information has come to light about your tenant in seven-B."

"What information?"

There was a gap in the conversation, or maybe whispers. Nadel tried to get a better angle but he could only see a portion of the woman in a long gown. Because of where she was standing, if he leaned out to see the detective, he would reveal himself.

Watching her expression, it seemed that she was comprehending something being signaled to her. Something silent. She shook her head, her face registering sudden fear. Then she blinked and nodded slightly.

"Won't you come in?" she asked.

*No! No! No!*

"Thank you," the detective replied. He walked inside and the door quickly shut behind them.

"What the hell?" Nadel hissed, turning to Loeffler.

"What just happened?" Loeffler replied, his hands open at his sides.

"They were talking and suddenly they went silent. I couldn't see that little shit but I think he was mouthing and miming to her, then she invited him in."

Loeffler peered around the bannister and used an accusatory tone. "Why did you let him go in?"

"Me? He's *your* little friend and he obviously isn't as enamored with your bullshit title as you'd thought."

Loeffler scratched his chin. "Maybe he just got spooked. Maybe he's in there levying the threats on her. It shouldn't take but a minute."

"Well, maybe he's not doing that. Maybe he somehow knows I'm not BKA. Maybe he knew what Raban Nadel looked like," Nadel said, gesticulating wildly. "Maybe he's in there calling in the rest of the Berlin Polizei to come down here and gun me down in this stairwell…what about that?"

Loeffler checked the volume on his handset before gripping his Walther again. "I'll know if it gets called in. For now, just wait."

"But he *was* mouthing something."

"Do you know that for sure?" When Nadel didn't respond, Loeffler said, "Just wait and see."

Nadel aimed his pistol through the spindles of the bannister, his intuition telling him they were being actively double-crossed.

***

When the door was shut, Werner spoke in a whisper. "No matter what I say, Frau Schaal, be very quiet."

"Why were you mouthing to me out there? What do you want?"

"I'll explain but you must be very quiet." He touched the bolt lock on the door. "If I twist this slowly, will it click?"

"What?"

"Is the lock quiet, or does it click?"

"It's quiet if you do it slowly," she said. Werner slowly turned the lock, satisfied when it seated with hardly a sound. When he turned, Werner recoiled so badly he nearly yelled out. Standing beside Frau Schaal, his arm and shoulder bandaged, was Martin Elder.

He wore only a pair of trousers. Even in the bluish street light that filtered through the filmy curtains, Werner could see the scars on the man's body, recalling what he'd read about the brutality that occurred at Kastellaun.

"Martin Elder," Werner said.

"Call me Marty, and if you're here to arrest me, detective, why are you acting this way? You're scaring her."

Werner reached into his shoulder holster and removed his Walther. "This is already locked and loaded. You'll need to cock the hammer. I assume you can handle it," he said, handing the weapon to the puzzled American. Werner turned to Frau Schaal.

"Do you have a telephone?"

"Right there," she said, gesturing to the narrow wall next to the kitchen.

"I don't have time to explain," Werner said, hurrying to the phone. "Just listen closely to my call." He lifted the earpiece and motioned his prosthetic to Marty. "If someone tries to come through that door, shoot them."

"What?" Marty hissed. "Those were cops with you."

"Do as I say, Marty."

Frau Schaal covered her mouth with both hands. "Detective, you're scaring me."

"I'm sorry, madam, but you *should* be scared."

"Go in there with Josh and lock the door," Marty said, cocking the hammer. He gestured to Werner. "Make your call because I want to hear what the hell's going on."

Werner dialed the operator and asked for the main dispatch at the Berlin Polizei. He listened for a moment before saying, "Who's the senior officer on duty?"

"Lieutenant Buchner," the dispatcher answered immediately. Werner dipped his head a fraction. Buchner was the deputy for homicide that had chided Werner when he'd first shown interest in the Felix Roth murder. Like Buchner's boss, Homicide Chief Leipziger, Buchner seemed to have no use for Werner. But he was the duty officer, and Werner needed his assistance.

"Ring Buchner now. This is Kriminaldetektiv Werner Eisch. I have a code alarm, officer and civilians in danger." Werner turned to Marty. "Our police have been stripped so bare I don't even rate a radio." He turned back to the phone.

There were a series of clicks before Buchner's voice came on. "Buchner here."

"This is Krimaldetektiv Werner Eisch, lieutenant. This is a code alarm. We have a critical situation in Steglitz with an officer and three civilians in imminent danger."

"Relay all facts," Buchner said sharply.

"This'll have to be fast. Without giving you background, suffice it to say that BKA Director Loeffler, who has been in our bureau all day, is corrupt. He's in bed with a former Schutzstaffel officer, Raban Nadel, who's been living in hiding since the war. They're trying to kill an American—the one who killed Felix Roth in Krofdorf-Gleiberg. The American has been here in Germany, trying to avenge the Massacre at Kastellaun."

"What?" Buchner shouted. "Do you mean to tell—"

"As I said, *two* German civilians, a woman and child, are in grave danger. Along with the American and me."

"This is hard to comprehend."

"It's fact," Werner said flatly. "If you send the reaction unit to Feuerbachstrasse fifty-one, right this second, you can take them in the stairwell. Approach with complete stealth—no sirens, no nothing." Turning his head to the door, Werner said, "There are *windows* in the stairwell. I'd recommend shooting CS gas into all the windows, especially the top windows, before breaching. The two men in the stairwell are armed, but the gas should incapacitate them. Hurry."

"If you're wrong, Eisch…"

"I take full responsibility for the entire op. Just send the team now or we're all going to die."

"Ten minutes, Eisch. We'll be there and we'll do it just as you said. Leave this line open and speak to me if anything changes. Got it?"

"Very good," Werner said. "I'm leaving it open and stepping away from the phone now."

Werner placed the earpiece on top of the phone. He turned to the American who was staring back at him, aghast.

Werner nodded. "Yes, what I just said is the truth. You were once Thomas Whiteside, the sole survivor of the Massacre at Kastellaun."

Marty only blinked.

"It wasn't a question," Werner said. "We just solved the puzzle a short time ago, just before I learned the BKA man was bent." He looked around. "And is there another gun here?"

The American rushed past him. "I'll find out." He was back seconds later. "No guns."

The detective turned to the door. "They're going to be very suspicious about why I came inside."

"Think they'll rush us?"

"They may."

"Then we've got to stall them until your people get here."

Scratching his forehead with his prosthetic, the detective said, "I assume you have a weapon upstairs?"

"There's a pistol just inside my door."

The two men created a hasty plan.

\*\*\*

Out in the stairwell, Nadel and Loeffler heard the door click back open. Then they heard the detective calling to them in a whisper. Nadel turned to

Loeffler, who nodded. The two men showed themselves on the lower stairwell, their pistols at the ready. The detective emerged with a woman.

"This is Frau Schaal," Werner whispered, gesturing with his prosthetic. "She was in the suspect's flat earlier."

"Why did you go inside her flat?" Nadel hissed.

"I didn't want…" Werner motioned upward with his prosthetic, "…our suspect to hear."

Loeffler and Nadel frowned at one another.

Werner continued to whisper. "Frau Schaal just informed me that our suspect has been gravely wounded. She attempted to patch him up but thinks he may be unconscious or even dead."

"H-h-he lost a great deal of blood," she nervously offered. "Someone sh-sh-shot him."

Werner whispered something to her, then retrieved a shiny object from her hand, his prosthetic twisting it in the scant light. "She's given me a key."

Nadel stepped closer, his pistol at the ready. "Lady, you're sure he's up there?"

"He could barely m-m-move when I left. I think he may be dead."

Loeffler narrowed his eyes. "Earlier, according to the detective, you were the American's *alibi*."

"He coerced me and I was scared of him. Petrified," she whispered, tears rolling from her eyes. "He's cr-cr-crazy."

"She was a nurse during the war. I think he took advantage of her tender nature," Werner added. "But with his injury she's quite confident that, at a minimum, he's incapacitated."

"So much blood," the woman said, dabbing her eyes with a tissue.

"How did he make it back here from Bayreuth if he lost all that blood?" Loeffler asked.

"The real bleeding began when I pulled out the bullet," she answered.

Loeffler's face registered optimism as he nodded at Nadel.

"Then lead on," Nadel said, gesturing his pistol up the stairs.

As the detective slowly crept up the first few stairs, the woman stepped back into her apartment and closed the door. "Eisch," Nadel whispered at the detective, who was halfway to the American's flat.

The detective turned.

"You trust that woman?"

"She's telling us the truth," Werner replied. "I'll go in first."

"What if he's not incapacitated?" Nadel asked.

"Then I'll shoot him."

Nadel and Loeffler followed, each of the men tiptoeing up the steps. Just as they'd passed the Schaal flat, the radio squelched. Loeffler lifted it, keying it twice, then he placed the speaker close to his ear.

Werner continued upward, with Nadel right behind. As Werner made the turn at the landing, Nadel said, "Where the hell is your pistol, detective?"

Werner's left hand was empty, though he was holding it as if it carried his handgun.

That was just as Loeffler, his eyes going wide, heard the urgent call from Deputy Buchner.

Werner sprinted up the last of the stairs to the top landing.

"It's a double-cross!" Loeffler bellowed, the sound reverberating in the stairwell.

Before Nadel had a chance to respond, Frau Schaal's door was yanked open. From it came the American, with Kriminaldetektiv Werner Eisch's Walther PPK aimed in their direction.

Nadel and Loeffler were facing the wrong way, standing a few steps up from the Schaal's landing. The American had the jump on them.

"Get your hands up. And if either of you so much as flinch, I *will* shoot you," the American said in flawless German.

While both men raised their hands, Werner yelled from above that he'd retrieved the pistol.

Director Loeffler and Raban Nadel had been bested.

# Chapter Twenty-Three

His good arm as steady as a Tiger II's main gun, the American stepped into the stairwell while Deputy Buchner's tinny voice continued to buzz on the private radio frequency, informing them that Kriminaldetektiv Werner Eisch had called in the entire situation by telephone. "I took the call and I'm containing it for now," Buchner said. "So hurry!"

Moving behind the two Germans, the American spoke with authority, saying, "Drop those pistols."

Neither man complied. They were facing away from the American, eyeing one another from the corners of their eyes.

"Very well." The American adjusted his pistol downward and fired it directly into the back of Loeffler's right knee. While the thunderous gunshot reverberated in the stairwell, the BKA man crumpled, dropping both the radio and the pistol as he tumbled back down to the landing in a screaming, cursing heap.

The American kicked Loeffler's pistol away and aimed his pistol at Raban Nadel's back. "Raban Nadel, *murderer*, drop that pistol or you're next."

*There's no way for me to turn and shoot without first getting shot*, Nadel thought, lifting both of his hands above his head. Rather than panic, he considered the problem academically. *He's got me, center mass. Damn it to hell. Of all the ways to go, defeated by a man I should have killed seven years ago. And if I'd listened to Loeffler and fled instead of facing this American head-on, he'd have never found me.*

The acidic pill of regret seared Nadel's throat and settled into his belly.

"You're now covered by two pistols, Nadel," Kriminaldetektiv Eisch said from above. He stepped around the bannister, showing himself and his handgun.

"So, you traitorous one-armed worm, you're in cahoots with this renegade American?" Nadel asked with a sneer. Down on the landing, Loeffler lay in the fetal position, whimpering as he gripped his leg.

"I'm not going to tell you again," the American warned. "Drop it!"

Nadel slowly turned to face him. He made sure he was calm, casual even, as he said, "According to Gloria Riddenger, you don't want me dead. Before I killed her, she told me you were fanatical about taking me alive."

"And you're about to lose your knee, just like your friend here."

Nadel glanced downward, eyeing Loeffler and snorting derisively. Then, knowing he had no other choice, Nadel released his pistol. It clunked harmlessly down to the landing as he laced his hands behind his head.

"I should have killed you when I had the chance," Nadel said to the American. "Back when I killed your spineless friends."

Unaffected, the American kicked the second pistol well away from Loeffler.

"Do my words not bother you?" Nadel asked.

Ignoring him, the American said, "Detective, did you hear the man on their radio?"

"No."

"He said he took your call and was *containing* the response."

"Buchner," Werner breathed. "Who else is on this man's payroll?"

"Come on down and cuff him," the American said. "Then maybe you can use their radio to call someone else."

"With pleasure," the detective responded.

Nadel continued to glower at the American as the detective cautiously approached from behind. Meanwhile, Loeffler's moans grew louder as he squirmed about, babbling about his own loss of blood.

"Careful, detective," the American warned Werner. "If he tries something, I'm shooting."

"Don't worry about me," Werner said. When he descended to Nadel, he slid the pistol in his waistband, unclipping his cuffs and grasping Nadel's wrist with his prosthetic.

Nadel felt the steel of the detective's prosthetic clamp on his wrist, pulling it down behind his back. There was a brief jangle before Nadel felt the handcuff snap around the same wrist.

*Boom!*

The stairwell echoed with another deafening gunshot.

Nadel felt the detective crumple into his back, his fall automatically thrusting Nadel forward. He stepped down to the landing, between the American and the bannister.

"Do not move!" Loeffler thundered.

Nadel turned back to see Kriminaldetektiv Eisch, facedown on the lower stairs. Next to him, stark even in the dim light, was the spatter of crimson on the spindles of the white bannister.

Gleefully stunned, Nadel turned his eyes back to the pale and sweaty Director Loeffler. As the director had been yelling and grasping his knee, he'd freed the snub-nose pistol from his ankle holster and redeemed himself. Now, despite his condition, he aimed the pistol at the American's back.

"Drop your pistol," Loeffler commanded the American.

Nadel's hands were still up as he eyed the scene. Eisch wasn't moving. The American stood between Nadel and Loeffler. He still had the Walther aimed at Nadel. But behind him, Loeffler aimed his compact pistol squarely at the American's back. Clearly, the American was in a position of weakness. But worrying Nadel were the American's intentions. *He could easily go ahead and kill me. Sure, he'd die, too, but such a prospect might not bother a man who'd come back to Germany bent on revenge, despite all that Gloria Riddenger had said.*

No sooner had Loeffler leveled his command than did the Schaal door open. Nadel glanced backward to see the Schaal lady and her son, both gaping at the ghastly scene.

"Go back inside," Loeffler ordered from his spot on the floor.

"We will not," the woman said.

"Are you okay, Mister Marty?" the boy asked.

Downstairs, a door could be heard opening. "What's going on up there?" a man yelled.

"This is the business of the Polizei and the BKA!" Loeffler shouted, maintaining his ruse. "Go back inside and lock your door until we ask you to come out."

"Herr Weiss!" the Schaal woman yelled. "Go back inside and call the American Military Police. Then call the Polizei. Call the feds. Call the fire department. Call any authority you can think of and tell them we have an emergency at this address!"

"What's wrong Frau Schaal?" yelled the unseen man.

"Tell them there are former Schutzstaffel here, shooting people! Please call now!" Herr Weiss's door could be heard slamming.

"You shot the one-armed policeman!" the boy yelled at Loeffler.

Nadel could feel his world spinning off axis. His eyes darted between the American and Loeffler.

"Don't anyone move," Loeffler bellowed. "I can shoot all three of you from right here."

Staring at the American, Nadel said, "You hand me that pistol or the woman and her kid die." He flicked his eyes to Loeffler. "Klaus, if he shoots me, shoot him then shoot this twat and her little bastard."

That got him. The American flinched at the threat. "You promise to leave them unharmed if I drop the pistol?"

"Of course," Nadel replied silkily.

"No, Marty," the Schaal woman entreated. "Don't believe him. He's not going to leave witnesses."

"You think I'm going to kill everyone in the building?" Nadel asked. "We'll leave everyone as they are and take you with us as our insurance policy," he said to the American. "Now hand over that pistol."

"No, Marty!" the woman pleaded.

"Let them go back inside, first," the American said.

"Why?" Nadel asked.

The American's eyes flicked to the mother and son before coming back to Nadel. "So they can protect the family jewels."

Nadel, his hands still above his head, screwed up his face. *"Was Juwelen?"*

"I just don't want you stealing their *family jewels*," the American said, nodding animatedly toward the woman and her son. "*His* very valuable family jewels."

Josh's face brightened.

Nadel was standing about four feet in front of the Schaal's door. Because of the way Werner had fallen into him, it made him actually stand with his legs slightly open. And when Josh, the unflappable teenager who hadn't seemed at all affected by seeing his American friend get shot, realized what Marty was implying, Nadel's body position was perfect for the resulting strike.

Josh stepped forward stealthily, unable to be seen by Nadel since he was almost directly behind him. His mother yelled a protest but Josh's leg was already rocketing upward. A fine soccer player, Josh's kick was true and powerful, striking Nadel in his most sensitive bodily region. Just before Nadel shrieked in pain, Marty yelled "Get back!" his warning aimed at Frau Schaal.

The gambit nearly worked.

BKA Director Loeffler, a former paratrooper, had always been a crack shot with any firearm. Although he appeared to be on death's door, he unleashed a round at the lurching American, catching him on his back, sending him tumbling forward into the falling Raban Nadel.

The resulting skirmish was sheer pandemonium.

*** 

Meanwhile, all across Berlin, urgent calls went out over numerous radios. The American military police, scattered all about the American sector, were instructed to converge on an apartment building in Steglitz. The building was German, but several American civilians resided there. There were reports of gunshots, Schutzstaffel, Americans—those who took the call were bewildered but responded with haste, if nothing else but to see what in the world was going on in Steglitz.

Despite Buchner's subterfuge at the Mitte Precinct, the Berlin Polizei had fielded several more calls about gunfire at the Steglitz apartment. Additionally, they monitored the open American frequency, and heard the calls from the military police. Three Polizei patrols in the area converged with great speed on Steglitz.

Also fielding a call was the BKA office at Treptower Park, over near Tempelhof. Normally they would allow the Polizei to initiate the contact, but the caller, a man named Weiss, had insisted they come, also. He claimed there was a man in the stairwell purporting to be BKA. The local section chief, covering for his subordinate due to a stomach bug, took the call himself and was now speeding southwest, toward Steglitz.

Finally, an engine from the Steglitz Fire Brigade, located only two kilometers from the Schaal building, roared from its garage, lights flashing and alarm blaring. They would be there in less than five minutes.

No one knew exactly what was happening at Feuerbachstrasse 51, but each authority that had taken a call knew it must be dire.

*** 

Marty dropped down and to the right, scrambling for the pistol he'd just dropped as Nadel crumpled to the landing. The former SS had hunched forward after the testicular strike and, already off balance, was propelled downward when Josh shoved him. Unable to come up with the pistol, Marty turned and pinned Raban Nadel face down.

As Marty adjusted himself for better leverage, he could see his own blood beginning to cover Nadel's neck and back. Marty chanced a look at the other man—the one who'd said he was BKA. He'd either fallen unconscious or was playing possum again.

"Needing a kid to help you," Nadel taunted, writhing underneath Marty.

"Josh!" Marty yelled as he contained the former SS. "Find the other pistol." As Josh scrambled to the steps, Marty noticed Werner staggering to his feet with the help of the bannister.

Feeling himself weakening, Marty was barely able to keep Nadel under control. "I need your help, detective," Marty grunted.

"Your cowardly friends squealed when they died," Nadel grunted, badgering Marty until the end.

Werner arrived just as Nadel was almost out from Marty's grip. Werner had been shot in his good shoulder, so he used his prosthetic to tug at Nadel's face, hooking his pincher into Nadel's nostril and pulling upward. The result was a satisfying shriek.

With the benefit of the detective's help, Marty could now regain control of the Walther pistol. He gripped it, staggering to his feet and supporting himself against the bannister.

"Let him go," Marty urged Werner. In the corner of his eye, Marty saw Frau Schaal ease out onto the landing.

As Werner retrieved the Russian pistol, he spoke to Frau Schaal. "Madam, please hang up your phone and call the United States Army Berlin." He shook his head disgustedly. "I don't know how far this man's tentacles reach but I doubt he has contacts there."

"In a minute," she said, touching Marty's back. "Marty, you're bleeding badly!"

Marty's vision was blurring. He asked Frau Schaal to go back inside, and to take Josh, and to do as the detective said.

"Shoot me!" Nadel suddenly dared, baring his teeth from his downed position. He'd slid backward, sitting against the blood-spattered wall beside Loeffler.

Then Marty felt Josh, grasping him around his waist. "Marty, come inside! Let the policeman deal with this."

Marty would have liked to acknowledge Josh somehow, but he couldn't allow Nadel the smallest of openings. Marty watched the defeated SS intently as he said, "I'll be okay, Josh. Please, go back inside."

Sirens could be heard.

Werner, his pistol also trained on Nadel, passed between the two dirty men. He untangled the pistol from Loeffler's hand and handed it to Josh. Then the detective touched Loeffler's neck.

"Hardly a pulse."

"Please, go inside," Marty said to Frau Schaal, blackness rimming the edges of his vision. "Do as the detective said and call the Army."

As the mother and son left the stairwell, Nadel bellowed again. "Come on, you American coward, and kill me!" He sat rigidly, leaning against the wall as he clenched his fists and pounded his chest like a threatening gorilla. "Do your job or should this German here do it for you?"

Marty's vision was now fully black at its periphery. His head was light and he suddenly felt nauseous. He'd thought about this moment for years, and now that it was here, he simply didn't have the time to savor it.

"You're a cold-blooded murderer," Marty rasped. "And you *will* stand trial for it."

"I'll never go to trial!" Nadel roared.

"Yes, you will," Marty whispered. "And when you walk in the courtroom, it'll be on crutches." He lowered the Walther and fired it directly into the top of Nadel's left shoe. While Nadel shrieked, Marty crumpled to the floor and rolled to his back.

As he stared up at the ceiling, a contented smile appeared on his mouth.

\*\*\*

Minutes later, Frau Schaal and Josh worked feverishly on Marty's chest. The bullet had entered in Marty's mid-back and, unknown to anyone involved, had nicked the large lower vein below the heart known as the interior vena cava.

The wound was mortal.

Per his mother's instruction, Josh dutifully raised Marty's legs, propping them on a kitchen chair he'd dragged into the stairwell. As Frau Schaal continued to work on Marty, she instructed Josh on how to provide a pressure tourniquet on Raban Nadal's foot. Nadel cursed Josh for trying, until the detective hammered the butt of his pistol down on top of Nadel's head, silencing him for the moment.

When the United States Army Military Police noisily entered the stairwell, Frau Schaal cradled Marty's head in her lap. Josh knelt across from her, and the small German family spoke final words to their American friend.

"I'm sorry," Marty whispered. "I'm sorry I brought all this to you."

"Don't be," Frau Schaal replied, pushing Marty's sweaty hair back. "Don't leave us with your sorrow."

"He's not going to die!" Josh yelled at his mother.

Marty managed a slight laugh as he gripped Josh's hand. "Hey buddy, I've been dead for seven years."

"What does that mean?" Josh cried.

Marty closed his eyes for a moment. When he opened them he spoke English to Josh. "Make sure you live, my friend. Be good for your mama...and make sure you live."

"Answer him, Josh," Frau Schaal said, her eyes full of tears.

She knew.

"I *will* live, Mister Marty," Josh managed. "I promise."

Marty closed his eyes again, taking shallow breaths. He didn't speak again.

As the military police tactically reached the sixth floor landing they found a woman. She was cradling a fallen man's head in her lap. The woman's face was streaked with tears. A young teen was across the fallen man, hugging him. The young man's wailing was muffled by the fallen man's blood stained shirt. And standing, a pistol aimed at the man propped up against the opposite wall, was Kriminaldetektiv Werner Eisch of the Berlin Polizei. Despite being wounded, the detective spoke excellent English and quickly relayed all that had happened.

Marty didn't officially die for three more minutes. Though the Schaals didn't know it, he'd heard almost everything they'd said to each other after he'd stopped talking. His mission complete, Martin Vincent Elder, formerly Thomas Wayne Whiteside, left this world with the satisfaction of knowing, though he'd been dead for seven years; on his final night, he truly lived.

*** 

## Final entry of Marty's journal:

Whoever reads this, please try to understand how difficult it was for me to explain exactly what happened leading up to, and during, the Massacre at Kastellaun. I'm pleased with my decision not to delve into too many details. There's no point in it and it would only serve to dishonor my friends' memories.

184 men suffered and died in those woods. Believe me. That's all that needs to be said about it.

More than anything, I wanted people to know something about my best friends, my namesakes. They'll always be a part of me as I walk this earth. Sometimes, I can even hear them speaking to me. No, I'm not referring to voices in my head—just memories. Things each one would say in certain situations, stuff like that.

While I've been here in Germany, other things have happened, too. The memories of my parents have been intense and difficult to set aside. My father was a strong man who spoke few words. Though I didn't have the benefit of a long life with him, I feel I take after him in many ways. My mother did her very best to raise me after Dad died. After processing all of my own grief, I'm now aware of the grief she was probably dealing with all those years. And, instead of comforting her, I acted like a real jerk, right up till I enlisted. She and I could have been so much closer. I desperately wish I had that time to live over again.

The professor has been on my mind, too. He didn't have to do all the things he did for me. Didn't have to feed me. Didn't have to compliment me by paying credence to my bizarre line of thinking. But he did. He cared for me and, even though I know he was trying to address his own demons, he also did his best to teach me as I went through the entire process.

I continue coming back to what he often said to me. I'd hazard he said this to me at least once a week, if not more. "Mister Elder," he would say, tilting his head the way he would always do when he was preparing to say something important. "Be cautious about painting an entire people with such a broad brush." He was referring to my hatred for the Germans, and would usually bestow this advice upon me after I said something particularly vile. "Don't forget, it wasn't so long ago that an organization painted my people with that same broad brush of hate."

I didn't listen to him. I didn't pay him any mind—not about that, anyway. And when I first arrived here to Germany, all I could find in the German people was the negative. If there were any positives, I certainly didn't see them. I was viewing the world through my own little filter. I hated the Germans. Hated all of them.

Now, however, having been here for some time, I was forced to consider exactly what happened in the recent decades in Germany. I melded that together with what I learned from the professor and at school. In summary, the Germans were a whipped country after the Great War, the First World War. The sanctions that were placed on them left many of them in a situation that wasn't sustainable over the long term. Millions of families were left without enough food for proper nourishment.

The sanctions created a power vacuum, and Adolf Hitler eagerly filled the void.

I'm not going to go into detail about the rise of Hitler and his Nazi Party. I'm no historian (I can visualize Professor Walden quickly nodding his agreement) and that information is readily available in just about any history book.

But it was Hitler and his minions, *criminals*, who took the mantle of power. The Schutzstaffel—the SS—was comprised of men chosen for their Aryan blood. There were other requirements, too, such as height, physicality and aggressiveness. But one need only do a small amount of research to find that many of the Waffen-SS were thugs. Villains. Men bent on violence who found a brotherhood of criminals in which they could ply their trade. Not all of them were that way. That much is obvious from the Massacre at Kastellaun alone.

But many were.

The Waffen-SS who slaughtered my unit shouldn't be classified as Germans, not for my purposes, anyway. They should be remembered as war criminals. The Americans have had war criminals. As have the Japanese. The Brits. I recall something that Gloria, Felix Roth's girlfriend, said to me. She said, "There are animals everywhere."

Indeed.

Back to what I've learned—there is a mother and son who live below me. The mother is my landlord. Although I did my very best to avoid them, they continued to push themselves on me. And, along with pushing themselves, they pushed friendship. They pushed caring. In a surprising realization that took months, I finally grasped that they're not bad people, not at all. In fact, they're some of the finest people I've ever had the pleasure of knowing.

They've changed me.

Ever since the massacre, I've claimed that my soul was dead. My body continued to function, pressing forward to complete my mission. All that time, however, I was missing something. I didn't know what it was, because I was blind to it.

But now I know, and it's changed me.

I was missing love. And every human, no matter their situation, needs love to be complete. Everyone. As cliché as it sounds, it's the truth.

My outlook has been changed, and I credit a woman I know as Frau Schaal, and I credit her son Josh. I owe them my life.

My new life.

# Epilogue

Raban Nadel was tried for war crimes nearly a year later, in the early summer of 1953. The trial lasted four days and the jury deliberated for only an hour. He was found guilty and, since Germany had outlawed capital punishment back in 1949, he was sentenced to spend the balance of his days in prison.

However, the balance of those days did not add up to many.

Raban Nadel was killed on the 31st day of his imprisonment. He'd been segregated at first, for his own safety. After a month, he'd petitioned the warden to insert him into the general population, boasting that he'd have the status of a hero. The warden, a jailer with nearly half a century of experience, granted Nadel's wish, smirking as he signed the order. On his second day in general population, Nadel was fatally beaten by a group of prisoners, all of whom were former German soldiers. Many of the men readily admitted to what they'd done, terming Nadel a monster, and a man who didn't deserve to call himself a soldier *or* a German.

Nadel's funeral was poorly attended. In attendance were the Lutheran minister from the local church and the mortician whose funeral home had the contract with the German prison system.

Neither man shed a tear.

THE END

# Acknowledgements

While this book is purely fictional, I based the premise around the Malmedy Massacre of 1944. In that massacre, 362 soldiers and 111 civilians were killed near Malmedy, Belgium. Those totals have been disputed through the years—an argument I will stay clear of. Though the Malmedy Massacre was my greatest influence, I also read about other massacres and imported elements from each into the pages of this book. Regardless, I hope you get the sense of what I was trying to convey. I wanted this story to mean a bit more than a typical Chuck Driskell fiction novel.

I owe a great deal of thanks to Scott Hortis for providing the initial idea for this book. Scott met one of the final living survivors of the Malmedy Massacre and suggested I do something with the story. Scott is a faithful reader and friend. He can also repair just about anything—a fine quality for a friend who happens to live nearby.

Charlie Mink did an excellent job of de-bugging the book, as he always does. I've always appreciated Charlie's unique perspectives. His contributions made this book better. I'm hoping to capture Charlie's hidden skill in an upcoming novel.

Charles Sims, Scott "Ranger" Rook, Mickey Dorsey and Lauren Knight assisted me with late reads after most of the changes had been made. I'm guessing my writing assisted them with their sleep during that time. Seriously, I owe them a great deal of thanks.

Elizabeth Brazeal, my editor (and possible T-1000 prototype) did a wonderful job as usual. Not only is she an excellent editor, she's also a wonderful reader and never afraid to put me back on the right path. Her assistance is invaluable.

Finally, I'd like to thank all my fellow soldiers from "back in the day." The stories and tales I heard and experienced helped me shape Marty's unit and friends. As I've mentioned many times, some of my strongest friendships were borne of my time as a soldier. And no matter where life has taken us, whenever we get together, we all fall back into that same camaraderie that I don't have the talent to explain. I've made few decisions in this life as positive as the one I made when I joined the United States Army.

I've said this before and I will say it again: The United States Army saved me.

God bless the men and women currently serving, as well as those who have served.

Until next time.

C.

## About the Author

Chuck Driskell is a United States Army veteran who
wishes he could write full-time. He lives in
South Carolina with his wife and two children.
*Seven Years Dead* is Chuck's eighth novel.

Made in the USA
Middletown, DE
20 July 2020